DAY FOUR

Also by Sarah Lotz

The Three

DAY FOUR

A Novel

SARAH LOTZ

Little, Brown and Company
New York Boston London

Copyright © 2015 by Sarah Lotz

Little, Brown and Company
Hachette Book Group
1290 Avenue of the Americas, New York, NY 10104
littlebrown.com

First United States Edition: June 2015
Originally published in Great Britain by Hodder & Stoughton, May 2015

Little, Brown and Company is a division of Hachette Book Group, Inc.
The Little, Brown name and logo are trademarks of Hachette Book Group, Inc.

The publisher is not responsible for websites (or their content)
that are not owned by the publisher.

The Hachette Speakers Bureau provides a wide range of authors for speaking events.
To find out more, go to hachettespeakersbureau.com or call (866) 376-6591.

ISBN 978-0-316-24294-3
LCCN 2015935825

10 9 8 7 6 5 4 3 2 1

RRD-C

Printed in the United States of America

For my dad, Alan Walters

(aka The Doc)

DAY FOUR

Welcome on Board *The Beautiful Dreamer!*

Congratulations on choosing a Foveros Cruise,
your one-way ticket to Relaxation and Fun! Fun! Fun!

★ ★ ★ ★

Start your Holiday of a Lifetime by treating yourself to a cocktail at one of our many sun-drenched bars while our musicians delight with their signature sounds. Then cool down in the pool and take a spin on Foveros's WaterWonder™ slides. Hungry? No problem! Our dining room and buffets will provide feasts galore, from five-star fare to yummy comfort food like momma used to make! And hey, don't forget to pamper yourself at our superb spa – you deserve it! Our cabaret performances will delight, so settle into your seats and prepare to be entertained like never before! Soak up the sun during one of our many exciting excursions, where you can shop till you drop at our many concessions, snorkel in turquoise seas, horse-ride along beautiful beaches, and enjoy al fresco dining on our fabulous private island. And why not take a spin in the Delectable Dreamer Casino? Who knows? It could be your lucky day!

DAYS 1, 2, 3

Cruise is relatively uneventful.

DAY 4

The Witch's Assistant

Maddie waited until Celine was midway into her opening mono-
logue, then threaded her way through the capsule chairs, making
for the empty area at the back of the Starlight Dreamer Lounge.
She'd almost made it when the cruise director's voice boomed over
the PA system, drowning out Celine's patter with his reminder that
the New Year's festivities would kick off in 'T minus two hours'.

'Voices from above,' Celine quipped, but Maddie wasn't fooled
by this show of good humour. Celine had been like a Rottweiler
with a sore tooth all day, sniping at the backstage tech after he'd
snagged her dress attaching the microphone's transmitter to her
wheelchair, and complaining that the spotlight wasn't in the
correct position to halo her hair.

'Know this,' Celine continued once the announcement had
petered away. 'When you all return home, rested and suntanned
and maybe a few pounds heavier,' – she waited for a ripple of
laughter to die down – 'you won't be alone. Friends, in all my
years of helping people connect with those who've crossed over,
there are two things I can tell you for sure. One: there is no death;
and two: the souls of those who've left the physical world are
always with us . . .'

With Celine back on track, Maddie allowed herself to relax. She
leaned against a pillar and massaged her neck, trying and failing
to dissolve the headache that had dogged her since day one of the
cruise. It was probably just a side effect of the anti-nausea medication she was taking, but the garish environment wasn't helping.
Whoever had designed the ship's decor had a hard-on for Vegas-
inspired neon and naked male angels; you couldn't go anywhere
without being blinded by an illuminated palm tree or leered at by

a cherub. Still – just one more night to get through and she'd be free of this floating hellhole. The first thing she was going to do when she got back to her apartment was run a bath and scrub the ship off her skin. Then she'd treat herself to a takeout from Jujubee's – splurge on the crab special with glass noodles and extra garlic. She could afford the calories; she must have lost at least five pounds this week.

'Hey, baby,' a voice stage-whispered in her ear. She turned to see Ray, his eyes fixed to her breasts. He'd jettisoned his usual shorts and navy T-shirt combo in favour of Levis and a flimsy cream shirt, which gave him the appearance of a seedy lounge singer.

'Shouldn't you be on the door, Ray?' Tonight's event was strictly for 'Friends of Celine' only – the select group who'd paid through the nose to cruise with 'America's Number One Psychic Medium' – and Ray knew as well as she did that Celine would flip if a non-paying passenger wandered in.

He shrugged. 'Yeah, yeah. So listen – you know when we stopped at Cozumel yesterday?'

'So?'

'So I got one of the waiters to smuggle me in a bottle of high-end tequila. The good stuff.'

A Friend sitting on the outskirts of the group scrunched around in her chair and shushed them. Maddie shot her an apologetic smile, and hissed at Ray to keep his voice down.

'Whatever. So, hey – party later, my cabin. You in?'

More heads were turning in their direction. 'Seriously, Ray, shut the—'

'Think about it,' he smirked. 'Going to grab a frosty while the boss does her *thang*.' Maddie watched him saunter off towards the bar, checking out a waitress en route.

Arsehole.

The atmosphere grew taut as Celine moved on to the highlight of the evening. She licked her lips, touched her chest and said: 'I'm getting . . . Who's Caroline? No, wait . . . Katherine? Someone with . . . it's a C or a K. Nope . . . it's definitely Katherine. Kathy, maybe.'

Maddie smothered a jab of guilt as Jacob, one of the older Friends, wobbled to his feet. She had a soft spot for Jacob. She admired his sense of style (he tended to dress as if he was a guest at a gay wedding), and he wasn't as pushy as some of the others. Celine had feigned illness for much of the cruise, barely showing her face at the various meet 'n' greets and cocktail events, so Maddie had been left to pick up the slack. Part of her job was schmoozing with Celine's fan base, but there was a world of difference between trading messages with the lonely and desperate online, and contending with their neediness face to face. Listening to the Friends' hopes that Celine would connect with their loved ones, missing relatives, and in some cases, deceased pets, had worn her ragged. 'Kathy's my sister!' Jacob called.

'That's what I'm getting,' Celine nodded. 'Know this, she's stepping forward right this second. Hey ... Why can I smell turkey?' She chuckled. 'And sweet potato pie. Good pie at that.'

Jacob gasped and wiped at his eyes. 'She disappeared in the late seventies, round about Thanksgiving. Is she ... is she at peace?'

'Yes. Know this. She has left the physical world and has gone into the light. She wants you to know that every time you think of her, her soul is with you.'

Jacob waited for more, but Celine just smiled blandly back at him and he nodded and sat down.

Celine touched her chest again. 'I'm getting ... It's getting harder to breathe. There's someone here who's ... they passed before their time. I'm talking about a suicide. Yes.'

Leila Nelson, a bony woman with mild hair loss, squealed and jumped out of her chair. 'Oh my *Lord*! My husband killed himself two years ago.'

'I want you to know he's stepping forward, my darling. What's with the breathing? I'm thinking ... did he asphyxiate? Does this make sense to you? I'm tasting carbon monoxide here.'

'Oh my *Lord*. That's how he did it! In the garage, in his Chevy.'

'In his Chevy.' Celine paused to ram this home to the Friends. 'What's the significance of April?'

'His birthday was in April.'

'So April's his birthday. Yeah, that's what I'm getting from him. A tall man, does that make sense?'

Leila hesitated. 'John was five eight.'

'That's tall if you're me, my darling,' Celine rallied. 'I'm getting that . . . Was John unhappy at work? Does that make sense to you?'

'Yes! He lost his job. He was never the same after that.'

'What's with the shoes?'

'Oh my *Lord*, he was always particular about his shoes. Always polishing them, been like that since he left the marines.'

'That's what I'm getting. A feeling like he was a very particular, precise sort of person. Know this, he wants you to know that what happened to him, the way he died, it was nothing you did. He needs you to move on with your life.'

'So he doesn't mind that I'm getting remarried?'

Shit. That was one detail Leila hadn't mentioned during last night's Friends of Celine cocktail event, but Celine didn't skip a beat. 'Know this, he's proud that you're doing so well.'

'He was such a jealous man, though. What I need to know is if he—'

'My darling, I'll have to interrupt you there, as Archie is coming through.' Celine pressed a hand to her throat. 'I can feel the weight of him. He's coming through strongly now.' Maddie suppressed a shudder. Fake or not, Archie, Celine's primary spirit guide – an urchin who'd supposedly died of consumption in late nineteenth-century London – gave her the screaming heebies. There weren't many mediums who channelled the voices of their guides these days, and secretly Maddie thought Celine sounded like Dick van Dyke gargling caustic soda whenever Archie's voice 'came through'.

Celine paused for dramatic effect. 'There's a bloke 'ere who wants a word with Juney,' Archie's voice rattled from Celine's throat.

Juanita, the Friend who'd shushed Ray, sprang to her feet. 'That's me! Juney is my nickname!'

Celine reverted to her normal voice: 'Juney, don't feel bad about leaving the insulin out of the fridge. He knows you didn't mean it.'

Goosebumps popped on Maddie's arms. Juanita hadn't said anything about insulin last night. Celine was adept at cold reading, but that was an unusually precise detail. She tended to stick to generalities.

Juanita's face creased. 'Jeffrey? Jeffrey, is that you?'

A blade of light sliced through the gloom as a man slipped through the doors on the far side of the lounge. He was two decades younger than Celine's core demographic, his legs clad in skinny jeans and boots, his arms scrawled with tattoos. Ray hadn't noticed the intruder; he was slumped on a bar stool, his back to the doors.

'Celine del Ray!' the guy shouted, striding towards the stage and pointing a camera phone in Celine's direction. 'Celine del Ray!'

Shit. The week after Celine had signed up as the cruise's guest celebrity, Maddie had heard via Twitter that there might be a blogger on board, and it looked like he'd finally decided to pitch up.

'Who is that?' Celine called, squinting into the audience.

'Any comment about the fact that Lillian Small is planning to sue you?'

A collective gasp. There were too many obstacles for Maddie to get to the guy easily, and she couldn't count on the wait staff to intervene. Thankfully Ray had realised what was going on and was hustling towards him.

'You know the story, right?' the man crowed to the Friends gaping at him. 'This so called *medium*, this *predator*, bombarded Mrs Small with messages saying that her daughter and grandson were alive in Florida, when DNA proves that . . .' he faltered. 'Proves that . . .' he clamped a hand to his mouth. 'Oh *fuck*.' With that, he whirled, shoved past Ray and ran out, the doors hissing closed behind him.

Ray glanced at Maddie and she gestured at him to follow.

Celine chuckled again, but it sounded forced. 'Uh. I tell you, that was . . . Give me a minute here.' She took a slug of Evian from the bottle in her wheelchair pocket. The room settled into an uneasy silence. 'You know, there are always gonna be doubters.

But I can only repeat what Spirit tells me. That situation . . . you know . . . Wait . . . I'm getting something else here. You know, sometimes the spirits come through so strong that I can taste what they're tasting, feel what they're feeling. I'm getting . . . Smoke. I can smell smoke . . . I'm hearing . . . Someone here lose a loved one in a fire? Does that make sense to anyone?'

No one spoke up. Maddie squirmed.

'It could be . . . yeah, you know, I'm smelling gas, think it might be a car accident. I'm getting . . . What is the significance of the I-90?'

A Friend called out that his second cousin had been killed in a head-on collision on that highway years earlier. Maddie allowed herself to breathe again. Ray crept back into the room and gave Maddie the A-okay sign. She checked her phone. Five minutes to go. She edged towards Celine, signalling that it was time to wrap it up. Ray had better do his bloody job and usher everyone out as fast as possible. The Friends were booked to eat at the second sitting, so they'd have to leave straight away if they didn't want a rubbery lobster tail.

Celine wished the Friends a Happy New Year and ran through her usual schtick about visiting her website where there were links to purchase her eleven books. Maddie leapt onto the stage before her boss could be engulfed in a tsunami of well-wishers. Celine's wheelchair wasn't strictly necessary (although she could propel it with the skill of a Paralympian if an over-zealous fan threatened to approach), but Maddie was glad of it this evening. Close up, Celine was really showing her age; her waxy skin had the look of an apple left too long in cold storage, her lips were the colour of old deli meat.

Maddie unplugged the mic and handed it to the tech before Celine recovered and lambasted him for the PA system screw-up.

'You okay, Celine?' she murmured.

'Get me the fuck outta here now.'

'Celine?' Leila bustled up to them before Maddie could intervene, waving a copy of part two of Celine's autobiography, *Medium to the Stars and Beyond.* 'I meant to ask you last night at the cocktail evening, but you were there so briefly . . . could you sign this?'

Celine smiled icily. 'It'd be a pleasure, my darling.'

'Can you put, "To Leila, my biggest fan"? I've got all your books. E-editions and audio as well.'

Maddie handed Celine a pen, glancing at Leila to see if she'd noticed Celine's shaking hands; fortunately she was far too busy staring rapturously at her face. 'You've helped me so much, Celine. You and Archie of course.' Leila pressed the book to her chest. 'You've really brought me peace. John . . . he wasn't the easiest and . . . I don't know how you do it.'

'It's a God-given gift, my darling. Know this, your faith and support means a lot to me.'

'And you mean a lot to me. That awful man who burst in here doesn't have a—'

'Celine is very tired,' Maddie interrupted. 'Connecting with Spirit takes a lot out of her. I'm sure you understand.'

'Oh, I do, I do,' Leila said, bobbing and bowing and scurrying off to join the other Friends bottlenecking the exit.

Ray approached. 'Sorry about that, Celine.'

Celine's eyes – already unnaturally hooded from a screwed-up eyelift in the eighties – narrowed. 'Yeah? What the hell, Ray? I pay you for *that*?'

'How was I supposed to know he was gonna show up? I checked out everyone else.'

'You should have been at the goddamned door, Ray.'

'Celine, like I say, I fucked up. Won't happen again.'

Celine snorted. 'Damn right it won't. Where'd he go anyway?'

'Ran into the restroom. Looked like he was gonna puke.'

Maddie's stomach rolled over. After stupidly reading a *Huff Post* exposé about ship-borne viruses, she'd only been able to cope by washing her hands at every opportunity and popping probiotics like an addict. Still, that explained why they hadn't been hounded by the blogger before. He must have been holed up in his cabin praying to the porcelain god for the duration of the cruise.

'You want me to escort you back to your cabin?' Ray asked.

'It's a suite,' Celine snapped. 'And no. Get out of my sight. Madeleine can do it.'

Ray nodded miserably and slunk away. Maddie knew very little about his personal life, but he'd mentioned something about having to pay child support to one of his exes. He may be a letch and a bullshitter, but she almost pitied him – he'd be lucky if he still had a job when they reached Miami. Celine's bodyguards never lasted long.

'Goddamned bloggers and undercover journalists,' Celine griped, twirling a hand in the air to indicate they should get going. 'Forty years I've been doing this. It's my God-given gift . . .'

Maddie let Celine ramble on as she manoeuvred the wheelchair out via the stage door exit, blinking as her eyes were blasted by the pink and gold neon signage splayed all over the Promenade Dreamz deck. Passengers streamed towards the staircase for the second dinner sitting, and twenty-somethings in tight white shorts and 'Foveros = Fun! Fun! Fun!' T-shirts flitted around, rumba-ing to the calypso music in the background and hawking plastic angel wings and devil horns for tonight's Heaven 'n' Hell themed New Year's Eve party. Maddie had no intention of going anywhere near the festivities. She planned on putting Celine to bed, ordering a grilled cheese sandwich from room service (her gut clenched at the thought of eating the mass-produced slop in the dining room and buffets) then heading up to the jogging track above the Lido deck. She hadn't yet found a gap to do her five miles today.

A trio of meaty men with fluorescent halos attached to their shaven heads made way for them as Maddie inched Celine into the elevator, which, as usual, smelled faintly of vomit. She pressed the button for the Verandah deck with her elbow and wheeled Celine as far away from the damp patch on the carpet as she could get. A reggae rendition of 'Rehab' plinked as they were propelled upwards through the atrium, the glass sides gradually revealing the lobby and cocktail bars below.

'Christ, I need a drink,' Celine said.

'Nearly there.'

Maddie dragged the wheelchair out of the elevator and headed in the direction of the VIP staterooms. A couple of giggly elderly women squeezed themselves against the corridor wall to allow them to pass. Maddie smiled brightly at them to make up for Celine's surly 'whatever' response to their Happy New Year wishes, and waved at Althea, the deck's cabin steward, who was exiting a neighbouring suite, a bunch of towels tucked under an arm.

'Good evening, Mrs del Ray and Maddie!' Althea called. 'Do you need any help?'

Celine ignored her, but Althea's smile didn't falter. Maddie had no clue how Althea remained so cheerful while mopping up after arseholes like Celine. Most of the staff exuded an exhausting (obviously fake) joviality, but Maddie was certain Althea's constant good mood wasn't a front.

After swiping the room card several times until the lock finally flashed green, Maddie hefted the wheelchair into the narrow entrance area and pushed Celine towards the balcony and her collection of booze.

Celine jabbed a talon at the TV. 'For Christ's sake change the goddamned channel. How many times have I told that goddamned woman not to touch it?'

On screen, Damien, the cruise director – an Australian with the fixed gaze of someone dangerously bipolar – was once again running through his tour of the ship. Maddie flicked past a *Saturday Night Live* parody of failed Republican nominee Mitch Reynard, and a shopping channel, where two middle-aged women were gushing over a reversible jacket, before settling on footage of the run-up to the Times Square ball drop. Without being asked, she scooped ice into a glass and poured Celine a double J&B.

Celine snatched it out of her hand and took a gulp. 'Christ, that's better. You're a good girl, Madeleine.'

Maddie rolled her eyes. 'Did I just hear you correctly?'

'Archie says you're thinking of quitting.'

'Celine, I'm always thinking of quitting. Maybe I wouldn't if you stopped calling me a useless bitch.'

'You know I don't mean it.' She gestured at the TV again. 'I don't need reminding that another year's over. Put one of my films on.'

'Which one?'

'*Pretty Woman.*'

Maddie connected the hard drive and scrolled through the menu until she reached the Julia Roberts folder. She still couldn't reconcile Celine's hard-bitten outlook on life with her addiction to nineties romcoms; Maddie had lost count of the number of scratchy motel chairs she'd sat in, waiting for her boss to fall asleep while *When Harry Met Sally* or *French Kiss* played out to their predictable conclusions.

Celine rattled the glass for a refill. 'So. What are we gonna do about Ray?'

'You're the boss.'

'You know he's got a thing for you, Madeleine.'

'Ray's got a thing for everyone with a vagina. He's a dickhead.'

Celine sighed. 'I know. The cute ones always are. He'll have to go. But that doesn't solve your problem, does it?'

'I've got a problem?'

'You need a man in your life, Madeleine. It's about time you put your past to rest.'

'Not this again. What the hell am I going to do with a man?'

Celine cackled. 'Well, if I have to tell you . . .'

'You want to tell me how I'm supposed to maintain a relation-ship when I'm on the road with you nine months out of the year?'

'Yeah, yeah, guilt-trip the old woman. You should go to the party tonight. See if you can snag yourself one of those cute crew members in their tight white pants. How long has it been? You know, since you last . . .'

'None of your business.'

'That's not an answer. You want me to ask Archie what he—'

'Enough with the personal stuff, Celine.'

'Just saying, you deserve better outta life.'

'Okay if I use your bathroom?' If she took her time in there, with any luck Celine would pass out in front of the movie and she'd be able to slip away without too much of an ear-bashing.

'Go right ahead.'

Maddie fled inside it and locked the door. It was three times the size of the one in her cabin, with a whirlpool bath and a pyramid of rolled white towels. She sat on the toilet lid and rubbed her temples. Thanks to that hipster guy, Celine would be in funk for the next week at least. And no doubt the footage he'd taken would already be all over YouTube. Celine had only signed up for the cruise to get away from the heat after the Lillian Small debacle, but they'd both known it could backfire on them.

After it had all blown up, Maddie had never said 'I told you so'. She'd warned Celine not to go on Eric Kavanaugh's *Black Thursday Remembrance Show*; the shock-jock was notorious for skewering psychics, scientologists and spiritualists. Plus, Celine had been one of the much-maligned 'Circle of Psychics' who'd joined together to 'use their combined energy' to ascertain the apparently mysterious causes of the four plane crashes that had occurred back in 2012. Kavanaugh had gleefully ripped the psychics a new one when the NTSB released its findings and it transpired that the psychics had struck out on all counts. To be fair, Celine had been holding her own until the subject of the Florida crash had come up. Maddie still had no clue what had possessed her boss to insist that Lori Small and her son Bobby, two of the passengers aboard the aircraft that had plummeted into the Everglades, were alive. Even when Bobby and Lori's DNA was discovered amongst the wreckage, Celine continued to proclaim that the mother and son were out there somewhere, wandering the streets of Miami, suffering from amnesia. She'd gone too far to back down. Tragically, Lori's mother, Lillian Small, had spent all her savings hiring private detectives to follow this dubious lead, and now an enterprising lawyer had taken on her case and was gunning for Celine.

It wasn't the first time Celine had got it wrong – but it was certainly the most high-profile of her blunders. But then . . . Maddie wasn't being entirely fair, was she? Celine *had* occasionally been right, hadn't she? There was tonight's insulin revelation for a start (but it was possible Ray had passed on that nugget – she'd have to check). She knew that statistically Celine had to hit on some facts that weren't fed to her by Maddie or whichever hapless ex-cop she'd hired to play the part of her bodyguard, but it still made her feel uneasy. And the guilt she usually managed to keep at bay was getting to her. Needling at her. It was a mistake getting to know the Friends. Maybe she should just quit. *And do what?* A shitty minimum wage job was the best she could hope for with her record. She could always move back to the UK, slink back with her tail between her legs. Her sister would love that: *I told you so, Maddie, I told you it would all end in tears.*

'You fallen in?' Celine shouted.

'Coming!' Maddie called. So much for Celine passing out. She was about to get up, when the floor lurched, forcing her to grab onto the toilet-roll holder. Her knees began juddering, a strong vibration hummed under her feet. The lights flickered, there was a long mechanical yawning sound and then . . . silence.

Pulse thumping in her throat, Maddie unlocked the door and hurried into the suite. 'Celine? I think there's something wrong with the ship.'

Maddie was expecting Celine to say something along the lines of: 'You're goddamned right something's wrong with the ship, it's a shithole,' but her head was slumped forward; her arms hung listlessly over the chair's sides. The glass lay on the carpet where it must have slipped from her fingers.

On screen, Richard Gere rolled down Hollywood Boulevard. Then the television blinked off.

'Celine? Celine, are you okay?'

No answer.

Maddie crept forward and touched the crepey skin on Celine's forearm. No response. She moved around to face her and sank to her knees. 'Celine?' Without lifting her head, Celine sucked in a breath, then began humming a jaunty, jazzy tune that reminded Maddie of Lizzie Bean, another (albeit less vocal) of Celine's spirit guides. 'Celine?' It was becoming difficult to swallow. 'Hey . . . Come on, Celine.'

Celine raised her head, a look of such raw terror in her eyes that Maddie yipped and fell back on her haunches. 'Jesus!'

Maddie leapt to her feet, meaning to lunge for the phone, but then the lights went out again, and she stumbled as the ship listed to the left. She fought to control her breathing, had almost done so when a voice cut through the silence. 'Ho-hum, me old ducky,' Archie cackled. 'This is going to be fun.'

The Condemned Man

Gary pressed his forehead against the wall, shivering as the cold water streamed down his back. The skin on his stomach and inner thighs stung from where he'd scrubbed at himself with Marilyn's nailbrush; the pads of his fingers were ridged and waterlogged. He'd been in the shower for upwards of an hour, and the reek of Pantene was becoming unbearable – he'd used all of the complimentary body wash and Marilyn's shampoo on last night's clothes, stomping on them like a demented wine presser. They were bundled in a ball in the corner of the stall: without bleach, there was no guarantee they didn't hold a trace of his girl's DNA. He'd have to dump them over the side as soon as possible.

Concentrate on the water. Think about the cold. But it wasn't working; the black thoughts were creeping back. Marilyn had bought his upset stomach excuse, but he doubted she'd let him skip the evening's festivities unless he was really at death's door. He supposed he could make himself vomit within her hearing, stick his fingers down his throat, but he was so consumed by anxiety he was beginning to think he wouldn't have to fake it.

Because they must have found his girl by now. The cabin stewards were thorough, servicing the cabins twice a day, and it'd been more than twelve hours since she'd—

A rumbling under his feet; a jolt. The shower water sputtered and Gary opened his eyes onto blackness. For a second he was convinced he'd gone blind – *a punishment from God!* – then, as a vibration rocketed up through the soles of his feet, it dawned on him that something was wrong with the ship. He shut off the water, fumbled for a towel, and listened. The background whir of the air-con was absent, which made his head feel lighter somehow, as if he could finally think rationally. He felt around the sink for his glasses, then edged his way out of the bathroom. He waited for his eyes to adjust to the darkness – but of course they weren't going to adjust, there was no natural light in the cabin; he always booked one of the cheaper internal staterooms. An alarm beeped several times, there was an unintelligible message crackling with static, and then: 'G'day, ladies and gentlemen, Damien your cruise director here. Just to let you know we are experiencing an electrical problem. There is no cause for alarm. For your own safety, please return to your staterooms and wait for further instructions, thank you. And like I say, there's no cause for alarm. We'll be updating you in more detail shortly.'

Gary inched his way to the door and eked it open. A bare-chested guy wearing plastic devil horns rounded the corner, a woman in a bikini and strappy gold heels jiggling after him. As they came closer, the emergency strip lights on the floor turned their skin a sinister greenish colour. The floor dipped and Gary stepped back, letting the door slam. Saliva flooded into his mouth. Outside, doors banged, a woman hollered, someone shouted for Kevin to 'get a fucking move on, dude'.

He shuffled back to the bed, flinching as the lights wobbled on. They were far dimmer than usual, and cast a sallow glow around the cabin. Water crawled through the hair on his legs, his panic now so intense he could almost see it as a physical thing in his peripheral vision.

It was just a mechanical glitch – it happened all the time, Foveros was notorious for them. And even if they had found her, the last thing they'd do is stop the ship. No. He was just letting paranoia get the better of him again. He squeezed his wrist, clung to the shallow thump of his pulse, made himself count back from a hundred. Then again. And again. Good. It was becoming easier to breathe.

The lock clicked, the door slammed open and Marilyn burst in. 'Gary! You're here!'

Speak. 'Where else would I be?'

'Honey, I reckon we should get out of here. Get to the muster station. I could've sworn I smelled smoke.'

'Damien said we're supposed to stay in the staterooms.'

'Didn't you hear me? I smelled *smoke*, Gary.' She was out of breath, her flat face greasy with perspiration. 'The elevators have stopped working – gotta be people trapped inside. What do you think's happened?'

'Some sort of mechanical fault. Nothing serious, you'll see.' His voice sounded uneven, a pitch higher than usual, but she didn't seem to notice. Marilyn wasn't the most observant of people – one of the reasons he'd married her.

Marilyn narrowed her eyes. 'Honey . . . why aren't you dressed?'

'Been in the shower.'

'Again? With all this happening?'

Deep breath, don't lose it. 'I was in the shower when it happened.'

'And you really think it's nothing serious?'

'Yeah. Remember what happened to *The Beautiful Wonder*? They fixed that in no time.'

'Oh. I guess . . . I still think we should go. Paulie and Selena said they'd wait for us on Eleven. Remember, hon, our muster station is right there.'

'Who the hell are Paulie and Selena?'

'They're just the cutest couple. We got talking at dinner. I decided to go to the Lido buffet instead of Dreamscapes, although the lines at the noodle bar were so long! That was how we got talking – in the line. We were sitting together on the Tranquillity deck when it happened. And hon, you'll never guess what.'

'What?' He did his best to sound and look interested. His cheeks were aching.

'They're Silver Foveros cruisers just like us, and they were on *The Beautiful Wish* last year – the Bahamas route – just a week after we went!'

'Amazing.'

'I know, right? That's what I said. They were really concerned when I told them you were feeling sick.' Typical Marilyn: she made it her mission to hook up with as many strangers as she could on their yearly cruise. Most of her new friendships were short-lived, she was fickle like that. Gary toyed with the idea of asking her if she'd noticed his absence early this morning. It wouldn't be that unusual, he'd been feigning insomnia for years, and she hadn't yet taken issue with his excuse that the only way to cure it was to go for a walk. But this was different. If she had woken in the early hours and noticed he was gone, would she be prepared to give him an alibi? He couldn't be certain. He pictured her seated in court, sobbing that she had no idea she'd married a monster.

'Gary!'

'Huh?'

'I *said*, I still think we should get going. Aren't you going to get dressed?'

'You go. I'll catch up.'

'But what if—'

'Just *go*, Marilyn.'

'You don't need to snap at me.'

Dial it back. 'It'll be fine, babe. Things like this happen all the time on cruises.'

'But I need you, Gary.'

'Hon, I'm still feeling icky,' he winced at the word – a Marilyn word – but it did the trick.

'Oh Gary, I didn't even ask how you were feeling.'

'I got sick again, had to use your shampoo to clean my clothes.'

'Oh baby, don't worry.'

Gary gave himself a mental pat on the back. 'Now, you go and join your friends and don't worry about me. Damien wouldn't have told us to stay in the staterooms if there was any real danger.'

'If you're sure?'

'I'm sure. If they tell us to head to the muster stations I'll come find you.'

'Okay. I hate leaving you, it's just . . . I don't think I could handle staying down here.'

She moved to hug him, and he leaned back, falling onto his elbows. 'Better not. I might be contagious.'

'You're so thoughtful. You know where to go, right, babe?'

'Uh-huh. I'll feel so much better knowing you're safe.'

He almost screamed with relief as the door closed behind her.

Now. Think coolly and calmly. Run through it again, and this time, don't lose it.

He'd chucked the remaining pills down the pan in the men's room outside the Sandman Lounge, so that just left his clothes, gloves and cap. He could get rid of those easily during the party when everyone would be whooping it up. But ... what if they cancelled the festivities? That would depend on whether they sorted out the mechanical glitch or whatever it was in time. They would. He couldn't worry about that.

Next – would her friends remember him? He hadn't drawn attention to himself, hadn't even spoken to his girl at the bar, and he prided himself on his bland appearance. He knew from years of careful study that people tended to fixate on obvious character-istics – a moustache, spectacles, garish clothing, a limp. The security cameras and face recognition systems shouldn't be an issue – he'd kept his head bent as he'd followed her to her cabin, and his cap would've hidden his bald spot. Once he'd disposed of his clothes, there'd be no way they could identify him, and in any case, his plain navy sports shirt and khaki shorts weren't particu-larly distinguishing, and could even be mistaken for the uniform worn by the low-level staff.

All good.

So why did he still have the feeling he was missing something? *Think.*

It hit him like a shock of ice water: the 'Don't Disturb, I'm Cruisin' n Snoozin'' sign. He had the sickening feeling that he'd already snapped off the surgical gloves when he slid it over the door handle. Ah, God. His DNA and fingerprints would be on it. Could he say he'd touched it as he walked past?

Yes. No. How would he explain what he was doing on her deck? Her stateroom was one floor above his, but it was situated halfway along a corridor that led nowhere.

It was his punishment for deviating from the plan. It was supposed to have happened tonight, New Year's Eve, when everyone would be drunk and occupied. He was usually so care-ful. Mr Contingency. He never took chances. He wasn't sloppy.

He had a system. But there she'd been, alone at the bar, staring wistfully at her friends, who were dancing and flirting with the rest of the singles group. It had been too good a chance to pass up. He'd given in to temptation, and now he had to pay. There was a very good reason he always did it on the last night of the cruise – the chaos as passengers were herded off the ship the following morning meant that the chances of a clean getaway were far higher. Most of his girls wouldn't fully recall what had happened to them until much later. Days, weeks, even. And by then it would be too late. Plus, he'd read on countless forums that the security staff were prepped to convince victims of on-board sexual assaults not to press charges. The last thing Foveros wanted was more adverse publicity.

But if they *had* discovered her, they'd be forced to investigate. Foveros already had a bad rep for safety on board, and then there were all those accusations that the company wasn't keeping up with hygiene requirements. They'd be stupid to try to hide this.

What had possessed him?

Perhaps he'd been lulled into a false sense of security because it had all been going so well up till then. On the first day, he was always especially attentive to Marilyn, arriving early and booking her into the spa so that she'd be occupied while he did his preliminary sweep of the passengers. Foveros's New Year's cruises always attracted a batch of eager singles, and he wasn't fussy about age. He preferred slightly larger ladies, blondes or redheads. No one too obviously confident; a follower rather than a leader. Over the years he'd become adept at picking out the ugly duckling at the party, the hanger-on, the afterthought bridesmaid at the bachelorette party. There were usually hundreds of Brits on the New Year's cruise, eagerly taking advantage of budget cabins and cheap cocktails. Brits partied harder than American girls, and (in his opinion) tended to have lower self-esteem.

He'd spotted his girl that evening during Happy Hour in the Sandman Lounge, had watched her out of the corner of his eye while Marilyn got steadily drunk on half-price Mai Tais. It always amazed him how he recognised his girls straight away, as if they were calling out to him. She was just his type, thirty or forty pounds overweight, stringy blond hair, hanging out on the periphery of a large group of thirty-somethings, laughing self-consciously at their jokes. On the second day he'd seen her in the pizza queue, her thighs and shoulders bright red from over-exposure to the sun, and it was even more obvious that she was being sidelined by the rest of her group (he'd rejoiced at the bleakness in her eyes). Another piece fell into place when she'd excused herself, and he'd followed, keeping his distance, as she made her way to her stateroom – taking the stairs rather than the elevator. Gary noted her stateroom number – M446 – and walked on past.

And last night, well . . . it was almost as if it was meant to be. Marilyn had been exhausted by the time they returned to the ship after the day in Cozumel. He'd signed them up for a beach resort excursion followed by a tour around some dull Mayan ruins (Marilyn had complained about the heat and the mosquitoes the entire time, as had most of their fellow cruisers), and doped by the unusual amount of exercise, she'd fallen asleep almost as soon as they'd returned to the ship. He'd sneaked out, intending only to continue his recce and make absolutely sure the girl he'd chosen was The One.

And there she'd been, waiting for him.

He always kept his tools on him – it wouldn't do for Marilyn to come across the little bag of goodies. It had been easy to saunter to the men's room, pocket his glasses and don the cap. Easy to check that the barman and the surrounding patrons were otherwise engaged. Easy to crumble the tablet into her cocktail glass. Easy to hang back and watch as she began to lose focus. Easy to wait for her to stumble out of the room. Easy to watch her weave her way into the elevator, while he made his way down to her deck via the stairs. Easy to trail her down the corridor, feeling his pulse quicken, anticipation twitching in his groin. Easy to lend a hand when she fumbled with the key-card. Easy to shoulder his way in, murmuring that he was just there to help her. Easy to—

Gary jumped as seven loud beeps echoed over the PA system, followed by: 'G'day, ladies and gentlemen, Damien your cruise director here again. We are now asking you to calmly and carefully make your way to your assigned muster stations. This is not a drill, but there is no cause for alarm. Crew members will be on hand to help you find your assigned stations, which will be clearly marked on the back of your stateroom doors and on your Foveros Fun Cards. I repeat, there is no cause for alarm. Your safety is our primary concern.'

The sound of raised voices, slamming doors and running feet floated in from the corridor. Gary didn't move, merely listened as the chaos outside petered away.

He counted back from a hundred again, had reached fifty when he heard someone – presumably a cabin steward – knocking on the doors. His fingers hurt from clenching and unclenching them. His bowels cramped. Should he hide? He could squeeze into the wardrobe. But what if the steward had been told to search the entire cabin? It wouldn't look good if he was found cowering in a closet.

His girl was supposed to have been number four. His lucky number.

He'd helped her over to the bed – she hadn't said much, murmured she was feeling sick, something like that. She'd slumped onto her back, her eyes glassy. When her face went slack, he began. He didn't allow himself to touch at first, just look. Then, lightly, softly, he ran his hands over her thighs, breasts and torso. Tight shorts, a strappy top. He yanked the top up, revealing a flesh-coloured bra. He'd have to roll her over to undo it, had been about to do just that, when she'd coughed, gurgled, and he'd jumped back as vomit spilled out of her mouth. She shuddered, coughed again. Choking. She was choking. He—

Bang, bang on his door. He sat absolutely still. Bit down on his tongue, hoping against hope that whoever it was would pass on. The lock clicked, the door opened and an Asian man poked his head inside. He wasn't their usual steward – a pretty Filipino girl Marilyn had taken an instant disliking to. 'Are you unwell, sir?' the steward asked. 'Did you not hear me knocking the door?'

'No. I'm fine. Just tired.'

'Sir. You have to get to your muster station. Do you know how to get there?'

'Are you checking all the cabins?'

The steward frowned.

Gary could hardly believe he'd said something so stupid. 'I mean, to make sure that everyone will be safe.'

'Oh yes, sir. Your safety is important to us.'

'I need to get dressed.'

'Please hurry, sir. I will come back.'

So this was it. If she hadn't been found, if by some miracle her friends or steward hadn't discovered her yet, there was now no chance she'd remain undetected. He pulled on a pair of shorts and a shirt, trying not to think about the sodden clothes in the corner of the stall. Then he sucked in a breath and slipped his feet into his sandals.

His only chance was to brazen it out.

He hadn't even checked to see if she was still alive, but he'd known. Known in his gut that she wasn't. His girl had choked to death while Damien chirped on the TV, the back of her hand flapping on the mattress, smack, smack, smack, '. . . *don't forget to check out our signature stand-up shows in the Starlight Dreamer Lounge . . .*' smack, smack. '. . . *and for a limited time only, Xenus watches will be going for a staggering forty per cent discounted price . . .*' After several unendurable minutes, a sound came out of her throat . . . not a death rattle exactly, but a hiss. A final, defeated exhalation. Without considering the implications of what he was doing, he'd used his foot to roll her off the double bed and into the gap between it and the wall, and threw the duvet over her.

That had been his greatest mistake. Now they'd know for sure that someone else was involved. If he'd just left her lying on the bed, more than likely they'd put her death down to alcohol poisoning.

He crept out into the now deserted corridor and waved at the steward, who was checking the last of the staterooms and sliding red cards into the key slots. 'Thanks for waiting,' Gary called. 'Sorry to cause any trouble.' Good. His voice sounded calm, controlled. *The man I encountered did not appear anxious or guilty,* he imagined the steward relating to the head of security – or God forbid the FBI or Scotland Yard or whichever agency was tasked with investigating British passengers' deaths.

'No problem, sir. Please hurry. Your life vest is there at your muster station.'

Gary walked stiffly towards the stairs, his sandals slop-shooshing on the carpet. It was gloomier here, the staircase's metal rails warm from countless hands. He sniffed. Marilyn was right, there was a smoky odour wafting from the lower level. He increased his pace, hesitating when he came to his girl's floor.

It would be so easy to hurry around the corner and peer down the corridor to her stateroom. He took a couple of steps towards the next flight, then whirled around and jogged back towards the entrance to her deck. His gut clenched again – he couldn't quite believe what he was doing, but something had taken him over and he couldn't stop.

The red cards indicating that the cabins were unoccupied were all slotted into the doors of the staterooms leading up to hers. The corridor stretched like an optical illusion, its end shrouded in darkness. He hustled along it, stopping dead when he saw the red card inserted into his girl's door, too.

Someone had checked the cabin. If they'd found her, he would have expected to see a security presence, unless the ship was already engaged in a cover-up. *Or perhaps she's not dead, after all. She could be in the medical bay, groggy and confused, trying to piece together the night's events.* He retraced his steps, moving as fast as he could, and it was only when he reached the stairwell that it hit him: he'd forgotten to shield his face from the security cameras.

The Devil's Handmaiden

Althea slapped on the smile she reserved for the most difficult passengers, and waited for the man lumbering down the corridor towards her. Mr Lineman; stateroom V23. He and his wife were truly disgusting, leaving their toilet bowl stained and sodden towels all over the floor. 'Hello, Mr Lineman,' she called, adding a respectful lilt to her voice. 'You should be at your muster station now.'

He huffed, his cheeks flushed from the effort of walking the hundred metres or so from the stairwell. The dim emergency lights accentuated the folds in his baggy face; his knees sagged under the strain of the load they were forced to carry. 'Just what in the hell has happened to the goddamned ship?'

'I am so sorry, Mr Lineman, but I don't know any more than you do.' This was almost true – she'd been napping at her station when the Bravo alarm had sounded – but she'd heard from Maria, her supervisor, that B Deck had been evacuated because of the smoke. Althea wasn't worried. In her four years of working for Foveros, there had been several similar incidents, and Maria had said the fire was minor.

'Why the hell can't we stay in our staterooms?'

'It's for your own safety, Mr Lineman.'

His jowls wobbled. 'I thought there was no danger? Damien said there was no danger.'

Smile still in place she said, 'That is true, but it is standard procedure for the captain to muster the passengers in a situation like this. I really must urge you to return to your station.'

'I had to come back for my medication. You people want me to get sick?'

No. I would like you to die a lingering, painful death. 'Of course not, Mr Lineman. A crew member should have accompanied you back to your stateroom. Would you like me to collect it for you?'

'I can do it.' He flicked the red card that she'd inserted into his stateroom's lock. 'What the hell's this?'

'It indicates that your stateroom has been checked and is empty, Mr Lineman.'

'Hmmmf.' He threw it on the carpet, slid his own card into the slot and slammed his way inside the suite.

She leaned against the wall and stretched like a cat while she waited for him to re-emerge. That bitch Maria would be on the prowl if she wasn't done soon, and she still had to check Trining's station on Five Aft – she'd meant to do it hours earlier. The lazy *puta* had come to find her at lunch, said she'd started puking half-way through her morning shift, but Althea suspected she'd been drinking again. Trining was already on a warning – it would be her third sick day this month – and she'd promised Althea fifty dollars if she'd cover for her. The extra money would come in useful, but today Althea could do without the hassle. Her limbs were heavy with exhaustion; she hadn't been sleeping well. She'd convinced herself that she was tired all the time because she'd been working too hard, taking on too many extra duties.

The alternative didn't bear thinking about.

Damien's voice droned over the PA system, repeating the same message yet again. The man was in love with his own voice. Althea had never spoken to him, but Rogelio, the only pinoy assistant cruise director, said he was an egoist with a nasty heart. Rogelio . . . now there was someone she should have married. Handsome, hard working, and always courteous. The opposite of Joshua.

The toilet whooshed in Mr Lineman's cabin, and seconds later he reappeared, a hefty Walgreens bag cradled in his arms. She smiled again, but he stomped past her without a word.

'*Putang ina mo*,' she said under her breath.

He paused and turned, his piggy eyes gleaming. 'What was that?'

Shit. 'Excuse me?'

'What did you just say? What language was that?'

'Tagalog, Mr Lineman.'

'Taga what?'

'Tagalog. It is a Filipino language.' *You ignorant pig-bastard.* 'I was merely wishing you good luck,' she lied.

'Learn to speak English, why don't you,' he muttered.

Althea wished that she could tell this stupid cone-head that she spoke English, Spanish and Tagalog fluently and could curse in five additional languages, whereas he could barely speak one, but she would lose her bonus if he gave her a negative rating. 'I am so sorry, Mr Lineman. I meant no offence.'

He looked slightly mollified. This time, she watched him carefully as he trudged away. The ship was listing more radically now, enough to affect his balance. *Good. Fall, bastardo, fall.*

She replaced the red card in his door and then checked the suite shared by the two seniors, Helen and Elise. Spotless – their twin beds were exactly as she'd left them when she'd serviced their stateroom earlier that evening. She expected a large tip from these two. Althea had worked on enough ships to recognise the big tippers, and it was never the ones who demanded extra bottled water every hour, bleated about the air-con temperature, or whined if she didn't fold a different fuck-darned towel animal every night.

She moved onto the last suite – V27 – the psychic's cabin. Devil's work, her mamita would have called it. Mrs del Ray was a grumpy old bitch to be sure, but she was generous – Althea had already made extra money by turning a blind eye to the bottles of alcohol in her stateroom. The second she inserted her master key-card into the lock, the door was yanked open and Maddie, Mrs del Ray's skinny assistant, lunged at her. 'Althea! I thought you were the doctor.'

'You are sick?'

'Not me – Celine. Mrs del Ray.'

Althea followed her into the bedroom, where Mrs del Ray was sitting in her wheelchair, staring slack-faced at the blank screen of the TV. The room smelled of alcohol.

'Celine? Celine? Althea is here,' Maddie said in a sing-song voice, as if she was addressing a child.

Mrs del Ray looked up, her head lolling back on her neck, her eyes unfocused. She giggled, and flapped a hand in a vague greeting.

'What's wrong with her?' Althea asked, her eyes drifting to the empty bottle of J&B next to the television. The woman drank too much – Althea was the one who lugged her empties to the glass crusher – maybe that was why she was sick.

'I don't know. She's acting confused. I called the fucking . . . sorry' – Althea nodded primly – 'I called for the doctor as soon as the ship stopped, but no one's come yet.'

'You have tried to call again?'

'Yeah. Haven't stopped. There's no answer at all now.'

Althea unclipped her radio and buzzed her supervisor. 'Maria? Come in, Maria.' Static hissed back at her. She tried again, with the same result. *Susmaryosep.* 'May I try your phone, Maddie?'

'Go ahead.'

Althea picked up the receiver and dialled the medical centre, but it just rang and rang. Next she tried Housekeeping and Guest Services, but both pipped with a busy signal. 'I will go to the medical centre in person and tell them to send the doctor.'

'Thank you.'

'You're welcome,' Althea said automatically. She didn't mind Maddie – Celine's assistant had always been courteous to her, without being patronising or over-friendly. And she was visibly worried. Perhaps there really was something wrong with the old woman.

Althea hurried out the stateroom, trying her radio again. Another gush of static. This was exactly what she didn't need. She checked the corridor on the port side for Electra, who serviced the staterooms in that section – but there was no sign of her. It would be faster to use the passenger staircase to reach the medical bay on Deck Three, although housekeeping staff were forbidden in the area. She'd take her chances. Most of the crew would be at their muster stations, herding the guests, or dealing with the issues in the generator room, so she should get away with it. Down and down she ran. She held her breath and ducked her head when she reached the landing on Six, where two engineers were helping several grumbling passengers out of one of the stalled elevators.

As she jogged towards the medical bay door, she caught a whiff of smoke drifting through the serrated sheeting that covered the adjacent entrance to the I-95. She pressed the bell next to the door and waited. Nothing. She tried the handle, and when it gave, she stepped inside. The narrow waiting area, pharmacy and reception desk were empty, but raised voices sounded from behind a door at the far end of the waiting area. She moved over to it, stood on her toes and peered through the frosted glass window. The new doctor was placing an oxygen cup over the face of a hysterical crew member in a pair of filthy blue overalls. Next to him, a male nurse was ministering to a fellow in officer whites, who was also attached to an oxygen tank. But it was the man on the gurney closest to her who grabbed her attention. He lay absolutely still on his side, his arm outstretched. Sloughs of skin like obscene lace drooped off his forearm, revealing a section of yellow and red weeping tissue. As if he could sense her gaze he shifted his eyes and looked straight at her. She offered him a look of sympathy, but he didn't react; his eyes were empty, as if he'd crawled inside himself to deal with the pain. She'd seen nasty burns before – she'd been visiting her mother in Binondo when a fire had ravaged a nearby factory – but the sight still made her stomach roll. The doctor hurried over to the burn victim and gently placed a hand on his forehead.

Shaking, Althea retreated back to the waiting area. The shouts from the room had become murmurs. The fire had to have been worse than she'd been told. And it was becoming rapidly warmer down here; the air-con was still out. Unsure what to do, she paced.

The last doctor, a Cuban man with bad teeth, had reportedly been fired for harassing one of the Romanian crew waitresses, but his replacement had a kind face. She wondered if she could ask him for help with her situation, then swallowed the thought. She couldn't think like that. She ran a hand over her belly. If she *was* pregnant, it was still too early to show. Two months at the most. Perhaps Joshua had made good on his threat to mess with her pills after all. *Bastardo.* They'd fought the last time she'd been home, when she'd refused to cook for him and his brothers. How dare he expect her to wait on him after she'd broken her back on the ships supporting them all! It still made her insides burn with fury. He knew her greatest fear was turning into her sister, who was grey-skinned and washed out, living in squalor in Quezon with five children. What did he think would happen if she got pregnant? She would be fired, that was what, the money would dry up, and then all of them would be one step away from the slums. Him and his whole fuck-darned family. *Well, guess what. That time will be coming sooner than you think.*

It was her own fault. She should have married an American with money, not a stupid pinoy who'd been dumb enough to get himself fired off the ships. But no, she'd fallen in love – ha! Love! – with a fuck-darned assistant waiter with a mole under his eye who'd promised her they'd rise through the ranks together. She might not be able to divorce him – their families would never accept that – but she could leave. She could save up and start a new life.

It was a plan – a good plan – but if she was pregnant, she could forget it. She was only two months into her tenth-month contract, so there was no chance she could hide it.

'What are you doing here?' Althea turned to see a large woman with dyed orange hair and a crumpled nurse's uniform bustling through the entrance door. 'Are you sick?'

Althea explained about Mrs del Ray's situation.

The woman gave her a tired smile. 'Ah. Bin must have taken the call earlier, before we were overrun.'

'The men who were injured in the fire,' Althea said, gesturing at the door. 'Will they be okay?'

The woman pursed her lips. 'You went in there? That area is for patients only.'

'So sorry,' Althea murmured, automatically sliding into her deferential act. 'No one was here. I was trying to find the doctor.'

'Ah. Okay.' The nurse ran a hand through her tangled hair. Dark circles ringed her eyes, and the skin on her nose and cheeks was florid with broken veins. A drinker. Althea knew the signs.

'My supervisor said that the fire was not bad,' Althea fished.

'Things look worse than they are, don't worry. I'd better get in there. Thanks for letting us know. V27, you say?'

Althea nodded, and dismissed, she ducked her way through the plastic sheeting and along the I-95. Trining's station was on Five Aft – a five-minute walk at least. She jogged along the passageway, aware that the air was becoming muggier, the smell of smoke stronger the closer she came to the engine rooms aft of the ship. She swapped greetings with a group of waiters who hustled past her, their arms piled with trays of water bottles, but they couldn't tell her more about the situation than she already knew. As she ran past the housekeeping offices, she heard the bark of Maria's voice. 'Althea!'

Althea froze, then turned to face her, eyes lowered.

'I have been trying to contact you, Althea.'

'I am sorry.' She tapped her radio. 'It isn't working again.'

'You have checked there is no one still in their cabin on your station? You have followed procedure?'

'Yes, Maria. But one of my guests is sick and needs the doctor. They called down to the medical centre, but there was no answer.'

Maria glowered as if she considered Althea personally responsible for engineering the passenger's ill health. One day, Althea promised herself, she would bring this *puta* to her knees. She would make her eat dirt and squirm. 'I will see to it. Which stateroom?'

'V27. It's the fly-in – Mrs del Ray. I've already been to the medical centre and told them. May I go, please?' Security must be checking that all the cards were in place by now, and Trining would blame her for the fact that her station hadn't been checked.

'Why didn't you tell me that Trining was sick?' Maria said in a dangerously soft voice.

Fuck-darned Trining. Althea was damned if she was going to cover for her this time. 'I thought Trining would have told you immediately.'

'She says you agreed to cover her station today.'

Althea put on her best innocent mask. 'She did?'

Maria raised the twin pencil lines of her eyebrows. They never matched – one was always drawn on higher than the other, and they clashed with her white-blond hair. *Learn to use a mirror, puta.* 'We are lucky there have been no complaints. She says she has not even begun the evening turn-down.'

'I'm so sorry, Maria. There must have been some confusion.'

'Paulo has checked that Trining's staterooms are empty, but I need you to ensure he has been thorough.'

'Will Security not do this?'

'You are questioning me?'

'No, Maria.'

'After you have done that, you must go to your muster station and wait for further instructions.'

'Yes, Maria. Thank you, Maria.'

How she hated to grovel, but she needed a good review if there was any chance of being promoted into a supervisor's position. Not that there was much hope of that on this ship. The paisano system would come into effect – Maria would only give breaks to other Romanians. That was ship life. Sometimes it worked in your favour, sometimes it didn't. And it didn't matter that English was her first language. Her nationality counted against her. Someone had to do the dirty work. It had taken her over two years to work her way up from a staff steward (and the cones could be disgusting, but they were nothing compared to some of the officers) and secure the coveted station on the VIP deck.

She pushed through the service door that led to the lower decks, catching another whiff of the smoky odour. She hated this section of stairwell – there were thirteen steps up to each landing, and she counted them aloud to banish the curse. She knew it was ridiculous, but she couldn't entirely shed her childhood superstitions – she still turned her plate whenever someone left the mess table.

. As she opened the door onto Trining's station, a blur of movement at the far end of the darkened corridor caught her eye. Someone was running towards her – a small figure. The light here was far worse than on her floor, but it looked like a child – a boy. How could that be? She'd been on cruises with spoilt American kids, running around like they owned the ship, the parents screaming at the staff every time one of the little snots got injured or lost, but the New Year's cruises were for over-eighteens only. The emergency lights flickered, plunging her momentarily into darkness, before hissing on again. The child, fair-skinned, dark-haired and barefoot – was now twenty metres from where she was standing. 'Hoy!' she shouted, wincing as the lights snapped out again. She fought the urge to dive back into the service corridor. The lights blinked on – brighter this time – but the child . . . the child was gone.

She crossed herself automatically, jumping as a tall figure rounded the corner at the end of the corridor. She breathed easier as she made out the white shirt and black trousers of one of the security personnel. Had she imagined the child? Was her mind playing tricks? She was running on less than four hours sleep a night, so it was possible.

The guard stalked towards her. One of the Indian mafia, his face made up of hard angles. He towered over her.

'Did you see a guest down here?' she asked him, amazed at how calm she sounded.

He stared at her blankly. 'No.' He indicated the red cards slotted into the slots. 'Have you finished?'

'It's not my station.'

'Then why are you here?' His hand strayed to the radio at his belt. 'All crew must report to their muster stations now.'

'I know. My supervisor asked me to check that everything was in order.'

'And is it?'

'I'm not sure.' She didn't want to tell him what she'd seen, in case it *had* been her imagination. But the child – if there even was a child – must have disappeared inside one of the neighbouring cabins, although she was certain she hadn't heard the crump of a door opening and closing. 'Do you mind if I recheck some of the staterooms? The steward who was sent to do it is new.' Good. A lie, but it sounded reasonable. She waited for the guard to argue, but he merely continued to stare at her – perhaps he'd read something in her face – then waved a hand as if to say 'go on'.

There were three staterooms that the boy could possibly have slipped inside when the lights went out. She opened the first, ducked into the bathroom, and then scanned the main area, opening the wardrobe to ensure that the child wasn't hiding in there. There was no sign of him, but the room was a mess, the sheets scrambled into a ball, the bin overflowing with empty Coors cans. It was clear Trining hadn't bothered to service her station at all that morning, and it was likely Paulo had just knocked on the cabin doors and then carded them without investigating properly. Trining must have God and all his angels on her side – it was a miracle no one had complained.

She glanced at the guard as she tried the next room, but he was fiddling with his radio. The second she opened the door, the acidic stench of vomit rolled out at her. She hesitated, then propped the door against its magnet and stepped inside. The bathroom was empty, and the rest of the space appeared to be unoccupied. She looked around for the source of the bad smell, aware that now she could also detect another odour: urine. It was faint, but unmistakable.

She crept around the edge of the dishevelled bed. The duvet was lumped between the wall and the side of the mattress, and poking out from the end of it, a pair of feet, the soles dirty and grey. She cried out and stepped back, bashing against the vanity unit and sending a make-up bag falling to the floor.

The guard was inside the room in seconds, scrunching up his nose. 'What is it?'

'Come here,' she whispered. 'Look.'

She watched the guard's face carefully as he took in the scene. He recoiled, and fumbled for his radio. 'Control, come in. Control.' A hiss and a crackle. He banged it on his hand.

Althea couldn't drag her eyes away from those feet. They belonged to a woman, and she found herself thinking about something her *lola* used to say when she was a child: that the shoes of the dead must be removed as soon as possible so that they are not weighted down on their journey to heaven. Barely aware she was doing so, she reached out to remove the duvet, but the guard placed a hand on her arm. His palm felt hot enough to burn her skin. 'Wait.' The guard climbed onto the bed, moved across it, and gently lifted the duvet covering the woman's head, revealing a scribble of straw-coloured hair. He leaned down to check for a pulse, then replaced the coverlet exactly as it was.

'Is she dead?' Althea whispered.

'Yes.'

They stood in silence for several seconds. The guard cleared his throat. 'I must go outside to see if I can get a better signal. Do not touch anything.' He softened his voice: 'Will you be fine to stay here by yourself?'

She nodded.

'Again, please do not touch anything.' He hurried out, leaving her alone with the body. The hairs on the back of her neck danced. Althea closed her eyes, crossed herself again, and for the first time in many months, she prayed.

The Suicide Sisters

Helen reckoned there were some benefits to being among the few over-sixties on board; she and Elise had been allocated sun-loungers, while everyone else at their muster station had to make do with the floor. She was comfortable enough, but she could do without the racket. Next to where she and Elise were sitting, a group of men and women were flirting aggressively with one another, vying to be the centre of attention. The loudest of the bunch, a thirtyish man with the build of a rugby player and a pair of angels' wings attached to his hairy back, was griping that the bar service had been suspended: 'It's why you go on a fucking cruise, innit?' he droned on. 'To have a drink and a laugh. And if the ship's going to do a Titanic, then I wanna be as pissed up as possible.' Nearby, an American couple, who resembled giant grumpy toads, were loudly complaining to whoever would listen that they would never sail Foveros again. She'd seen them once or twice in the dining room, ordering every entrée on the menu; they'd never once thanked their waiter.

And then there was Jaco, the ship's one-man marimba/rock/ reggae band (or whatever was required), who was wrapping up an off-key acoustic rendition of 'By the Rivers of Babylon'. He'd arrived twenty minutes ago, presumably sent by Damien to distract them from ideas of mutiny while they waited to be dismissed from the muster station. He didn't appear to be fazed that no one paid him the slightest bit of attention. In fact, being universally ignored appeared to be part of his job description as far as Helen could make out. She'd seen him all over the ship, hosting the Michael Jackson tribute evening, or lurking in the background during karaoke. She caught Elise's eye and they both gave him a small round of applause. As if to punish them for their generosity, he launched into a clumsy version of 'Jail House Rock'.

'It's a shame musicians are no longer required to go down with the ship,' Helen said crisply, and Elise laughed.

The crew allocated to their muster station – a plump Australian woman with flinty eyes and a Filipino man with cheekbones like a supermodel's – had long since given up telling passengers not to film the proceedings on their mobile phones, and were now chatting amongst themselves, occasionally offering bored platitudes to the passengers who harassed them for information. No doubt the people waving their iPhones around were hoping to sell the footage to one of the networks if the ship did indeed 'do a *Titanic*'. Which was unlikely. If *The Beautiful Dreamer* was going to go down, Helen was sure it would have done so by now. She and Elise had been in the dining room deciding on their starters when the ship had shuddered to a stop and the lights died. There had been a few seconds of stunned silence, a single high-pitched scream, and then, in a clatter of dropped cutlery and raised voices, their fellow diners rushed – almost as one – for the exits. She and Elise had stayed seated and calmly finished their obscenely expensive champagne cocktails while the other passengers streamed past their table, rudely shoving the equally bewildered waiting staff out of their path. Few people appeared to heed the cruise director's pleas to return to their cabins; most fled straight to the Lido deck where the lifeboats were situated. But now, a couple of hours since they'd all been instructed to head to their muster stations, that initial panic had turned into boredom and irritation.

'Time?' Elise asked.

'Ten minutes past eleven.'

'That late, huh?'

They shared a sigh.

'We can't do it now that the ship has stopped moving,' Helen said, stating the obvious. 'They'll just fish us out again.'

'You think they'd bother?'

'If someone saw us, it's conceivable.' They'd scoped out where to do it on the first day of the cruise – the Tranquillity deck, aft of the ship. The main party was scheduled to take place on the Lido deck, and they'd agreed that no one would notice two old women slipping over the railings at midnight. Only it didn't look like there was going to be a party after all.

'There's always the sleeping tablets,' Elise said.

'Too risky.' But it wasn't just that. Helen had set her heart on doing it like they'd planned. A watery grave. She'd done her research, and she knew that drowning wasn't painless – far from it – but the sleeping tablets would help, and it meant that no one would have to deal with the memory of coming across their bodies. If they did it right, they'd simply disappear without a trace.

'Well, it ain't over till it's over,' Elise said.

Helen closed her eyes and tried to drown out the background noise. Now that their plan was scuppered, she needed to take stock. She'd assumed that as the hours slipped away, the enormity of what they were planning would eventually hit home. It hadn't. She was well aware that her attitude to ending her life was psychologically abnormal, and she still felt a trace of the giddiness – not happiness exactly, but close – that had infected her since she'd made the decision five months ago.

It had been Elise's idea to do it on a cruise. Helen had never been on one before, and she was drawn to the idea of spending her last days on a luxurious vessel with Egyptian cotton sheets and five-star meals. It would be her version of Blanche Dubois, who longed to die after eating a poisoned grape while holding the hand of a handsome ship's doctor. But it wasn't to be. Elise had booked them on a Foveros cruise – she had happy memories of cruising with the company in the eighties – and for someone as Internet savvy as Elise, *The Beautiful Dreamer*'s vast number of one-star reviews on CandidCruisers.com had somehow passed her by. Helen had been appalled when she'd read some of them – one passenger had discovered urine leaking from the bathroom tap. But she'd thought: what did it matter? How bad could it be?

Bad, but not awful. And to be fair, the first three days of the cruise had been less odious than she'd expected, although she'd had a few dark hours when they'd stopped at Foveros's private island on the second day. 'Isn't it beautiful?' a couple sitting in front of them had sighed as the tender boats ferried them to the harbour, but Helen saw only a tawdry mess, a once beautiful island cancerous with shops selling mass-produced tat. Two other Foveros cruise liners were docked next to *The Beautiful Dreamer*, and Helen was aghast at the number of people pouring out of their innards and streaming into the duty-free compound. She and Elise had found a shady spot next to the pirate-ship-themed beach bar, and although she'd put on a brave face, she'd been listless all day. Back on board, she was more aware than ever of people around her stuffing their faces with junk food, gulping down iridescent cocktails, and leaving half-eaten meals on tables for others to clear away.

Then, on the raised stage on the Lido deck, she'd seen a woman dancing alone, hamming it up unselfconsciously to a pop song. A friend had brought the woman a plate of food, and she'd continued to dance, casually cramming fries into her mouth without missing a step. Helen had caught Elise's eye, and they'd both roared with laughter. She still wasn't sure why this scene had snapped her out of her existential crisis or whatever it was, but suddenly, she wasn't so filled with despair. It was a contradiction; she was going to die – she'd made that decision – but she didn't want to die feeling like that. She didn't want to be just another sad old woman who'd booked herself on a cut-price cruise in order to kill herself.

Yes, that was the only time she could honestly say she felt down. She'd thoroughly enjoyed yesterday's trip to Cozumel. They'd rented a rickety jeep from a decidedly dodgy car-hire outlet, and she'd driven them around the island, stopping at a deserted stretch of beach where they'd paddled in the waves. After two margaritas each at Fat Tuesdays, they'd giggled their way back through the compulsory duty-free mall that led to the ship, egging each other on to find the ghastliest curio. After dinner they'd amused themselves at the gallery, posing for photographs. You could have one taken with a dancer with fruit piled on her head, or in front of a grand piano. It tickled them both that those ridiculous photos would be the last piece of evidence of their lives, proof that they were happy, right up to the end.

She was jerked out of her thoughts by the blare of the PA system: 'G'day, ladies and gentlemen, Damien your cruise director here. We'd like to thank you for your patience. As you've probably gathered, we're still working on the technical problem, but it should be resolved shortly. The captain has decided that bar service will be resumed as we count down to . . .'

Damien's voice was drowned out by an ear-splitting cheer, and the area emptied as there was a stampede for the bar.

'You want something?' she asked Elise.

'No thanks.' Elise yawned. 'Oops. I'm getting sleepy. Last thing I thought I'd be feeling tonight.'

Helen checked her watch again. Eleven thirty. She was certain there would still be too many people milling around near the Tranquillity deck to take the risk, and in any case, they couldn't do it until they'd taken the sleeping tablets and given them half an hour or so to kick in. The Zopiclone was still in their stateroom – Elise had forgotten to slip the pill container into her handbag when they'd been instructed to head to the muster station.

The hairy-backed angel returned to his group, triumphantly carrying three buckets of beer, closely followed by a woman in a flimsy red tunic bearing a tray of shot glasses filled with purple liquid. Hairy Back downed two of the shots, grabbed the woman in red, and started slobbering over her. She giggled, and pressed herself against him. He clamped his mouth onto hers, and ran his hand up under her dress, revealing a flash of sunburned thigh and a blurry tattoo of what looked to be Elmer Fudd.

'Would you ever have dreamt of behaving like that in public?' Elise tutted.

Hairy Back's friends were now cheering him on, and the sight of his thick jabbing tongue was making Helen faintly sick. 'Let's go back to the stateroom and decide what to do next.'

'They haven't said we can go yet,' Elise said.

'Since when do we need to follow the rules?'

Elise laughed. 'Damn right. Let's go. At least then we can have a drink. And I don't mind telling you, I could use the bathroom right now.'

Helen got to her feet, wincing as pain needled down her legs. Poor circulation. She'd suffered it for years (but hopefully not for much longer). She held out a hand to help Elise up.

'Thanks,' Elise huffed. Her weight was the only issue they tended to skirt, and Helen's main concern about their plan was the mechanics of it – she wasn't sure how Elise was going to heave herself over the railings when the time came. 'Look,' Elise nudged her. A slender, dark-haired woman was darting through the crowd, heading for the crew members. 'Isn't that the woman who was with the psychic earlier? Celine somebody.'

'Celine del Ray.' A fake name if ever Helen had heard one. They'd seen Celine's air-brushed photographs all over the ship promoting her 'Friends Only' events. And Celine had been rude, damn rude, when they'd encountered her in the passage as they were heading for the dining room.

Helen attempted to eavesdrop, but the woman's words were drowned by the hoots of the increasingly drunk people around her. The Filipino crew member she'd approached unclipped his radio and spoke into it. He frowned, tapped it, and then shook his head apologetically. After a heated exchange, the woman threw up her hands and scanned the crowd, her eyes locking on Helen's.

'Uh-oh,' Helen murmured to Elise. 'Looks like she's heading our way.'

Sure enough, the woman wove her way through the knots of revellers towards them. She greeted them with a small, tight smile. 'I'm sorry to bother you, but I kind of met you earlier. You're on my boss's deck.' A trace of a regional accent – Midlands, perhaps – corrupted with the odd American vowel.

'Oh yes,' Elise said. 'The psychic.'

'She's actually a medium.'

'Is there a difference?'

'Of course,' Helen chimed in. 'Mediums talk to the dead, psychics see into the future.'

The woman gave Helen another tight smile. 'Yeah.' She blew a strand of hair off her forehead. Helen could see every muscle on her forearms – she was far too thin, borderline anorexic, and she crackled with nervous energy. 'Listen . . . I know Celine was rude to you earlier and I apologise. She can get like that sometimes. Only . . . she's been taken ill.'

'I'm sorry to hear that, honey,' Elise said.

'I was wondering . . . look, I need to go and find the doctor and make him come and see her. They sent a nurse, but he only stayed for five minutes and I'm still worried. Would you mind sitting with her while I go and get him?'

'What's wrong with her?' Helen asked.

'I'm not sure. She's not herself, been saying some really weird things. I've been waiting for over three hours now. If she's had a stroke or something like that, I don't want to leave her alone.'

'I could go fetch the doctor for you,' Helen said.

'It might be best coming from me. I won't be long, I promise.'

Helen caught Elise's eye. 'We're not doing anything else, are we?'

'Not right now,' Elise replied.

The woman's face relaxed, the lines in her forehead smoothing out. 'I really appreciate this. I'm Maddie, by the way.'

'I'm Helen, and this is Elise.'

They followed Maddie across the deck, down the ramp to the Verandah level and through the grubby glass doors that led to the stairwell and elevator station. 'You sure you want to do this, Helen?' Elise murmured, already out of breath.

Helen linked her arm through Elise's. 'Perhaps we can ask Celine to tell us what our future holds.'

Elise giggled, and Maddie, who was striding ahead, turned to look at them.

'Don't mind us, hon,' Elise said.

Maddie hurried along the VIP corridor, unlocked a stateroom a couple of doors down from their cabin, and ushered them inside it. It reeked like a brewery, but apart from that, the suite itself was a carbon copy of theirs – right down to the turquoise colour scheme and the generic angel-themed watercolours. Celine was sitting in her wheelchair next to the television, her head back; her mouth slightly open. But Helen didn't miss that her hooded eyes followed their progress into the room.

Maddie touched her boss's hand. 'Celine. This is Helen, and this is Elise. They're going to stay with you while I go get the doctor, okay?'

Celine grunted. To Helen, Celine looked less like a psychic and more like an elderly beautician. A tower of bleached hair, blood-red talons, and skin that told of decades of facelifts and chemical peels.

'Do you know where to go?' Elise asked Maddie.

'Yeah. I've got the deck plan. I really appreciate this.' With a last grateful look, Maddie ran for the door. 'I'll be as quick as I can.'

Elise sat on the bed and mouthed, 'Now what?'

Helen approached Celine's wheelchair. 'Hello, Celine. How are you feeling?'

Celine's gaze slid away from her, and she moved her mouth as if she was chewing on something.

'You think she could have had a stroke?' Helen asked Elise.

Elise shrugged, and mimed pouring a bottle into a glass and drinking.

Helen took Celine's wrist and felt her pulse, which was strong and steady. Close up, she could see the thick make-up coated over the fine lines on Celine's cheeks, the folds of floury flesh under her chin, the hands and neck betraying the true age as they always did. A snatch of a poem she'd always loathed popped into her head: *Oh fat white woman whom nobody loves . . .*

Celine lifted her head, licked her lips, and stared right at her.

'Celine? Can you hear me?'

Helen was certain she caught a flash of something in the woman's watery blue eyes.

'You think it's okay if I use the bathroom, Helen?' Elise said.

'Of course.' Helen smiled at her. Elise was one of those people who always announced whenever she had to go to the bathroom. Helen found it endearing rather than annoying.

'Helen?' Elise said, hesitating outside the bathroom door. 'Helen? I think there's someone in there.'

'There can't be.'

Elise knocked on the door. 'Hello?' Elise pressed her ear to the door, then gestured for Helen to join her. 'Listen.'

Elise was right. A faint sound was coming from within – a woman's voice humming a jazzy tune. Al Jolson, something like that. Helen dampened a spark of grief before it spread – Graham would have been able to identify it. She knocked on the door. 'Hello? Is someone in there?' The humming stopped abruptly. 'It might be coming from the cabin next door.'

'You think?'

'What else could it be? Here, try the handle.'

'Uh-uh,' Elise said. 'You do it.'

Helen hesitated, then opened the door. The scent of lavender wafted out, but the bathroom was empty.

Elise shivered. 'Ugh. That gave me the jitters.'

She disappeared inside and Helen made her way back to Celine. The air inside the cabin was stifling, and she moved towards the balcony to crank the door open, catching her breath as a flicker of movement caught her eye. There was someone behind her – a man – she could see his reflection in the glass of the balcony door. Tall, broad-shouldered, his face a blur. Slowly, heart in her throat, she turned around.

The room was empty.

She almost screamed when the toilet whooshed in the bath-room. Elise emerged, shaking her hands to dry them. 'Helen? You okay?'

Helen forced herself to smile. 'I'm fine.'

'I tell you, I hope Maddie hurries up. I'm going to get us a drink.'

While Elise poured them both hefty doubles, Helen glanced at the balcony door again. Stress, that was all it was. Exhaustion. Her mind playing tricks on her.

'Here's mud in your eye,' Elise winked, handing her a glass. Helen wasn't much of a whiskey drinker, but she knocked it back gratefully, the burn as it slid down her throat bringing her back to herself. They perched on the bed.

The sound of a cheer filtered down from the Lido deck above them, and Elise clinked her glass against Helen's. 'Happy New Year, hon.'

'Happy New Year.'

'Happy New Year, Celine,' Elise said.

Celine raised her head slowly, and then she gave them a smile full of intelligence, and, Helen thought, something that looked very much like malice. 'It will be,' she said. 'You'll see.'

The Angel of Mercy

Jesse still didn't dare breathe through his nose. He'd seen (and smelled) far worse – he'd interned at Makiwane Hospital, for fuck sakes – but the odour of stomach acid and decomposition in this confined environment was really getting to him. His first death on board, and right in the middle of everything else he had to deal with.

Ram, the more senior of the two security guys waiting at the door, cleared his throat. 'How much longer will you be, doctor?'

'I'm about done.' Jesse hated to admit it, but the ship's security staff intimidated the crap out of him, and none more so than Ram, who was something of a legend. According to Martha, the font of all ship gossip, Ram was an ex-Gurkha, a veteran of Afghanistan, and someone you seriously didn't want to mess with. Devi, the guard with him, was more of a mystery. He was almost a head taller than his boss, and unlike the other security staff, was clean-shaven – the others tended to sport identical moustaches. Jesse hadn't spoken to him before, although he'd seen him once or twice in the crew bar.

'Can you tell us time of death?' This from Devi. His boss glanced at him sharply.

'I'm not a pathologist,' Jesse sighed. He'd taken the girl's core temperature, factoring in that the air-con would have been blasting out before the ship stopped. The purplish red of lividity was evident on the girl's thighs and stomach, and rigor was still present, but he didn't have the equipment to do much more. The body showed signs of being dead for twelve hours at least; more like eighteen or even twenty. He needed to tread carefully; he couldn't risk this backfiring on him. 'Don't quote me on this, but I'd say from twelve to twenty hours, give or take.'

'She died early in the morning?' Ram asked.

Jesse shrugged. '*Ja*. I would say so. But again, I can't be sure.'

'Could the body have been moved?'

'Doubtful. The signs indicate that she has been here for a while. Why didn't the steward discover her hours ago?' Paulo, Jesse's steward, serviced his cabin twice a day.

'We will be looking into that,' Ram said. 'We will be talking to the girl's steward and the others in her group.'

'Group?'

'She was part of a singles group on board,' Devi said. 'We will also need to—'

'The covering that was on top of her,' Ram interrupted. 'Could she have pulled it on top of her when she rolled off the bed?'

'No, sir,' Devi said, before Jesse could answer. 'I took photographs of the scene after I checked her condition. It was obvious that someone wanted to hide her.'

'We cannot say that for sure,' Ram said.

Jesse noticed Devi's lips tightening, but he didn't contradict his superior.

'Who found her?' Jesse asked.

Devi glanced at Ram, and then said: 'A steward and I discovered her when we were checking that the cabins were unoccupied.'

'Is there any sign of interference?' Ram asked.

'Sexual assault?'

'Yes.'

'Her top is pushed up, but otherwise her clothes are intact. There are no obvious injuries. We won't know until an autopsy is done.' Which wouldn't be his problem, thank God. 'She'll have to be taken to the morgue. We can't leave her here in this heat.' He ran through the procedure in his mind, grateful that he'd bothered to study the agency guidelines. The captain would need to be apprised of the situation, and he'd have to instruct the engineering department to freeze the morgue, if that was even possible with the power outage. *Christ.* Security would get hold of the authorities in Miami and the Bahamas, where the ship was registered, but it would be up to him to inform the insurance company, head office, the agency, and the passenger's family, although how he'd achieve all that seeing as the entire satellite and radio system were down was beyond him. He'd discovered this new twist on the shit-storm that was rapidly becoming his night after he'd tried to contact Ground Support to inform them about the casualties of the fire.

He wiped his face; the anxiety was coming off him in waves. Never – not even when he'd come within a hair's breadth of being struck off – had he felt so overwhelmed. He wasn't good with stress. He knew what it could lead to.

'And you cannot speculate on the cause of death?' Devi asked.

'I can speculate all you like,' Jesse said, earning himself a frown from Ram. Nervousness was making him flippant. 'It could be that vomit obstructed her airways. It's possible that this killed her.'

'Do you think there were drugs involved?'

'Without blood work being done, I couldn't say.'

'Perhaps one of her friends tried to conceal her,' Ram said, staring at him with a worrying intensity. 'Perhaps they had all been drinking together, perhaps the girl was taken ill, and they were concerned that they would find themselves in trouble. Is that possible?'

'I'm not a detective.'

'But it is possible that she died from drinking too much alcohol, perhaps taking some drugs?'

'It's possible. But that doesn't explain who put the duvet on top—'

'Thank you, doctor,' Ram cut him off.

'I'll make sure the body is removed to the morgue.'

'Yes. It will be best to do this before the passengers are given the go-ahead to return to their cabins. We will secure the scene.'

'Do you need anything else from me?'

'That is all for now.'

'Should I inform the captain?'

'That has already been done.'

'Right. I'll . . . I'll be on my way then.'

Jesse squeezed out past the guards. He ducked through the service door, paused, and slammed his fists on his thighs. *Breathe. You can handle this.* He wasn't alone, he had to remember that. Bin and Martha would have his back. He could depend on them. They'd warned him that the New Year's cruises could be rough, but they weren't expecting anything more serious than alcohol-related issues and the usual spate of food allergies – he'd quickly learned that his most valuable piece of equipment on the ship was an EpiPen.

He clanged down the steps towards the I-95, the air becoming increasingly fetid as he went lower. Day or night, the service corridor that stretched the length of the ship buzzed with activity, but tonight, apart from a couple of exhausted waiters puffing on vaporisers in an alcove next to the purser's office, it was deserted, the emergency lights masking the dullness of the scuffed floors. The floor seemed to undulate under his feet, although whether this was from the stabilisers not being operational (he had a weak grasp of the ship's mechanics) or because he was exhausted, he couldn't be certain. And there was little chance of a break anytime soon – Bin had brought him a bowl of vegetable curry earlier, but it had ended up congealing on his desk. His fingers itched. *Don't let it in, don't give into it.* Because he knew how it went: *Hey, Jesse. C'mon, bru. Just one more time. No one has to know. Take the edge off, you deserve it.*

No.

They won't miss it. They'll never know.

No.

He forced himself to think about the casualties from the fire. The assistant purser and mechanic who were suffering from smoke inhalation were stable, but he was still concerned about Alfonso, the engineer with the second-degree burn. He'd treated it with a burn pad, but the guy had been listless, like he'd gone into shock, which had surprised Jesse. He didn't know Alfonso well – the engineer tended to fraternise with the other Italian officers – but he'd treated him for a nasty ear infection a fortnight ago, and Alfonso had taken that in his stride, acting tough and making jokes. Then there were two cases of vomiting and diarrhoea – one a passenger, the other a steward. He prayed they weren't looking at the beginnings of a virus. Outbreaks on cruise liners always hit the news, and coupled with the fire, this could mean the end of what little reputation Foveros still had.

He pushed the medical bay door open with his shoulder, receiving identical frayed smiles from Bin and Martha, who were slumped on the waiting-room couch. He dumped his bag on the desk, and Bin immediately got up to sterilise the equipment.

'How are they?' he asked Martha, nodding at the door that led to the treatment room.

'Sleeping. I thought it best to keep them here for the rest of the night.'

'The burn as well?'

'Yeah. I gave him something to calm him down and he went out like a light.'

'Good.' That was something, at least.

'And the girl?' Martha asked.

'Dead. Looks like she's been that way for a while.'

'Ach, no. How long?'

'Twelve, eighteen hours?'

Martha cursed, and even the usually unshakable Bin stopped what he was doing, sucked air through his teeth, and asked: 'She was in her stateroom?'

'*Ja*. She was found at the side of the bed.'

'That is strange. The steward should have discovered her hours ago.'

'I know. It's a fuck-up. Looks like foul play might be involved.'

Martha swore again. 'What happened?'

'I'm not sure. Could be a sexual assault gone wrong.'

'She was raped?'

'I don't know. We'll have to wait for the autopsy.'

'Poor girl.' Martha had told him that over the years she'd had to deal with several cases of suspected rape on board – there were rape kits in the supplies – but as far as she knew, none of the cases had resulted in a conviction.

'Christ. I hope I did everything right. Ram seemed quite keen for me to say that it was death by misadventure.'

Martha bristled. 'The last thing they want is any bad publicity.'

'I'm still not sure I did everything I could have done. I'm not exactly a pathologist or crime scene technician.'

'Don't beat yourself up.' Martha patted his hand. 'You're doing *grand*. We'll be back in port tomorrow.'

'You reckon? I've got to call this in. Is the Wi-Fi up yet?'

'Nope.'

Christ. 'Nothing? What about the radio?'

'All dead.'

'What does the IT guy say?'

'Everyone is flummoxed,' Bin said.

Flummoxed. A typical Bin word. 'So we're cut off from civilisation?'

'For now. But don't worry,' Martha said without much conviction. 'They'll sort it out, so they will.'

'I hope so. And the girl – she'll have to be removed to the morgue.'

'That's going to be fun without the lifts working,' Martha sighed. 'Bin and I can do it. We know the drill.'

Jesse shot her a grateful smile. 'Anything else I should know about? How are the two passengers who were complaining of vomiting?'

'They are the same,' Bin said. 'And I went to see the suspected stroke—'

'The *what*? Why didn't I know about this?' Bin flinched, and Jesse held up a hand. 'Sorry, Bin.'

'Don't be blaming Bin, now. It's my fault,' Martha said. 'I didn't tell you because you had so much on your plate. It's the psychic.'

'The what?'

'The fly-in. One of the special groups on board.'

'And?' he asked Bin.

'All I saw were signs that she was intoxicated.'

'No FAST signs?'

'I know what to look for, Jesse,' Bin said, without sounding defensive. 'There was no drooping of the face or loss of sensation, and her pupils were normal. She smelled very strongly of alcohol. I gave her two aspirin.'

'Which will help with her hangover,' Martha sighed.

Jesse swiped a hand over his face. 'What a fucking night.'

'Relax, Jesse. Really, you're doing grand.'

'Yeah?'

'Yes.'

'Thanks.' He didn't know what he'd do without Martha. She'd had his back from the second he came on board, patiently showing him the ropes, the slang, the shortcuts, the ship culture. Bin had been equally kind to him, but tended to keep himself at a slight distance, and Jesse found the man's work ethic a little intimidating. He knew both nurses were curious as to why a doctor from a thriving private practice had chosen to work for Foveros – the bottom of the cruise industry barrel – and once or twice he'd almost confided in Martha. Blurted out the whole sorry saga. She liked a drink; he doubted she would judge him. And everyone made mistakes, didn't they? It could've happened to anyone. Occasionally he found himself fantasising about what it would be like being married to someone like her – solid, dependable, warm, funny, non-judgemental. But she had a husband back in Ireland, two grown-up sons, and was hardly his type (if he even had a type these days). She was always encouraging him to hook up with one of the British dancers or the statuesque Eastern European human resources staff. He got the impression she'd had a fling or three over the years – casual hook-ups were, after all, one of the perks of ship life.

But sex was the last thing on his mind. All he cared about was keeping his nose clean. *One step at a time.* 'I'd better get started on the paperwork.'

The door opened and a tall, skinny woman with a mass of black hair burst in. She jabbed a finger at him. 'You the doctor?' Before he could respond she continued: 'Don't you give a shit about your passengers? I've been waiting for you to come and see my boss for two hours now!'

At a loss, he took a step back from her. 'I—'

'The suspected stroke, doc,' Bin said.

'Calm down,' Martha said, stepping between Jesse and the woman. 'The doctor will come when he's ready.'

'When he's ready? Are you kidding me?'

There would be a world of *kak* if Bin was wrong about the patient being intoxicated. They weren't set up to deal with a major cerebral event – a distress signal for off-ship support would usually be sent for anything that serious – but he wasn't about to share that information. 'Of course,' he said. 'I'll come now.'

'Well . . . good,' the woman said, swiping her hair away from her face. Striking rather than pretty – not dissimilar in looks to Farouka. *Don't go there.*

He turned to Martha and Bin. 'Can you deal with the other matter?'

Bin nodded.

'Can you give me the patient's details Ms . . .?'

'Maddie. My name's Maddie.' She glared at Bin. 'That nurse has got all her details.'

Martha mouthed 'sorry' at him as he grabbed his bag and followed Maddie out of the medical centre. She strode ahead and steamed up the stairs, forcing him to run to catch up with her. He kept meaning to use the gym on the ship, but hadn't yet bothered. Now that he was off the pethidine diet, he was running to fat; he could feel the waistband of his ridiculous white trousers biting into his gut. *If only Farouka could see me now. She'd be back like a shot.* He wondered what she was doing this evening. Laughing it up in Kalk Bay, maybe. A party with friends. Her friends, who used to be their friends.

The faint sound of a cheer echoed through the ship.

'Happy New Year,' he muttered.

Maddie paused at the top of the third flight and looked over her shoulder. 'Is it?' She waited for him to puff his way up to her.

'Not really, no. It's been a hell of a night. How old is the patient?'

'Celine tells everyone she's sixty-five, but her passport says she's ten years older.' She gave him a fleeting smile.

'And any history of illness? Strokes, heart attack, anything like that?'

'No. She has bad hips, so she tends to use a wheelchair to get around. She can walk, but not far.'

'Drinking, smoking?'

'She likes a drink.'

Maddie bounded up the next flight, and he followed her down the corridor towards one of the VIP suites. She unlocked the door and impatiently waved him inside.

He was greeted by two elderly women, one skinny, one obese (Aunt Sponge and Aunt Spiker, he thought uncharitably) who were sitting on the edge of the bed, clutching empty whiskey tumblers. Another woman – who had to be the patient – sat in a wheelchair next to the television, her eyes closed.

'Is she okay?' Maddie asked the women anxiously.

'She seems fine,' Aunt Spiker said in a crisp British voice. He put her at seventy, skin browned from an outdoorsy life. 'She was sluggish when you first left, but she's talking now.'

'Oh my, is she talking,' the other woman said – American, about the same age. Kind eyes, the flushed face of the hypertensive. 'She's been saying some really screwy things.'

'Like what?'

'For one, she said that she wasn't sure if it would work.'

'If what would work?'

'It. That's all she said.'

'Celine?' Maddie said. 'The doctor is here.'

'Hello, Celine,' Jesse said. 'I'm going to examine you, make sure you're all shipshape.'

Celine made a sound somewhere between a grunt and a laugh. He extracted his penlight, and examined her irises. Both normal. Next, he reached into his bag for his sphyg and attached the cuff to her upper arm. 'I'm just going to take your blood pressure, Celine.'

'You don't need to talk to me like I'm retarded, doc.'

'Celine! You're talking,' Maddie breathed.

Celine chuckled. 'Why wouldn't I be talking?'

'You've been . . . a bit out of it for a while. I've been worried about you.'

'No need to worry.' She waggled her fingers at the two older women. 'I've been hanging out with my new friends, isn't that right? Just us girls, getting to know each other.'

'Any headache, weakness or numbness in your limbs, Celine?' Jesse asked.

'Nope. All shipshape, doc.'

He pumped up the cuff. 'I'm just going to ask you a few questions, that okay? Let's start with an easy one. What is your full name?'

She gave him a wide, toothy grin. 'Celine del Ray, medium to the stars. What's your name?'

'Dr Zimri.'

'Zimri. Unusual. King of Israel, am I right? And your first name, doc?'

'Jesse.'

'Jesse. After the outlaw?'

'*Ja.* My father was big on Westerns.'

'That so.'

She certainly appeared to be on the ball. 'Can you tell me today's date, Celine?'

'Depends what time zone you're in, doc.'

'Who is the president of the United States?'

'What's with all the questions?' Celine pressed her fingertips to her forehead. 'Wait . . . I'm getting . . . Someone's stepping forward from the other side. Who's the young woman in your life who's crossed over, doc? There's a sadness about her. A betrayal of some sort. And pain. Physical pain.'

Jesse blinked, the sensation of icy breath tickling the back of his neck. 'I'm not sure what—'

'She's a medium,' Maddie said.

'I see dead people,' Celine said with an exaggerated wink. 'Only, as I always say, there is no death. Isn't that right, Maddie?'

Jesse cleared his throat. 'Any pain in your head or neck, Celine?'

She cackled. 'No pain, no gain. You know, doc, I've always

wanted to die holding the hand of a handsome ship's doctor, after eating a poisoned grape.'

The British woman gasped.

'That mean something to you?' Jesse asked her.

'It's a quote. Blanche Dubois. From *A Streetcar Named Desire*.'

'Helen sure knows her shit, don't she?' Celine howled in an exaggerated Uncle Tom voice that made them all wince. 'Oh lawdy, yes she does!'

'Celine!' Maddie glanced at Jesse apologetically.

'I think it's time we left,' Aunt Spiker – Helen – said. The two women got to their feet.

Maddie, who was still staring at Celine in a mixture of exasperation and relief, stood up to see the two women out. 'Thanks for everything.'

'You're welcome, Maddie,' Helen said stiffly. 'Good night, Celine.'

As the women exited, Jesse heard Celine mumbling something under her breath. It sounded very much like: 'Sleep tight, don't let the rug-munchers bite.' She winked at him again. 'Do I get a clean bill of health, doc?'

'For now. I'll come and check on you tomorrow.'

'Lovely. Can't wait.' Celine gestured at Maddie. 'Could you get me my comb from the bathroom, Madeleine?'

'Of course.'

Jesse packed his sphyg back into its case. 'I think that's it. Let me know if—'

Celine's hand shot out and grasped his wrist. She pulled him towards her with surprising strength. 'You've been a naughty boy, haven't you? Time to put things right. You're gonna be tested again, doc. You're all gonna be tested. Question is, will you pass or won't you?'

The Keeper of Secrets

The girl continued to sob, her make-up running down her cheeks in muddy tracks. She picked at her hair, attempting to disentangle the devil horns stuck at an angle on her head. 'How did it happen? Was it an accident? Did she have a fall when the ship stopped or something?'

'It was not an accident, Ms Williams,' Devi said, glancing at Ram for approval. His superior had instructed him to reveal as little as possible about the facts of the girl's death.

'Oh God. Oh no. She didn't do herself in, did she? *Kill* herself?'

'Is there a reason why you would jump to this conclusion, Ms Williams?'

'Emma. My name's Emma. No . . . God. Did she, though?'

'No.'

'What then? Was it . . . oh my God . . . was she murdered? What the *fuck*?'

'No one has said it is murder, Ms Williams,' Ram broke in. 'It was more than likely death by misadventure.'

'What does that mean?'

'It is possible that she had too much to drink.'

'What, you mean she died from alcohol poisoning?'

'We cannot be certain until more investigation has been done.'

'God. Kelly. Poor Kelly. She was so . . . I've never known anyone who died before. Except for my nan, but she was really old. So . . . when we get back to Miami, will I have to talk to the police? The FBI and that?'

Ram sighed. 'We cannot say at this point.'

She adjusted the straps on her flimsy red dress and licked her lips, her tears forgotten. Devi could now read excitement in her eyes, and judging by the look of distaste on Ram's face, so could he. Devi sighed inwardly. It was obvious this girl didn't know anything. After she'd been identified as the closest associate of the deceased passenger, Ram had sent Devi to track her down. He'd eventually located her on the Tranquillity deck, perched on the wall of one of the Jacuzzis, her arm around a bare-chested man, both of them swigging from a Walgreens' juice bottle – a favourite method for smuggling alcohol on board.

Devi surreptitiously stretched his back and rubbed his eyes, which stung from lack of sleep. He'd been on duty for over twenty hours now, and had only managed to grab a sandwich and a Coke since lunchtime. Ram, as usual, showed no sign of fatigue, despite being well into his second shift. They'd already spoken to Trining Aquido, the deck steward who serviced the girl's cabin, but she had little to add. She said that she'd fallen ill halfway through her morning shift, which explained why the body had only been discovered so late. Aquido had also insisted that Althea Trazona, the steward who'd discovered the body, had promised to take over her duties, but according to their supervisor, Trazona had denied this. Whatever the truth, Devi was certain Trazona was hiding something. He was convinced the shock on her face when she'd discovered the body was genuine, so he doubted she was covering for someone, but of all the cabins on the deck, it was too much of a coincidence that she'd chosen to check that one. For now – although he wasn't entirely sure why – he was keeping this to himself until he had a chance to talk to her again.

There was a knock on the door and Ashgar, who was supposed to be monitoring the security cameras, poked his head inside the room and gestured to Ram. 'May I speak with you, sahib?' Through the half-open door, Devi caught a glimpse of Rogelio leaning against the wall in the corridor outside, and their eyes met briefly. As Damien's second-in-command, Rogelio facili-tated most of the singles group's activities, and Ram must have called Rogelio in for questioning while Devi was searching the ship for the girl.

Ram stood up and waved at Devi to continue.

'When did you last see Kelly Lewis, Ms Williams?' Devi asked, relaxing slightly now that Ram was out of the room.

'Um . . . last night. Night before, I mean.'

'Why did you not report her missing earlier?'

She crossed her arms defensively. 'I didn't notice, did I?'

'Why is that? Were you not friends travelling together?'

'Yeah. But we weren't, like, best mates or anything. She only came with me because Zoe dropped out at the last minute. Kelly works – worked – in our salon on reception, and when Zoe dropped out she said she'd take her place.'

'And you were both part of the singles group?'

She sniffed and wiped her nose with the back of her hand. 'Yeah.'

'Where did you last see her?'

'The Sandman Lounge. Bunch of us decided to go after we got back from Cozumel. Kelly wasn't keen, but she tagged along in the end.'

'Had she been drinking?'

'We all had, yeah? But not that much. Just a few cocktails and that.'

'No roommate?'

'No. She wanted her own cabin, although me and Zoe were planning on sharing. Kelly paid the extra and everything. I'm sharing with another girl in the group – Donna, she's American.'

'Was Kelly enjoying the cruise?'

'Yeah. I guess. I dunno. She was dead excited about going, she'd never been to the States, but soon as we got on the ship, she wasn't so keen. Said she felt a bit sick a couple of times. Didn't always join in. I just thought . . . Does her mum know? She was always going on about her mum.'

Devi hesitated. 'Her family will be informed as soon as possible.' There was no point spreading the news that the satellite system was malfunctioning.

'God. They're going to be so upset. Do you think they'll blame me? Cos like . . . it was only because of me she came along.'

'Was there anyone who showed her special attention during the cruise?'

'Who, Kelly? No. There was this one guy she quite liked at speed dating, but she didn't hook up with anyone.' The girl looked up at him, sniffed again. 'Hang on . . . why are you asking me this? I thought you said she died from drinking too much?'

Devi kept his face blank. 'I am merely wishing to know more about her background.'

'Oh. What's happening with the ship? They fixing it or what? Cos, like, I've got a flight tomorrow. Will we be back by then?'

'The engineers are working on the problem,' Devi said automatically, but all he knew was that the fire had disabled the cables that ran from the engine to the generators. *The Beautiful Dreamer* was one of the older vessels – but even so, this shouldn't have happened with the back-up system in place. Madan, his cabin mate, was part of the fire crew, so he was certain to have more information.

'Where is she now?' the girl asked.

'What do you mean?'

'Kelly. Where is she now?'

Ram reappeared, saving him from answering. 'Devi. Please come outside so I may speak with you.'

The girl slumped in her seat as Devi left the room and joined Ram in the corridor. Rogelio had left – Devi wasn't certain if he was relieved or disappointed. 'Yes, sir?'

'The captain has called an emergency meeting for all the heads of department. Can I trust you with this situation? We must show that we have followed procedure all the way through.'

'Yes, sir. Should I talk to the others in the singles group now, sir?'

'We can do that tomorrow if we have to.' Ram let the implication hang. The ship was due to dock at eight a.m. – six hours from now. Whatever happened, they would be late, which would mean disgruntled passengers, and extra duties for all the security staff. In the usual course of events, their role would be to secure the scene of the incident and take statements from any possible witnesses; the rest would be left to off-ship agencies.

'Is the satellite working now, sir?'

Ram wiped a hand over his eyes, for the first time showing a sign of exhaustion.

'No. There is still no Internet access or radio communication.'

'How can that be?'

Ram shrugged. 'They have sent out emergency signals, so by morning we should receive off-ship support if we need it. For now, I am asking you to contain this situation.'

'Sir. I think it is best if I check the security camera footage from this morning. It is possible that we can identify whoever was in her cabin.'

'You are not in the crime squad now, Devi,' Ram said softly.

Devi fought to keep his expression neutral. He'd often wondered how much Ram knew about his past. His boss had never asked why a sub-inspector with a promising career ahead of him had chosen to become a shippee, and Devi sometimes wondered what he would say if he was asked. After all, he was overqualified for his position. Without exception, the other guards were only trained for security. Ashgar, for example, had worked for one of the tourist hotels; the others had used their connections for recommendations.

'We must be seen to have done all we can,' Ram continued. 'But I will not be pleased if rumours spread throughout the ship that there is a predator on board. I am relying on you to be discreet.' Ram paused and looked straight into Devi's eyes. 'You of all people are adept at this.'

Devi licked his lips, but his mouth was dry. 'Understood, sir.'

'Good. Please escort the guest back to her cabin.'

Ram stalked away, allowing Devi a minute to breathe. *You of all people are adept at this.* Could Ram have meant that as an ex-member of the notoriously corrupt Maharashtra police force, Devi would be practised at keeping his own counsel? It was the only explanation – he'd taken every possible precaution. Not even Madan knew of his hasty liaisons with Rogelio.

Devi returned to the security office and informed the girl that she was free to go to her cabin. Neither of them spoke as he walked her through the service corridors and out onto the main deck on level five. Without the air-con working, the air hung heavy, but the mugginess didn't bother him – he despised the artificial iciness that blasted through the ducts. It was one of the reasons he didn't mind working the exit point on port days. The work was dull to the point of insanity, but the fresh air made it worth it.

Her cabin mate came to the door the second it was opened. 'What's going on?'

'It's Kelly,' the girl howled. 'She's *dead.*'

Devi left them to it. It was pointless to instruct them to keep the news to themselves.

He retraced his steps, ducked into the service corridor and headed for the surveillance offices instead of peeling off towards his cabin. Ram hadn't specifically told him not to review the CCTV footage, and as the monitors and motion-capturing cameras were directly linked to the back-up systems, they would still be running on emergency power.

The security room stank of sweat and sour breath. Ashgar was snoozing, his head on his chest. On the screens, passengers were still milling around the Lido deck – a group sat huddled next to the stage, others dangled their feet in the pool. A couple were entwined in one of the Jacuzzis on the Tranquillity deck, which should have been closed off an hour ago. Someone would have to request that they leave the area, but that could wait. He moved a chair next to Ashgar and sat down. His earlier tiredness had washed away, and he felt oddly energised, the way he used to feel before his mind became rusty from the daily routine on board. There was rarely any excitement on the shorter cruises: the occasional alcohol-fuelled fight or minor incidences of alcohol or drug smuggling – mostly marijuana.

The doctor said the girl had been dead for twelve to eighteen hours. That meant he'd need to call up the footage from two a.m. until six to be safe. Fortunately, the cameras on the passenger decks were motion-sensitive, which would save him from fast-forwarding through hours of empty time. He typed in the command, and sat back to review the action.

3.01 a.m. An African-American couple stumbled down the

corridor, laughing. The woman playfully slapped the man, who pressed her up against the corridor wall. They shared a passionate kiss, and then he followed her into a nearby stateroom.

3.32 a.m. A room service waiter slid out of the service door that led to the staff elevator, balancing a tray piled with plastic-covered dishes. He knocked on a door midway along the corridor, which was opened by a white man wearing a towel, and disappeared inside it. The waiter returned two minutes later, made an obscene gesture at the cabin door, and disappeared back into the service elevator.

4.17 a.m. A woman who fitted the body type and colouring of Kelly Lewis rounded the corner from the direction of the stairwell. A man wearing a baseball cap appeared behind her thirty seconds later. The woman moved unsteadily, trailing her hand against the wall for balance.

Sweat prickling his scalp, Devi paused the footage and zoomed in: it was definitely the victim. She dropped her card on the floor and the man hurried to help her. He pushed the door open and followed her into the cabin.

4.38 a.m. The man reappeared, placed the 'don't disturb' notice on the door handle, and jogged back towards the stairwell.

So now he knew for sure that she had been targeted. Devi made a note to check the footage from the Sandman Lounge, which was undoubtedly where the man had found his prey. Devi ran the footage again, hoping that the face recognition software would identify Kelly's assailant. But there weren't enough points for the computer to match up. The man's face was hidden beneath his cap, and he'd kept his head lowered. Devi would need to check who in the singles group resembled the man's description: white, stocky, approximately six feet tall. Rogelio would know who fitted the description.

And what of the 'don't disturb' notice? He didn't recall seeing it. Perhaps the steward who'd been sent to check the rooms had removed it.

You are not in the crime squad now, Devi.

Ram was correct. It could be left to the US authorities, but . . .

but. Perhaps this was his way of putting things right. A way to make amends for what he had done – or what he had not done. He could still see the girl, limp-bodied, eyes blank, not much older than his cousin Misha. The woman who'd brought her into the station was hysterical, couldn't understand why her charge was bleeding. He could have fought for the girl. He *should* have fought for her. But he chose his family's sensibilities over justice.

Coward.

But he couldn't help anyone if he let his mind pick over his past like a bird eating a corpse.

There had been two sexual assaults on his last ship, both crew-related. A waitress had accused one of the assistant engineers of attacking her on the loading deck, and a crew member had been detained for following a teenager into one of the elevators and making indecent suggestions to her. The guy had been flown back to India at the next port – standard practice to avoid involving the American authorities and the press seizing hold of the story. The teenager's family had been comped, and that had been the end of the matter. But this was different. The man who had stalked Kelly had known exactly what he was doing.

If he wasn't stopped, he would do it again.

He ran the footage once more, then typed in the approximate time he and Althea Trazona had discovered the body. Trazona had been on edge when he'd first encountered her in the corridor. He should have questioned her more closely, but tomorrow would suffice.

The screen flicked to an image of Trazona stepping through the service door, a few minutes before Devi had encountered her. She paused, a hand to her throat, moved forward, and her lips moved as she said something. Confusion, then fear, flashed over her face. The lights in the corridor died, and the infra-red kicked in, rendering her eyes ghoulish black spheres. There was a flicker of static, black and grey, and then—

Devi yelped and jumped back in his chair, disturbing Ashgar, who jerked, murmured, 'Wha?' then fell back asleep.

Fingers shaking, Devi clicked back to the footage, and steeled himself to re-run it. What he'd seen – or thought he'd seen – was impossible.

But there it was again: a hand, the palm of a hand, covering the camera lens.

DAY 5

The Wildcard Blog

Fearlessly fighting the fraudulent so that you don't have to

Jan 01

Happy New Year.

Only it's not. For me, anyway.

First: apologies. I know I promised daily updates about my takedown of The Predator, but a lot has happened.

I'm going start with the big one. The ship is fucked and we're officially stranded somewhere in the Gulf of Mexico. Yeah, you read that right or you will when I can post this. The Wi-Fi's down and there's no network coverage. Thinking this may be intentional to avoid people sending angry anti-Foveros tweets, but we'll see. The crew I've spoken to seem to know as much (or as little) as we do. The ship is supposed to dock in Miami in five hours from now (8 a.m.), but that's not going to happen as we're still dead in the water. All we can do is wait for more news, which will be relayed by Damien, the cruise director, who not only has his own TV channel, but starts every sentence with 'G'day'. He's Australian and wants all of us to know it. Don't mean to diss Aussies – to be fair, Damien's the only one I've ever found irritating – dude probably got thrown out of his country for being a dick. Other shit is going down. After spending hours at the muster station last night with a bunch of frat boys who were smoking weed through vaporisers (wasn't tempted – see below) I went back to my stateroom (a gloomy cave on Deck Five aka the 'Majestic' deck), to find that a cabin three doors down from mine had been sealed by Security, the door covered in tape, crime scene-style. Took a pic, will also post that when I can.

And the reason why I haven't been in touch? I've been sick. The kind of stomach flu where you beg the gods to take your life. Felt like my entire body was trying to turn itself inside out. It started an hour after the ship left Miami. I was sniffing around, looking out for any sign of

The Predator, when . . . OK, you probably don't want to know the details. Think Jackson Pollock, only out of both ends. Yeah. Big props to Trining, my cabin steward. Woman has a stomach of iron. A nurse came to see me on day 2 and charged me 97 dollars to basically tell me there was nothing I could do apart from keep hydrated. Still a bit shaky.

OK. On to the stuff you're reading this for:

As you know, I didn't get the chance to sign up as one of The Predator's Friends, seeing as the spots were booked up minutes after the 'Cruise with Celine del Ray' was mentioned on Zoop and FB, and last night, thinking it was my last chance to confront her, I dragged my aching body out of its sickbed, and lurched along to gatecrash her last event. Subtle, I wasn't. I managed to slip inside the Starlight Dreamer Lounge (which looks as cheesy as it sounds) and walked straight into The Predator doing her Artful Dodger impression. Still feeling like crap, and suspecting I was gonna puke at any second, I confronted her about Lillian Small. Didn't get much footage as nature called with a vengeance.
But the fact that the ship has stopped isn't a bad thing for me. It'll give me another chance to confront the old fraud.
Will update when I know more.

The Witch's Assistant

Maddie sat up too quickly, blinking as sunlight needled into her eyes. Her neck throbbed from sleeping on the couch in Celine's suite, and her T-shirt clung to her back. She had no recollection of dropping off – she must have passed out while waiting for Celine to fall asleep. But now the bed was empty, the coverlet barely creased. 'Celine?'

No answer. She must be in the bathroom. The PA system beeped, making her start, and then Damien's voice smarmed down at her:

'G'day, ladies and gentlemen, Damien, your cruise director here. Just to give you an update on the situation. As you will have noticed, we're still experiencing an electrical problem, but there is no cause for concern regarding your safety and well-being. We are aware that some of you have flights to catch this morning, and we'd like to assure you that this issue will be addressed shortly. We respectfully request that you refrain from bringing this up with Guest Services at this time. We also regretfully report that as the dining rooms are currently closed, breakfast will be served at our Lido buffet, where our staff are doing all they can to ensure you are comfortable and well fed.'

Maddie checked the time on her cell: ten past eight. She and Celine were booked on an early afternoon flight back to La Guardia, so there was still a chance they'd make it if the ship got going in the next hour or so. She stretched until she felt her back muscles twang, then got to her feet, stumbling as she was forced to adjust her balance. Christ, the ship was now listing slightly to the left – not a good sign that the situation was under control. She padded to the bathroom door. 'Celine? You in there?'

She peered inside, a faint trace of Poison, Celine's perfume, wafting out at her. No Celine, but her make-up bag was in disarray – the box containing her false eyelashes was open next to the sink – so she must be feeling better this morning. Still, it was strange for her to go anywhere on the ship alone: who knew when a Friend could approach and ask for an autograph or an impromptu reading? She couldn't have gone far, just to the pool or main decks, the only places on the ship with wheelchair ramps. Unless she'd decided to walk, which would be a first. And that wouldn't explain the missing wheelchair.

Maddie avoided looking in the mirror (she'd had enough bad news for one morning), splashed cold water on her cheeks, squirted a pea of toothpaste on a fingertip and rubbed it over her teeth. The ever-present headache continued to nag, and she dug in Celine's vanity case for the extra-strength Tylenol. Next, get coffee. Find Celine. Find Ray, who was noticeably absent last night. Head down to her cabin to shower and change. Then check on the Friends, something she should really have done last night.

She stepped into the corridor, narrowly avoiding colliding with an overweight couple who were barrelling towards the stairwell. Maddie mumbled an apology, although it was hardly her fault. She'd encountered them before in the elevators a couple of times, and she'd never yet seen them smile. This morning, in an act of passive-aggression that Maddie reluctantly approved of, they were both wearing oversized 'I *heart* Foveros Cruise Lines' T-shirts.

'What do you think about this, now?' the man grumped at Maddie. 'I tell you,' he carried on, before she had a chance to answer, 'this is typical Foveros. No answer from room service.' He waved his breakfast card. 'Six a.m. I wrote down here. Six a.m. No one showed up to fetch it.'

'If the electricity is out, they might be having issues in the kitchen,' Maddie said.

'Huh. It's unacceptable. We have a flight back to Galveston at one thirty.'

'One thirty exactly,' the woman echoed. Maddie assumed they

were married, but with their similar short haircuts and large builds, they could be brother and sister. 'Heads will roll if we miss it.'

Helen poked her head out of her door, saving Maddie from answering. 'Oh, it's you, Maddie. I thought it might be Althea.'

With a curt nod at Maddie and Helen, the couple waddled off to the stairwell.

'Is Celine feeling better today?' Helen asked.

'She must be. She's not in the stateroom. You haven't seen her, have you?'

'No. Elise and I have only just woken up.'

'Thanks again for all your help last night. I don't know what I would have done without you.'

'It was nothing.'

Elise appeared at Helen's shoulder. 'Oh hey, Maddie. How's Celine doing today?'

Maddie repeated what she'd told Helen.

'I'm glad she's up and about. Maddie, may I ask you something? It's going to sound strange.'

Maddie almost laughed. 'I've been working for a medium for three years, strange is my middle name.'

'Last night . . . Helen and me, we had a very strong feeling someone else was in the cabin.' Helen nudged Elise and told her to hush. 'There's no harm in mentioning it, Helen,' Elise tutted.

'What do you mean?' Maddie asked, not sure she really wanted to know.

'Well . . . this is going to sound kooky. But we heard music. Someone singing. Helen thought it might be coming from one of the other cabins. I can't get it out of my head.' She hummed a tune that sounded very much like the one Celine had sung just after the ship stopped – the tune that reminded Maddie of Lizzie Bean, Celine's less vocal spirit guide. Celine's guides made quite the pair of stereotypes (her boss was anything but subtle): Archie the tragic Cockney urchin, and Lizzie the tragic 1920s socialite who could have tumbled out of the pages of *The Great Gatsby*. And then there was Papa Noakes, although Maddie had never actually heard his voice coming through. An 'ex-slave from Mississippi', Papa Noakes had dropped out of Celine's repertoire years ago – Maddie only knew about him at all from a first edition of Celine's memoir (he'd been eradicated from the e-editions and reprints). She thanked her lucky stars he'd been shelved before the Internet boom; she could only imagine the field day Celine's army of detractors would have with him. Then again, Celine had put on that awful voice last night, embarrassing everyone, especially the doctor, but she'd never exactly been politically correct. Occasionally, Maddie wondered if Papa Noakes was the real reason Celine had hired her; having an assistant of mixed race might offset any possible accusations of racial insensitivity.

'Perhaps Celine was humming it,' Maddie said. She was surprised they hadn't thought of that explanation.

Helen shrugged. 'Perhaps. It doesn't matter. I'm sure it was just our imaginations working overtime.'

'Were you two planning on flying home today?' Maddie changed the subject.

Elise sucked in a breath and she and Helen exchanged a glance Maddie couldn't read. Maddie had been too stressed last night to dwell on the relationship between the two women. They clearly weren't related – for one thing Helen was British and Elise was American. Perhaps they were lovers – there was definitely a bond between them that went beyond friendship.

'Let us know if there's anything else we can do,' Helen said.

'I will. Again, I really appreciate all your help.'

Maddie walked carefully to the end of the hallway, peered over the glass balcony and down into the atrium. A queue of grumbling people snaked from the Guest Services desk to the cocktail bars. Several of the complainants were still dressed in their fancy dress – beer-bellied men wrapped in white sheets, women in gold sandals and blond wigs, the odd devil here and there. The brother-and-sister couple had joined the end of the queue, adding their voice to the chorus.

She could see from her vantage point that the Catalina Coffee outlet was shut, which meant she'd be forced to drink the free vile brew served in the Lido buffet. She cut through the photo gallery, where garish signs begged her to remember that 'Memories Last Forever!' and pushed through the glass doors that led out onto the pool deck, breathing in salty air tinged with diesel. She clanked down the spiral staircase and out onto the main deck, which was far busier than it usually was at this time of day. Every sun-lounger held a body, and cleaning staff darted to and fro, scooping up trash and handing out bottles of water. Most kept their eyes lowered to minimise interaction with the passengers, moving furtively like soldiers creeping through land mines.

She picked her way past the groups gathered around the Jacuzzis and exterior stage, scanning faces for any sign of Celine. She tended to hold her breath to avoid the foul gust of broiling hotdogs and boiled tomatoes that blasted out of the interior seating area 24/7, but there didn't appear to be any hot food on offer. Only one of the buffet stations was operational – a line of sweating chefs slapping sandwiches together. People stared at her resentfully as she squeezed through them to the coffee station, closing ranks and clutching their plates to their chests. The coffee sputtered into the cup. She could tell immediately it was cold. She carried her cup back outside, stepping over discarded water bottles and what looked to be the jellyfish body of a used condom, and headed down to the Tranquillity deck. It was doubtful Celine would have made it to this level, but it was worth a look.

If anything, this area was even more populated, the Jacuzzi stuffed with a crowd of rowdy British men.

No Celine.

She was about to backtrack, when a dark-haired man sitting on a lounger next to the towel station caught her eye: the blogger from last night. Head bent, he was fiddling with his iPhone. Fuelled by a surge of resentment, instead of moving on, she found herself saying: 'Feeling better?'

''Scuse me?' He looked up, and she stared at her reflection in the twin lenses of his retro aviator glasses.

'After last night. Celine's event.'

He looked her up and down. 'You were there?'

'I'm Celine's PA. So yeah. Hope you're happy.'

He shrugged. 'Not really. Been sick as a dog pretty much since I came on board. Still not feeling great.'

'Oh, what a pity.'

'The PA, huh? Do you write her excuses for her as well?'

Maddie was scrambling for a retort when there was a beep signalling another message from Damien: 'G'day, this is your cruise director Damien speaking. It may not be the greatest start to the New Year, so how about we shake off the blues with an extra game of Bingo?'

'Thank God for Damien,' the blogger said. 'What the fuck would we do without him?' He gave her a sardonic grin, taking her off guard. 'Can you believe this shit?' He waggled his phone. 'No signal. No Internet. Can't log on.' There was the sound of a squeal and Maddie looked over her shoulder to see two women in bikinis jumping into the Jacuzzi on top of the men. 'You don't think it's weird we haven't seen anyone?' the guy continued. 'Like a helicopter or another cruise ship? They should have sent something by now. I was up here most of the night. The Gulf is lousy with drilling rigs, but nothing. No lights. Nada. Zip. Something's going on that they're not telling us.'

'Foveros gets a lot of bad press. They're probably trying to keep it quiet. Avoid it being splashed all over the news.'

'You'd know all about that, wouldn't you?'

'Nice. You got me.' She'd asked for it. What the hell was she doing talking to this guy anyway? If he'd bothered to book himself onto the ship, he must be one of the tenacious debunkers who spent hours trying to lure Celine into responding to him on FB, Zoop and Twitter. Maddie, who ran all these accounts, never bothered to engage with them, or refute or comment on any of their blogs. The Friends had that covered. Time to move on.

'Hey! Hey wait. I'm sorry.' She hesitated, then turned back. The guy took off his glasses. Dark-blue eyes, fair lashes – his hair was definitely dyed. 'I suppose an interview is out of the question.'

'You suppose right.'

'You're from England.'

'You're sharp.'

Another wry smile. 'How long you been working for Celine?'

'I said no interview.'

'Off the record then.'

'Yeah, right.'

'Look, I'm just doing my job. You got to admit, what happened with Lillian Small was fucked up. It's proven without a shadow of a doubt that Lori and Bobby Small died on Black Thursday and yet Celine—'

'Like Celine says, she can only use what Spirit tells her.'

He grimaced and Maddie took a step back. 'Don't worry, I'm not going to hurl. That was my gross-out face. I don't get it. Why do you work for her?'

Because no one else in their right mind would employ me. 'None of your business.'

'She's a predator. Preying on the grieving.'

'She brings hope and closure to people,' Maddie said automatically.

'Does she? Did she bring hope and closure to Lillian Small?'

'I don't need to listen to this.'

'You're right. You don't. But don't you think you should? Celine has made a goddamned fortune feeding off the grieving.'

'People want hope. They need to know—'

'That there is more than this? That there is an afterlife?'

'Yes.'

'That I can understand. But telling a mother her daughter and grandson are still alive after there's incontrovertible proof otherwise? C'mon.'

'It's not foolproof.' Maddie mentally winced.

'That's no defence and you know it. Admit it. It's all bullshit.'

'Maybe I do believe she has a gift.'

'I don't buy it for a second. You're too switched on for that. You don't look like the type of person who'd wilfully deceive anyone.'

'Nice try.' The appeal to her ego was a smart move. He wasn't to know that her ego had gone the same way as her self-respect a long time ago. 'I think we're finished here.'

'Wait. What's your name?' He grinned, disarming her once more. 'Just so I know who I'm bad mouthing.'

'You first. Just so I know who to sue.'

'I go under the name Xavier.'

'You "go under" the name Xavier? What are you, twelve?'

He laughed – a low grumble that she wouldn't have expected from him. 'You don't think it's cool? Stripper-name cool? It's my real name, by the way.'

'Sure it is. Enjoy writing your story. Looks like you might have a real one this time.'

He laughed again, and she found herself smiling back. She wasn't a moron. She knew that she'd be ripped to shreds in the guy's next blog, but their exchange had made her feel oddly buoyant. 'Catch you later,' he said.

'Don't count on it.'

She walked back through the interior buffet seating area. Celine had to be on this level somewhere. Unless . . . *Shit.* Why hadn't she thought of it before? She could have left the suite and fallen ill again – perhaps she'd been taken to the medical bay. Ray. It was about time the bastard pulled his weight. Like her, he was ensconced in one of the cheaper cabins in the bowels of the ship. She dredged her memory for his cabin number, then padded down the stairs, past the entrance to the Promenade Dreamz deck, the casino and the art gallery. The neon lights had been disabled, and without them the interior of the ship looked drab; an ageing showgirl scrubbed of her make-up. She jogged down several flights of stairs, trying not to breathe through her nose. The air down here was a foul humid broth, seasoned with a tinge of effluence. She made her way along the corridor that led to the odd-numbered staterooms, and knocked on what she hoped was Ray's door.

'Yeah?' a sleep-muffled voice shouted. It sounded like Ray's voice.

'It's Maddie.'

More than a minute passed before Ray opened it, a towel around his waist. 'Hey, Maddie,' he said, preening and trailing his fingers over his bare chest. 'Hot, isn't it?'

A giggle came from within the room, and a woman's voice called: 'Hurry up, Ray.'

Ray turned his head. 'Be there in a minute, babe.'

A plump woman in skimpy underwear appeared behind him, wrapped her arms around his torso, rested her chin on his shoulder, and stared unselfconsciously at Maddie through panda eyes. Her skin was a patchwork of red and white criss-crossed tan lines. 'Hi.'

'Hi.'

'This is Maddie, babe,' Ray smirked. 'We work together.'

'Oh yeah?' The woman yawned and unpeeled her arms. 'Gotta have a shower.'

Ray winked at Maddie. 'I'll join you in a second.'

The woman giggled again and disappeared into the bathroom.

Maddie gave Ray a look. 'You've been busy.'

Ray shrugged, smirk still in place. 'Decided to have my own party, seeing as you didn't take me up on my invite. We met at the muster station. Hey, where were you, anyway?'

'Nice of you to notice.' And thinking about it, it was nice of Foveros to notice. She didn't recall any of the staff doing a head count. 'I was with Celine. Our boss, remember? She . . . something happened to her last night.'

'Oh yeah? What?' He scratched his stomach and shifted his position, allowing Maddie space to view the interior. The floor was an apocalypse of beer cans and plates smeared with sauce the colour of dried blood.

'Have you seen Celine this morning?'

'What does it look like? Like you pointed out, I've been busy.'

'I need to find her.'

'Good luck.'

'You're not going to help me?'

'How hard can it be? You're on a ship. She's in a wheelchair.'

'It's your job, Ray. I hardly slept last night.'

'Makes two of us.'

'Fine. You know what? Forget it. Thanks for nothing.'

'Listen, Maddie. You know what? You can shove your bullshit.'

'Excuse me?'

'I'm sick of you sneering at me, looking down at me.' This was a side to Ray she hadn't seen before.

'Fine. Whatever.'

'You think you're so superior, don't you? Well, babe, let me put you straight on that. You're just some stuck-up Brit with a chip on her shoulder. You know what you need, don't you? A good fu—'

The rage was instant and overwhelming. Maddie thrust both palms into his chest. 'I'll tell you what I need, you bastard, you out of my *fucking* face.' Flecks of her spittle peppered his face. His shocked expression turned to amusement, incensing her even more.

He held up his hands. 'Yo. Easy there, tiger. I was only kidding around.'

'Fuck you.' She whirled and ran towards the stairwell, shaky, a roaring in her ears. Sod going to her cabin to collect her belongings; she couldn't face that now. She clung to the handrail. Bloody *bloody* Ray. She couldn't let him get to her. She paused to get her bearings – she'd need to head back up to the atrium to cut down to the medical bay. She'd barely made it up one flight when a man came sprinting down past her, his hand clamped over his mouth as if he was about to vomit.

Jesus. Oh God. Maddie crossed her arms under her armpits and ran, desperate to reach fresh air. Her scalp was tingling, her palms were beginning to sweat and she could feel her throat closing. She stumbled over to the atrium balcony, and tried to slow her heart, which felt like it was attempting to force its way out of her mouth. The floor beneath her pitched, and her guts rolled lazily.

'Maddie?' She looked up, and saw Eleanor, one of the Friends, bearing down on her. 'Are you okay?'

Maddie couldn't speak at first, *Jesus.*

'C'mon, come and sit down.' Eleanor rubbed her back.

'I'm fine. Just . . . I'm fine.'

'Are you sure?' Eleanor was one of the pet fanatics; desperate to get in touch with the spirit of her dog. Maddie dredged her memory for its name – Denny or Dirk or something; a name that sounded like it should belong to a porn star. 'Can I get you some water? It's awful close in here, isn't it?'

'I'm fine.' Saying the words seemed to help. The pinprick in her throat widened. 'Thank you, Eleanor. I just felt a bit dizzy for a second there.'

'I'm not surprised. You're too thin, Maddie. Have you had breakfast yet?'

'No.' And she'd missed dinner last night – hadn't ordered that toasted cheese after all.

'I've been looking for Celine.'

'Well honey, she's in the Starlight Dreamer Lounge.'

'Huh?' That couldn't be right. 'What the . . . what's she doing there?'

'Well, I tell you, this morning I was up early, went to the buffet to see if I could get myself some granola – I slept so badly last night with all that's going on, despite Damien telling us all there's nothing to worry about – and I saw her on the Lido deck. She asked me to gather all the Friends together.'

'Celine did *what*?'

'Bless her heart. She's been with us for two hours now, really making us feel comfortable. Quite a few of the Friends were really worried, specially the ones who have flights today, but Celine told them all would be just super. I was on my way back to my cabin to take my vitamins, but that can wait. You want me to take you to her?'

'I can manage.'

Eleanor tsked. 'I'm not leaving you alone in this state.'

She hooked a plump arm through Maddie's, bathing her in the scent of Lily of the Valley.

'How did Celine get down there?'

'Why, she walked of course. She took her time, but she said she felt up to it.'

'And her wheelchair?'

'Oh, Jacob and Jimmy helped with that.' Maddie let Eleanor lead her past the deserted casino and along the passageway towards the entrance to the lounge. A small group of Friends were gathered outside it, and Jacob came scurrying up to them, dressed in a lavender waistcoat, pink tie and a pinstriped shirt.

'Maddie's not feeling well, Jacob,' Eleanor said, releasing Maddie and patting her arm.

'Oh, you poor thing. Well you've come to the right place. We'll look after you.'

Maddie did her best to smile. She tended to think of the Friends as losers – human jigsaw puzzles missing a crucial piece of blue sky – but here they were, propping her up.

'I was just telling Maddie how wonderful Celine's being to us,' Eleanor said.

Jacob nodded enthusiastically. 'Oh yes. Celine *and* Archie. Archie's been very vocal today. Celine says that Spirit wants us to know that we need to take all this in our stride.'

'Jacob,' Eleanor said, 'tell Maddie what Archie said to you about Kathy.'

'Kathy?' Maddie asked.

'His sister. You remember, Maddie. She stepped forward last night – she went missing at Thanksgiving.'

Of course. How could Maddie have forgotten that? She'd been the one who'd passed on the details to Celine after Jacob had confided them to her during their first meet 'n' greet. Another jab of shame.

A faraway look came into Jacob's eyes. 'She came forward with Archie this time. He said she was wearing her favourite white dress and she wanted me to know exactly what had happened to her.' Maddie's fingers were tingling again, and she dug her nails into her palms. 'Archie told me the whole story. Kathy ran away to San Francisco, lived there for a while, but fell in with a bad crowd.' His voice thickened. 'She died alone in a boarded-up apartment, a year after she left us, from a drug overdose.'

'I'm so sorry,' Maddie said. What the hell was Celine playing at? She dealt in hope, not despair.

'Don't be sorry. I wanted to know, I *needed* to know. Kathy's waiting for me to join her. She'll be there at the moment I cross over into the next world.'

'So inspiring,' Eleanor breathed.

The glass doors were wedged open just enough for Eleanor to squeeze through – anyone larger would have a problem – and Maddie followed her into the lounge's shadowy depths. Annabeth and Jimmy, one of the few couples who'd signed up to Cruise with Celine, clucked around her. Maddie murmured a vague greeting and approached the stage, where Celine was deep in conversation with Leila.

Celine looked up and caught her eye. 'Thank you, my darling,' Celine said to Leila. 'Madeleine needs me now.'

Without a murmur and only the slightest smile in Maddie's direction, Leila drifted away as if pulled by an invisible string. Maddie clambered onto the stage.

Celine cocked her head on one side and assessed her. 'You look tired, Madeleine. Didn't you sleep well? You were sleeping like the dead when I left this morning.'

'Yeah, about that. Why didn't you wake me?'

'You needed to rest.'

'How are you feeling, Celine? Should you really be doing this?' Whatever the hell this was. It wasn't right – Celine had spent the entire cruise dodging the Friends, and now here she was, their new best friend.

'I'm feeling wonderful. Just wonderful. Like a new person.'

Maddie had to admit she did look better than she had for months. Her make-up wasn't as garish as usual, which made her look younger, less jaded. 'Jacob and Eleanor said you asked them to bring all the Friends here this morning. What are you playing at?'

'People are worried, Madeleine. We must all do our part.'

'Okay. Can the real Celine please come back now?'

'Oh she's around. She'll show herself soon enough. And know this, I plan to help as many people as I can.'

'What do you mean by "help"?'

'People need to be shown the way, Maddie. They need guidance. I'm here to provide them with a helping hand. Me and Spirit, of course.'

'Tell me you're taking the piss, Celine.'

Celine took her hand. Her boss's fingers were icy, although the lounge, like the rest of the ship, was stultifying. 'Where's Ray?'

'In his cabin.'

'Well, he'll show up soon enough. They all will if they know what's good for them.' Celine winked at her. 'Go grab a pew. Watch the show. Think you're gonna enjoy it.'

'I don't think you should be doing this, Celine.'

'My darling, this is what I was born to do.'

'Last night—'

'Go on and sit down, Maddie,' Celine said, her voice turning from honeyed to brittle, which was reassuring. Maddie could cope with irritable Celine. 'You don't want to make a scene, do you?'

'Celine, please tell me what you're—'

'Enough. Go on, now.'

Maddie didn't have the strength to argue. Celine had to be playing this part for reasons of her own. Perhaps it had something to do with the blogger's accusations last night. Perhaps she was hoping that the Friends would flock to her defence when Xavier (or whatever his real name was) vomited the clip all over the networks. Perhaps something had snapped in her mind, uncovering a new altruistic side.

Maddie made her way over to a booth at the edge of the room. She spotted the technical guy – the kid Celine had sniped at last night – lost in conversation with Juanita, who gave Maddie a little collusive wave. She slumped onto the seat, the headache now pulsating in her temples, and waited. A hush fell over the Starlight Dreamer Lounge as Celine wheeled herself across the stage, and Maddie couldn't shake the feeling that she was about to watch a deranged, wheel-chaired prophet addressing her acolytes.

The Condemned Man

Gary lay as still as he could, watching the sweat beading the hairs on his belly. Marilyn had left the stateroom an hour ago, complaining that she couldn't breathe. He was planning to hole up in the cabin until they fixed the problem, but without the air-con, it was fast becoming a sauna. The heat and his low blood sugar were making him nauseous; he wouldn't be able to stay down here much longer in any comfort. And sleep was out of the question. Unable to staunch the running dialogue in his head, he hadn't done much more than doze since he and Marilyn had returned from the muster station last night. At least he'd emerged from that unscathed. He'd been on continual high alert, twitching every time a security guard or a crew member walked by, but Marilyn hadn't commented on his behaviour. He supposed he could thank her cruise buddies for that. They'd monopolised her attention, providing a non-stop stream of unasked-for commentary about the state of the Minnesota housing market, leaving him free to lurk in a darkened corner, attempting to be as unobtrusive as possible.

They would have come for you by now if they were going to. Relax.

But what about the 'don't disturb' sign? What if they've got that?

What if they have? Even if they do test it for fingerprints, yours aren't on file anywhere.

When we get back to port they might take everyone's fingerprints.

So what if they do? It's purely circumstantial. They've got other things to worry about. You're home free. You're over the worst of it.

The footage – they might recognise me.

No chance.

Really? What about last night? How will I explain walking to her cabin?

You were in shock, disorientated by the ship's sudden stop.
And DNA. My DNA will be all over her stateroom.
They're not going to test everyone on board.
You don't know that for sure.
They'll want to keep it quiet. You know the drill. By now they've convinced themselves that she died of alcohol poisoning. Why else aren't they interrogating the crew and passengers?

He had to believe that.

He sat up, and hobbled into the bathroom, slightly thrown by the fact that the ship was now listing to the left. He adjusted his balance and tried not to look at the clothes he'd left lying in the stall last night, which Marilyn had hung on a line in the shower. The water spattered out of the tap, and he splashed it over his cheeks. He decided not to bother shaving – anything he could do to change his appearance would help. He sprayed himself with deodorant, slipped on a fresh shirt and pair of shorts, and made his way out of the cabin and towards the stairwell. A crew member polishing the handrails eyed him warily as he passed, stumbling as the listing floor unbalanced him. He cut through the atrium, pushing through a clump of angry people who were waiting for their turn to shout at the Guest Services staff. The woman at the front of the line was yelling: 'My dogs are in kennels. Kennels! I was supposed to fetch them today!'

A wall of noise hit him as he stepped out onto the Lido deck. The place was heaving with people, every sun-lounger taken up. The light stung his eyes, and framed by the railings, the ocean undulated sluggishly.

'They'll come soon,' a middle-aged man was saying to a group of women who were gathered round him, slathering each other in sun cream. He stepped over the outstretched legs of a passenger fanning herself with a copy of Damien's daily entertainment bulletin, and scanned the area for Marilyn.

'Gary!' He craned his neck, and spotted her next to the entrance of the indoor buffet seating area, waving her arms over her head. 'Gary! Over here, hon!' As he made his way towards her, people turned to look at him, and he coloured and kept his head lowered.

She was sitting at a table with a couple who were flashier and younger than last night's pair. No surprise there; he'd expected that Marilyn would have moved onto fresher pastures.

'Hey, hon,' Marilyn said. 'This is Samantha and Mason Patchulik.'

The guy – late twenties, flinty eyes, crewcut, scorched scalp – nodded at him. 'Some vacation, huh?'

'You gotta see it as an adventure, baby,' the woman – Samantha – crooned, crossing her legs and giving Gary a calculated smile. Fake breasts, fake hair, bleached teeth. A manufactured woman. Not Gary's type. 'Just wish I could tell my folks what's going on. You think Foveros will have let everyone know? They'll be leaving to fetch us from the airport in an hour.'

Gary looked around for an empty chair, but they were all taken. He had no choice but to stand awkwardly next to the table.

'Samantha and Mason are from Michigan,' Marilyn said, oblivious to his discomfort.

'Oh really? That's nice.'

Mason shook his head as if Gary had said something woefully stupid. 'You think? Been freezing our asses off back home. Thought we'd get some sun, booked at the last minute, got a good deal, but look what else we got. Stranded. Gonna miss our flight. They'd better fly us home business class now to make up for this. Or at the very least give us a comp cruise.'

Marilyn's eyes lit up. 'Oh, I didn't think of that. You think they'd do that?'

'If they don't want their asses sued, they will. Gonna get them for missed earnings as well.'

Good luck with that, Gary thought. He'd read the contract when he booked; he read it carefully every year, and he knew Foveros had its ass well and truly covered. The company could practically sell the passengers to Somalian pirates and the consumer wouldn't have a case.

'So, Gary,' Mason continued. 'Marilyn says you're a teacher, huh?'

'I am, yes.'

'High school?'

'Middle grade.'

'Those who can't do, teach, am I right?'

Gary managed a rigid smile. 'Something like that.'

'Hey, don't mind me. I'm just messing with you. I'm in construction.'

'He has his own business,' Samantha preened, rubbing his thigh.

'Yeah. Started my own business. Own boss. Get to make my own hours.' Mason was clearly one of those guys who had to one-up everyone – Gary knew the type. He saw fledgling Masons in the schoolyard every day. He'd never been one of them – or one of their victims, for that matter. He knew how to keep his head down, disappear, blend into the background. He was practised at avoiding the staffroom dramas and the occasional parental gripes at work. And he knew what his students thought of him: Mr Johansson, the world's most boring teacher. He rarely had trouble in his classes; got the impression the students didn't see the point. They'd figured out that he was just going through the motions.

He glanced around, looking for anyone from his girl's group. It was possible they were hunkering beneath one of the sheets that several people were attaching to the railings as sunshields.

'You seen what they're putting on for breakfast?' Marilyn said to no one in particular. 'Sandwiches!'

'I know, right?' Samantha gasped. 'I asked one of the guys serving and he said there wasn't much they could do as there was no electricity.'

Mason (what kind of a name was Mason, anyway?) shook his head. 'Should have had a redundancy in place.'

'Redundancy?' Marilyn asked.

'A system that would kick in during a situation like this one. It's the regs. Saw it on Cruise Critics. All Foveros ships were supposed to be equipped with them after the incident with *The Beautiful Wonder.*'

'How clever of you to know that!' Marilyn said, eyeing Mason with awe. Gary hated her for it.

'The least they could do is send one of their other ships to check on us. A helicopter, something,' Mason said. 'Hey!' he shouted at a passing crew member who was stepping through an obstacle course of prone bodies collecting plastic soda cups and discarded water bottles. 'When the hell we gonna hear what's going on?'

'The captain will be making an announcement soon, sir,' the crew member said in a voice leached of any inflection.

'That's what we've been hearing all morning. This is bullshit.'

'Hon,' Samantha said. 'It's not his fault.'

'I'm sick of this shit. I paid good money to be here.'

'I know, baby. I'm just saying—'

'And I don't need you telling me what to do.'

'I'm not.'

'Yeah? Sounds that way to me.'

'Sorry, babe,' Samantha said, with a little girl pout.

Marilyn's eyes were gleaming at this unexpected entertainment. Mason puffed his chest out like a rooster and waved the crew member away. The man drifted off, only to be accosted by a group sitting at the neighbouring table, who asked him the same question.

'It's gonna be a hot one,' Samantha mumbled, fiddling with the straps of her top.

'That reminds me,' Marilyn said, turning to Gary. 'Hon, I left my hat in the cabin. Could you get it for me? I'm gonna cook out here without it. And you'd better go to Guest Services and find out what's going on.'

'Sure.' At the very least it would give him a chance to get away from the Patchuliks. Hopefully Marilyn would tire of them soon. If not, he'd feign illness again and find a place in the ship to hide that wasn't as stuffy as the cabin. 'I could be a while. The line looked like it—' he froze as a security guard strolled past the pool deck; Gary could have sworn the guy looked right at him.

'Hon?' Marilyn and the Patchuliks were looking at him curiously. 'You okay?'

'Sorry. Sure I am. I'll go right now. See you later.'

Gary picked his way through the herd and headed into the heart of the ship. The line for Guest Services had almost doubled, as had the clamour of raised voices. He cut past the art gallery and padded down towards his deck. In contrast to the racket outside and in the atrium, the lower decks were eerily silent. A door banged, making him jump. He told himself not to be ridiculous; he'd only just been down here. The low ceilings and endless corridors didn't usually bother him, in fact he liked the idea that he was bobbing in a subterranean underground, surrounded by miles of ocean, but for some reason he was beginning to feel on edge. The lights were dimmer than they were before – he was almost sure of it, and the screen-printed murals, all of which showed angels wrestling with each other, were now a blur of lumpy limbs and holes for eyes. The garish carpet seemed to be breathing. A door banged again, and then he heard a steady thumping sound. A sick heartbeat. As if someone was running up to him.

He turned. No one there. 'Hello?'

With no warning, his bowels cramped. He fumbled for his room card, dropped it on the carpet. The hairs on his arms and the back of his neck bristled, his heart sped up. Gary didn't think of himself as possessing an overactive imagination, but it really did feel as if he was alone down here; the sole passenger on an entirely empty ship. *Thump, thump, thump* – he whirled again, but the corridor was deserted. He couldn't decide where it was coming from: beneath his feet or from one of the cabins, perhaps. He tried the card again, and this time it opened. He propped the door open on its magnet and flicked the switch. The lights were out. His shirt was now soaked through, and he stripped it off and fumbled in the closet for another one. He was swamped with a strong, urgent sense that he had to get out of there, but his bowels cramped again, and he had no choice but to hurry to the bathroom. He barely made it. The flush button plinked hollowly. He tried it again. Nothing. Screw it.

Get out get out get out.

He lurched into the hallway, was about to hurry away when he realised he'd forgotten Marilyn's hat. Reluctantly, he returned. The cabin reeked of his own waste and he gagged. The hat, a pink straw thing that she'd bought from a vendor in Cozumel, hung innocently over the edge of the television. He ran for it, almost had it in his grasp, when he heard the door slam behind him. He looked around wildly, thought in the blackness he could sense movement, getting the impression of two darker shapes twitching at the far end of the space.

Gary backpedalled, the backs of his knees bashing against the bed.

It's okay, it's okay, it's okay. No one's coming to get you, there's no one there, you're just—

He screamed and bit down on his tongue as a weight landed on his chest, squashing the breath out of his lungs. He tried to thrash out, but his arms wouldn't – or couldn't – move. Paralysed, there was nothing he could do as icy breath tickled his cheeks and cold fingers slowly spidered up his thigh.

The Devil's Handmaiden

'I haven't been able to spare anyone to service your cabins this morning,' Maria said to Althea by way of a greeting. 'Trining is still sick, and Joan says she is unable to work today.'

Althea nodded in response. There were no eyebrows on Maria's face today, just a smudge where they should be. It made her look as if her facial features were slowly disappearing. Perhaps tomorrow her nose would be gone, then the eyes, then the mouth, and then just smooth, blank skin. Althea mentally shook herself – what thoughts were these? She ran her tongue over her teeth. She'd been plagued with hyper-real nightmares last night; a man with rusty pliers – she couldn't see his face – yanking her teeth out one by one. She could still hear the crunch of each root being ripped out of her gums in her mind. Her *lola* firmly believed in finding meaning in dreams, and Althea had heard somewhere that pregnant women were more likely to suffer nightmares. And then there was the boy . . . he hadn't haunted her dreams, but somehow, that was worse.

'Althea? Are you listening to me?'

'Sorry, Maria. Could you repeat what you just said?'

'I said that Security would like to talk to you as soon as possible.'

'Yes, Maria.' Althea was expecting this. She needed to get her story straight. She could hardly tell them that a ghost boy had led her to that particular cabin. Or admit that she was going loco. After she'd been dismissed by the tall security guard, who'd returned to the dead girl's stateroom accompanied by a senior officer, Althea had fled to her cabin. Grateful that Mirasol, her cabin mate, was absent, she'd rolled herself in her blanket and shut her eyes tight, feigning unconsciousness. She was practised at that, it was what she did at home when she wanted to avoid Joshua's attentions. Sometime later – it could have been minutes, or hours – she'd fallen asleep. She had a vague recollection that Mirasol had tried to wake her this morning, but when she finally crawled out of bed – three hours late for her shift – the cabin was empty. And now her brain felt like overcooked rice; she needed to clear her head, sharpen her wits.

Maria wiped a finger over the bald patch where her left eyebrow should be. 'I know what occurred last night. I know about the dead passenger.'

'Security informed you?' Althea hadn't yet told anyone about the girl, but she was not surprised that Maria knew. Maria made it her business to know everything about her staff, and it made sense that Security would have spoken to her.

'Yes. They needed to talk to Trining. It must have been a shock. You are fine to work today?'

Althea considered saying that no, she was not fine to work, but what else was she going to do? The only other option was to sit in her cabin or the mess canteen and obsess about the boy while they waited for the engineers to fix the problem or for Foveros to send a rescue boat. She felt a twinge in her lower belly. A swift, sharp pain. A reminder of what else she had to worry about. 'I can work.'

'Good.' A small smile. It struck Althea that she had never seen Maria smiling before. 'You are the best I have on my team.'

Althea blinked, surprised at the thrill of pride she felt at this unexpected compliment. 'Thank you, Maria.'

'You should know. Trining will have to go. She will be taken straight to the airport when we return to port.'

'But . . . she is a good worker,' Althea said, as she knew was expected of her, although she couldn't care less if Trining was fired. That stupid *puta* should have been the one to find the girl, not Althea. Sure, she would miss the extra cash Trining paid her for picking up her slack, but there were plenty of ways to make extra money – Althea wasn't afraid to get her hands dirty. 'You have told her?'

'No. But soon. And there is something else. Several of the vacuum pumps that work the sanitary system are malfunctioning.'

'Which areas?'

'Issues have been reported in most of the public restrooms and the staterooms mid and aft of the ship.'

'Not the VIP section?'

'Not as far as I know. But your guests will have to be informed. There will be an announcement shortly. I have already briefed the others. You know the procedure.'

Althea did. She and the other stewards would be sent to hand out waste bags to the passengers, which would add another layer of misery to her day. She'd dealt with a situation like this a month into her last contract, when a propulsion issue disabled the sanitation system and resulted in the stranding of the ship in Cozumel for several days. But in that instance there were no passengers to deal with; they were all disembarked while the problem was addressed. Althea toyed with telling Maria that she couldn't work, after all. Then again if she proved herself to be reliable, the chances of getting that promotion might increase. *You are the best I have on my team.* 'Maria . . . do you know when help will arrive?'

'No. I have not been informed.'

Althea was certain Maria knew more than she was letting on. Paulo, one of the crew stewards, had told her he'd seen Maria slipping into the second officer's cabin on more than one occasion. 'The passengers will want to know.'

'Tell them that there will be an announcement as soon as we know more.'

Althea doubted that would cut it. It was nearly midday, four hours past the time they were due to dock in Miami. 'Should I go to Security first?' Althea wasn't sure which was less appealing: being interrogated by the Indian mafia or facing the wrath of the passengers when they learned they would have to do their business in plastic bags.

'No. Make sure your guests are comfortable first before you go to Security. I will tell them that you will go there when you have finished your shift.'

'Thank you, Maria. May I please go to the mess hall first and have something to eat?' Althea wasn't hungry – the twinge she felt in her belly wasn't from lack of food – but she wanted to regroup before she faced the day.

'Yes. But hurry. And Althea . . .'

'Yes?'

'If . . . if things get worse, I can count on you, can't I?'

Who was this new Maria? Althea struggled to imagine how things could get worse. Surely it wouldn't be long before Foveros swung into action and sent a support crew. 'Of course.'

She left the housekeeping office, narrowly avoiding colliding with a couple of crew members hefting bales of the red plastic waste bags out of the storeroom. Mirasol was helping to unpack them, and she flinched when she caught sight of Althea. 'I am so sorry, Althea,' she said in a rush. 'I tried to wake you this morning, but you would not get out of bed.'

'I know. I'm not angry.'

Althea noted Mirasol's sigh of relief with amusement.

'Althea . . . is it true that a guest on Trining's station is dead?'

'Who told you that?'

'Angelo.'

Of course. Angelo, one of the assistant waiters, and an old gambling buddy of Joshua's, could sniff out gossip like a rat detecting rotting meat. 'Don't listen to everything Angelo says. And stay away from him, Mirasol.'

'Why?'

So that you don't end up like me. 'He likes to take advantage.' The girl was too naïve, had only been with the ship a month. Althea had meant to take her under her wing, but hadn't yet found the time. She remembered how bewildered she'd felt when she'd started on the ships, which was part of the reason why she'd accepted Joshua's attentions. She'd been lured in by his confidence. Stupid. No. She must keep a close eye on Mirasol, especially with everything that was happening now.

And it never hurt to have people owing you favours.

'He heard it from Paulo, Althea. One of the security men was asking about the "don't disturb" sign on the guest's door. They were angry at Paulo because he said he put it with the others in Trining's station. Why would they do that?'

Because they think whoever killed her touched it. 'I am sure they have their reasons.'

'Angelo said that Paulo might get in trouble because he didn't check the rooms properly before he—'

'Angelo shouldn't talk so much.'

'Did Maria put you on a warning for being late, Althea?'

'No. It's fine.'

'Maria says I must do Trining's station after I have finished mine. I don't like it down there. The passenger who died . . . is it true that she was murdered?'

Fuck-darned Angelo. 'We don't know how she died.'

'Althea . . . what if her spirit is still trapped down there? Also, Angelo said that one of the maintenance-crew men had seen the Lady in White when he was—'

'That is crazy talk.' But who was the one who was really going crazy? After all, Althea was the one who was seeing imaginary boys – or the ghosts of imaginary boys. No child had ever died on any cruise ship she'd worked on – that was for the elderly and the suicides. An assistant waiter had thrown himself overboard on her first ship after a fight with another crew member, but as Foveros ran shorter routes, there were usually very few deaths. But, she thought, that didn't stop superstition taking hold, and the Lady in White was the most popular ghost story amongst the staff. The Lady, the vengeful spirit of a deceased passenger who dressed, for some unaccountable reason, as the majority of Foveros's ships had been built in the eighties, in a Victorian gown, had been present on all of the ships she'd worked on. A very busy spirit, that one. She'd had enough of this talk. 'You know what to do with the bags, Mirasol?'

The girl nodded.

'And be polite to the passengers. Some of them will be angry with you.'

'I know. Maria told me. But most of them have moved out of the lower decks.'

'To where?'

'Outside.' Mirasol scrunched up her nose. 'They are saying that it stinks down there. Pah. They should be down here.'

'I must hurry. I will help you with Trining's station later when I am finished.' Which would give her an opportunity to check out Deck Five again – where she'd seen the boy.

'Thank you, Althea.'

The atmosphere in the mess was subdued, several people were lying with their heads on their arms, dozing. She slid her tray along the rack, past platters of bread, sliced cheese and olives. There was no cooked food. She dished up a bowl of yesterday's rice, cold and glutinous, some chopped tomatoes and a sliver of dried fish. Over by the recycling bin, Angelo was gossiping with Pepe, one of the kitchen assistants. He was trying to catch her eye, and waved her over, but she pretended not to see him. She wasn't in the mood to listen to him today. Instead, she made her way over to where Rogelio was sitting alone at a table in the corner – he was entitled to use the officers' mess, and she liked him more for continuing to eat with his paisanos.

She greeted him, but he barely acknowledged her. 'Are you okay, Rogelio?'

He shrugged, and wouldn't meet her gaze, which was not like him. Rogelio was usually full of energy, smiling and upbeat even when he was off duty and could let his mask slip. He often hosted karaoke crew parties long into the early morning in his own cabin, and she rarely heard anyone bad-mouth him.

'Do you know anything more about the situation?' He was Damien's right-hand man, after all.

'They're working on the problem.'

'Come on, Rogelio. You know more than that.'

He shook his head.

'We should have been in Miami several hours ago.' When the last ship she was on ran into difficulties, it had only been a matter of hours before Ground Support flocked to help.

'I know nothing.'

'What does Damien say?'

Rogelio grimaced. 'He is spending most of his time on the bridge with the captain.'

As if summoned by magic, an announcement came from Damien himself. The clattering and murmurs in the mess ceased as everyone heard the bad news. But it was Althea and the other stewards who would be in the firing line.

Rogelio pushed his plate away from him. 'I must go. We are putting on extra activities for the guests.'

Althea automatically turned her plate as he left the table. Stupid. She was already married – she didn't need superstition to keep the spectre of spinsterhood away. The rice sat in her gut in a hard ball.

Angelo sidled up to her the second Rogelio left the mess hall. 'What did pretty boy say to you, Althea? He won't talk to me.'

'Nothing.'

'Ah, come on.' Without being invited, he sat opposite her and leaned over the table. 'Pepe says that the kitchen crew were told this morning that they had to be extra careful with the supplies.'

Althea snorted. 'What does Pepe know? He works in the side kitchens.'

'He says it is in case we are stranded for a long time and they have to send tugs. Pepe says they're preparing just in case it takes as much as two days to get back to port.'

'It will not come to that.'

'You don't know that. It is lucky that we're stocked for the next cruise.'

'Mirasol says that you've been gossiping again.'

'What else is there to do?'

'She does not need to hear your ghost stories.'

'Whatever.' Angelo smirked. 'Perhaps Rogelio will get more information from his boyfriend.'

'Damien is not his boyfriend.'

Angelo pursed his lips and cocked his head on one side. 'Believe that if it makes you happy. But someone is.'

'I don't have time for this, Angelo.' She stood up, dumped the remains of her food in the recycling bin and headed back towards the service area. Unable to use the elevator, she would have to heft the bags up the stairs. She collected a pile and clunked up towards her station.

She would start with Mr Lineman, who would be the worst by far to deal with. Holding her breath, she knocked on the door. No answer – the angels were on her side this morning. She propped the door open and slapped the bags down on the couch. The suite wasn't its usual pigsty, their belongings were packed away; their luggage piled neatly next to the closet. She straightened the bed, brushed away a stray grey pubic hair – she wouldn't bother changing the sheets – and then wiped a cloth over the TV stand.

She heard them before she saw them: the slam of the bathroom door, followed by the liquid spatter of vomit and groaning. Mr Lineman's wife, a woman with a dumpling face and quick little eyes, barely glanced at Althea. 'Jonny?' she was saying to the bathroom door. 'Jonny, you okay in there?'

Althea shuddered. She hoped there wasn't a virus going around. Perhaps Trining was telling the truth after all and really was sick. 'May I do anything to help?' she asked Mrs Lineman.

'We were in the queue when he said he felt bad. It can't be something he's eaten, we didn't even get a chance to get to the buffet.' The lavatory whooshed. The woman eyed the bags. 'What you got there?'

Here we go . . . Althea put on her most innocent expression and explained what they were for. While Mrs Lineman stared at her in undisguised horror, Althea briskly opened one of the bags and slid it inside the metal trashcan.

'I will not take a . . . take a . . . *you know what* in a bag. I'm not an animal.'

'It is just in case, Mrs Lineman. You are fortunate, the conveniences on this floor are still working.'

'I should think so. These are the VIP staterooms. We were upgraded on account of our stateroom was smaller than advertised.'

'Mrs Lineman, as I say, as of now your deck has not been affected—'

'You people won't hear the last of this.'

Althea put on her best smile. 'Is there anything else you need?'

'Just give us some more water and towels.'

'Thank you, Mrs Lineman.'

Mrs Lineman harrumphed.

Althea scurried past her, had almost made it when Mrs Lineman called her back.

Shitballs.

Althea turned, readying herself for a volley of abuse, but Mrs Lineman was now looking contrite. 'Don't mind me. I'm sorry for shouting at you. I'm just rattled, is all.'

For a second, Althea was worried the woman was about to start crying. She was not in any mood to put on her sympathetic act. 'There is nothing to worry about, Mrs Lineman. It will all be fine, you will see.' The lavatory flushed again, making them both jump. 'Let me know if there's anything else I can do.'

Mrs Lineman nodded distractedly, and Althea slipped away.

Her favourite two seniors, Helen and Elise, were absent, and she was gratified to see that their beds were made as usual. She left the red bags in their room, along with an extra bottle of water. She wouldn't charge them for it. Her radio buzzed, and she was tempted to ignore it – it would only be Maria, checking up on her. She clicked on receive, expecting to hear the usual gush of static, but Maria's voice came through clear and strong. 'Althea, come in, Althea.'

'I'm here, Maria.'

'Get to my office now, over.' There was a slight wobble in Maria's voice. Althea attempted to radio a response, but found she was talking to dead air once more. She would have to go all the way down to find out what the stupid *puta* wanted.

She bagged the dirty towels, and hauled them down the service stairs, cursing at the lack of an elevator. Her shoulder muscles would be burning by the time the day was done. Raised voices drifted towards her as she neared the alcove at the bottom, a popular gathering spot. Paulo and a couple of other stewards were huddled together in the corridor. 'What is happening?' Althea asked.

'It's Mirasol,' Paulo said. 'She was attacked by a passenger.'

'What? When?'

'Not long ago. I was the one who—'

'Where is she?'

'Maria has taken her to her office.'

Althea hurried along the I-95, and flew into Maria's office without knocking. Mirasol was sitting in front of Maria's desk with her head back, pressing a ball of tissues to her nose. Maria was standing over her, and on any other occasion, Althea would have relished the disconcerted expression on her usually smug supervisor's face.

'Is it true?' Althea asked. 'Did a passenger attack her?'

Maria looked up. 'Yes. It is true.'

'Why is she not in the medical bay?'

'No one is there. They are dealing with the passenger.'

'What happened?'

'He went to attack her when she walked into his stateroom to clean it.'

'He was crazy,' Mirasol said. Her voice was muffled. She hitched a breath and took her hand away from her face. 'Is it bad, Althea?'

Apart from the bloody nose, Althea could see no other injuries. 'It is not bad. You will live.'

'Can you look after her, Althea?' Maria asked. 'Security is dealing with it, but I need to inform the hotel head, the staff captain and Guest Services.'

'Of course.'

Althea noted that Maria's hands were trembling. She was bad in a crisis. This was useful information. A rare smile, and then Maria clacked her way out of the room with obvious relief.

Althea crouched next to Mirasol. The girl's eyes were bloodshot. 'Where did this happen? Trining's station?'

'No. It was at my station.' Mirasol sniffed again, and Althea grabbed the box of tissues from Maria's desk. She always kept it full. People did a lot of crying in this room. 'Before . . . before I opened his door, already things didn't feel right. I felt all the time like I was being watched.'

'I know that feeling, Mirasol. It is the security cameras. It takes a while to get used to them.'

'No. That isn't what I meant. I had to keep checking no one was coming to sneak up on me. All of my staterooms were empty and some of the mattresses were gone. People had moved out because of the smell. Have you been down there, Althea? It is becoming worse. Some of the carpets are wet, and there are blockages so that the toilets are overflowing. They must send Maintenance down there soon.'

'And the man who attacked you?' Althea tried not to show her impatience.

'I knocked on his cabin. There was no answer, so I walked in and . . . I could not see his face, but he was screaming and crying. He hit me, but I think that was an accident, I don't think he even saw me, and then I ran. He was scared, Althea. Something had scared him very badly.' She paused and wiped at her eyes. She really was very pretty. Althea would have to be watchful to ensure that Angelo didn't ruin her.

'Go on.'

'I think I know what it was. I saw something as I was running away, Althea.' Mirasol crossed herself.

'What did you see?' Althea felt another twinge in her stomach. 'A boy?'

'A boy?' Mirasol shook her head. 'No. I saw *her*, Althea. The Lady in White.'

'You couldn't have seen her, Mirasol.'

'I did, Althea. She smiled at me. She was—'

'There is no such thing as the Lady in White, Mirasol,' Althea snapped, her voice sounding harsher than she meant it to. Mirasol looked down at her hands. 'I am sorry. But it is just your imagination. Angelo put the idea in your head, and when you were frightened that's what you thought you saw.'

'Really?'
'Yes, really. There is no Lady in White, Mirasol.'
Just like there were no *duwende*s, or evil spirits, or witches.
Just like there were no ghost boys.

The Suicide Sisters

Damien the cruise director's announcements were coming thick and fast, each one more inane than the last: 'The shower is fun if you need a number one, and the red bags will do for a number two.' Helen suspected he might be enjoying the situation for some warped reason of his own. And she hadn't missed that there was a lack of real information – no message from the captain yet, or an explanation as to why no one from Foveros had come to rescue them, or tow them back to shore. She eyed the pile of red plastic bags that had been left while she and Elise were out. Thankfully their lavatory was still in working order, but it had made an alarming grinding sound the last time she'd flushed it.

'Helen?' Elise called from her bed. 'Could you get me some water?'

'Of course. How are you feeling?'

Elise gave her a brave smile. 'Better, thanks. It was just the heat getting to me.'

They'd been on the Lido deck queuing for breakfast when Elise said she felt faint. Helen had helped her back to the suite and encouraged her to lie down for a while. She didn't look well; her face was flushed and she could barely keep her eyes open.

'You sure?'

'Uh-huh. Think I'm gonna take another nap for few minutes. That okay?'

'Of course.' Helen poured her a glass of tepid water – their bar fridge was no longer working – and placed it next to the bed. Restless, she straightened up the room, then took her laptop and Kobo out onto the balcony. It was a couple of degrees cooler out here than in their stateroom; a slab of heat had hit them when they'd returned from the main deck. Still, they were among the lucky ones. At least their balcony suite – albeit with the view partially obscured by a lifeboat – provided them with a modicum of fresh air. The ship was still listing, and they didn't appear to be moving at all. The ocean was utterly still, the water coated with a greasy skin that reminded her of the top of a discarded cup of tea.

She sat and fired up her laptop. Her suicide note was still on the screen, waiting to be copied and pasted into the body of an email. It had taken her weeks to write the three lines, intending to send them to her friends and Graham's nephews who kept her up to date with their lives on Facebook. She supposed she could always just change her FB status to 'dead' instead.

Not funny.

I have decided I don't wish to live anymore. I am of sound mind. Please do not feel any guilt about my decision, it was not made lightly.

A lie of course. She wasn't someone who did anything lightly, but that decision had been . . . she searched for a way to describe it – almost flippant.

It had struck her randomly on an unseasonably humid day in June. She'd been gardening, talking to Graham in her head like she always did. She'd clipped a stem, and then thought, why bother? Who cared if the hedges were trimmed or not? The rest of the day loomed ahead of her, planned with military precision so that she wouldn't have too much time to think. Gardening from ten to twelve, then a drawn-out trip to Waitrose, a meeting with the local Save the Badger society for which she acted as secretary, then she'd read from three to five p.m., watch a couple of hours of television, cook herself a lonely dinner for one, take a sleeping pill and do it all over again the next day. She was tired of living from hour to hour, trying to fill the chasm. She had her friends, of course, but she was intensely conscious of not being a burden, and they were busy with their own lives and grandchildren. Filled with a peculiar sense of elation, she'd brushed the dirt off her hands, hurried inside and switched on her laptop. She was staggered by the amount of information available for the potentially suicidal. There was Exit International and Dignitas of course, scores of counselling services and hundreds of websites listing the top ten foolproof ways to do the deed. She'd stayed up for twenty hours straight, eventually landing on Bettertogether.com, a forum for 'those who don't want to die alone'. A message from 'Recently Widowed' caught her eye, a bittersweet account of how the poster attempted to fill her days: finding novel ways to extend her shopping trips, volunteering at every local charity she could find, signing up for correspondence courses to learn Spanish and French. A kindred spirit. It had taken Helen hours to frame a reply, and she'd refreshed the page every thirty seconds in the hope of a response. It had come ten minutes later: 'How lovely to meet a fellow swan!' That was what Elise called the pair of them: swans. Forever locked in the limbo of mourning their other halves.

They'd chatted online every day for weeks – discussing everything from the minutiae of their daily lives to long, frank exchanges about why they'd both ended up on the site. Curiously, although they now had each other in person, she missed receiving Elise's emails, and Elise admitted that she missed her messages, too. There was an intimacy in writing that was somehow absent from personal interactions, although she couldn't complain. Strange to think how nervous she'd been about meeting Elise for the first time. They'd planned on spending a couple of days together at a modest hotel in South Beach before the cruise, and as she waited in the bar for Elise to arrive, her stomach had fluttered as if she was about to meet a lover. Which, in a sense, she was. What could be more intimate than dying with someone? She'd come to rely on their daily exchanges, and she feared that in person, things would change. After all, on paper, they couldn't be more different: Elise, the Pennsylvanian housewife; Helen, the retired tax lawyer. Helen: British, bookish and reserved (she knew she'd been nicknamed the ice-queen in her firm); Elise: open, warm and unashamedly addicted to confessional magazines and the soaps. Helen the lifelong atheist; Elise the regular churchgoer. Neither had children, but unlike Elise, who she knew mourned this aspect of her life, Helen had never seen the point of passing on her genes. Really, it was a wonder they had anything to talk about at all. But the second they met, they immediately fell into the easy camaraderie they shared online – proof that opposites could balance each other out.

She let her cursor hover over the delete button.

Yesterday – eleven hours ago – she was supposed to be dead. She flexed her fingers. She was now officially living on borrowed time.

I want to die holding the hand of a handsome ship's doctor while eating a poisoned grape.

How could Celine possibly have known that Helen had been thinking about that quotation earlier that evening? She hadn't brought a copy of *A Streetcar Named Desire* with her, and she always kept her e-reader with her in her handbag. That whole night had been disturbing. The music they'd heard in the bathroom, and the shadows she'd seen in the balcony glass. It could all be explained, but that fear she'd felt – a primitive, powerful sense that she should run – still made her uneasy. She closed her computer, fanned herself, then tried to lose herself in *Persuasion* again. It might be her last chance to read it, and she was hit with a pang for all the books on her e-reader that would never be read. She spent a few minutes deleting the more embarrassing selections – amongst her Graham Greenes, Jose Saramagos and David Mitchells lurked a thriving nest of bodice-rippers. Unable to settle, she went back into the room.

Elise murmured something in her sleep, twitched, and then opened her eyes. She looked around blearily as if she was trying to figure out where she was.

'How are you feeling?' Helen smiled down at her.

'Helen . . . I was dreaming of him. He was talking to me.'

'Peter?'

Elise nodded and drew breath. 'It was so real, Helen.'

'I know.' But Helen didn't know. She didn't dream of Graham, but sometimes, just sometimes, she thought she could smell his scent on her pillow in the mornings.

'He said I should stop feeling guilty.'

'Guilty? About what?'

'Stepping out when he died. I wasn't there.'

Another thing they had in common – Helen hadn't been with Graham either when he drew his last breath. 'That's not your fault.'

'I know, hon. Helen . . . you still want to do it?'

Did she? Again, Helen searched inside herself. Her only other choice was to go home. She'd turned off the immersion heater, emptied the fridge and the freezer. She imagined catching a taxi from Heathrow, arriving at her door on a drizzly evening, placing her keys on the hall table where Graham used to keep his secret stash of cigarettes, walking through to the cold kitchen, stripped of any personal touches; stripped of any traces of his presence. 'Yes. I still want to do it. Do you?'

'Yeah, hon. I do.'

Elise was in a far worse place than she was in many ways – Peter's medical bills had wiped her out. Helen would gladly have helped her if she'd ever asked, but she never had. And why *would* she ask? It wasn't as if Elise had to worry about falling further into debt. They'd been resolute about their plans. As for Helen, with no children or close relatives alive, she'd considered leaving her substantial savings to charity – a cats' home, maybe – but was there such a thing nowadays? It was at moments like these that she could hear Graham's voice clearly – almost as if he were standing right there, talking to her. *Don't be so bleeding daft, girl.*

'Going to sleep again, Helen,' Elise said, her eyelids already drooping. Helen held Elise's hand until her breathing steadied. Love. That was what she felt for Elise. And she knew it was recip-rocated. They'd once discussed moving in together, living out their days in a Florida condo, perhaps, or a cottage in St Ives. But that would only be putting off the inevitable. Rather do it now while they were both mobile and fully compos mentis.

She stood up and paced. Claustrophobia nibbled at her. She wasn't used to being so inactive. She didn't relish the thought of wandering through the ship alone, but a quick walk wouldn't hurt. She scrawled a note for Elise, who was now snoring softly, and stepped outside cautiously; she was becoming used to the ship's sloping gait. She wandered to the balcony and looked down into the atrium. The Guest Services counter was now closed, and several passengers were drifting aimlessly around in the area; untethered balloons. She walked down the main staircase, and along past the IT room and the shops, their interiors black, the doors locked. She hadn't found a single thing she wanted to own in them, although Elise had oohed over some gewgaws, then joked that she wouldn't need coral earrings where she was going.

She took a turn at random, and drifted into the library, which was decked out to resemble a Victorian drawing room. It wasn't entirely unpleasant; the subdued lighting suited the dark – obviously fake – antique furniture, and it somehow felt cooler in here. She scanned the books locked behind glass cabinets, most of which were battered Jeffrey Archer and Jodi Picoult paperbacks. She was about to sit on one of the leather armchairs when she realised she wasn't alone. There was a group of people huddled around a table in an alcove, their eyes shut and holding hands. A prayer circle of some kind. Uncomfortably aware that she was intruding, Helen picked up a copy of *The Five People You Meet in Heaven* that was sitting forlornly on one of the coffee tables, and left the room.

Next, she wandered past the closed casino and the shuttered bar, nodding at Jaco, who was readying himself to sing on the small raised stage next to the casino's bar. Again, she felt a twinge of pity for him; he had no audience, just a couple of crew members who were polishing the fixtures. She walked on, skirting the Dreamscapes Dining Room, which was slathered with 'closed' signs, and slid into a booth outside the Duty Free shop, next to a huge picture window that framed the sluggish ocean. A well-dressed couple of around her age rambled past. Helen could sense that they were looking at her and she pretended to be absorbed in the book.

'Hi there,' the woman said.

'Hello.' Helen willed them to move on.

'I hope you don't mind me saying, but you look a little lost. I've seen you in the Dreamscapes Dining Room – you're also late dining, aren't you?' The woman's bright blue eyes looked almost radioactive against her deeply tanned skin.

Helen nodded and looked pointedly at the novel, hoping that the woman would get the message.

She didn't. 'You shouldn't be alone.'

'I'm fine. I'm reading.'

'Oh! You're from England!'

'Yes.' *Go away.*

The woman slid into the booth next to her, and her companion – a saggy-eyed fellow who was presumably her husband – sat opposite. The woman took out a phone and started scrolling through it. 'I was in London last year. I just love it. Wait. Look at this!' The woman thrust the phone in Helen's face, and she looked down at a picture of the woman's husband posing unsmilingly next to Princess Diana. 'What's this place called again, Jimmy?'

'Madame Tussauds.'

'That's it. Madame Tussauds. I'm Annabeth and this is my husband Jimmy, by the way.'

'Helen.'

'Helen! Lovely name. I had an aunt called Helen, once. You remember her, Jimmy?' A nod. 'Are you travelling on your own, Helen?'

'No. I have a friend with me. She's taking a nap in the cabin.'

'Uh-huh, that's right. I recall seeing you with someone in the dining room now I think about it. I don't blame her. It's awful hot, isn't it? Jimmy and I live in Florida, so we don't have to worry about missing our flight home, but so many people aren't in the same boat as us. Oh, Jimmy, did you hear what I just said?'

Jimmy gave her a long-suffering smile.

'You shouldn't be here by yourself, Helen. People are getting antsy. And that business about the bathrooms not working. Why don't you come along with us? There's a nice group of us, we're all looking after each other. Most of us are seniors, although there are some younger ones now too.'

A waiter approached, and silently handed them each a bottle of water. Annabeth gripped the waiter's arm, veins like earthworms under her tanned skin. 'Thank you. How are you? How's all the crew doing?'

'We are all fine, thank you, madam.'

'We're grateful for what you're doing for us. Is there any news?'

'No. I am sorry, madam.'

She loosened her grip and patted his forearm. 'I'm sure Damien will let us know when they fix the ship.'

The waiter nodded and wandered away.

'Helen. We're going to take you under our wing. Come along with us and meet the rest of the gang.'

'No. I'm fine. Thanks, though.'

'I'm not going to take no for an answer. I know you English, so polite. C'mon and meet everyone. We're a friendly bunch. And you can meet Celine.'

'Celine del Ray?'

'Yes! You know her?'

'I met her last night.'

'At your muster station?' Jimmy said, looking almost surprised that he'd managed to get a word in.

'Oh, that's just wonderful,' Annabeth laughed. 'That's why me and Jimmy are on the cruise. A friend of ours, Leila, signed us up as soon as she saw on Facebook that Celine was going to be cruising with Foveros. Celine's helped us so much, isn't that right Jimmy?' Jimmy nodded. 'We lost our daughter, you see,' the woman said, matter-of-factly.

'I'm so sorry.'

'Seven years ago, breast cancer.'

'I'm so sorry. How awful for you.'

'Oh, aren't you sweet to say that. And I thought ... if only I could speak to her one more time, and know for sure that her suffering was over, I'd be able to carry on. Jimmy told me I was crazy the first time I went to a psychic. He didn't believe that it was possible to talk to those who've crossed over. And you know, I think in my heart I didn't really believe. The ones we'd been to, they ... you could tell they didn't really know what they were doing. And we had our doubts about Celine as well, didn't we, Jimmy?' Annabeth leaned forward. 'We'd heard the stories.'

The man's chin wobbled. Annabeth reached over and squeezed

his hand and they shared a look of such devotion that Helen couldn't help but feel touched. 'But what she said this morning to us . . . she has something special. A real gift. It was as if Julia was right there with us. I'm sure she'd do a reading for you if you asked her.'

'Really, I'm fine.'

'There must be someone you want to contact.'

'There isn't.' And even if there were, the rude and disturbing woman she and Elise had spent time with last night would be the last person she'd ask.

'You don't believe in Spirit, Helen?'

'I'm not sure what I believe.' A lie. She just wasn't in the mood to be proselytised to. Sometimes she wished she did believe in God and heaven. Occasionally she envied Elise, who was certain that Peter would be waiting for her when she died. Helen had no such reassurances. And what would she say to Graham if she did see him again? It had been so sudden. A heart attack. In the gym of all places. A casualty of the forty-a-day habit he'd kept up since he was sixteen. After the grief had come the fury at him for leaving her. Graham had always been there for her, chivvying her along, laughing at her, making life lighter. It was a cliché, but he was her best friend; they did everything together, didn't need anyone else. Without him, life was . . . grey. That was it. Dull.

Helen stood. 'I really should get back to my friend.'

'Five minutes, Helen. Let us show you where we are, then you can always come later.'

It would be easier just to go along with them. She had nothing to lose and nothing to gain either way. As soon as the ship started moving again, she and Elise could revise their options.

Helen allowed herself to be herded towards the entrance to the Starlight Dreamer Lounge, where she was greeted by a small group of cheerful middle-aged men and women. The room was fairly full, with most of the lounge chairs taken up. On stage, a plump man in his twenties was fiddling with a mini portable generator. She spied Maddie sitting off to one side, her head bent.

'I know her,' Helen said to Annabeth.

'Maddie? She's lovely. She's also from England. Celine wasn't herself on the first few days of the cruise and she really took care of us all.'

'I'll just go over and have a word with her. Excuse me.'

'You will come back though, won't you? I want to introduce you to everyone.'

'Oh, I will,' Helen lied. She'd have a word with Maddie and then she'd get the hell out of here before Celine made an appearance. Some of the people sitting in the chairs were dozing, but most gave her friendly smiles as she passed them. It did seem like an oasis of peace. Subdued lighting, the air less fusty than in her suite, which was strange, considering the number of people inside the lounge. Maddie didn't look up as she approached her table and Helen was forced to touch her on the arm.

She jerked, sending her water bottle flying. 'Helen. What are you doing here?'

Helen looked over at the table where Annabeth and Jimmy were watching her. 'I was invited.'

'The Friends found you, did they? Rounded you up.'

'The Friends?'

'Friends of Celine. The group who paid extra to cruise with her.' Maddie flapped her hand. 'It doesn't matter.'

'Where's Celine?'

'Backstage. Preparing. I left her to it.'

'Preparing for what?'

'She's going to do another reading. Her third today, if you can believe that.'

'So she is definitely feeling better then.'

'Oh yes. In fact, I would go so far as—'

With no fanfare or announcement, Celine wheeled herself out onto the stage. 'So how are we all feeling?' her voice carried through the room. Helen glanced longingly at the exit. She decided to wait until the audience was distracted, and then slip away. 'I'd first like to welcome all of our new friends. I'm so happy you could join us. We're all gonna look after each other here. This is a safe place. Long as we all stick together, we're gonna be just fine. Know this. Every single one of you has your own guardian angels and guides who are watching over you. Maybe you can't see them, but you can sense them, can't you?'

A ripple of assent ran through the room. Helen glanced at Maddie, but she was examining the backs of her hands. Everyone else was staring fixedly at Celine.

'Know this, your guardians and guides and the spirits of those who have passed over are stepping forward. Know this, there is no death.' Celine paused, and Helen was almost certain the woman was looking straight at her. 'But this doesn't mean that life isn't a precious gift.' A sardonic smile. Helen shifted uncomfortably on her seat. 'Wait . . . my guides, Archie and my very own Lizzie Bean, are letting me know that there are some urgent messages and connections that need to be made.'

The audience barely appeared to be breathing.

'A man . . . A man is stepping forward. Yes. Know this, there's someone here he's trying to connect with. Does the letter "G" mean anything to anyone? Wait . . . Oooh. He's a tall man. A handsome man. Slight paunch, but we're all human, aren't we? We can forgive those little details, can't we, Friends?'

The crowd rippled with laughter. Helen felt a creeping sensation trickling over her skin. She knew what was coming. 'And know this, the physical body isn't something we need to worry about when we cross over. Now . . . I'm getting . . . Forgive me here, but I feel like I need to sing. My voice isn't the best, but the man who's stepping forward, he wants me to sing it. "She was right next door, and such a strong persuader . . ."' Celine paused. 'Does that mean anything to anyone?'

A hand gripped Helen's heart, and for a second, she was certain she was going to be sick. Calm down, she told herself. They were clever, psychics and mediums. They were adept at cold reading and con games.

'No one? I'm getting it really strong now. And you know, I feel like I want to cough.' A low laugh. 'I quit smoking years ago, but I tell you, right now I'm feeling a strong need.'

Helen stood up stiffly. 'I'll see you later, Maddie,' she heard herself say.

Maddie looked up. 'You okay?'

'I just need to get some air.'

Helen hurried out, bashing her shin on the edge of a table in her haste. She barely felt it.

'Helen? Where you going?' Annabeth's voice trailed after her.

Wiping the tears from her eyes – not sure if they were from shock, fury or sorrow, Helen ran. She bolted past the casino and the closed black doors of the Sandman Lounge, her gaunt reflection in the glass momentarily startling her. There was no way Celine could have known that song. She must have been in their suite, perhaps she'd looked her up on Facebook – there was a picture of Robert Cray on her wall, from the last time she and Graham had seen him play live in London years ago. That was it. She began to relax. Cheap tricks.

By the time she reached the Verandah deck, her breathing had steadied, but she composed herself before she entered the suite. The last thing she wanted to do was worry Elise. 'Elise?'

Elise's bed was empty, the sheets and pillows in disarray.

'Elise?'

A strangled cry came from the bathroom. Helen yanked open the door. Elise was lying on the floor, her skirt rucked up. 'I'm not feeling so good, Helen. My head hurts. I think, I think I'm . . .'

The Angel of Mercy

The man was now out for the count, but Jesse knew he'd have to monitor him closely. Christ, what a scene that had been. Adrenalin still tingled in his bloodstream from when he and Bin had been hustled up to the man's cabin to sedate him. They'd found him curled in the corner of his stateroom, screaming every time one of them came near. It had taken two security guards to hold him down while they waited for the sedative to take effect.

And it wasn't just the new arrival who was concerning Jesse. Alfonso was still borderline catatonic – he'd barely reacted when the hysterical passenger had been brought into the treatment room. Jesse couldn't get a word out of him. The burn pad would do its job – Jesse would only need to change it tomorrow at the earliest (and please God they were out of this situation then) – but Alfonso had barely touched the yoghurt and banana Martha had brought him earlier, and nor had he used the commode they'd set up in the small bathroom. Short of flying in a psychologist, there wasn't much else Jesse could do.

A psychotic passenger, a dead girl, the norovirus, and an engineer who was borderline catatonic. *How much more shit can we add to the pile?*

Martha banged her way into the treatment room, and threw her gloves into the bin. 'We've got another one, Jesse.'

'Noro?'

'Noro.'

'How many now?'

'Six in total. Three crew and three passengers. I'm worried about this one. Patient is overweight and elderly. She's weak. Her friend found her collapsed on the floor of the bathroom.'

'You want to bring her down here?'

'No. It's always best if we keep any cases quarantined in their cabins.'

'You want me to go check on her?'

'You've got enough on your plate.' She flapped a hand at the psychotic. 'How's your man doing?'

'The midazolam is working, thank Christ.'

'We know what caused it? He got a history of psychosis?'

'We don't know yet. Security is trying to track down his wife.'

'Any injuries?'

'I've only had a chance to do a superficial examination. Bruising on his upper thighs and wrists, contusion on his forehead. Probably sustained during the struggle. Took two security guys to restrain him.'

'Shite. And Bin?'

'He's dealing with the steward the guy attacked before we brought him down here. Nothing serious, but she's understandably traumatised.'

Martha looked him up and down. 'You found time to rest?'

'Nope.' He was surviving on cold coffee and endless cans of Coke, the jittery caffeine high just about keeping the exhaustion at bay. 'Should I tell the captain we should go to red alert?' There weren't enough cases of noro – yet – to warrant it, but better safe than sorry, especially considering the situation with the propulsion system. He'd put in a request to meet with the captain yesterday, but so far it had been ignored.

Martha leaned against the gurney. 'That'll go down well on top of everything else. But I think we should suggest it. At the very least the passengers should be instructed to use the hand-sanitisers.'

Yeah, right, Jesse thought. In all his time on the ship, he had never once seen anyone using them. 'How long can this go on for?'

'God knows.'

'You heard anything more?'

'No. Communications are still down.'

'I'm worried about the morgue. With no power, we could have a problem there.'

'Don't worry about that. It's below the water line. It'll stay cool enough.'

For now.

There was a knock on the door and a man in white officer's garb stepped in hesitantly. Like the majority of the crew on the bridge, he looked like a stereotype of a good-looking Italian, crisp white uniform and smooth dark hair; effortlessly attractive. The officers tended to make Jesse feel hopelessly inadequate. 'Excuse? May I visit with Alfonso?'

'He's sleeping. You should not be in here.'

'I am sorry.' The man's eyes strayed to Alfonso, who was lying perfectly still, his eyes closed. 'I knock on the outside door, but no one came.'

Jesse exchanged glances with Martha, who gave him an 'up to you' shrug.

What would it hurt? Perhaps the man would get Alfonso to talk. 'Go ahead.'

Martha gave Jesse a supportive smile, and left the room.

The officer strode over to Alfonso's bedside and let loose a barrage of Italian. Jesse's Italian basically boiled down to *Nessun Dorma* and the odd bit of slang he'd picked up, so he had no clue what the man was saying, but whatever it was didn't seem to be helping.

The officer – Baci, according to his name badge – turned to Jesse. 'Why is Alfonso not awake? What is wrong with him? I see the arm, but there is something else?'

'He's been sleeping most of the time. It's possible he's having a reaction to the pain meds. Is he a good friend of yours?'

'He helped me get on the ships. We are from the same area. He is like a father to me. But I am worried. We need him to do his job. He has worked in the control room for five years. Nobody knows the engine and generators like Alfonso.'

'Do you know what the issue is?'

An exaggerated shrug. 'The redundancy did not work as it

should. Now the ship is run only from the two emergency generators. There is no power.'

'But you can fix it, right?' Jesse didn't see why not. He'd been
given a tour of the ship when he first started – although he wasn't
allowed to go down into the thumping depths of the engine room
– but he'd seen the workshops, the areas full of spare parts.

'Maybe. I do not know. I work on the bridge. Third officer.' He
said something else to Alfonso in a slightly more strident tone of
voice, but still the engineer showed no reaction. 'I can try wake
him up?'

'You can try.'

'Alfonso!' Baci shook his shoulder with more force than Jesse
would have liked. But then Alfonso's eyes flickered and he jerked,
letting out a strangled cry. Fear – there was pure fear in his eyes.

'Tell him we just want to help him,' Jesse said. 'Ask him if he is
in any pain.'

Baci softened his voice, Alfonso appeared to look right through
him, and then, finally he seemed to see him and take in his
surroundings. Baci asked him a question, and Alfonso responded
in a low, shaky voice. They conversed for several minutes, Alfonso's
eyes darting around the room. Baci appeared to be getting more
and more agitated by Alfonso's responses.

'What is he saying?' Jesse broke in.

Baci turned to face him. 'I do not know how to say this.'

'Can you at least try?'

'He says that he saw the devil.'

'The what?'

'He was there when the fire started.'

'The devil was in the generator room?'

A shrug. '*Si*. He calls him the dark man.'

'Right. Um . . . Is this normal for him?'

'No. He is a religious man, but he is not . . .' Baci waved his
hand around his head.

'Delusional?'

'*Si*.'

'Can you ask him if he is in any pain?'

'He can speak English.'

'*Ja*. But he's not speaking to us at all.'

Alfonso said something else.

'He says the dark man is here with us now.'

Jesse looked around. 'You think he means the other patient?'

'I do not know.'

Abruptly, Alfonso turned onto his side and shut his eyes. Baci tried to elicit a response from him for the next couple of minutes, but Alfonso was silent.

'You will take care of him?'

'Of course.'

'I will come see him again soon.' Baci smoothed his hair with both of his hands. 'This is not good. I must get back.'

Jesse followed him out. 'When are we going to get some answers?'

'*Scusi?*'

'When are we going to be back online? At the very least I need to inform off-ship support.'

'You have spoken with the captain?'

'I have tried to speak with the captain.'

'He is very busy.'

Jissus. 'Listen, can you ask him to get hold of me as a matter of urgency?'

'I will do what I can. I am only the third officer on the bridge, so I do not have much authority.'

'I need to meet with him.'

'I will do what I can,' Baci repeated.

Jesse was aware he was haranguing the poor guy – Martha, who was writing reports at the desk was watching him with interest – but short of going up to the bridge and hammering on the door, he wasn't sure what else to do. 'Do you at least know where we are?'

'*Scusi?*'

'In the sea. We've been drifting. You know where we are?'

'We can use manual navigation.'

'And have we drifted off course? Is that why no one has found us?'

'We are drifting, but we can track how fast and far we are moving.'

'And?'

'I must go back to the bridge.'

Jesse let him go.

'Did he get Alfonso to talk?' Martha asked.

'*Ja*. A little.'

'And what did he say?'

'Only that the devil is on the ship.'

'I could have told him that. But seriously, now, what did he say?'

'I'm being serious. He said the devil started the fire.'

'Jaysus.'

He downed the dregs of his latest caffeine fix and tried not to think about the delicious escape valve hiding behind the pharmacy door. He must look like shit. He needed to shave. He needed to shower. His whites were rumpled and grubby and stained with last night's hastily consumed cold curry.

He returned to the treatment room. Alfonso's eyes were shut once more, his breathing slow and regular. The psychotic was still out for the count. Jesse eyed the third empty bed. It looked inviting. He could curl up on it, and by the time he woke, they could be back in Miami and all this would be over. He shut his eyes tightly and saw stars popping and dancing in his lids.

Raised voices floated through the door from the reception area, and seconds later Martha poked her head through the door. 'Gary Johansson's wife is here. She wants to see him.'

'Whose wife?'

'Your man, there.'

A high-pitched howl penetrated the room. 'Where is he? I wanna see him!' A woman with short dark hair, shorter shorts and a bad attitude burst into the room.

'Ma'am,' Martha said to her. 'I told you to wait out there.'

'Where is he?' A tired-looking security guard hovered behind her. He wasn't one of the guys Jesse had encountered when he was called to the girl's cabin. This one – Pran – was young, with a patchy moustache.

The woman had spotted her husband. 'Gary!' She flip-flopped her way to his bedside, then turned to glare at Jesse. 'What's with the drip?'

'We need to keep him sedated, madam.'

'Sedated? Why?'

'He was agitated.'

'A steward said that he attacked her,' the security guard said – unwisely.

'Huh? Attacked her? She's lying. Gary would never do anything like that. He's a lamb.'

'Calm yourself now,' Martha said. 'We have another patient in with him, and we don't want to be upsetting anyone, do we?' She smiled at the woman, and she appeared to become less agitated.

'Gary? Gary, can you hear me?'

'He'll be out for a while,' Jesse said.

'What's wrong with him?'

'We're not sure. Does he have any history of mental instability?'

'No! What are you saying?'

'I'm just trying to get a clearer picture of what we're dealing with here.'

'Well he didn't attack anyone. No way.'

'Is he allergic to anything?'

'What?'

'Does he have any allergies we should be aware of?'

'No. No he doesn't. Oh, wait. He doesn't like cheese.'

To Martha's credit, she managed to suppress the smile.

The woman shot a spiked glance at Jesse. 'Aren't there any American doctors on board?'

'Dr Zimri is more than capable,' Martha said.

The woman didn't look convinced. 'You'll look after him, won't you?' she whined to Martha.

'Yes, ma'am. Go on, now. We'll get a message to you when he wakes up, so we will.'

'I'm not staying in my stateroom. I'm up on the Lido deck with friends.'

'We will make sure that you are contacted.'

Martha ushered her out, the security guard following in their wake.

And this time, Jesse did flop down on the empty gurney. Five minutes, he promised himself. He'd barely slept at all last night. That crazy old psychic woman had rattled him. And he'd spent hours obsessing about Farouka. Building monsters about her in his mind, imagining her with other men, happier than she'd ever been, telling everyone how grateful she was to be out of their marriage. Perhaps he'd spend the rest of his life dragging the wreckage of his old life behind him like a tattered wedding dress.

Weak. He was weak.

'Can you come, doc?' This time it was Bin.

'Is it the steward?'

'No. It's the morgue. The laundry workers say they heard a noise coming from inside it.'

'Don't be ridiculous.'

'Doc, I'm just telling you what I heard.'

'Have you checked it out?'

Bin shook his head. 'No, doc.' It struck Jesse that it was the first time he'd ever seen Bin look anything but serene and controlled. 'I think you should come.'

'Seriously?'

Bin nodded apologetically.

A cluster of men were gathered just outside the laundry room entrance, talking amongst themselves. They fell silent as Jesse and Bin approached. The morgue itself – a single bay, the door of which resembled a giant metal bread bin – was situated inside a storage area behind a metal door to the right of the laundry room.

Jesse felt the weight of everyone's eyes on him as he heaved open the storeroom door. Space was precious on a ship, and the floor was littered with tins of tomatoes and red hazardous-waste bags that had presumably been kept inside the morgue until it was needed. Unlike the cadaver drawers in most morgues, this one was fitted into an alcove sideways on. Its hatch was firmly shut.

'Looks fine to me. You sure it was coming from in here?' Even if someone was hammering on the door (like who?) from inside the storage area, it was unlikely that the sound would carry.

One of the men, a pot-bellied forty-something fellow with smoker's teeth, murmured something to Bin.

'He says it was most certainly coming from inside the morgue. They opened the storeroom door and heard it.'

'Well he must be—'

Bang.

Jesse flinched. 'What the fuck?'

Bang. A long pause and then, this time, a metallic *bong.* They all jumped.

'We should get Security,' Bin said, his voice cracking with fear.

'No,' Jesse said. 'It's the heat down here. Making the metal expand.' He touched the morgue's handle, then ran his hand over the front plate. It was cool, but not cold. They hadn't frozen it yet – the engineers had forgotten, or it was possible it wasn't connected to the emergency power source.

'Don't open it, Jesse,' Bin whispered. The pot-bellied smoker was muttering what sounded like a prayer under his breath. The others had scarpered.

The lid slid up easily, revealing the body bag. Jesse stared at it, half-expecting it to twitch.

Crazy.

What did he expect to find? The girl alive in there? Bollocks, as Martha would say. He might be a fuck-up, but he wasn't that inept.

'They say that she is haunting the ship,' Bin whispered. 'That she is a restless spirit. That she is bringing other bad spirits to join her. They say she is bringing bad luck and it is because of her that we are stranded.'

'Jesus. This is bullshit.' But despite himself, Jesse unzipped the bag. The reek of decomposition boiled out at him. The girl's face was slack, her eyes white. Her mouth was open, rigor locked in, revealing a row of old-fashioned cheap fillings in her lower molars. He stood back to let Bin and the laundry guy see for themselves.

'See? Dead.' Well and truly *morsdood*.

The pot-bellied man grimaced and backed up. Bin – reliable, level-headed Bin – looked as if he was about to faint with relief. Had Jesse misjudged him all this time? No. He was just spooked. Hell, Jesse was spooked as well.

He zipped the body bag up, unclicked the hinges that kept the lid from falling, and stood back to let it slam closed. 'Can we all go back and just—'

Bang.

The Keeper of Secrets

Devi stared up at the metal base of the bunk above him. Madan and Ashgar had papered the walls and the areas above their bunks with lewd photographs, but he had nothing but the scratched ghosts of ancient graffiti to distract him: several versions of 'Fuck u', 'Monica does it doggy style', and an etched drawing of what looked to be a half-naked woman fused to a Ferrari.

He'd slept for three hours before jolting awake, convinced someone had shaken his shoulder. Since then, he'd drifted in and out of a doze, trying to get his thoughts in order, and breathing in the hum of stale smoke, which drifted off Madan's coveralls dumped on the floor below. The day had run away with him; he hadn't yet found the time to double-check last night's security footage. His time had been eaten up interviewing the singles group and the steward who had supposedly checked the rooms, and patrolling the main and Lido decks. He was exhausted from fielding complaints about the lack of hot food, paucity of information, and the most popular gripe of all – the fact the bars were shut. In Devi's experience, most passengers couldn't go without food or drink for more than an hour without misbehaving.

Ram had sent Devi a message via Madan a few hours ago insisting he take a break. His superior had spent much of the day meeting with the captain on the bridge, and Devi hadn't yet told Ram what he'd learned from the footage. One thing he wouldn't be mentioning or putting in the report was what else he'd seen – the palm of a hand, a small hand, covering the camera's lens. It was not possible. The cameras were placed high up on the ceiling. It had to be a trick of the light, interference from another CCTV feed, maybe. There was always a rational explanation. And he still hadn't spoken to that steward – Althea Trazona.

He closed his eyes and scrubbed his hands over his face. He should clean up and then get something to eat before he went back on duty. He'd need his energy and—

The cabin door opened, and Devi fought to hide his dismay as Rogelio entered the room.

He swung his legs off the bunk and stood. 'Rogelio, you can't be in here. Ashgar or Madan could arrive at any moment.'

'They are not around. I checked.' Rogelio stepped over Madan's gear and moulded his body against Devi's. 'I had to see you.' Devi needed a shower, he could smell the sour tang of his own sweat, but Rogelio didn't seem to mind. He never did. 'Why did you not come to me last night? I needed you.'

Devi disentangled himself. 'I had to work. I am sorry.'

'I'm scared, Devi. This situation is bad. Damien . . . Damien made me promise not to say anything, but he says the captain is very worried. There is still no Internet, Devi. No radio. Nothing is coming in from the ships that must be in the area. They should have come to look for us hours ago after the emergency signal was sent to the radio beacon.'

'Perhaps there is bad weather in port and they are unable to get to us.' He glanced anxiously at the door again. He had to get Rogelio out of here. 'Please, you must leave.'

Rogelio pouted. 'Why do you always push me away? You are ashamed of me?'

'No. Of course I'm not.' If he was ashamed of anyone, it was himself. *Coward.* He knew what Rogelio wanted; he knew he would never be able to give it to him. 'You know my situation.'

'And why did you not come and find me to tell me about Kelly Lewis last night? I had to hear it from that horrible Ram, and he spoke to me like I was a criminal.'

'I'm sorry. It was out of my control.'

Rogelio sighed with his whole body. 'I am sorry for Kelly. It must have been frightening, dying alone like that.'

'Did Ram tell you how she died?'

'Just that she'd drunk too much alcohol. The singles groups always drink too much.' A shrug. 'It is sad. A waste.' Rogelio slid a finger down the buttons of Devi's shirt. 'You should have told me.'

'I know. What was Kelly Lewis like?'

'She was nice. Quiet. Not like some. You should hear the names I have been called today, Devi. You would be furious.'

Devi toyed with telling Rogelio the truth about how he believed Kelly had died. As a member of the entertainment crew, he interacted daily with hundreds of passengers and it was possible he might recognise the man on the CCTV footage.

Devi's radio crackled, followed by the sound of Ashgar's exhausted voice, broken up by static. 'Come in . . . control . . . Altercation . . . crew bar . . . now.'

'I must go.' He managed to usher Rogelio out of the cabin. The corridors were usually busy, with many crew members using them as informal meeting places, but tonight they were empty.

'Can you meet me later?'

'I will try.'

Another pout.

Devi let Rogelio walk ahead of him, the knot of trepidation loosening in his chest as they reached the stairwell that led to the I-95. Rogelio blew him a kiss and headed towards the crew mess.

Devi had to put an end to it. Gossip would spread fast, especially through the Indian mafia network, which had ties throughout the entire cruise industry. It was possible that it could get back to his family, he had a cousin who worked in the kitchens on *The Beautiful Wonder*. And then there was what Ram had said last night . . . It was safer to be paranoid. He would end it before they were caught in the act. That was how they'd trapped him last time. He'd let his guard down; taken chances. They'd followed him to Matungas Road Station. Waited for him to disappear inside the bathroom stall. And when he emerged with the boy – a skinny twenty-two-year-old whose face Devi can no longer recall with any clarity – they'd pounced. They'd given him an ultimatum: desist from investigating the rape of the child, or Devi's family would be told of his proclivities. The boy had fled, barely escaping

a beating, and Devi had quit the squad and signed up to be a shipp-
pee, preferring exile to the other alternatives. Coming out wasn't
an option. It had never been an option for him. It wasn't the fear
of prosecution – there was a thriving gay community in Mumbai:
it was the thought of his parents' disgust that he couldn't bear.
They were deeply conservative; they wouldn't understand. His
brothers were all dutifully married, busily producing grandchildren. His parents had been aghast when he told them he had
signed on to Foveros, just as they had been disappointed when he
chose to join the police instead of settling down with a wife and
following his brothers into the business. But that would be nothing compared to how they would feel if they knew about this
secret part of his life.

The sound of shouts greeted him as he hurried into the darkened depths of the crew bar. Ashgar was pushing against the chest
of a skinny white guy, who Devi recognised as the assistant chief
of the IT department. Jaco, the ship's musician, was being
restrained by two of the bar staff. On the few occasions Devi had
visited the bar, he'd found Jaco to be pleasant and friendly. The
tension was getting to them all. A female casino croupier was
sobbing in the corner, her hair drenched with beer.

'Fuck you!' the IT guy shouted, lunging for Jaco.

'You should do your job and fix the fucking Internet!' Jaco
roared back.

'I've told you! There's nothing to fucking fix.'

Ashgar was struggling to restrain the man, and Devi was
about to step in, when Ram materialised, and moved between
the furious crew members. It was all he had to do. No violence.
Just a look.

'You will be calm?' Ram said without raising his voice.

'He started it,' the IT guy moped.

'Are you going to stop? Do you want me to close the bar?'

A food and beverage manager, drunk beyond reckoning and
sitting with a group of staff waitresses, booed. There was no brig
on this ship, so Ram instructed Ashgar to take the IT guy to his
cabin. He assessed Jaco. 'Are you calm now?'

'Yeah. I'm sorry, okay?'

'Good. Do not let it happen again.' With barely a glance at Devi, Ram headed for the door. Devi followed.

'Sir!'

'What is it, Devi?'

'May I speak with you?'

'Did you rest?'

'Yes, sir.'

'Good. And you have eaten? You will need your energy for tonight.'

'Sir, about last night. I looked at the footage again. A man most definitely followed Kelly Lewis to her cabin.'

'I need you up on the main deck, Devi. Madan and Pran are the only ones up there.'

'But, *sir*. The footage.'

'We cannot concern ourselves with that now, Devi. We have followed procedure. Did you see the man actually assaulting the girl?'

'No. But it is clear that he conned his way into her cabin.'

'Then the FBI will deal with that when we reach port. We cannot risk a rumour like this getting out into the public domain. The passengers are disgruntled enough.' Ram nodded and turned away.

Devi could no longer retrain himself. 'Sir! There is a murderer on board!'

Ram paused and wiped his fingers slowly over his moustache. 'I will forgive this insubordination once, Devi, but do not make a habit of it. Go up to the main deck. Then you can relieve the control room.'

'Sir—'

'That will be all, Devi.'

'Yes, sir.'

Twitchy with adrenalin, Devi watched as his superior walked away. How could Ram be so bull-headed about the situation? Was he simply concerned about needlessly panicking the already frightened passengers, or was this the first stage in an attempt to cover it up? Still unsettled, he made his way into the passenger area and through the atrium. The Guest Services counter was closed and shuttered, as were the cocktail bars that ringed the space. A passenger stopped him as he was heading up the stairs. 'When will the bars be open?'

'There will be an announcement soon.'

'That's what everyone says!'

Devi mumbled something about being needed elsewhere and moved past her.

On the Promenade Dreamz deck, applause spattered out of the Dare to Dream Theatre. A beefy fellow standing outside it nodded at him as he passed. A couple had moved their mattress into the hallway next to the elevator by the VIP deck. They were not blocking the stairs, so he left them to it.

If anything, the main deck was even more populated than it had been when he was on duty. He strolled past the pool, making for where Madan and Pran were trying to explain to a passenger why he could not block the entrance to the muster station with a corral of sun-loungers and pillows.

Madan greeted him with a tired sardonic smile and Pran raised his hand, as if he was about to salute and then thought better of it. Devi knew very little about him. One of the younger guys, he'd just started his first contract and was officially still in training. With his beaky face, a struggling moustache and eloquent eyes that should have belonged to a girl, Devi doubted Pran had the backbone for the job.

'*Gandu*,' Madan muttered under his breath to the sun-lounger hoarder's back. 'It's bloody awful, Devi. Crazy cones.'

'I was up here this morning.'

'Pran and I had a *badbad* situation this afternoon. Had to restrain a lunatic.'

'What?'

'A passenger attacked one of the stewards. Pran almost soiled himself, didn't you, boy?'

Pran looked down, embarrassed.

'What did he look like?' Devi asked.

'Who?'

'The man who attacked the steward. What did he look like?'

'Why you asking that?'

With only a moment's hesitation, Devi filled him in on what he'd seen on the footage. Madan whistled through his teeth. 'It would not be the first time some fucker spiked the ladies' drinks, eh? But I do not think my lunatic is your guy. This one was out of it. The man you are speaking of sounds organised.'

Devi had to admit Madan was right. 'Ram wants to keep it quiet.'

'I am not surprised.'

Madan gestured at a group of men who were haranguing one of the waiters handing out water next to the towel station. 'Pran. Go talk to them.' Pran nodded and did as he was told. 'There will be trouble soon,' Madan said to Devi.

Madan was right. There were only five security personnel on this ship, and Madan and Ram were the only two who Devi knew would be of any use in a crisis. Madan had no police background, but he was cool in a crisis. They had the MRAD device, but he wasn't sure that even Ram had experience with that. Devi had had a fair amount of experience dealing with riots in his old life: a flare-up over the murder of a Muslim businessman in Dharabi; an anti-rape march that had turned violent. It didn't take much for the crowd mentality to kick in and turn into a mob, and on a ship, there was nowhere for a crowd to disperse.

Another guest sidled up to them. 'When will they be opening the bars?'

Madan let all emotion leak from his face. 'There will be an announcement soon, sir.'

'And my wife needs to charge her iPhone.'

'There will be an announcement soon, sir.'

'When?'

'Move along, sir,' Devi said.

The man huffed, but did as he was told.

Madan gestured for Devi to follow him to the side deck that housed the muster stations. He took out an e-cigarette and dragged the vapour deep into his lungs. A firing offence if Ram caught him, but Devi knew that Madan was adept at bending the rules and taking chances. 'Listen . . . this situation. It is not right. The fire. It was small – and nothing like the ones we dealt with during training. They think it started from a fuel leak, but I have connections, Devi, and that wasn't it.' Madan waved at the ocean beyond the railings. 'The gulf is busy, Devi. There are always ships.'

He was right. There were no lights anywhere in the distance. 'What are you saying?'

'I am thinking that the ship has drifted off course. It is the only explanation for why they have not come for us yet.'

A bickering couple emerged from the side deck, their arms filled with pillows and duvets. The sky was suddenly a burst of light. Whoops and cheers came from the main deck.

'Why would they set off fireworks?' a woman called.

But Devi knew. Those weren't fireworks. They were flares.

The Wildcard Blog
Fearlessly fighting the fraudulent so that you don't have to

Still stranded. Still no Wi-Fi. Still no signal.

The pool deck is overrun with hung-over passengers, who have dragged mattresses and sheets into the open air as the lack of air-con has turned the cabins on the lower decks into sweatboxes. Place is beginning to resemble a Middle American refugee camp.

So far we've got: a dead passenger, missed flights, flares, a smell so bad it makes you want to cry. And did I mention that the propulsion system that runs the toilets is down and we have to 'poop' (Damien's favourite euphemism) in bags? So there's that too.

Been scrawling notes on the back of the entertainment flyers as have to save the battery. Just over 4 hours left. I have the spare, but I'm not taking any chances. I'm sending this the second I get online, warts n all. People need to know what's been happening here. And I'm going to be the first to tell them.
Going to break the day's total insanity down for you in a timeline:

9.30 a.m. Just had an encounter with The Predator's PA. Frosty, but I think we made a connection. Helps that she's cute ;). Possible in to Celine???
Was still feeling ropey, decided to start my hunt for The Predator after I'd had a shower.

10 ish. En route to cabin, saw a girl crying hysterically at one of the tables inside the Lido buffet, a group of people around her. Stopped to eavesdrop. She and her buddies are part of the singles group and one of the girls in their group died yesterday. Security are saying it's alcohol poisoning but the group isn't convinced. Could be more

sinister. There's been no PA message about this yet, but this must be why there's that sealed cabin on my floor. Gonna hunt down Trining to get more info. Didn't see her this morning.

10.20 a.m. Cabin stinks as there's no airflow. Had a shower, no hot water. Still no Trining, but spoke to Paulo, the harassed steward working on the other side. Said he knew nothing about a dead passenger (could tell he was lying) and told me Trining is sick (hope to Christ I didn't infect her).

10.30 a.m. Shit. Literally. Message from Damien. Propulsion problem with the ship. Toilets not working. 'Use the shower for a number one, a red bag for a number two.' Red 'hazardous waste' bags will be handed out. Tried to flush my toilet – made weird gurgling noise. V relieved stomach no longer explosive. Need to find a way to talk to an officer or even Damien. Deafening silence from the captain about the situation. Thinking maybe it really is a cover-up and some kind of conspiracy with Foveros head office to keep the news we're broken down out of the press. This story could be a real coup for me. Asked Paulo if he could find a place where I could charge my laptop/phone. Gave him 50 dollars to grease the wheels.

Had a nap, woken by the sound of screaming at 11.30-ish. Couldn't find where it was coming from.

11.45 a.m. Went back to the Tranquillity deck (altho is it tranquil? Is it fuck). Massive lines for Lido buffet (sandwiches and hotdogs – no thanks) so ate a bag of Cheese Curls I brought on board. They stayed down.

My 2 main goals are to track down The Predator and find out why the fuck no one's come for us yet. There should be helicopters, a tug at least, maybe another Foveros cruise ship. Everyone around me complaining about missed flights, the crappy cold food, no coffee, and no booze.

Day Four

12 p.m. Decided to check out the Bingo. Damien on stage. Smaller in person and with tragic facial hair. Kept making jokes about poop bags. Have to hand it to the guy, he had everyone eating out of his hand. Said if we're not out of there soon, there will be extra cabaret. Awesome!

1 p.m. Wandered around, checked out the Starlight Dreamer Lounge. Lots of people with Friends of Celine lanyards hanging around. Could tell they recognised me so decided to leave them to it. Went up to the mini-golf course. Hung out with the singles group again. Most of them are on the deck lower than mine. Said some of the cabins were flooded with sewage water.

Heard via one of the singles (Donna from Providence) that Celine del Ray was going to do an open event at 2 p.m. Asked where she heard it from, and she said a couple of old men were going around telling everyone. The girl who was crying (Emma or Amanda or something, a Brit) says she wants to try and 'get in touch with Kelly and find out for sure how she died and if she has a message for her mom.' Tried to explain to them the concept of cold reading. They didn't take it on board.

Saw a guy pissing over the side.

2 p.m. Tried to get into the Starlight Dreamer Lounge to see The Predator strutting her stuff, but was stopped by a couple of oldies on the door who recognised me from the night before. Thought about arguing, but too fucking tired, no energy. Will try later. Looked around for the PA, couldn't see her. Hung around for a while hoping to catch Celine coming out of the stage door. No such luck.

4 p.m. Queues for food intense. Managed to get myself a ham and tomato sandwich and a banana.

5 p.m. OK. This is getting crazy. We're not in the Antarctic in 1917. We're in the Gulf of fucking Mexico. Why has no one come for us yet?

6.30 ish. Trouble brewing. People are not only scared (because hey, we were supposed to back at port almost 12 hours ago), but getting snappish with each other. Couple of men almost came to blows over a fucking sun-lounger.

Joined 'my' group again.

7.30 ish. People crowded on the Lido deck, pool deck and around the jogging track and waterslides to watch flares going off.
Dumb bastards kept cheering.
If I needed any proof that we were fucked, this is it. Spoke to a sensible-looking guy, older than a lot of the passengers, who said he reckoned the captain has got us lost or that we've drifted out of the high traffic area. He says if that was the case we could easily get washed down the Gulf Stream as the current is pretty strong there and end up in the Bermuda Triangle. That's when things got weird and he went all conspiracy on my ass. Tried to explain that the BT is just a myth and is all bullshit, but he kept going on about those WW2 planes that had disappeared for no reason.
Gave up.
Never fuck with the nuts too much.

8.30 p.m. Lined up for food. Took an hour.
Here are the choices:
Cold hotdogs
Deli meat sandwiches and wraps
Pre-cooked (and now defrosted) lobster tails & shrimp. Fucking buckets of the stuff. People were falling over themselves to get bowls of them. Guess they have to get eaten. Not risking that shit after getting sick.
Sliced tomatoes
Potato salad
Bread, olives, sliced peppers
Piles and piles of desserts. Melting cheesecake and chocolate gateaux leaking cherry blood.

Day Four

The desserts were gone in thirty seconds.

9.30 p.m. Sat with the singles group, who have all decided to sleep up on the deck. Think Donna tried to hit on me. They were passing round a bottle of cheap vodka. I didn't have any.

Felt gross again so returned to my cabin. I'm the only person on this deck. It stinks, but too tired to move for now.

Night.

DAY 6

The Witch's Assistant

The lavatory in Celine's suite had packed up at around four a.m., signalling its demise with a disconcertingly human-sounding groan. Maddie had held off for as long as she could, but eventually she'd had no choice but to relieve herself in the shower. Thankfully the water was still running, and she stripped off her clothes and doused her skin with Celine's body wash, the cold water doing nothing to clear her head.

She hadn't been able to sleep for more than a few minutes at a time, despite taking one of Celine's sleeping pills. She couldn't stop obsessing about what the hell her boss was up to.

Unable to stand the happy-clappy atmosphere in the Starlight Dreamer Lounge any longer, she'd returned to Celine's suite at around six p.m. last night (there was no way she was going to brave her own cabin in the rank depths of the lower levels – she'd made an attempt to go down there to retrieve her stuff, but only made it halfway down the corridor before the stench sent her scurrying back to the higher levels). Maddie had tried to speak to her boss several times during the day, but Celine kept blanking her, concentrating her energies on encouraging the Friends to go out and find others 'who might need our special kind of support'. Others like Helen, who had clearly been deeply affected by whatever pernicious crap Celine had been spouting. Because that was the thing – Maddie had no clue where Celine was getting her information from. It was possible that she'd convinced Jacob and Juanita and the gang to go fishing for facts for her, but Maddie doubted her boss would take a risk like that. It couldn't be Facebook or Zoop – they were still offline. But somehow, Celine managed to trot out a series of disturbingly accurate readings for the random strangers the Friends collected on their outings. And her group was growing – by the time Maddie left, it had almost doubled in size. Among the new arrivals were a honeymooning couple from Kansas ('Know this, your grandmother forgives you for not coming to the funeral'); a morbidly obese woman, whose petulant 'go on then, entertain me' expression had slowly morphed from shock to wonder ('Know this, your husband wants you to have the surgery'); and a man in a wheelchair accompanied by a woman who wore a perpetual mask of martyrdom ('Know this, your sister doesn't blame you for the accident'). A few, Helen among them, didn't stay long, but the vast majority settled in for the long haul. Part of it was the atmosphere. The Friends worked hard to make the newcomers welcome, handing out water and sharing snacks, and even a couple of the waiting staff had hung around well after their shifts. Celine – the old Celine – knew how to work a crowd, but this was taking it to a whole new level. She seemed to be genuinely interested in what she'd always professed to do – helping people.

She didn't bother to towel off, and wrapped in one of Celine's robes, she stepped out onto the balcony. The sun was limping into the sky, the hazy light revealing a sea livid with the red bodies of used plastic bags. *A jellyfish shit swarm. Lovely.* She slumped into the plastic balcony chair and put her feet up on the railings. She needed to run – she was always cranky if she didn't exercise every day – but there wasn't any hope of that with the jogging track being used as a campsite. The ship was quiet: the catcalls and shouts that drifted from the Lido deck above had died down at around three a.m.

Her thoughts returned to Celine. Her boss never did anything without a reason or the promise of a payday. And Maddie was honest enough with herself to admit that she was hurt. Why hadn't Celine told her what she was planning? Maddie had been her confidante for three years, but for some reason Celine was cutting her out.

Maybe this was what she needed. The final push; the nudge she needed to quit her bloody job. Yeah. She'd hand in her notice when they finally made it back to port. She'd go back to the UK – she didn't need to return to Nottingham, she could live in any city she chose; she had enough saved to keep her going for a couple of months. And if she got lucky, maybe her next employer wouldn't dig too deeply into her background and unearth the two years of probation she'd got for basically being a dumb bitch – another woman who'd fucked up her life by falling for the wrong man.

Yes. She was done with being Celine's lackey.

She put her head back and shut her eyes.

She was woken by a spattering sound. She jerked and opened her eyes in time to see a stream of liquid arcing over the balcony. Some arsehole was urinating off the top of the Lido deck above her.

'Oy!' she yelled. 'Stop that!'

A burst of derisive laughter.

She gagged and went back into the room, slamming the balcony door behind her. Disgusting. How long could this go on for? People on land must know that something was amiss – no way could Foveros hide it for so long. She checked the time on her phone – it was getting on for nine a.m., later than she thought it was – and downed a slug of tepid water from the bottle next to the bed.

There was a knock on the door, followed by: 'Housekeeping,' and Althea entered the room. Maddie wasn't surprised to see that she was more subdued than usual. A situation like this must be hell for the staff. Maddie couldn't imagine what the conditions must be like in the crew quarters. At least here she could breathe. Down there it must be stifling. It must be intolerable.

Maddie tried to smile at her. 'Good morning.'

'I am sorry, I can't bring you any clean towels as we cannot use the laundry.' Althea placed a bottle of water next to the table, along with a pile of red bags. Christ. Maddie prayed it wouldn't come to that. It had been revolting enough peeing into the shower. 'Where is Mrs del Ray?'

'She's in the Starlight Dreamer Lounge. She's been there all night.'

'She is feeling better?'

I have no fucking idea what she's feeling. 'Yes. Thank you.'

'She was sleeping in there?'

'I have no idea.'

Maddie had no clue if Celine had slept at all. And, come to think of it, she hadn't seen her drinking anything other than water. That alone should have set alarm bells ringing if they weren't already screaming in her head. Her stomach rumbled. She'd had nothing to eat since yesterday apart from a packet of shortbread biscuits that she'd found in the bottom of Celine's suitcase. 'Is there any news about when we might get moving again?'

'I am sorry. No news.'

Maddie didn't question Althea further. She looked beyond exhausted. Distracted and wan.

Althea began straightening the bed. 'Don't bother with that, Althea.'

'You are sure?'

'Yes. You must have loads to do with all this going on.'

'Yes.' A sigh that seemed to come from the pits of her soul. 'There are two people who are sick on this deck.'

Maddie swallowed. Oh God. 'There's a virus going around?' Xavier had been ill for several days. It was possible. And she knew from her reading how quickly something like that could spread.

'I think so. The old woman in V25 is very sick.'

'Which woman? You mean Helen or Elise?'

'Yes. The fat one. The American.'

Elise. 'Has the doctor been to see her?'

'I think the nurse came yesterday.' Helen and Elise had been there for her when she needed them. The least she could do was see if they needed anything. The last thing she wanted to do was expose herself to the virus, but she could take precautions. As long as she didn't actually enter their cabin she should be fine. 'Many people are getting sick,' Althea continued. 'But you will be okay if you are careful what you touch. I would advise you to keep some cutlery that only you use. As well as a plate. Just in case.'

'Thank you, Althea. I appreciate that.'

'It is not a problem.' She began spraying and wiping the top of the mini-bar cabinet.

'You don't have to bother cleaning in here.' Maddie wasn't just being altruistic. She didn't like to think about the germs that might lurk in the cleaning rags.

'You are sure?'

'Yes. And I'll make sure you're reimbursed for all your hard work.' *Christ, way to sound patronising.*

'Thank you.' Giving Maddie a tepid smile, Althea left the room.

Maddie perched on the bed. What now? Checking on Helen and Elise was her first priority, and then she supposed she should go and find something to eat, although Althea's mention of a virus was making her feel even more bilious. She couldn't wear yesterday's clothes, and she still didn't feel up to retrieving her belongings from her cabin. Which reminded her, she hadn't seen Ray since their altercation the day before – he certainly hadn't been in the creepy group in the Starlight Dreamer Lounge. He'd have to move out of his cabin sooner or later. Without air-con, it would be stifling down there.

With only a moment's soul-searching, she dug through Celine's closet. She found a lilac shirt embossed with jewels in the shape of a cat – six sizes too big, but so what? – and pulled it over her head. Her jeans would have to do for another day – Celine's slacks and skirts would fall off her. In the drawer, she found a pair of black leather gloves ready for when they returned home to the cold weather. She wrapped one of Celine's silk scarves around her neck: she could use it to cover her mouth. Germs could get through it, but at least she'd be able to block out the smell of the ship. She must look ridiculous, like the invisible man. But rather that than spend the next few days projectile vomiting.

She left the suite before she lost her nerve, and knocked on Helen and Elise's door.

It took Helen a while to answer it, and when she did, Maddie had to step back and put her hand to her mouth. She could definitely detect the stench of vomit coming from the room. 'I'm sorry. I'm not good with . . . you know, illness, smells.' That sounded terrible. 'Sorry.'

'I understand.' Helen's mouth twitched as she took in Maddie's outerwear.

'Althea said Elise was ill.'

'Yes. A virus of some kind.' Maddie was shocked by her appearance – she looked as if all the moisture and colour had been bleached out of her skin.

'How is she?'

'Not good.'

'Can I do anything to help? Get you something to eat, maybe?'

Helen touched her throat. 'I'm not very hungry.'

'You should try to keep your strength up.'

'Perhaps just a sandwich. If that isn't too much trouble?'

'No trouble.'

Maddie hesitated, unsure if she should mention Helen's encounter with Celine yesterday. She decided against it. Helen would have brought it up if she wanted to talk about it. She didn't strike Maddie as someone who was afraid to speak her mind.

Tightening the scarf around her mouth, Maddie made her way up the staircase and out onto the main deck, which was now a sprawl of makeshift tents and mattress enclaves, spreading all the way up onto the jogging track and mini-golf course. The queue for the meagre buffet – again there appeared to be only a couple of stations open – snaked out of the door of the indoor seating area and reached almost to the pool. She joined it, trying not to think about the germs that were flying everywhere. Under her gloves, her palms were wet.

The queue zombie-shuffled forward. The man in front of her – a British guy with a wide, plain face and a sunburned nose – turned and gave her a grin. 'Nice gloves. Smart. The virus, right?'

'Yeah.'

'My girlfriend's got it now. It's bloody horrible. Doctor says the best thing for her is to stay in the stateroom. We're lucky we've got one of the suites on the upper deck. It's them buggers down below I feel sorry for.'

Maddie nodded in agreement and half listened to his theories on why the ship had broken down as the queue inched forward.

Maddie took two plates from the denuded stack, jumping as someone tapped her shoulder.

'You can't do that,' the woman behind her snapped.

'Do what?'

'Hoard food. You can only take one plate.' She crossed her arms across her chest and glared at Maddie.

Maddie attempted a conciliatory smile. 'I'm not hoarding. I need to take some food to a friend of mine. She can't leave her cabin.'

'Then you have to wait in line twice.'

Jesus. 'I'm not doing that. Look. I didn't eat anything yesterday, so it's not as if I'm—'

'That's your problem. You can't hoard food.'

A murmur of agreement came from the people standing behind her. Maddie looked to the friendly guy in front of her, but he'd turned his back. Maddie suddenly felt tearful. *Don't give into it.* She wouldn't have lasted very long as Celine's PA by being a complete pushover. Maddie squared up to her. 'So what is my friend supposed to do? She can't leave her cabin.'

'That's not my problem.'

The anger came hot and quick. 'It's everyone's problem, you dumb bitch.' Maddie was shocked at herself. First Ray, now this.

The woman blinked. 'What did you call me?'

'You heard me.'

'You . . . you can't—'

'You're the one who's getting in my face. Why don't you mind your own business?'

'There's a system here.' The woman outweighed her by forty pounds or so, but hopefully it wouldn't come to that. Maddie glanced around for a security guard, but there was none in sight. 'You can't just help yourself to stuff like this when we all have to line up. It's not fair!'

A man stepped in between them – the blogger, Xavier. He touched Maddie's arm and said, 'Thanks, babe.' Before she could respond he said to the disgruntled woman: 'She was keeping my place.'

The woman wasn't mollified. 'She's got two plates. She's hoard-ing. She can't do that. And you can't keep places.'

'Yeah. Sorry about that. I was . . .' – he tapped his stomach – 'you know.'

The woman twisted her mouth. 'Don't do it again.'

'Hey, I won't. Thanks for being so understanding.'

'Yeah.'

The woman stared at her a little longer, but Maddie didn't rip her gaze away. 'Something else bothering you?'

The woman dropped her eyes. 'No.'

The man in front of Maddie turned and said, 'Tempers are running high.'

'Yeah, thanks for all your help, dickhead,' she said, surprising herself again, and Xavier snorted. The man coloured and looked away.

'Thanks for doing that,' she murmured to Xavier.

'No problem. Smart with the gloves. Wish I'd thought of that. Apparently you can get the norovirus again. Wouldn't that just take the fucking biscuit?'

Finally they reached the head of the queue. A deli meat sandwich flopped onto each of her plates, but at least the bread looked fresh. She thanked the server, but he stared at her blankly, mask in place.

'You really going to eat that?' Xavier asked.

'I haven't eaten since yesterday.'

He gave her an assessing glance. 'Come with me. I want to show you something.'

'What?'

'It's interesting.'

She held up the plates. 'I have to take this to my friend.'

'I'll come with you.'

'No. Wait here. I won't be long.' She didn't know him; it wasn't a great idea to show him exactly where Celine's cabin was located.

He gave her a sardonic grin. 'Cool.'

She hurried back into the atrium and across to the VIP deck. A clump of soiled red bags was dumped outside one of the suites, and she tried not to look.

Helen took the food with a tired smile, and Maddie returned to Celine's cabin. She took a bite of the sandwich, the bread like carpet on her tongue, and put the rest in the bar fridge – pointless, as it wasn't working.

She could just stay in here. Did she really want to get entangled with that blogger? But she had to admit, part of her was curious about what he wanted to show her. Sod it. What else did she have to do?

He gave her a cocky salute as she walked up to him. 'Thought you might have changed your mind.'

'What is it you want to show me?'

'C'mon. It won't take a second.'

He waved her towards the stairs that led up to the jogging track. A young woman in a bikini greeted him and gave Maddie a curious look as they zigzagged their way through the mattresses and chairs covering the deck. Several people glared at them as if they were trespassing on private property. Self-conscious in her outlandish outfit, Maddie kept her eyes glued to Xavier's back as he strode over to the viewing deck. She joined him and looked down at the passengers and crew littered over the Lido and main decks, feeling a twinge of vertigo.

'Look.' Xavier leaned closer to her and pointed towards the bow of the ship. On the far left side, a small band of crew members were fussing around one of the crew lifeboats.

'What are they doing?'

'Someone's going out there. Someone's planning to go and see what the fuck is going on. Which can only mean we're in deep shit.'

'They're sending out a lifeboat?'

'A tender boat. One of the lifeboats that's equipped with a larger engine. You know, the kind they used to take us across to Foveros Island. That pretty much tells you all you need to know about the situation. If they knew the cavalry was on its way, why send out a boat? It's got to mean we're not where we're supposed to be.'

'Why haven't they just radioed for help?'

'Wi-Fi's down, maybe the radio's also poked. It's not right.

Remember when *The Beautiful Wonder* got stranded?' Maddie didn't, but she nodded anyway. 'One hour into that ship losing power, the whole world knew about it. We're on day two of this mess, and nada. We're on our own. They're not going to be able to put a lid on this much longer. They must be thanking their lucky stars for the norovirus. You saw what it was like in that line. It's only a matter of time before there's a full-on mutiny. There are no guns on ships.'

'It won't come to that.'

'Yeah? You think?'

A beep, and then: 'G'day, ladies and gentlemen. Damien your cruise director here. I'd just like to let you know that the captain will be speaking to you shortly about developments. In the meantime, our guest celebrity on board, Celine del Ray, has generously offered to put on a show for any of you who would like to join her. She'll be appearing in the Dare to Dream Theatre in thirty minutes.'

Xavier gave Maddie a look. 'That's three times the size of the Starlight Dreamer Lounge of hell. She must be expecting quite a crowd. I tried to get in there yesterday, but got blocked.'

Maddie snorted. 'Big surprise.'

'What is she doing, starting a cult?'

'I don't know what she's doing. This isn't like her at all. She's had a radical change of personality overnight. She says she's help-ing people.'

'Yesterday you said that that's what she does, period.'

Shit. But what did it matter what she said to Xavier? She was going to quit; she had her plan in place. 'Yeah, but she's helping people without being paid. That's not like Celine.'

'Ah.'

'And I don't know where she's getting the information she's using.'

'She usually googles this stuff, right? And I'm guessing the rest is cold reading.'

Maddie shrugged. She wasn't prepared to go that far yet. 'Maybe.' Could Ray be doing her dirty work? She hadn't seen him anywhere near the lounge after her run-in with him yesterday, but it was possible Celine had sent one of the Friends to find him.

Down at the tender boat, an officer in whites was gesticulating to a couple of men in blue overalls.

'I wouldn't mind having a chat with her,' Xavier said.

'I bet.'

'You could get me in there. C'mon, you owe me a favour. I got you out of hot water in that line, right?'

He smiled at her again. He wasn't exactly what she'd call attractive, and he certainly wasn't her type (not that she had one these days) but nor was he completely vile, as she and her friends used to say at school. Christ, where had that come from? Maddie thought about it. Celine was more than a match for Xavier, and it might be interesting. 'Why not? You want to meet Celine? I'll take you to Celine.'

'Awesome.'

As they left the main deck and headed down towards the theatre, Xavier continued to pester her with questions about Celine's methods, but Maddie kept him at bay. She wasn't going to make it that easy for him.

A small but steady stream of passengers were making their way into the theatre. There was no sign of Jacob or Eleanor or any of the other Friends, but as the last group passed through the doors, she saw Ray standing outside them, his arms folded across his chest, his legs slightly apart. A bouncer pose.

'Let me deal with this,' she murmured to Xavier.

Ray greeted her with one of his cheesy grins. 'Hey, Tiger. Celine said you'd show up. What the hell are you wearing?'

'I thought you didn't give a toss about Celine. What are doing here?'

'Well, babe, turns out this is where it's at. Got a job to do.' Something flicked over his face.

'She say something to you, Ray?'

'Nah.' He was lying. Celine could easily have used a fact from the file his security agency would have sent her. Twisted it, so that it sounded like something she could never have known. But

Maddie didn't get it; Ray knew how Celine operated. Maybe he really was that dumb. Or maybe there was another explanation as to why he was doing his job.

'How much extra is she paying you?'

A crafty smile. 'Hey. A bonus is a bonus, right?' He appeared to see Xavier for the first time. 'You the guy who tried to bust in here the other night?'

'Yeah.'

'What you doing with this asshole, Maddie?'

'We want to see Celine.' Maddie moved to step past Ray.

'Sorry, babe. Celine don't want to see you.'

'What are you talking about?'

'You can't come in here. Not till she says you can.'

'She's my boss.'

He shrugged. 'My orders. Don't bother trying the other door, Maddie. Been secured. Celine says you're not ready yet.'

'Ready for what?'

'Just passing on the message, babe.'

'Let me through.'

'Can't do that, Maddie.'

'How about we pay you?' Xavier asked.

'You offering me money?'

'Yeah.'

'You a rich boy?'

'I do okay.'

Ray nodded. 'I getcha. You figure a dumb old ex-cop like me would go for a bribe.'

'Not what I'm saying.'

'Listen, Ray,' Maddie jumped in. 'There's no reason why this has to get nasty. I've worked for Celine for years and you—'

'It's a public space, you can't stop us,' Xavier spoke over her.

'Watch me.'

Maddie realised that people were bottlenecking behind them. They wanted a show, she thought, and now they were getting one. She tried the charm offensive. 'Come on, Ray. Just a quick look. We won't stay long. You can tell Celine we sneaked past you.' Why was she even bothering? All she knew was that it was suddenly very important to her that she get in there.

Xavier pulled two hundred-dollar notes out of his wallet and fanned them in front of Ray. 'Take it.'

'I don't want your money.'

'Take it.'

'I *said*, I don't want your money.'

'Come on, dude. Two hundred dollars, where would a guy like you—'

Ray lunged, grabbed the blogger's shirt, pulled him towards him and head-butted him in the face. Xavier staggered back, clamping his palms over his nose. Maddie froze, only moving to help Xavier steady himself when one of the women behind them screeched.

Ray leaned towards her. 'Get the fuck away, Maddie.' She could now smell the alcohol on his breath. 'Get the hell away from here now.'

The Condemned Man

Snuggly. Warm. Dreamy. Gary liked it in here, it was cosy and quiet. White walls, warm air, stuffy, but not unbearably so. He shuffled onto his side. A man lay in the bed next to him, a thick bandage on his arm. The man was swarthy, like a pirate, and he was staring straight ahead, his mouth open. Gary craned his neck to follow his gaze.

A large black man wearing dungarees and with a rumpled face was standing against the wall opposite, his head bent, wringing his hands. Gary couldn't see his eyes, they were hidden in the folds of his face. A distant part of his mind registered that this should have been alarming, but it somehow wasn't. 'Hey,' Gary croaked.

The dungareed man darted a grey tongue out of his mouth and put a finger to his lips. 'Shhhhhh.'

'Sorry,' Gary whispered. 'Do you work here?' Wherever here was. The ship. Of course! He was on the ship. The cruise. Ooooh. His head. Swimmy. It was all jumbled.

'Shhhhhhh.'

'I won't say anything.'

The large man giggled, and Gary giggled along with him. Friends all together. He liked this man. Like the kids at school would say, he was cool.

Was it night-time? Daytime? What time was it?

Who cares? And mmmmm. He felt nice, as if he'd been rolled in cotton candy; as if he was floating in a large tub of warm water. He snuggled deeper under the sheet covering him. Ow. Something was pinching his arm, and he looked down to see a tube snaking out of the crook of his elbow. A needle. Ugh, no. Get it out. He pulled and pulled, but it wouldn't come free. Tape. It was taped in there. Pick it off. His fingers didn't want to work, but then he understood. They weren't his fingers! They weren't attached to him. Someone else's fingers. All numb. He could work them, though. Yes. Work the other person's fingers with the power of his mind. Pick, pick, get the edge up and . . . riiiiip. He snatched out the needle, watching as a rivulet of blood lazed down his arm. It was very red. That was okay. That was better. He tried to lift his head to get a better look at the man with the bandaged arm, but it was heavy. Tired. Sleep. Yes, that would be nice. He'd have a little nap.

A nudge at his shoulder. He opened his eyes. Had he slept? He couldn't tell, but his head didn't feel quite so cumbersome anymore.

His neighbour moaned and muttered something in a language Gary didn't understand.

Gary blinked and looked around the room again. The white walls. Of course. Now he understood. The huge man in the dungarees was closer now. Gary still couldn't see his eyes. 'Am I in hospital? Did I fall?'

'Shhhhhhhh.'

And then the man was over by the door, finger to his lips, beckoning for Gary to join him.

'Time to go?'

The man didn't answer.

Up, up. Get up. He kicked away the sheets, which tangled in his legs. He was about to ask the man to help him, but he was no longer there. The blood was drying on the inside of his arm. Rusty flakes. He wiped it with the sheet. Slowly, slowly does it. Ooh. The floor beneath his feet was spongey. He tripped over a bag half-hidden beneath the bed. Clothes. And his glasses. Where were his glasses? Never mind. He wasn't blind without them, just got headaches.

'Going now,' he said to the man with the bandaged arm, who was now curled up like a child. 'Bye, bye.' His mouth tasted funny, as if he'd been sucking on chalk. How did he get here? Maybe he'd fallen. Had a little accident. Oops.

He shuffled to the door, drifted through it and floated past a desk and on towards another door. This one was heavy and it took him several tries to get his hand to turn the handle. Out into a hallway.

Two people came blurring towards him. A man and a woman. Black and white, ebony and ivory. He liked the look of the woman, she was—

No.

The man had a bloodied face.

'Is the doctor in there?' the woman asked him.

Gary couldn't speak, and he had to move on. The man in the dungarees was waiting for him at the foot of the stairwell. He crooked a finger and Gary followed. Up the stairs, the floor moving again. He walked on in his floaty way. It wasn't unpleasant. His friend was beckoning him on. He didn't want to lose sight of him. He had the feeling he knew the man. From where? A gap in his memory.

Marilyn. He should find her. Which way?

He turned a corner, passing a woman who was rubbing at the carpet. Pukey smell. 'Are you okay, sir?'

'Yes. Need to find Marilyn.'

There were two women ahead of him, talking excitedly and blocking his view of his friend. One of them turned to look at him. The skin on her face was like a cracked vase – so many lines on it! 'Help you?' she said.

'Going up,' Gary giggled. His friend was bouncing up the stairs in front of the couple. Gary pushed past them to catch up to him.

'Hey!' they called after him.

He rounded another corner, but the man was gone. Where now? He had a cabin, maybe Marilyn would be in the cabin, but he couldn't go down there. He couldn't bear the thought of that. Something had happened down there, but all that came to him was the memory of a nasty smell. He went up and up until he reached the atrium. He remembered this area. He tickled his fingers against the Christmas decorations that were woven through the railings. Mmmm. Pretty. He'd never really stopped to look at them before. Christmas, he liked Christmas.

Then he made his way outside, pushing against the greasy glass. Sea – he loved the sea. He drifted over to the railing, tripping over a pair of outstretched legs.

'Watch it, mate!' a grumpy voice sniped in his direction. Gary ignored it. How would he ever find Marilyn in this crowd? His chest tightened. He needed his friend to guide him.

He stood as still as he could, looking down at the waves. There was something floating in the water. Bobbing and drifting like him. Something red and shiny. The sun beat down on his head. He lifted his face and closed his eyes. Mmmm.

'Gary!'

'He belong to you, love?'

'Gary! Is that you?'

He opened his eyes and turned around. He was now standing next to a line of people. How did he get here? Marilyn. There she was. His wife. God, he loathed her. Things were woolly, but he could remember that. Sunburned face, mouth like a scar, her lips too thin. Not like . . .

No.

'Gary. You've been out for over twenty-four hours. Honey. I've been so worried.'

He squeezed the words out. They sounded distant, as if he were hearing them through a tube. 'What happened to me? I fall?'

Marilyn had been joined by a man with dull blue eyes. Gary dredged up his name: Mason. 'They let you out, then, Gary?'

Gary nodded. Had they?

'What happened to me?' His distant voice sounded tearful, but he didn't feel like crying.

'You don't remember?' Marilyn asked.

'No.'

Marilyn glanced at Mason.

The itch of a memory at the back of his head. *Fingers.*

'Honey . . . you'd . . . I don't like to say it. You were passed out in the cabin, and when they tried to move you, you started scream- ing. They gave you some kind of tranquilliser.'

Nudging in the back of his head. Fingers. Fingers and—

No.

'I was so worried. I came to see you, you remember that? Brought you some clean clothes last night. Hon, Mason's been so good to me. He came down to the cabin with me to get the rest of my things.'

'Stinks down there,' Mason growled. 'You're not going to freak out on us again, are you?'

'What happened, Gary? Did someone attack you? Did someone spike your drink with some dangerous drug or something? We can sue.'

'Yeah. Safety is an issue on these goddamned things. They need to do more. There was that girl as well.'

'Girl?' Marilyn asked.

His girl. They were talking about his girl, but she was—

'Found dead in her cabin. Sam heard it from one of the girl's group when she was in the line for hotdogs this morning.'

Marilyn touched her throat. 'Oh my Lord. What if whoever did that came after you, Gary?'

'Hey, what are you wearing, bud? Going for the *Miami Vice* look?'

Gary looked down at himself. He didn't remember getting dressed. The fly on his shorts was open, a whorl of pubic hair poking through the zip's mouth. His shirt was unbuttoned. 'I . . .'

Mason slapped him on the shoulder. 'You come with us. We're getting ourselves organised. We have a safe place.'

Marilyn took his arm and led him towards a metal staircase. His friend – where was his friend? He looked around for him, but he was gone.

'We're using the Tranquillity deck, hon,' Marilyn said. 'Mason's making sure it doesn't get too crowded.'

Mason grunted. Mason had a wife, Gary remembered that. A plastic woman, like a doll.

'We have to poop in bags. Isn't it awful? Mason keeps trying to speak to the captain, but they keep fobbing him off.'

'I'll get there. They got no right to keep us in the dark like this. And they're lying to us. Guy in our group is a cellphone technician. Came equipped with state-of-the-art tech. Can't get it to work. Says the whole lot is down.'

'We're just drifting, honey. We can't go back to the cabins, so most of us are up on the deck . . .'

Gary let the talk wash over him. The sun was flashing into his eyes.

'. . . we think we're going to have to go up to the bridge through the crew bar. There are staircases that will lead us up there.'

Someone shouted: 'Look!'

A beep and then: 'G'day, ladies and gentlemen. Damien here, your cruise director. I'm sure you're really grateful to all your wonderful crew members . . .' Gary fought to concentrate on the words, but it was hard. '. . . thank you for your patience. The captain of the ship, Guiseppe Leonidas will be speaking to you shortly. As you will have noticed, one of our tender boats is about to drop over the side.' A long pause, a crackle and then a heavily accented voice: 'Ladies and gentlemens, I am sorry not have been speaking to you sooner. We have been working very hard on trying to fix the problem. In short, what it is is an issue with the generator. A small fire which caused a break in the connection. Until this is fixed we do not have power to move. We have also attempted many times to call to our control for help, but there has been no answer. We have tried in many ways. We are sure that . . .'

Gary's vision wavered. He wanted to lie down, go back to sleep.

Marilyn's voice drifted in and out. '. . . mean, Mason? . . . a good sign?'

'At least they're doing something . . . hey . . . so good . . . down here if he's got the . . .'

The sound of a cheer. 'There's a boat!' People shoved past Gary to get closer to the railings, their skin rasping against his. He was left alone next to the Jacuzzi. He stared at their bodies, all lined up. His friend wasn't with them, but . . .

His girl. His girl was there.

No nononononononononono.

Blonde. His girl was blonde. Overweight. She was standing

there, her back to him. Teasing him. He stalked up to her. She was alive after all. He knew it.

He grabbed her arm. She squealed and turned around. Not his girl. It wasn't her. 'What the fuck you doin'?' she yelled.

'Sorry. Sorry.' He backed up, got his legs tangled in a chair behind him. He felt himself falling in slow motion, crumping on his tailbone. He looked up, the sun turning the people staring down at him into ghosts. He could see their faces, but none of them had any eyes.

Marilyn said: 'Oh *Gary.*'

And then a hole inside his head opened up, and dragged him under.

The Devil's Handmaiden

The laundry room, usually a hive of activity, of sudsy smells and voices and the whir of the giant machines, was deserted and dark and reeked of mildew. Althea hefted the bags containing the filthy sheets and towels and dumped them in the corner. *Somebody else's problem now.* Most of them belonged to the Linemans. Mrs Lineman hadn't lifted a finger to help her, and didn't seem at all embarrassed that her stateroom was a slovenly mess of soiled towels, sheets and body fluids. It had taken her over an hour to put it straight. Still, the thought of that stupid *bastardo* being forced to void his bowels in a bag almost made up for all the extra work. In contrast, Helen had insisted on changing the sheets herself, and had respectfully asked Althea if she could bring her a bucket, chlorine spray and rags so that she could clean up after Elise should the need arise. She must go and check on Elise and Helen again later, ensure that they had everything they needed.

She was surprised the ship hadn't gone into red alert; she'd been through two norovirus outbreaks over the years and it was standard procedure. Althea had no intention of getting it. It was simple: wash and disinfect your hands; don't touch any surfaces without wearing gloves and be liberal with the chlorine bleach spray. There were two more sick passengers on the starboard side – Electra hadn't shown up to service her station – and Althea had made sure the guests wanted for nothing. When the ship eventually limped home to shore, the fact that they'd been stranded for so long would be a big story. And when it was all over, it would be Althea the guests would remember. She hadn't abandoned her station once. But it was taking its toll. The exhaustion felt like a slow acid crawling up her legs. She hadn't slept well. How could she? The boy had come to her last night in her dreams (at least she hoped it was in her dreams). He'd curled up at the foot of her bed, and she'd barely dared to breathe for fear of disturbing him.

Then Mirasol had returned from the bathroom, slamming the door, and the boy . . . the boy was gone. Perhaps the boy she was seeing was hers. The child in her belly. The baby she was going to have. Telling her that she must accept her fate. She shook her head. Loco. There was no madness in her family, although her sister was of a nervous disposition and had become moody, irrational and withdrawn after she'd had her third child. But that was normal. Althea had seen it many times. No. It was just the stress. This situation was frightening. Even the old hands who had been on the ships for years were spooked. The Internet was still down, and Angelo said it wouldn't be long before the emergency generators ran out of juice. Paulo had a short-wave radio in his cabin and even he couldn't get a signal. Many of the crew were choosing to sleep out on the crew deck or the airier loading decks, the smell of unfiltered sewage and the fear of the unknown driving them out of their cabins. The stories were raging around the crew decks: the ship was haunted, the dead girl in the morgue had come to life and was lying in wait to scare the foolhardy to death. The water was still running, so it was possible to have a shower, but that was it. She was relieved it was not up to her to clean the communal staff bathrooms.

She forced herself to move, and made her way down to Maria's office. The door was open and raised voices came from within. She hesitated, planning to hang back and eavesdrop, but Maria spotted her before she could slip out of sight. 'Come in, Althea.'

Mirasol, who had clearly been crying, smiled with relief when she saw her. There was only the faintest bruise below her left eye from yesterday's attack.

Maria folded her hands on the desk in front of her. 'If you won't do your work then I will have no choice but to let you go.'

'But I have told you, I can't go down there!'

'I understand that you had a shock yesterday, Mirasol. I asked you if you were fine to work. You said yes. Now you say you are not. Which is it?'

'There are no guests down there. The carpets are wet. The toilets have overflowed. And . . . and the spirits are down there.'

Maria sighed.

'I can do it,' Althea spoke up. 'I will go down there.' She could do without the extra work, but she needed to set her mind at ease about the boy. That was where she had first seen him.

'Althea, you can't,' Mirasol whined. 'The Lady is there. I told you.'

'I'm not afraid.'

'Please leave, Mirasol,' Maria snapped.

With an anguished look at Althea, Mirasol fled the room.

'You are sure you are willing to do this, Althea?'

'I'm sure.'

'Good. Thank you.' The faintest smile of gratitude. 'I need you to remove the linen. Mirasol is correct. The toilets have backed up down there.' She sighed again. 'Maintenance is refusing to go down there too. This is a mess.' No eyebrows today. For an instant, her facade cracked to reveal the worry beneath – an expression Althea would have paid money to see just days ago. Maria was losing her grip. Good. About time the *puta* had a fall. But Althea would stay strong.

'Is there anything else I can do, Maria?'

Maria looked at her sharply. Perhaps Althea was laying it on a bit thick. 'It is fine, Althea. You may go.'

Mirasol was waiting outside for her. 'Do you think I will lose my job, Althea?'

'No, of course not. Maria is stressed and is taking it out on you. Ignore her.'

'But a word from her and I will be off the ships. I can't afford to lose my job, Althea. I owe the agency all that money.'

Althea sighed inside. The girl was becoming a drain. 'Trust me. It will all work out. You will not lose your job. You were attacked by a guest. Of course you do not want to go down there.'

Mirasol opened her mouth to say something, no doubt to go on and on about the Lady again, but Althea cut her off. 'They told you what to do if there was a virus on board during the training lecture, didn't they?'

'Yes.'

'Make sure you keep to it.'

'Yes, Althea. Thank you. How can I repay you?'

Althea smiled. She'd think of something.

She hurried along the I-95. There was a certain laxity about the atmosphere down here. A group of Indonesian workers from Maintenance and the garbage room were gathered in a tight little group and talking in hushed whispers. One of the officers, his white shirt stained with what looked to be coffee, hurried along, almost banging into her. There was none of the single-mindedness that was usual for this time of day. She would need to collect another box of surgical gloves out of her cabin. If it was as bad down there as they said, she would need as much protection as she could get. As she made her way to her cabin, she noted that the door to Trining's cabin was open, no doubt to circulate what little air there was down here. Althea hadn't seen her since Trining had asked her to take over her duties on the day the ship broke down, which now felt like forever ago. Had Maria told her she was fired yet? Curious, Althea paused and looked in. A strong smell of chlorine wafted out of the tiny bathroom. Good. Someone had had the sense to clean in here.

Trining was lying on her side, her back to the door. 'Hello, Trining.'

'Go away, Althea.'

'Why do you speak to me like this?'

Trining rolled over. She didn't look that sick. If it wasn't for the bucket and scrunched tissues next to her, Althea would assume she was malingering.

'I know that you lied.'

Shitfuck. 'I did not lie.'

'Maria said you told her I hadn't asked you to do my station.'

Althea widened her eyes. 'She did? I don't know why she would say that. Have I ever let you down, Trining?'

'No.'

'It's just a misunderstanding. That is all it is. I will talk to Maria.'

Trining was no fool. She didn't respond to Althea's smile.

'I am going to do your station now, Trining.'

'I am not paying you extra for that.'

'Of course not.' Althea kept the smile in place. 'Trining ... On your station. Did you ever see anything strange?'

A flicker of interest. 'Like what?'

'Did you ever get the feeling that someone was watching you?'

'No. Have you been listening to the ghost stories, Althea? Angelo has told me what those stupid peasants are saying about the dead passenger.'

Wait till I tell you about the ghost boys.

'I was the one who found the girl, Trining.'

'You did?'

'Yes. It was very shocking. You are lucky you were ill and didn't have to see what I saw.'

Althea noted with amusement that Trining's morbid curiosity had got the better of her resentment. 'What did you see?'

Althea mock-shuddered. 'I can't speak about it.'

A flash of disappointment. 'I understand. I liked her. The passenger who died. She was one of the nicer ones on my station.'

Althea shrugged. Good or bad everyone had to die sometime. The boy was her concern. 'I'm worried about you, Trining. You must come and find me if you need anything. And I do not expect you to pay me for that.' *Like hell.*

'Thank you, Althea. I am sorry I was rude to you.'

Althea exited, snapping off the smile the second her back was turned to Trining. That had been almost too easy.

She went into her cabin, shoved another handful of the purple gloves into the pockets of her cleaning smock, and made her way back up to the I-95. She paused as she reached the end of the corridor. The security guard who'd been with her when she stumbled upon the girl's body was standing in an alcove next to Maria's office, shaking his head as if he was having a serious conversation with someone. He hadn't yet come to find her, but she was not surprised. The security and housekeeping departments were bearing the brunt of this situation. She waited until he walked away, then moved in the opposite direction, almost bashing into Rogelio, who emerged from the alcove.

She greeted him, but he barely acknowledged her. His eyes were downcast, and he looked as if he was about to cry. He practically ran into the crew mess. Why would the security man want to speak to Rogelio?

And then she understood. She hadn't seen it because she hadn't wanted to see it. Angelo was right about Rogelio, after all. Only it wasn't Damien he was involved with. She stored this piece of information away. It might come in useful one day. She liked Rogelio, of course she did, but the world was tough and in her situation she needed to use every piece of ammunition she could gather.

The smell that greeted her when she emerged out of the service door into Trining's station was worse than she'd anticipated, the lack of air-conditioning adding a potent edge to it. And the light down here was dimmer than she remembered. The floor was now scattered with passengers' belongings. A pink flip-flop, a pillow, a pair of plastic angel's wings. Mirasol was right; there were no guests down here. She slowly made her way over to the dead passenger's cabin, the one that was sealed with tape. If the boy was anywhere, she suspected it would be in there, but she didn't dare break the seal. There were cameras on these floors and that would be a firing offence.

'Are you here?' she whispered. 'Show yourself.'

A thump came from somewhere in the heart of the ship. She walked forward cautiously. Halfway down the corridor a door stood ajar. That shouldn't happen. The doors were weighted to close unless they were hooked onto the magnets. Holding her breath, she stepped inside it, waiting for her eyes to become accustomed to the murky light. A gush of fear filled her chest when she saw him. He was sitting in the corner, his knees up to his chest. His face was wet with tears, and she couldn't make out his eyes. The only light came from the green emergency lights, not enough for her to see him in any detail.

'Hello.'

The fear drained away, replaced with relief. She wasn't going loco. He was here. He was real. She approached him slowly. 'How did you get in here? Where is your mother?'

With no warning, he jerked, uncurled his limbs, and flashed towards her on all fours like a spider. Too fast – no one should be able to move that fast. She screamed and leapt for the door, flailing out into the corridor. A giggle came from behind her. She spun. He was standing a few metres away from her, nearly outside the dead girl's cabin.

Impossible.

He sniffed. Now that he was standing in the light, she could make out his clothes: a fraying buttoned-up shirt, and trousers that stopped way above his ankles. Grime was worn into his bare feet and arms.

She walked towards him, a hand outstretched as if he were a dangerous animal. She expected him to run, but he didn't. She reached down to touch his arm, half-convinced that she'd encounter empty air. But no. He was real. Flesh and bone.

He giggled again, skipped away from her, and ran towards the service door.

'Wait!'

He hesitated, then disappeared through it. 'Wait!' she tried again, then followed.

She could hear the skitter of his feet moving lower down the stairs, but she'd lost sight of him. He was waiting for her at the junction to the I-95; he smiled, covered his mouth with a hand, and darted straight across the passageway. A couple of maintenance engineers glanced at her curiously as she ran past them. She followed the sound of his footsteps, barely taking note of where she was going, until she reached a low corridor lined with white piping. She didn't know where she was. Althea really only knew the crew area and the Verandah deck well – she was not allowed in the passenger areas and had no reason to venture into this part of the ship.

A giggle, and then she saw him again. He was right next to her. She felt a cold pressure on her hand, and looked down to see he was gripping it. He led her through another door and along a corridor lined with crew cabins. One of the doors was propped open and she walked past it as if she was in a dream, barely glancing at the couple writhing on the bed inside. The boy led her through a door that opened out onto a wide, dark space. Curtains billowed in front of her, large black boxes with steel edges were piled against the walls, and then she understood. They were at the back of the stage.

She found her voice. 'What are we doing here?'

The boy wiped at his nose. He pulled out of her grasp and disappeared down a short flight of stairs. Althea stumbled after him and stepped into a low-ceilinged area, the glow of the emergency lights catching the spangles and sequins on the racks of costumes lined up against the far side of the room. Very occasionally the entertainment crew put on a show for the staff, but she'd never been to one. This was a part of the ship that was alien to her. She was always working.

Where was the boy? She moved towards the costume rack to see if he was hiding in there, when a low laugh came from behind her. She was not alone. She whirled, and something shifted in the dark corner next to the doorway. Mrs del Ray. Sitting in her wheelchair. Watching her. She rolled forward. 'Althea, so nice of you to come.'

The boy reappeared, took Althea's hand and rested his head against her side. A flush of warmth ran through her. She should have been repelled, but she wasn't. 'He likes you, Althea. And he's a good judge of character. You should see what he does to those he doesn't like.'

Althea's throat was dry, but she made herself speak. 'Did you bring him on board?'

'Celine did. In a manner of speaking.'

'I don't understand.'

Mrs del Ray patted the back of her hair and smiled. There were too many teeth in her mouth. Wisps of blond hair wafted out of the hair-helmet that Althea had thought was as solid as a block of wood. 'I have a proposal to make to you, Althea. You can help me, and I can help you.'

'Help me how?'

'Help you get what you want. Sometimes we do that, give

people what they want. Sometimes we give people what they deserve.'

'I don't understand what you are saying.' The woman was talking in riddles.

'I know you have a secret. A secret you don't want anyone to know. But they will in about seven months.'

Althea's stomach dropped like a brick. Ghost boys, now this. 'How did you know I'm pregnant? Not even I am sure.' She was proud that her words came out calmly.

A wink. 'Ain't much I don't know, me old duck. Things are going to get a lot worse before they get better. I'm the only one who can get you where you want to go.'

'And where is that?'

'Away from this. Away from Joshua.'

'How do you know about Joshua?' Had Angelo been gossiping about her to Celine? No. The woman was psychic. Perhaps she really could see into her head. Althea crossed herself. A *bruha*, a witch. Like the ones her *lola* used to tell her about, that would send insects to burrow under your skin, eat your baby alive in your womb.

'No. I can't see into your head, my darling. But close enough. Now, are you interested in dealing?'

The boy popped a thumb in his mouth and peered up at her. The woman was the devil. Althea could feel it. She could sense it. But not the devilry she'd been brought up with – a different kind. An alien kind. Mrs del Ray wasn't evil, exactly – Althea had met evil before and this woman wasn't it – but something was not right about her. She almost laughed – *something wasn't right!* She was clasping the hand of a ghost boy and all she could think was that *something wasn't right.*

'We all have to adjust our mind-set, my darling,' Celine said. 'It is a bit of a jump to take all of this in. We all had to go through it at one stage or another. Even me.'

'And what do you need me to do?'

'Oh, this and that. Nothing that's too far out of your purview. You have three things I need, my darling. You're clever and you're connected.'

'That's two things.'

'The third will come in time.' Mrs del Ray ran her tongue around her lips. 'And I can pay you. Perhaps I should have said that at the beginning?'

The boy snuggled even closer to Althea. 'Again, I ask you, what do I have to do?'

'Come closer and I'll tell you.'

Moving awkwardly, the child stuck like a limpet to her side, Althea did as she was told.

'Now listen.'

And Althea listened.

The Suicide Sisters

Helen bundled up the soiled towels she'd been using to protect Elise's mattress and sheets, and carried them through to the shower. She squeezed the last of the shampoo on top of the pile and let the water run. The pressure was weak, but she was grateful that there was still water at all. She didn't want to trouble Althea for yet another round of clean linen; the poor girl had looked exhausted the last time she'd seen her.

Helen's hands shook as she ran a facecloth under the tap. Several times last night, she'd been convinced that Elise had gone. Died. Passed on, or whatever euphemism people tended to use. She'd heard them all after Graham died, along with: *I'm so sorry for your loss; the pain will pass; if there's anything I can do . . .* Stock phrases that she'd used herself many times. *I'm sorry, you're sorry, we're all fucking sorry.* She gasped in a breath and clutched at the sink. There was a constant ache just below her solar plexus. If Elise died she'd be totally alone on this bloody ship. The thought of that made her feel as if she was teetering at the edge of a tall building, looking down. She had the sleeping tablets, but she knew from her research that they might not do the trick. They might not be enough. And she didn't want to do it alone.

Better together.

She didn't think she had it in her to do it alone.

The tears wanted to come, but they would just be tears of self-pity, and she couldn't allow herself to slide all the way down. *That's right. Buck up, girl,* Graham's voice came to her. *You're strong, you can get through this. You're stronger than you think.* The pain in her chest deepened, and she was hit with a sudden, unexpected flood of homesickness.

There's no home to go back to.

Packing up the evidence of her and Graham's life together had been one of the tasks she'd made herself complete the week before she left for Miami. At first she couldn't bear to throw out anything he'd ever touched – it had taken every bit of resolve she possessed just to sort through his desk, or remove anything that could possibly retain an iota of his scent – but after she'd managed to box up his shirts for Oxfam (a task that made her weep for a whole afternoon), she turned a corner, and she'd ended up chucking things out with wild abandon. Better that than leave it up to Graham's nephews, who would eventually inherit the house.

She smothered the emotion, washed her hands and face, and went back into the bedroom. She knew she was in real danger of infection. The nurse who had come to check on Elise this morning – a harassed, brisk redhead who smelled faintly of stale alcohol – had told her how easy it was to pass on the norovirus. Helen had been careful, but she doubted she could continue much longer without catching it. She'd insisted that Elise be taken to the medical bay where she could be monitored closely, but the nurse said that Elise was better off in the suite than down in the medical bay. At least here, with the balcony, there was the possibility of fresh air.

'Helen,' Elise croaked, fumbling for her hand. Her skin was hot and clammy, her nightdress damp from sweat.

'Do you need to go to the bathroom?'

'Nuh-uh. Thirsty.'

Helen held the glass to Elise's lips. She managed three small sips, which was better than nothing. She should really change Elise into another nightdress. The first time she'd done it, she'd been shocked at how much of her life Elise had kept hidden from her. Naked, the body revealed secrets. The mastectomy scar, a cruel slice of raised flesh, had shaken her. Elise had never told her about it, and Helen had never noticed – or been too self-absorbed to notice – if her friend wore a prosthesis. Yet Elise's body was beautiful in its own way, the smooth thighs and belly, bulky, but devoid of the cellulite that had plagued Helen no matter how many hours she spent walking.

The PA system beeped, signalling another of Damien's interminable messages. There'd been one earlier from the captain (about bloody time, she'd thought), saying that as all communication systems were still disabled, a tender boat had been dispatched to alert the coastguard of their position. It was clear they were in far more serious trouble than the crew was letting on. She tried not to listen while Damien ran through his usual excuses and platitudes, but then something else caught her attention:

'. . . helping to keep our spirits up, our guest celebrity, the wonderful Celine del Ray, will generously be performing again in the Dare to Dream Theatre in just half an hour. All are welcome!'

Helen shuddered. Just the thought of Celine made her feel queasy. The woman was a fraud. A sick, manipulative con artist.

Someone rapped on the door – perhaps it was Maddie again, checking up on them. Celine might be a monster, but Maddie had been kind. She peered through the peephole and saw the doctor – the one who'd come to see Celine on New Year's Eve – standing a little to the side. About time.

'May I check on the passenger?' he said, when she waved him in. His eyes were tinged with yellow and striated with veins, and a surgical mask hung limply around his neck. 'I believe she was seen by a nurse yesterday?'

'That's right.'

'How has she been?' He stifled a yawn.

'Not good.'

'Vomiting? Diarrhoea?'

'Yes. But not for the last hour. That's a good sign, isn't it?'

He made a noncommittal sound. 'Her name? I'm sorry, I know you told me what it was last night . . . the night before. Lost track of time as well.' He tried to smile and failed. Helen almost felt sorry for him. Almost. 'Her name is Elise. Elise Mayberry.'

'Sorry.'

'Please just take a look at her, doctor.'

Helen watched anxiously as he listened to Elise's chest and attached the cuff to her upper arm and took her blood pressure. 'Well?'

Another noncommittal grunt.

'Doctor, I need to know. Is it possible that . . . that she could die from this?' *Don't leave me, Elise. Don't leave me.*

'It's very unlikely. Her pulse is fairly strong. I'm not too worried about her blood pressure, but you must make sure she has enough fluid intake. If she doesn't improve then I might put her on a drip.'

'When will all this be over?'

He sighed and stood up. 'I wish I could tell you. This must be very hard for you. Are you getting enough rest?'

'I'm fine.' Not true. She'd barely slept since Elise had fallen ill. But this wasn't about her.

She saw him out and then lay down on her bed. It would be so easy to do. The sleeping pills were in Elise's handbag, hanging over the chair. But they couldn't slip over the side now, even if Elise was up to it. Even if they could ensure no one would fish them out again. The water that lapped around the ship was as flat as a stagnant pond, its surface sullied with red plastic bags. If she jumped, she'd gulp down someone else's waste. No. She had to be brave. It couldn't be much—.

There was someone – a man – on the balcony. She let out a small scream, remembering that dark figure she'd seen in Celine's room on New Year's Eve. She squinted her eyes to reduce the glare from the sunlight, and peered at him. He looked familiar, and then it came to her. Jaco, the musician. She hurried over to the door and slammed it shut, just as he turned and offered his hand to a tall blonde woman, who was climbing across from the metal ladder leading up to the lifeboat directly in front of the suite. It had never occurred to Helen how easy it was to access the state-room from the deck below them.

Jaco tapped on the glass and gave her a wide grin. 'Hey. Can we come in?'

'What . . . why are you here?'

'It's hell out on deck. We just need a quiet place to chill for a while. I'm Jaco and this is Lulia. Lulia's one of the dancers.'

'Hello. Pleased to meet you,' Lulia said. Long bleached hair and full make-up. The woman had what Graham would have called 'shifty eyes'. He was always judging people on their appearance and to her knowledge he'd never been wrong.

'You shouldn't be up here. My friend is sick. She needs to rest.'

The woman recoiled slightly, but Jaco clung to her wrist. 'We were wondering if we could sit on your balcony for a while. Maybe get something to drink.'

'Like I say, my friend is very unwell.'

'We won't stay long.'

'Please,' Lulia said. 'People are getting sick everywhere. We just want somewhere quiet to sit while we wait for it to be over.'

'There must be somewhere else you can go.'

'No. The crew area is bad. The air is bad.'

Helen's gut told her to get rid of them, but what kind of person would she be if she didn't at least offer them a drink? Reluctantly, she unlocked the door. 'Come in. But only for a minute.'

'Thanks,' Jaco grinned at her. 'I really appreciate it.'

'It stinks,' Lulia said, flapping a hand in front of her face. 'We should have tried to get into the owner's suite.'

'I told you my friend was sick. She's contagious.'

'We'll be careful,' Jaco said.

'What is your name?' Lulia asked.

'Helen.'

Lulia sat down on the couch and crossed her legs, which were spray-tanned and riddled with stubble. She was barefoot, her toes almost freakishly long. 'You have seen the shows?'

'Yes.' A lie. She loathed cabaret with a passion. Elise had gone to see the 'Daydream Fantastique Extravaganza' or whatever its ghastly name was on the first night, and had said it was 'interesting', which was about as critical as Elise ever got.

'We have to sing *and* to dance.'

'You were very good.'

'Thank you. Your friend, she is your lover?'

'No. We're just friends.'

'Why you on this cruise? It is for young people.'

'Enough questions,' Jaco laughed. 'Again, really appreciate this, Helen. People are freaking out all over the place. Seeing ghosts.'

Helen blanched. 'Ghosts?'

'Yeah. Lots of superstitious people on ships.'

'And it stinks so bad,' Lulia said. 'People poop everywhere. They are dirty, like pigs.'

Jaco waved at the mini-bar. 'You mind if we grab some water? I'll go out and get you some more.'

'Go ahead.'

He dropped to his haunches and peered inside it. 'Champagne. Never got to drink it on New Year's Eve, huh?'

'No.'

'Tell you what. You help us, we'll help you. Sound like a plan?'

'I'm not sure that's really a good idea.'

He turned his head and grinned at her. 'Hey. You can trust me. I'm a musician.'

The Angel of Mercy

Martha was waiting for him when he slogged back to the medical bay after doing his rounds. Her hair was tied back in a messy bun, and she was picking at a flake of dried skin on her lower lip.

'What now?' He wasn't sure he could cope with any new developments. On top of the noro cases there were two fairly serious cases of heatstroke and a suspected broken toe. He needed a caffeine injection. He needed a shower. He needed to sleep for more than two fucking hours.

'Ah, Jesse. We have a bit of an issue. It's the new patient. The fella that came in yesterday.'

'What about him?'

'He's gone, Jesse.'

He was struggling to take in what she was saying. 'You discharged him?'

'No. I came back after getting something to eat, you know? I wasn't gone long. And he wasn't in his bed.'

'But he was doped up to the eyeballs.' Jesse had made the decision to increase the midazolam dosage last night, after the man had woken and started acting erratically. Other than locking him in his cabin, where he could easily cause harm to himself, Jesse didn't know how else to restrain him. It was a ship, not a bloody mental ward.

'I know. I can't explain it.'

'Where's Bin?'

'Sent him for a couple of hours' rest. He was on duty all night, poor soul. You know what he's like, you have to drag him away from his post.' She pulled at her lip again. 'And that's not all, Jesse.'

A sinking feeling in his gut. 'Go on.'

'Alfonso is also AWOL.'

'Seriously? Where the hell has he gone?'

'I don't know. I checked his cabin and went down to the generator and control rooms, but no one's seen him.'

'So we've lost two patients now?'

'Looks that way. Sorry, Jesse.'

'It's not your fault. How in the fuck do they expect us to deal with all of this?' They weren't set up for it. Strictly speaking there should be two doctors on board, but Martha said that the shorter cruises tended to ignore this stipulation.

'You look desperate, Jesse. Are you sure you're not getting ill?'

He shook his head. He was tired, that was all. Sure, he felt sick to his stomach, but he'd been living on Coke Lite and Pringles for the last three days. And he should be grateful that the whole ship wasn't overrun with the virus. It tended to spread fast, and considering the conditions it was a miracle they weren't all down with it. He'd used a red bag, furtively in his cabin last night. Not wanting to leave it for Paulo to clean up, he'd carried it down to the incinerator room. Why he should be so embarrassed about something like that, he had no clue. *You're a doctor.* 'I'm worried about the elderly patient. Elise Mayberry,' he said. 'Her pulse is erratic. Does she have a history of heart disease?'

'Not that I know of.'

He should have asked her friend, the woman he'd cruelly dubbed Aunt Spiker, but the patient he'd seen just before Elise – a middle-aged man on the same floor – had been abusive and abrasive, which had rattled him more than he liked to admit.

'You wanting to get her down here now?' Martha asked.

'Maybe. There are three other cases on that deck alone. How many crew have it?'

'Seven in total. Maybe more. Problem is that most of them don't want to stay in their cabins.'

'It'll spread like wildfire if they don't.'

They were interrupted by a message from Damien, informing them that Celine del Ray would be holding yet another performance (or whatever the hell it was that she did) in the Dare to Dream Theatre.

Madness. Encouraging people to clump together in large gath-
erings while noro raged through the ship was unbelievably
short-sighted. He sighed. 'That's it. I'm going to insist we go to
red alert. You heard anything else about when we might expect the
cavalry to fucking arrive?'

'No, Jesse. Still no Wi-Fi. They sent out a tender boat this morning, but that's all I know.' Jesse couldn't understand why anyone
would think that sending out a tender boat was a good sign. The
whole thing made no sense. At the very least, Foveros should have
sent one of *The Beautiful Dreamer*'s sister ships to check up on
them. 'Jesus Christ,' he breathed.

'We could use him now all right.'

'Fuck this. I'm going to see the captain. I'm not taking no for an
answer.'

'What do you need me to do?'

'You'd better stay here. I'll be back now-now.'

'Good luck.'

Jesse sprayed his shirt with a liberal dousing of deodorant –
shower in a can, the best he could do for now – and got moving.
He momentarily lost his way – he wasn't thinking about where he
was going – and had to double back, cutting past the crew bar. It
was full, he could smell the beer and hear the rowdy voices.
Another one-way ticket to spreading infection all over the ship.
The bar would have to be shut. The food stations would need to
be disinfected from top to bottom, and anyone showing symptoms would need to be isolated. Jesse had heard about what a
nightmare the extra duties were for the crew and staff, but fact
was, they didn't have a choice.

Ram was standing outside the door that led to the bridge, his
implacable mask in place. 'Can I help you, doctor?'

'I need to see the captain immediately.' There was only a slight
wobble in his voice. Good.

Nothing showed on Ram's face. 'He is in a meeting.'

'It's an emergency.'

Ram stared at him for several seconds, then gave a minuscule
nod. 'Wait here.'

'Okay, but I—'

Ram was already gone, slamming the heavy bridge door in Jesse's face before he could slip through it. Jesse wiped his sweating palms on his trousers.

A few minutes later, the door clunked open again, and Ram waved him inside. Jesse had only been on the bridge a couple of times since he'd joined the ship. A huge area sided with floor-to-ceiling windows, the air felt fresher in here, although Jesse was certain it was only his imagination. The captain – a tubby man in his late sixties with flamboyant white hair – was standing, his back to Jesse, over by the navigation console, gesticulating at a group of men in officer's whites. Jesse recognised the hothead – the hotel director – a sniffy Greek who looked as if he was incapable of smiling, one of the IT guys (who was sporting a spectacular black eye and a cut on his right cheek that looked like it was festering), and Damien. A bolshy little man, Damien always entered the crew bar as if he expected everyone to cheer. Jesse hadn't had much to do with him out of choice, and Martha described him as 'a total gobshite'.

The rest of the bridge officers, including Baci, Alfonso's visitor, who gave him a nod of recognition, were gathered discreetly over by the window. Jesse took a second to drink in the view. Nothing but wide, endless ocean. No ships. No oil rigs. Not even the wispy tail of a passing plane in the sky.

Finally, the captain acknowledged him. 'How is Alfonso, *dottore*? Can he work now?'

Wrong-footed, Jesse blinked. 'He left the treatment room this morning.'

The captain barked something in Italian at Baci, who shook his head.

The captain stared accusingly at Jesse. 'He is not in the control room.'

Jesse breathed in. He couldn't allow himself to be railroaded. Alfonso wasn't why he was here. 'I have been asking to see you since day one of this mess, captain. You must be aware of the situation. There are more cases of the virus daily.'

'How many?'This from the hothead.

'As many as twenty, maybe more.' Damien sucked his teeth. Jesse let a second pass before he spoke again: 'I need you to put the ship on red alert.'

'No. That is not possible,' the captain said.

'Sir, respectfully, if you don't, we're going to be looking at a major—'

'The staff are stretched to the limit,' the hothead said. 'We cannot give them extra duties.'

'So you want the whole of the ship to get infected? How will that look when we get back to port?'

'Do not raise your voice to the captain,' Damien dived in.

Jesse was aware that Ram was watching him carefully. Fuck. He hadn't expected this reaction. 'I am not raising my voice, I am saying that we need to—'

The hothead spoke over him again. 'Morale is very bad. If we give my staff extra duties and restrict them to their cabins, they—'

It was Jesse's turn to interject. 'Just how long are you expecting this situation to continue?'

The captain sniffed. 'Not long.'

'A day? Two days? A week? What? Does anyone even know we're stranded out here?'

'The situation is under control, *dottore*.'

Bullshit. The Coke Jesse had been living on was turning to acid in his gut. 'Are we lost? Is that it?'

The captain's eyes hardened. 'We are not lost.'

'So why hasn't anyone come to see where the hell we are?' There must be some way they could track the ship even if the power and communication systems failed. *The Beautiful Dreamer* wasn't a state-of-the-art vessel in anyone's book, but it must be equipped with transponders and beacons.

'There is bad weather in the home port. They will come soon.'

'So you've been in contact with Ground Support?'

'It will not be long before help will be here.'

Jesus. Jesse swallowed a lump in his throat. He couldn't tell if the captain was spinning him a line or not. 'Look, all I am asking is that the passengers be informed about the virus and encouraged to dispose of the hazardous-waste bags in a hygienic manner, and food preparations be monitored and restricted. And anyone showing early signs of the virus should be confined to their cabins. That's vital.'

'Where do you suggest we put them, doctor?' the hothead sniped. 'The lower cabins are uninhabitable.'

The IT guy snorted. 'Yeah, and most of the crew are seeing ghosts all over the goddamned ship.'

Ram shot the man a warning glance.

'Many of the crew are superstitious. It is to be expected,' the captain said. 'There is no basis for this . . . unusual phenomenon.'

Like dead girls banging on the inside of the morgue? Or maybe stroke patients who can read minds.

'Can we at least ask passengers not to congregate in large groups?' Jesse turned to Damien. 'The performance in the theatre should be cancelled immediately.'

Damien shook his head. 'No no no. It's keeping people busy and occupied. We can't disrupt that.'

'They'll be busy enough when they're puking their guts up.'

Damien shook his head again. A goat. A little goat. *Ja*, that was what Damien reminded him of. Cloven hooves and bulging wicked eyes. 'Absolutely out of the question. We can't cancel any of Celine del Ray's shows. Or our other events. The passengers depend on them.'

The captain held up his hand. 'Enough. *Dottore*, of course we are appreciating your concern. We will tell the kitchen staff to be vigilant. We will increase the chlorine levels in the, ah, fluid for cleaning. We will put out additional hand sanitisers.'

Jesse's face was growing hot, and a trickle of sweat tickled the back of his ear. 'Captain, I must insist that—'

'That is all we can do for now. Thank you for your time.'

The captain turned away from him, and Jesse was left staring at his back. Ram took a step towards him, and not sure what else to do, he left the bridge, the door clanging behind him.

He'd barely made it to the entrance to the I-95, when there was a beep and Damien's voice oozed through the speakers:

'G'day, ladies and gentlemen, Damien your cruise director here. Just to let you know that we're continuing to endeavour that you're as safe and as comfortable as possible at the present time, and we really value your patience. A little reminder to please use the hand sanitisers that are placed at the entrance of all of the common areas whenever possible. And don't forget that Celine del Ray will be appearing in the Dare to Dream Theatre in five minutes. That's five minutes, folks.'

Bastard. It was almost as if the fucker wanted people to get sick.

It wasn't good enough. If they weren't going to do anything, he would. At the very least he could have a word with Celine del Ray or whoever was in charge of the event, and try and make them see sense. Neither the captain nor Damien the Goat could stop him doing that.

Without stopping to fill Martha in on the meeting with the captain, he flew along the I-95 and up the stairs to the atrium, increasing his pace every time a passenger appeared and putting on his 'medical emergency' face. The lower doors to the theatre were locked, so he headed up to the next floor. Only one side door was open, several seniors milling about in front of it. Two women and a man dressed in a fantastic tweed suit and violet tie gave him a friendly greeting.

'Hello, doctor,' the dapper fellow grinned. 'Are you coming for the show?'

'No.' Jesse explained his concerns about the virus spreading through the theatre.

'Oh, you don't need to worry about us, doctor,' the man said. 'None of Celine's group are sick. We're being very careful. The bathrooms we're using are scrubbed twice a day with chlorine solution and we all use the hand sanitisers.'

'We know what to do,' a Hispanic woman in her fifties broke in. 'I've been on a cruise before that was hit by a virus, doctor. We even have extra waste bins for the bags.'

He'd had patients like this woman. Know-it-alls. Convinced they knew his job better than he did.

'That's all wonderful, but I'd really like to speak with Mrs del Ray.'

'She's communing with Spirit right now.'

'I'll just go in and see, shall I?' Jesse smiled and shoved past her.

It took a second to acclimatise to the theatre's shadowy depths. The atmosphere was so heavy and sombre, it was like walking into a cathedral. He made his way slowly down the aisle. The place was almost full, passengers and several low-level members of staff filling the booths and chairs, whispering amongst themselves and staring expectantly at the stage. He could only imagine how fast the virus could incubate in here. Someone familiar caught his eye, and he paused. Alfonso was sitting slumped in a seat halfway along a row. The elderly woman next to him was clutching his wrist and whispering into his ear, but he stared straight ahead and made no response. Jesse thought about approaching him, but that wasn't why he was here. He'd inform Baci where to find his missing father figure after he'd spoken to the del Ray woman. Alfonso wasn't a prisoner: he couldn't make him go back to work and fix the bloody ship, could he? Several people sitting on the edges of the rows gave him welcoming smiles, and Paulo, his steward, who was standing next to a crate of water bottles and a box of bananas, gave him a wave.

Jesus. They were really set up here.

There was a click, and then lights bloomed on stage. As Jesse moved nearer he could make out what looked to be a complex set-up of car batteries – possibly from the forklifts on the loading bay – attached to standalone halogen lights. Clever.

With no fanfare, Celine del Ray wheeled herself into the middle of the stage. She cleared her throat, beamed at the audience and said: 'Just a little bit of housekeeping. I'd like to welcome all our new friends, especially those who've been working very hard to keep our space clean and comfortable for us. Let's help them out by doing our bit.' Jesse was amazed at how well her voice carried without a microphone. 'Now. While we've all been dealing with this stressful situation, I want to ask you, old friends and new, have I let you down?'

In unison, the audience murmured a long, drawn-out 'noooo'. Unnerved, Jesse crept to the side of the theatre.

'Have I lied to you?'

'No.'

'No. I haven't. Some of you say that you've been seeing strange things on the ship and are frightened. There's no need to be frightened. Know this, you are simply experiencing Spirit drawing you to me so that I can help you come together and get through this. Some of you want to know where I get my gift from, and how it is that I'm able to connect with Spirit. Know this. What I do is not evil. I am as in tune with God, whatever your conception of Him – or Her – is, as you are. You all come from many faiths and I urge you to lean on them now. Look into your hearts, ask your own guides and your own loved ones who have passed on for support.'

Celine paused for breath, cocked her head, and Jesse had the skin-crawling impression that she was staring straight at him. 'Wait . . . I have to interrupt myself as Archie's coming through and letting me know there's a message for someone here. I'm getting . . . yes, a young girl is stepping forward. She's crying.' Celine touched her throat. 'Ooh. There's a pain in my belly, she's saying. A bad pain. I'm getting . . . She's wearing some kind of uniform. A school uniform. Blue. Does that make sense to anyone?'

Now he was absolutely certain she was staring right at him.

'She's saying . . . she's saying that how she died, it was avoidable. She's saying it wasn't an accident.'

The crawling sensation on his skin was getting stronger. And for a second, just for a second, a snapshot of the girl's face jumped into his mind. She'd come to see him straight after school. She'd sworn that she wasn't sexually active, but how could he have known she was lying? He should have asked her mother to stay with him in the consulting room, or instructed the nurse to sit in. He hadn't been thinking clearly; he was well into his pethidine habit by then.

Jesse reeled up the aisle, almost colliding with a heavy-set guy who was now standing, his arms crossed, outside the door.

'Hey, careful there, buddy.'

Face hot, Jesse walked blindly back to the stairwell, shrugging off the passengers who tried to harangue him en route. When he reached the atrium, he clung to the railing and breathed in deeply through his nose.

Chill the fuck out. But there was only one thing that really chilled him out, wasn't there?

No.

He was just letting the day's shit-fest get to him, that was all. Celine could have gotten the story off the Internet. Only there was no Internet, was there? Perhaps she'd googled him before she even came onto the ship, investigated as many of the crew and passengers as she could. Dug out their stories.

Unlikely – but he had to hold onto something. It was more feasible that she'd just been fishing for information, casting around until she hit on a target. *Ja.* That had to be it. Every doctor had something dodgy in his or her past – a misdiagnosis, a patient who'd died unexpectedly. And just how precise had she been, exactly? Not very. A school uniform. Big deal.

That was all it was.

Or maybe he was looking for an excuse to break down so that he could give into the lure of Lady Demerol. No. He'd just got spooked and fallen for an old woman's con-tricks.

Martha was out when he returned to the medical bay, but there was a can of Coke, a sandwich and a note on the reception desk: 'Another one.'

Great.

He cracked the Coke can and slung his feet up on the desk. He should really return to the theatre and prise Alfonso out of there. That whole scene had reminded him of some sort of cult activity. At the very least he should get a message to Baci. If Alfonso was well enough to leave the treatment room and find his way into the clutches of that creepy old woman and her acolytes, then he was well enough to get his arse down to the generator room and fix the fucking ship. Get all of them out of this situation.

'Doc?'

Jesse turned to see Bin hovering in the doorway. His skin was tight on his bones, his eyes hollow. Christ, Jesse hoped he wasn't getting the noro. 'We have a problem, doc.'

How many times had he heard that today? 'What is it now?'

'The girl in the morgue. They—'

Oh, for fuck sakes. 'Not this again. It was just the metal expanding in the heat.'

'Doc. Jesse – they are saying they are going to throw her body overboard.'

The Keeper of Secrets

With Ashgar now sick and confined to the cabin, Devi was the only security presence on the main deck, and the passengers' resentment and fear boiled around him. The guests either refused to look in his direction or stared at him with open hostility, and the other staff were receiving much the same treatment. There were fewer cleaning crew on duty than usual, and the filth and rubbish was piling up. Some worked their way vigilantly around, picking up the plastic cups and smeared plates, but they received no thanks and were forced to field endless questions about when the bars would be open or when they could be expected to be air-lifted off the ship. Thankfully, there had been no major altercations for a couple of hours, although Devi had had to caution a group of young men – part of the singles group he'd spoken to after the girl's death – for smoking marijuana on the exercise deck. Several passengers were now using the children's fun room as a makeshift lavatory, and he'd had to ask several guests to desist from urinating over the side of the ship. Ram had instructed the security staff to only intervene in serious incidences; in these conditions they could not consign the perpetrators to their cabins and spare the manpower to guard them.

He passed a group of people crouched around a plastic table, holding hands, their heads bent, and made his way towards the buffet area. The pool was turning a sickly green, but this hadn't stopped passengers from using it. In the Jacuzzi (which should really have been cordoned off as there was no power to circulate the water) a woman, whose bikini top had slipped to reveal a brown nipple, was sleeping with her mouth open. She jerked awake as the PA system beeped:

196

'G'day, ladies and gentlemen, this is Damien your cruise director here. Again, I'd like to thank you for your patience while we sort out the issues we are still experiencing. The captain will be addressing you all again shortly. I'd like to take this opportunity to remind you to use the hand sanitisers whenever possible, and to please let a crew member know if your tummies are feeling funny at any stage. On a brighter note, Keri and Jason, two of our brightest stars, will be showing you how to do the rumba on the Lido deck stage in a few minutes, and the wonderful Celine del Ray will be holding another show in the Dare to Dream Theatre this evening, if any of you would like to join her.'

While he patrolled, Devi kept an eye out for anyone who resembled the body type of Kelly's assailant. Devi had already decided to visit the medical bay when his shift was over to ensure that the passenger who had attacked the steward couldn't be the same man.

'Hey! Over here!' A man standing at the top of the stairs that led down to the Tranquillity deck was waving him over as if Devi was a servant. Devi sighed inside. The fellow was one of those overconfident American men, of which there was never any shortage on the ships. Grumpy if there was a long queue on the embarkation ramp. Brimming with self-righteousness. The type who treated the security guards as if they were invisible unless they had to wait more than five seconds to be allowed back on the ship after the day trips.

Devi took his time walking over to him, taking the opportunity to lean over the railing and assess the group gathered on the deck below. He estimated there had to be around fifty people or so, and they looked to be well organised, with mattresses neatly lined up. He scanned the men he could see – he was unable to look beneath the overhang – but none fitted the profile of Kelly's attacker.

'Hey!' the man shouted. 'Hey. I'm talking to you.'

'Can I help you, sir?'

'Yeah. I need to see the captain.'

'Sir, I do not have the authority to make that happen.'

'Well who the hell does? I paid good money to be on this ship and you treat us like this?'

Devi let the man's words roll over him. At the far side of the Tranquillity deck, a skinny woman with sun-streaked skin was crouching next to a bucket. The woman next to her was stroking her back, and holding her hair back while she vomited.

The man finished his diatribe. 'Well?'

'There will be an announcement soon, sir.'

The man shot him a look of disgust and swore under his breath. Devi headed back towards the indoor area. At the front of the buffet line, a passenger was screaming that the lettuce was brown. Eyes averted, the server was apologising over and over again in a toneless voice. Devi readied himself to get involved, but with a snappish: 'Whatever,' the passenger backed down.

His radio crackled, and Pran's tremulous voice sputtered: 'Need assistance . . . crew . . . Laundry.'

Devi waited for someone else to respond – he was reluctant to leave the main deck – but there was nothing but silence and static. He'd have to check it out. He ducked through the service corridor next to the buffet kitchen, and hared down to the crew decks.

A crowd of about twenty men, the majority Indonesian, but with a smattering of Eastern Europeans among them, were pushing and shoving in the corridor outside the laundry. Pran, who was attempting to force his way through them, was being roundly ignored, and Devi spotted the doctor on the edge of the crowd, yelling at the men to 'get the hell away from here'.

A door slammed, a cry went up and then the mob drew back. Through the gap that had opened up, Devi saw that two men were hauling a large black bag out of the storeroom.

A body bag.

Pran elbowed his way through the mob to join him, his face etched with relief. 'They want to throw the body into the sea, Devi. They say the dead woman is the one haunting the ship.'

Devi had seen and heard his share of superstition in his months on the ships; it didn't surprise him, but he was angered at the lack of respect they were showing the girl. She had been through enough.

'Hey!' he yelled, projecting his voice. 'Hey!'

The men looked up, and several peeled away from the group and tried to make themselves less visible. The two dragging the bag were clearly the core instigators. He eyed the man he judged to be the leader – a fellow with a round belly, his name tag reading 'Benyamin'. 'Step away.'

Benyamin muttered something and gestured at his now reluctant cohort to continue.

'Anyone who touches the bag will be taken off the ship,' Devi said, keeping his voice low and authoritative. It was an empty threat as things currently stood. 'If you do not desist, I will personally ensure that you never work on the ships again.'

Several of the men ducked their heads and hurried away. They couldn't risk losing their jobs. Most of them would be supporting extended families.

'We cannot stop!' Benyamin yelled. 'She is doing this! We will never get back to shore if she stays here!'

'It is not the girl,' Devi said. 'The ship stopped before she died. Is that not so, doctor?' Devi gave the doctor a pointed look, and thankfully he played along.

'That is so.'

Another few men peeled away.

Devi tried a different tack. 'How would you feel if this was your mother, or the body of your wife or sister?'

'We have all seen it. What she is doing . . .'

But Devi saw he had won. Benyamin was running out of steam. 'This will be over soon. If you continue, you will have no job. You will have to go back to your family with nothing. You know what the agency will do. Do you still owe them money?'

'Yes. But . . . no one is coming for us.'

'They will come.'

Benyamin stared at him resentfully for a few seconds, then his shoulders dropped. Without a word, he walked away, the others following.

'Thank you,' the doctor said. The male nurse with him – who Devi hadn't taken note of before – bowed his thanks. 'How can we stop them from coming back here?'

'They will be back. We can't stop them. We can't post a guard here.'

'Why not?'

'We don't have the manpower.'

The doctor nodded tiredly. 'Come on, Bin. Let's put her back.'

The doctor and the nurse each took one end of the bag, and shuffle-walked into the storeroom.

Pran was staring at his shoes. 'I did not handle that well.' He picked at his patchy moustache. 'I was in the surveillance room, but no one came when I called for assistance.' He jumped as the morgue door slammed closed.

The doctor wiped a hand over his mouth and approached Devi. 'Listen . . . we have another issue.'

Devi waited for him to continue.

'The patient who attacked the steward. He left the medical bay without being discharged.'

'When?'

'Some time this morning.'

'Doctor, in your opinion . . . Could he be the same man who killed the girl?'

The doctor's eyes widened, and Devi swore inwardly. Ram would be furious if he found out Devi was spreading rumours that there was a predator on board. But Devi found he no longer cared. 'So now you definitely think she was murdered?'

'We're considering all options.'

'Jissus.'

'I checked that, Devi,' Pran said, still picking at his moustache. 'I spoke to the passenger's wife. She said he was with her all night.'

'Did Ram ask you to do that?'

Pran looked at his feet. 'No, sir. The passenger did, after all, attack the steward, so it seemed like a logical question to ask.'

Perhaps Pran wasn't so useless after all. 'Good work. Good thinking.' But people had been known to lie to protect their loved ones. 'Did you believe her?'

Pran shrugged. 'I think she was telling the truth. She seemed to think that her husband was the victim in all of this.'

Devi considered this, then turned back to the doctor. 'I will see if I can locate the passenger, doctor. Can you describe him?'

'His name is Gary Johansson. Forty or so. White. Slightly overweight. Thinning hair.'

That description could fit seventy per cent of the male passengers on board, but it was also not dissimilar to the man he had seen on the footage.

The doctor thanked Devi again, and headed back towards the stairwell.

'What are your orders now, Pran?'

'I was supposed to be off now, sir, but Madan . . .'

'Madan?'

'He did not come and relieve me.'

'He is sick?'

'No . . . the last time I saw him he was in the bar.'

'I will go and talk to him. Stay in the surveillance room until I get there.'

'Yes, sir.'

'Good man.'

And, Devi thought, he could also get Pran to look at the footage of the morning of the attack. The image of the girl's stalker wasn't clear, but it was possible that Pran might pick out a characteristic that would confirm or exonerate the patient who had absconded from the medical bay.

Devi made his way up towards the crew bar. As usual, the interior was a haze of vaporiser smoke. One of the assistant waiters was lying slumped next to the foosball machine. Casino workers and Steiners – the women who staffed the spa – were gathered around the tables, talking furtively. And over in the corner, sitting alone, was Madan, a tower of empty Heineken cans piled around him.

He waved Devi over. 'Devi. Devi. Have a drink.'

'You know I don't drink, Madan.'

'First time for everything, my man.'

'Pran says you were supposed to relieve him.'

'Get Ashgar to do it.'

'Ashgar is sick.'

'So am I. Been on eighteen hours. Need a break.'

'If Ram sees you here, you will be disciplined.' No, he would be fired.

Madan laughed. 'No he won't. I'm his right-hand man. You know that. We have a history.' Devi hadn't known that. 'And anyway, he is with the captain. He is always with the captain. You haven't noticed? Our beloved and dutiful' – Madan leaned over to spit on the floor – 'captain is paranoid that the passengers will mutiny and overrun the kitchens and crew quarters. Let them. It is shit down here. And why would they come here? What could they do?'

'They just want answers.'

'There are no answers. I have to get off this ship, Devi. This is a bad boat. It's sick.'

'They sent the tender boat out. Someone will come soon.'

Madan burped. 'You are so naïve, Devi. I like that about you. It's good to be like that. Me, I'm not like that. I'm . . . I'm not like that. You're a good person. You have honour, an honourable man.' He belched again, and wiped his mouth with the back of his hand. 'I'm not going back to my post. Fuck that. You think we're going to get overtime for this mess? Fuck that, Devi. The captain has fucked up, got us lost. We could be anywhere.'

'The Gulf of Mexico isn't that big—'

'But you can get swept into the Gulf Stream, Devi, all the way along, end up . . .' he waved his hand. 'End up fuck knows where.'

'We don't even seem to be drifting that far.'

'We've drifted a long way, my man. We're lost.'

'Impossible.'

'Like I say, we're fucked. C'mon, have a drink with me.'

'No. Madan, you must—'

Madan reached over to slap Devi on the shoulder, missed, and sent the pile of cans crashing to the floor. No one looked up to locate the source of the noise.

'And there are other things going on too. You've seen it, Devi. You must have seen it. It isn't right, I tell you. The ship is sick,' he said again. Madan was not someone who Devi would have said was superstitious. If anything, he would have said he was the opposite. He rarely mentioned anything about religion or spiritual matters. He'd been on the ships longer than all of them: seven years at least, and in that time had cultivated a deeply cynical side. 'I have to get off this ship, Devi. And I will.'

'What did you see?'

'It was not so much seeing as feeling. They're all feeling it.'

The hand that covered the camera lens. The crew who were convinced the dead girl was haunting the ship. The reports from some of the Indonesian and Filipino staff about the Lady in White floating through the guts of the vessel, taunting passengers and crew alike.

There was a rational explanation for all of it. There had to be.

'We're fucked, Devi,' Madan said. 'Fucked.' He laughed humourlessly. 'And then there is the matter of the generator. They are saying there is no significant damage. They are saying that there is no reason for the ship's engines not to work.'

'So why is the ship disabled?'

Madan leaned towards him. 'It isn't.'

None of what Madan was saying made any sense. But whatever was happening with the generator or the ship's power was out of his control. Finding the man who killed Kelly wasn't.

'Someone wants you, Devi.' Devi turned to see Rogelio standing next to the entrance to the bar. Madan smirked and raised his eyebrows. Devi's heart dropped. He knew. Madan knew. Too bad. There was nothing he could do about that, other than beg Madan to keep it to himself.

Devi stalked over to Rogelio before he could make a scene. He'd been hoping to avoid running into him this evening. Rogelio had cornered him that morning in one of the public areas, where anyone could have seen them, complaining that Devi hadn't found time to meet with him last night. But how could he? He'd barely had time to return to his cabin and sleep. He did not need Rogelio's neediness on top of this, but he only had himself to blame. Before Rogelio could speak, he ushered him into the deserted IT room. 'I am busy, Rogelio. I'm on shift.'

'You have time to go to the bar, but you don't have time to see me?'

'Rogelio. Please. I don't need this.'

'Why won't you talk to me, Devi?'

'You've seen what it is like out there, Rogelio. The passengers need reassurance.'

'*I* need reassurance, Devi. What if this never ends? What if we're stuck out here until we run out of food and . . .' He slumped. 'I'm sorry. I know I'm being impossible.' He looked up through his fringe. 'You must hate me.'

The anger that had been festering inside Devi since he found Kelly's body surged up. 'Rogelio, you have to understand, I have something I need to do, and I can't have you hounding me like this.'

Rogelio flinched, and Devi prepared himself for a round of recriminations. Instead he asked: 'What do you need to do?'

Devi hesitated, and then let it all pour out. He didn't even try to stop it. He told him about the Merinda girl – the child who had been raped by her uncle – and how he'd allowed the family and his superiors to cover it up to save his own skin. He told him about the man he'd seen on the footage, the monster who'd followed Kelly Lewis back to her cabin. He told him about his fear that the man would get away with it, that her death would be submerged under the media storm that would ensue once they were finally rescued.

Rogelio listened, and then simply said: 'Go. Do what you have to do.' And then he left the room.

Devi made his way back to the surveillance office. His chest felt lighter – as if he was unburdened. Perhaps he should have confided in Rogelio from the start. Perhaps he'd underestimated him. He supposed he'd always assumed Rogelio was as shallow and empty as the entertainments he facilitated – the karaoke nights, the line-dancing, the singles' events. Little more than a pretty face.

'Devi.'

He looked up to see Ram standing outside the security offices, his hands clasped behind his back. 'What are you doing away from your post, Devi?'

'There was an incident in the storeroom next to the laundry, sir.' Now was his chance to make Ram listen. 'Sir. I must speak with you, sir.'

'About what?'

'The man who murdered Kelly Lewis.'

'There is no murderer, Devi. I have said this many times now. The girl drank too much.'

'Sir. I have proof. The CCTV footage—'

Ram didn't raise his voice. 'You are here to make sure the passengers and crew do not get out of hand. That is all. I have told you once, I will not have insubordination. Are we clear? There will be repercussions if you do not act in accordance with what I have said.'

It was futile. He could see that now. 'Yes, sahib.'

'Good. I hope we understand each other.'

Devi watched his superior walk away towards the bridge. But he would not give up, whatever Ram said. He could not give up.

Pran was staring at the monitors when he stepped inside the surveillance area, and Devi was certain he must have overheard their conversation. He looked up. 'Devi . . . there is . . . look. Screen seven.'

Devi peered over Pran's shoulder. The screen showed the corridor on Five.

And every single cabin door was wide open.

The Wildcard Blog
Fearlessly fighting the fraudulent so that you don't have to

Jan 02

Still no helicopters, rescue boats, nada.

Big news of the day: got attacked by Celine's bodyguard. Going to sue the shit out of The Predator and her monkey. She doesn't know who she's messing with. Guy just attacked, no warning, didn't have a chance to defend myself. Face feels like it's exploded.

Recovering in The Predator's cabin if you can believe that shit. Going to mine Maddie for every bit of info I can get.

Captain Useless sent a tender boat out this morning and we're all waiting for it to return with a fleet of rescue boats and helicopters. The reasons why we haven't been rescued are obvious: captain fucked up, got us lost and we're drifting where they don't expect us to be (and no, not the Bermuda Triangle); OR: something even bigger has happened on land and they can't get to us. A storm, maybe.

Maddie says I can sleep on the couch in The Predator's suite if things carry on like this.
Can I emphasise how much my face hurts? The nurse says my nose might be broken. Didn't bother going to Security. The cops can deal with it if we ever get the fuck home.
Here's today's rundown:

3 p.m. Had a nap (painkillers knocked me out).

4 p.m. Message from Damien: Predator doing another show. And there will be hotdogs available at the Lido buffet.

Went back to my cabin to get my spare battery. No sign of Paulo or Trining. Stinks down there, toilets still overflowing. Jesus. Heard a rumour there might be working bathrooms next to the spa. Went to look. Bad idea. Shit and paper boiling up out of the pan and all over the floor. Felt really sorry for the guys cleaning it up. Saw a perfectly coiled turd just sitting on the carpet outside the art gallery. WTF is wrong with people? Nearly puked.

6 p.m. Going stir crazy. Maddie not in the mood to talk. Won't leave as she's paranoid about getting sick. I'm heading out for a while.

10 p.m. Just got back to The Predator's cabin.

After I left here, I joined the singles group camped out in mini-golf land. People have now really formed into solid little groups. There's the bible group who pray all the time; the stoner group who smoke pot all the time; the Tranquillity group who stop people from entering their territory all the time. You get the idea. The singles group isn't too bad – at least they really look out for each other. Donna and Emma (the friend of the girl who died) have made sure they take turns to go for food and water runs.

At 9ish or so, Dane and Carl from 'my' group (BTW, they look exactly like their names suggest) came back from fetching their dope supply out of their cabin (Deck 5) looking spooked. Said they saw a woman and a kid staring at them and then the lights went out.
They looked genuinely rattled, convinced they'd seen ghosts.

Said I'd go check it out.

It wasn't pitch dark like they said – the emergency lights were on when I got there. Stank like death. All the doors were open on the deck, which I guess was supposed to look creepy. Had to hand it to Dane and Carl. Don't know how they pulled it off. They denied it of course.

Day Four

No ghosts, but ran into a security guard dude as I was leaving. He asked me if I'd seen anyone else down there. Said no. He was intense.

Nose is killing me so going to turn in.
Night.

DAY 7

The Witch's Assistant

Last night, alone in Celine's suite, Maddie had managed to convince herself she'd caught the virus. Her body broke out into a cold sweat, her guts churned and she couldn't stop herself from swallowing convulsively. Little by little she got herself under control. It was only the thought of having to use the red bag that snapped her out of it.

Celine still hadn't returned to the suite. Should she take her a change of clothes? No. Celine wasn't her bloody boss anymore. She had to stop thinking like that. It still burned that Celine was shutting her out. They'd been through so much together; they had a history. The fallout from the Kavanaugh show, made worse by the fact that Celine continued to insist to whoever would listen that Bobby and Lori Small had survived one of the four Black Thursday crashes. The stalker who'd showed up outside Celine's house every night for a week, begging her to put him in touch with the spirit of Johnny Carson. The journalist who'd taped one of Celine's readings and then debunked it, line by line, on YouTube. Those bloody awful romcoms. The endless, endless messages she'd answered from the Friends and the desperate on Facebook.

Three years she'd been loyal to her, and for what? No, that wasn't fair, Celine had offered her a way out of a bad situation. A way out of that shitty cocktail bar in Long Island, the only place that would hire her after Neil destroyed her life. Celine and her then PA, a pinched-faced girl who rarely spoke, came into the bar once a week or so, and Maddie had heard from the other staff that Celine was some sort of psychic, a Sylvia Brown type. She'd found Celine amusing, with her bouffant hair, long red nails and false eyelashes. Thought of her as the weird woman in a wheelchair. All sorts frequented the bar – corporate types looking for a fling; blue-collar workers; out-of-work musicians. But Celine stood out.

One night, while Maddie was wiping down the tables, Celine had grabbed Maddie's wrist, and said: 'Know this, it will get easier for you, my darling.'

Taken aback, Maddie snatched her hand away, but then, with no warning, and before she could stop them, the tears came. She'd sobbed, right there in the bar, while the punters ate chicken wings and downed tequila slammers. Celine instructed the PA to fetch Maddie some tissues from the bathroom, and then said: 'The girl's an idiot. No conversation. No charm. I need someone who can talk. Has some chutzpah about them. Someone I can trust.' Celine had pressed a card into her hand. 'Call me tomorrow.'

She'd googled Celine that evening. The books, the interviews. An old TV show, *Celine del Ray, Mindhunter*, which hadn't lasted more than one season. And Maddie had called her. Of course she had. Celine invited her to her house. Expecting either a shaggy colonial or a gleaming mansion, Maddie had been surprised to find herself parking next to an unremarkable suburban villa in East Meadow. Sitting at the counter in Celine's bland kitchen, Maddie had come clean. She told her all about her past; about Neil. About meeting him in a pub in Hackney (she'd thought it was love at first sight, and continued to cling to the idealised memory of the moment she'd first seen him even when it all turned to shit). About throwing in her job, moving to the States, the lavish wedding that was never paid off. About his endless money-making schemes that never went anywhere. About his investment firm, that wasn't a firm at all. About the day when she finally woke up and saw him for what he was. About her decision not to leave. About extracting the last of her sister's savings, mining her friends for cash, all with the promise of a payday that would never come. She told Celine about Neil skipping out just before the axe fell. The two years of probation she'd received for being an accessory.

Celine had listened, and then she'd offered Maddie the job, on condition that she sign a non-disclosure agreement. Celine had seen something in her. A lack of morality, perhaps. A desperation that she knew she could exploit. Maddie had almost quit several times in the first month. The sympathetic woman who'd listened to her that day in the kitchen had quickly morphed into a demanding autocrat. But she'd stuck it out.

More fool her.

She stood up and stretched. Xavier was fast asleep on the couch, his mouth open, his laptop on the floor next to him. The bruise above his nose was turning yellow. She almost hadn't let him in last night, but she hadn't wanted to be alone. And it felt good – reassuring – to have someone with her, even someone she hardly knew, and certainly didn't trust. She'd rummaged through his things earlier, unearthing nothing more incriminating than a driver's licence showing a photo of him with blond hair and an address in South Beach, Miami.

A beep, and then another bullshit message from Damien: 'G'day, ladies and gentlemen. It seems that bad weather at home port is delaying any rescue operation at this time . . .' She tuned him out. She could detect the insincerity in his voice. Celine had taught her that skill.

She needed to shower. Her skin was clammy after last night's panic attack, and she'd kill for some fresh gear. She could always ask Xavier to bring her suitcase up from the lower levels, although maybe that wasn't a great idea. The smell might have infested her clothes. He'd been down there last night, and when he returned to the suite, his shoes reeked of sewage. She'd made him put them out on the balcony.

She padded into the bathroom, shutting the door behind her.

She couldn't get her brain to accept it at first.

There was a woman in the bath.

There was a woman lying in the bath wearing a shift dress – a Gatsby-style dress – beaded with tiny white pearls. Her skin was as white as the dress, the pores clogged with dark matter, like black pinpricks.

'How did you get in here?' Had Celine given someone her key-card, perhaps? But no . . . After she'd let Xavier in, she'd drawn the security bolt across the door.

The woman opened her eyes wide – and God, oh God they were white as well – and bared her teeth. They were tiny, pointed and quite dark. She snapped them together with a clearly audible 'click' and then started humming, softly at first, then louder and louder until it was all that Maddie could hear.

A woman in 1920s garb, like Lizzie Bean, Celine's Lizzie Bean, Celine's roaring twenties cliché, was lying in her bath.

Maddie understood that she was having a nervous breakdown. She'd always wondered what one felt like, and now she knew. She reached for the door behind her, fumbled for the handle, and backed out. The humming stopped abruptly. Her whole body was shaking. A distant part of her mind noted that pure terror really was icy.

She ran over to the couch and shook Xavier's shoulder. He woke with a start, his mouth snapping shut.

'Xavier. There's someone in the bathroom.'

He sat up, took one look at her face and jumped to his feet. 'Huh? Someone's in here?'

'In the bathroom.'

'Who?'

She pushed him roughly towards it. Xavier gave her a look, walked over and flung open the door.

'It's empty.'

'What?'

'There's no one here, Maddie. C'mon. Take a look.'

Digging her nails into her palms, she peered past him. The bath really was empty. 'Look behind the shower curtain.'

He ripped it back. Nothing.

'She was there. Lying in the bathtub. A woman. A . . . a dead woman.' No one alive had skin that colour.

Xavier snorted. 'Are you fucking with me?'

'Do I look like I'm fucking with you? I know what I saw.'

'A dead woman in the tub? Like in *The Shining*?'

'It was . . . I think it was Lizzie Bean.'

'Huh?'

'You know, one of Celine's spirit guides.'

'Maddie . . . seriously. You hit your head or something?'

Hysteria surged, but she forced it down. 'Maybe Archie and Papa Noakes will show up too.'

'Who the fuck is Papa Noakes?'

Maddie hesitated, the old loyalty kicking in. But sod Celine. 'Spirit guide number three. He was around in the seventies and eighties.'

'So tell me about this . . . what's his name again?'

'Papa Noakes.'

'He's an ex-slave.'

He laughed. 'Oh Jesus. Really?'

'Listen . . . I know how it sounds, but I saw her, Xavier. I know what I saw. And you said people were seeing things on the lower decks.'

'I went down there, Maddie. It's just a bunch of guys fucking with everyone. All that was down there was a really, really bad smell.'

'But—'

'Listen, Maddie. You haven't been sleeping well. None of us have. You ever heard of lucid dreaming?'

'Don't patronise me.'

'I'm not. But what you're saying . . . what's the most logical explanation? That Celine's spirit guide was hanging out in the tub, or you had a nightmare that felt so real you were convinced you actually saw a ghost?'

'It was so *real*.'

'Maddie. Listen to me. It was only your imagination. You of all people should know this.'

'Maybe I should go and talk to Celine. Maybe . . . maybe she was sending me a message.'

'Hello? Earth to Maddie. You know she's a fraud. How can you even be saying this?'

Maddie paced, avoiding looking at the bathroom door. And hadn't Helen and Elise said they heard humming as well? Yeah. She was losing it. 'I just want to see her.'

'After what her henchman guy did to me?' Xavier looked almost childishly aggrieved.

'I just . . . I think I should talk to her. I'm not the only one who's—'

'Bad idea. Listen, I know what's going on here. You've been affected by the stress of what's going down and Celine's taking advantage of it. I'm talking about mass hysteria. Mass psychogenic illness. The only explanation for why people are seeing things is that Celine is feeding some kind of shared delusion.'

Maddie paced again. 'I know Celine. I know how she does what she does. It's all bullshit. But some of the things she was saying on the day after the ship stopped . . . she couldn't have known them.'

'And that other dude, Ray? He couldn't have told her? It's all cold reading, Maddie. People believe what they want to believe. People are scared. This whole situation is weird. They're flocking to someone who seems to know what they're doing.' He drew breath. 'She's taking advantage of the situation, Maddie. After all this is over, she wants to be seen as the big hero.'

'I want to talk to her.'

'Seriously, Maddie . . . You think her goon Ray will let you in to see her?'

'I can talk him round.'

'And then what?'

Yeah, then what? 'I don't know, Xavier, okay?' She risked a glance at the bathroom door. 'But whatever happens I've got to get out of this cabin.'

'Maddie, there's nowhere else to go. It's fucking awful out there.'

'There must be someone we could go. The gym, maybe. The spa.'

'Nope. Been there. It's a mess.'

'I don't care! I have to get out of here.'

Xavier assessed her for a couple of seconds. 'Okay, okay. If you want to see Celine, we have to play this carefully.'

'We?'

'Yeah. We.'

A wash of relief. She didn't trust him, but at least she wasn't alone. 'What do you suggest?'

'We can't just go in there all guns blazing.' He gingerly touched the top of his nose. 'I could do without getting whacked in the face again, it's not a good look for me. I'm thinking, how about we try and get to the crew area through one of the service doors?'

'You think we can?'

'We can try.'

While Xavier collected his shoes, she wrapped the scarf around her neck and pulled on her gloves. Xavier was probably right about her mind playing tricks on her. He had to be right. Fear did strange things to the brain.

But it had seemed so *real*.

They stepped into the corridor. She hadn't been out of the suite for hours; the least she could have done was check up on Helen and Elise again. She promised herself she'd do that later. Maybe. Xavier attempted to open Althea's service door, but it was tightly sealed. 'No go. Hey . . . maybe we can try down on my deck.'

'Doesn't it stink down there?'

'Yeah. Bad. But that means there won't be any crew down there to stop us. When I was down there last night the place was deserted. Well, I saw a security guy, but he didn't stick around.'

'Okay.'

A man and a woman were lying snoozing on a naked mattress outside the elevators, crusty plates and soda cups littered around them. God. At least she hadn't had to go through that. She followed Xavier down the stairs and onto the Promenade Dreamz deck, gagging as the smell of vomit wafted her way.

Talk. Speak, take your mind off it. 'What's with your obsession with Celine, Xavier? Do you have some kind of personal history with her or something?'

He gave her a half-smile. 'No. I just don't like what she does. I don't like what she did to Lillian Small.'

'Yeah. That was . . . That wasn't like Celine, either. She usually stays away from anything that can be proven.'

'So what was her motive for that, you think?'

She shrugged. 'Publicity, maybe. Notoriety. Perhaps she just wanted to be part of the whole Black Thursday circus.'

'Figures. By the way, it isn't just Celine. I don't like what any of them do. Vultures. Predators. Telling the parents of missing children their kids are still alive. It gets to me.'

'How did it start? Your interest in all this, I mean.'

He hesitated. 'I wanted to be a magician when I was a kid.'

'Really?'

'Really.' He grinned self-consciously. 'Didn't have the patience. But I got into Ouija boards, messed about with the arcane. You know. A stage. And I saw how easy it is to fool people.'

They'd now reached Deck Six. The smell of mildewed carpet coated her nostrils. 'So what do you do for cash?'

'I have my blog.'

'Yeah, no offence, but I'm guessing that doesn't keep you in champagne and caviar.'

'My grandfather left me some money.'

'You're a trust-fund kid?' No wonder he had so much time to devote to chasing down Celine.

'I hate that word.'

'You're rich?'

'I'm not rich. I've got enough to live on.'

The smell on Deck Five's landing was just as bad as she'd expected, and the entrances to the passageways housing the cabins were hidden in darkness. She hesitated on the bottom step. She hadn't realised just how dark the interior of the ship could get. A velvety blackness – no, that was bullshit. There was nothing soft about it.

'Wait here. I'll go see if any of the doors are unsecured.'

'How are you going to see down there?'

He grinned and held up a mini flashlight attached to a keychain. 'I've got it covered.'

Gripping the railing with a gloved hand, she watched as he was swallowed up by the shadows. The fear was dissipating; she couldn't maintain it.

A spirit guide come to life. Ridiculous. Now she was out of the suite, had some distance, she could see that. She was even becoming used to the shitty smell down here. The light came darting back towards her. 'We're all set. There's one open down here.'

She followed him down the passageway, keeping her eyes on the beam of the torch and holding a hand over her mouth. And God, the carpet was wet, squishy. Her feet seemed to sink right into it, as if the ship was trying to inhale her. Xavier held the door open for her, and she stepped through, crossing a small landing and moving down towards a narrow stairwell. She moved aside to let Xavier squeeze past. Grubby white walls hemmed them in; the fluorescent emergency lights on the ceiling flickered. It was a different world from the passenger areas: utilitarian, stripped back to the ship's skeleton, and the air felt twice as heavy.

Xavier stopped abruptly, and she almost crashed into his back. Footsteps were clumping towards them. A small Filipino man was running up the stairs, halting when he spotted them. 'You shouldn't be down here. No passengers down here.'

'We need help,' Xavier said.

'You need a doctor? You must go back.'

Maddie peered around Xavier to read his name tag: Angelo.

'Not a doctor. We need to get to the stage. The Dare to Dream Theatre?'

The man frowned. 'Why not just go around the front?'

'We have . . . reasons.'

'It is that woman? Mrs del Rio?'

'Del Ray. Yeah.'

'You know her?' Maddie asked.

'No. But I know about her. How does she do what she does? A trick?'

'Yes,' Xavier said.

'So why is it you want to see her?'

'Tell you what, if you show us how to get there, I'll make it worth your while.'

'How much?'

Xavier took out a hundred-dollar bill, and the guy made it disappear. 'I will show you. But if we see any security, then you are to say that I didn't try to help you.'

'Thank you. We will. We won't get you into trouble, I promise.'

The man backtracked, and waved at them to follow him down

another two flights of stairs. He ushered them through a heavy metal door, and they emerged into a low-ceilinged corridor that stank of paint, cigarette smoke and worse. The floor was scuffed, the red paint worn down.

She jumped at the sound of voices. Angelo was striding ahead, and she and Xavier had to jog to keep up with him. The air was becoming hotter; her whole body was slick with sweat. The slam of metal against metal, a clatter. They passed several small tiled rooms. In one, two surly-faced men wearing plastic gloves were slicing green peppers, discarding the slimy pieces. They glanced at her with little interest.

'How much food is left?' Xavier asked Angelo.

A shrug. 'Some of the fridges are still cold. There is cereal. Stuff that was frozen. We need the electricity to cook, but there are some hotplates we can use.'

They whipped through another passageway, and now she was completely disorientated. The air wasn't getting deep enough into her lungs.

Oh God.

She couldn't breathe.

Angelo opened another white metal door and pushed them into a wider, featureless conduit that appeared to stretch on forever.

Angelo pointed to the left. 'So what you must do is to—'

Their guide froze. And then he ran.

A stocky figure was stalking towards them, barking into a radio. 'Stop!'

'Oh shit,' Xavier muttered as a security guard, his hand on the baton at his belt, approached at speed.

'You can't be down here. How did you get down here?'

'I'm sorry,' Maddie tried. 'We got lost.'

The man – Ram, according to his name badge – had the darkest, hardest eyes she'd ever seen. 'How did you get down here?'

'Chill out,' Xavier said. 'We were just—'

'You cannot be down here.'

'Look. You guys aren't telling us anything. We have a right to know—'

'If you do not lower your voice, I will be forced to subdue you.' Xavier clamped his mouth shut. It was clear that Ram meant every word. 'I will escort you out of here. If you are found here again I will make sure you are locked in your cabins.'

He motioned harshly for them to walk ahead of him.

'Shit,' Xavier muttered.

They weaved through another series of passageways, up another narrow metal staircase, and then the man flung open a door and pushed them through it. Maddie got her bearings: they were on the Promenade Dreamz deck. The air smelled like a fresh meadow after the depths of the ship.

Ram slammed the door behind them.

'Now what?' Maddie pulled off her gloves and wiped her hands on her jeans.

'We could go up onto the exercise deck, I know some people there.'

She thought about it, remembering the woman in the Lido buffet queue, the crowds pushing and shoving. People pissing over the side. No. She couldn't bear it. They wandered past the casino, where a small group of people had set up a mini corral of mattresses next to the slot machines. A woman with a stricken face and clutching a bucket was making for the blackened doors of the dining room. They rounded the atrium, and Maddie could make out the entrance to the theatre. Ray was at his usual post, and he stood aside to let a small man with black hair styled in a quiff and a woman in a steward's uniform enter. With a jolt, Maddie recognised Althea. And she realised that the man with her was one of the assistant cruise directors. She'd liaised with him a few times about the technical details of Celine's performances. She'd been charmed by his cheerful demeanour.

'Don't go there, Maddie,' Xavier said.

'I have to know, Xavier.'

'Know what?'

'Why Celine's cutting me out. Why she's . . .'

'Let's get out of here, Maddie. Go back up to Celine's suite.'

She couldn't. She couldn't go back there. The tune Lizzie Bean had been humming drifted through her mind. She shivered. 'Wait here.'

Ray gave her a broad grin as she walked up to him. 'Hey, Maddie. Round two? Or you gonna try to bribe me with something else?' Then his expression changed, became serious, and he leaned towards her, taking her off guard. 'Listen, you're better off, trust me. You don't want to be part of this scene. They're treating her like Jesus fucking Christ.' His eyes locked on something over her shoulder and his face shut down.

Maddie turned to see Jacob walking towards them, a bottle of cleaning spray tucked under an arm. The purple surgical gloves he was wearing matched his bow tie.

He gave her a smile that appeared to be genuine. 'Maddie! I haven't seen you for ages. I hope you've finally decided to join us.'

Jacob's eyes flicked over to Xavier, who was leaning against a pillar at a safe distance from Ray. Maddie had no clue whether Jacob recognised him from the New Year's Eve reading. It was likely. Xavier's old-school hipster look didn't exactly help him blend into the ship's crowd.

'Jacob. Listen . . . has Celine said anything about me to you?'

'No. Why would she?'

'Do you know why she doesn't want to see me?'

'We're welcoming everyone, Maddie. We all have to stick together.' He leaned forward conspiratorially. 'Celine says it won't be long now. We'll be out of this mess very soon. And about time.' He snapped off his gloves. 'Just between the two of us, I'm getting heartily sick of tomato sandwiches and baloney.'

'How are the others? The other Friends, I mean.'

'We're all doing wonderfully. It's been such a tonic being able to share Celine's gift with so many. Some of the crew are joining us now, Maddie. They've been working so hard on the ship and we're doing all we can to put their minds at ease. Spirit will take care of us.'

Jesus. She glanced at Ray, but he was staring off into the distance. 'Listen . . . Jacob, I owe you an apology.'

'An apology for what?'

'I told Celine about your sister.' Maddie fished for her name, came up empty. 'You remember? You told me all about her at the meet 'n' greet. Celine uses information like that, spins it to make you believe that she's talking to the dead. It's a con.'

Jacob gave her a sad smile. 'You'll come round, Maddie.' Shaking his head, he walked off to the entrance to the theatre. Maddie tried to catch Ray's eye again, but he was clearly avoiding looking in her direction.

'Well?' Xavier asked when she re-joined him.

She shook her head.

'Back to the suite?'

'Yeah.' Xavier was right. There was nowhere else to go.

The Condemned Man

He'd made himself a nest in a shadowy area under the overhang, near to the towel station. After he'd fallen yesterday, someone had given him a couple of tablets and a bottle of water, and Gary had spent much of the night and the morning drifting in and out of consciousness. He hadn't wanted to take the tablets or drink the water, but Marilyn insisted. The curious cloud that kept the black thoughts at bay was slowly clearing. He didn't want it to go. There were things he'd rather not think about waiting on the other side of it. He still felt weak, and the whole of his body ached, but the physical pain helped keep his mind from latching onto the dark thoughts. And he kept having strange, hyper-real dreams. Last night he'd dreamt he'd woken to see Marilyn – he was sure it was Marilyn – naked and shrieking, her arms around someone in the Jacuzzi.

He scrunched his knees to his chest and wrapped his arms around his head. Time went smoother if he slept.

When he woke, his friend from the medical bay, the big black man in the shabby dungarees, was leaning against the railings. He grinned at Gary, then pressed a finger to his lips. *Shhhh, don't tell.*

I won't, Gary mouthed back at him.

Don't tell what?

A hot stone in his gut.

Of course.

The girl. His girl. Did the man know what he'd done?

How could he?

A whisper of fear tickled over his skin. And the fear was real. Something else had happened. Something that had caused him to end up in the infirmary, but it was slippery, and he couldn't get hold of it.

Good. He didn't want to get hold of it. Let it swim away. Swim, swim.

A shadow loomed over him and he looked up to see Mason looking down at him. 'How are you today, buddy?'

'Okay.'

'Yeah? You don't look okay. Saw you talking to yourself.' Mason leaned closer. 'You lose it down here again, I'll throw you off the fucking side, hear me?'

Gary swallowed. 'I'm fine. I'm not sick. Nothing happened to me. I'm fine.' His mouth felt as if he'd been drinking a bottle of glue; gummy and foul.

'Good. Then you can pull your weight. Go line up for food. We all gotta take turns.'

Marilyn skittered up to join them, a pink hat slouched on her head. Fingers prodded in his mind. He remembered that hat, that hat was—

No.

'Gary. You're awake.'

Mason folded his arms and flexed the muscled on his forearms. 'Gary's gonna help us out today.'

'Oh good.'

'I don't like your hat,' Gary whispered to Marilyn.

Marilyn laughed. 'What? You were with me when I bought it, Gary.' Gary saw her fingers stray to Mason's shoulder, then stop, mid-stroke. 'You remembered anything else about that morning before they took you to the medical room, hon?'

'No.'

Mason sniffed. 'Selective memory. Seen it before.' He tapped his head.

'Sandy says you should take these.' Marilyn handed him two blue tablets. 'Good of her, as she doesn't have many left. They helped you last night, hon. You were' – she shared a glance with Mason – 'not yourself.'

Gary shook his head. 'Don't want to.'

'It'll help you, hon. You had a bad experience. C'mon. Do it for me?'

He placed them on his tongue and sloshed warm water in his mouth, trying not to gag. But he couldn't get them down, they got stuck in his throat, and he had to spit them into his palm – Mason staring at him in disgust – and try again. He managed it the second time.

'Well, go on, buddy,' Mason said, clapping him on the shoulder. 'Time to get to work.'

Gary hauled himself to his feet, looking past Marilyn to see if his friend was still there. He wasn't.

Mason pushed him up the stairs. 'Make sure you get a big portion. Don't let them railroad you.'

The two men stationed at the top of the stairs stood aside to let him pass. At first everything was just a blur of noise and faces and the smell of chlorine and other, nastier things. A crowd was gathered around the buffet area. Three men in dirty chef's whites, their faces hard masks, were sweating behind the counter.

'Back of the line,' a face loomed into his.

'Okay.'

He turned and trotted back. The line stretched all the way to the pool. Some of the people in the queue were laughing with each other, but most wore grumpy clouds above their heads. As he reached the end, he stepped in a puddle of water and skidded, but he managed to right himself. He could do this. It was easy.

He looked into the green water, trying to make out his reflection. Two plastic bottles bobbed next to a red bag. They looked happy together. The woman in front of him turned and smiled. Her sun-glassed eyes made her look like a bug. 'Baloney again. But it's not all bad. Heard they were sending a ship to restock us today. That's gotta be good, right?'

Blah blah blah. The sun on his head. He should have a hat. His cap . . . he had a cap but he couldn't remember what he'd done with it. Fuzzy wuzzy.

A shriek behind him, and he turned to see a man falling in slow motion into the pool, scattering the plastic threesome. The man jumped up and shook his head. He was laughing. 'Fuck you!' he shouted.

Then Gary saw him. His friend. He was standing next to the glass doors that led into the inside of the ship. Gary waited for him to beckon him over, but he didn't.

Shuffle shuffle. The line inched forward, the insect woman had given up talking to him. Good. The air wavered. He zoned out, felt a prod in his back. A gap had opened up between him and the insect lady. He caught up to her.

Then, shouting. The lady in front of him moved back, the whole line rippled and fractured. Gary stepped to one side to see what was going on. A couple of men were wrestling with each other next to the raised stage. Pulling and pushing and grunting. Some people in the line were staring, some were cheering. Another man in a blue shirt tried to pull them apart. Two men in white shirts and black trousers were running towards them. A squeeze of panic. Uh-oh. Security. The uniforms. He remembered them. Time slowed down, sound disappeared. One of the security men nudged the other and pointed at him.

Gary felt all the strength, what little he had, draining away. *Gogogogogogogogogo.*

His friend. He had to get to his friend. He ducked and ran, shoving through the people queueing behind him, fighting his way through the line.

He reached the doors and pushed, falling, almost falling.

'Stop!' someone shouted.

But Gary didn't stop. His friend was at the top of the main staircase, smiling and beckoning. Gary zipped across to join him. Then, down and down – his friend would show him the way. Round a corner, into the bottom of the atrium. His friend was gone again. He looked up at the glass elevator cubes frozen above his head. Which way now?

He whirled. There! His friend was standing next to a golden pillar, a row of dark doors behind him. Gary knew that place. Marilyn had taken him there once. The theatre. He blinked. His friend was gone.

Gary paused. Was he supposed to go in there?

'Yo. You coming in or what?'

A big man, with the same empty eyes as Mason, was staring at him. Gary didn't remember walking up the stairs that led to the doors.

'Yes.'

'Got any concealed weapons on you?'

'No.'

'Hey, chill. I'm kidding. Barefoot huh?'

Gary looked down. He hadn't noticed that his feet were bare and covered in nicks. His big toenail was almost ripped off. How had that happened? 'Yes.'

The man hooted. 'You're going to fit right in, my man.' He opened the door, and waved Gary inside.

Dark. Lights at the front on the stage though. A woman was speaking, her voice booming. He didn't listen to her words: he couldn't hear them, the blood was still pounding in his ears. Disorientated, he ran down the aisle steps and then back up again. At a loss, he made his way to a stool on the back row. The woman next to him turned and smiled. 'Welcome,' she whispered.

Gary dug his fingers into his palms. Shut his eyes.

A sound, like rain. No. Applause. The people around him were clapping. The woman's voice was speaking again: '. . . going to be panic. There is going to be chaos. I want all of you who are here with me to know that I will take care of you.'

He shouldn't be in here. Every instinct was yelling at him to get out. But his friend had shown him. And now, what he thought of as his real self was slipping back in, chipping away at the lovely woollen warmth he'd cultivated. No. He wouldn't let it. He didn't want to remember.

The girl. His girl.

'As usual, I'd like to say a big welcome to our new faces. It will seem strange at first to you, so just imagine how it was for me the first time I heard Spirit coming through!'

The people around him laughed. Someone handed him a banana. It was squishy and the skin was half-black, but he ate it anyway. He sat back in his seat. Better. He felt better. Calmer. He let the woman's words wash over him again, and then began to listen. She was telling a story about a cat she had once had called Francine, and how it could also sense spirits. 'All animals are spiritual beings. The ability to do so is inside all of us.' Gary wasn't a fan of animals, especially cats. Marilyn had wanted one, years ago, but he'd said no. All animals did was leech off you. What did they give back? '. . . even animals know that. Death is not the end, people. You never really die. We all just go round and round. Into the spiritual realm and out again. Know this, there's nothing but the finest layer of vibration between realms. Light and energy, my friends. That's all we are. And some of us have the ability to choose how we want to . . . Wait . . . my guides are coming through.' Gary felt a ripple of anticipation rush through the audience around him. He didn't like it. '. . . telling me something . . . A woman is stepping forward. She's a young woman. Oh. She passed over recently. Very recently. She's still bewildered. Hold on . . . she's asking for . . . her name. I'm getting a K. Does that mean anything to anyone? Died very recently. In fact . . . I'm getting that she died on this very ship.'

Someone shrieked. 'It's Kelly! Oh my God.'

Gary craned his neck. In one of the lower rows, a woman had leapt to her feet.

The woman on stage touched her throat. 'I'm getting . . . She's . . . she's finding it hard to breathe. She's choking. Choking. And sorrow. So much sorrow. So much pain. So much loneliness. She's a restless spirit, I'm afraid, my love.'

His bowels cramped. His scalp prickled. *Get out.*

'Her mum . . . does she want to say anything to—'

'Sorry to interrupt you, my darling, but she's got a message for the person who was with her when she died. She's saying that—'

Get out get out get out get out.

Cold, cold, fear. It filled every vein, every artery – it pulsed through him. He threw himself out of the seat, and hobbled up the aisle. He didn't want to hear it, he didn't want to hear it.

The Devil's Handmaiden

The man almost knocked her over as he ran out of the door, his elbow bashing into her side.

A large woman with a broad kind face hurried over to her. 'Honey, you okay?' she stage-whispered. Althea retrieved the box of Wet-Wipes the man had knocked out of her hands as he'd hurled his body past her. 'I am fine. Thank you.'

'Sometimes it can be too much for people.'

What the woman said was true. Not everyone liked what Mrs del Ray had to say. Right now she was saying something about healing and coming to terms with the 'demise of the physical body'.

'But we got to stick together, am I right?' the large woman was going on. All the people here were loco. Out of their minds.

'Yes.' Althea gave her a professional smile.

The woman patted her arm and went back down the aisle. Althea took the box over to a booth in the far corner. Pepe had done well. There were now several salamis, a box of American cheese slices and a crate of fresh tomatoes, peppers and bananas. She'd heard from him that the head chef had deserted his post, and the sous chefs were left to ration out what remained. There couldn't be much food left. Soon they would be fishing off the side. She hoped it wouldn't come to that. The water surrounding the ship was disgusting.

She helped herself to a bottle of water and a slice of baloney and leaned against the table. The theatre, which was on two levels, wasn't completely full, but it wouldn't be long until it was. Most of the people here had decided not to return to their cabins, and were making themselves nests out of duvets and pillows. Some of the staff were doing the same.

It had been easier than she thought it would be. It couldn't have been easier, in fact. Celine had asked her to bring crew members to the Dare to Dream Theatre 'to join the gang', and no one she'd spoken to so far had refused. And why would they? It was comfortable, it didn't stink. Celine's group of elderly men and women were making sure that the bathrooms just outside the upper level were kept clean. They even had a system for disposing of the bags. All Celine asked was that the staff help collect supplies and water from the kitchen. Paulo and Pepe had been her first targets. They'd been reluctant only because they were afraid they would be disciplined for straying into the passenger areas, but Althea hadn't had to spend too long convincing them. Security was too busy dealing with the mob on the main deck to worry about a few stewards leaving their posts. And they were helping keep the guests happy, weren't they?

And the news had spread. They were safe here. There was no Lady in White. No devils, no girls trying to crawl out of morgue bags. No angry passengers abusing them. Angelo had been more sceptical, but she'd expected that. She'd assured him that Mrs del Ray would pay well for anything he could do to help, and she knew that he would go where the money was.

She left to check on Mirasol, who was supposed to be disinfecting the two bathrooms just outside the theatre. As Althea feared, she was giggling with Ray, one of the men who guarded the entrance. At least she could see straight through Angelo. She was wary of Ray. He hadn't bothered her, but she didn't like the way his eyes followed some of the women. He reminded her of Joshua.

'Mirasol,' she snapped, making Mirasol start guiltily. Althea noted with distaste that her shirt was stained. Althea had made an effort to maintain her appearance. The water was sporadic, but she had no problem washing out of a bucket, and her smock – unlike those of many she'd seen – was still neat and clean. 'Please tell Paulo that we will need to bring more water up here.'

'Yes, Althea.' Mirasol scurried away.

Ray took a sip out of the flask he kept in his back pocket and stared at Althea. She stared right back at him. Perhaps she should tell Mrs del Ray about his drinking. There was no point. She already knew. She knew everything.

'You got a problem?' he asked.

'No.' Lies. She had many problems, and the biggest one was in her belly. 'Do you?'

He snorted. 'Crazy lady.' Althea couldn't tell if he meant her or Mrs del Ray. She sensed that he didn't buy into Mrs del Ray's act. She could almost respect him for this. Althea shoved past him and strolled down the aisle, looking for Rogelio. She was curious to see how he was reacting to Mrs del Ray's performance. She'd snagged him in the mess canteen this morning. She could see he was broken. Distracted, worried. She now realised that she'd been wrong about him, and his cheerful exterior was in fact nothing but a mask. She could see he wanted someone to talk to, and she knew how to listen. Years of dealing with the fuck-darned cone-heads had taught her that skill.

She spotted him in the front row, sitting in between Annabeth and Jimmy, two of the seniors who made up what she thought of as Mrs Del Ray's core group.

Mrs del Ray creaked closer to the front of the stage. 'So many secrets in here. So much sadness and unresolved issues. Know this, those of you who are here, who have had the bravery and foresight to join us will be rewarded . . .'

Althea had no idea where Mrs del Ray got all her energy from. Althea had never once seen her sleep. Or, for that matter, use the bathroom. 'My guides are letting me know that someone wants to come through. A small woman is stepping forward. Dark hair. Long dark hair. I'm getting that she's proud of her hair. And . . . wait. She's touching her forehead. Does she have a scar on her forehead, perhaps? Does that mean anything to anyone? Don't be shy.'

Althea watched as Rogelio stood up. Strange, because she had not told Mrs del Ray about a scar, only that Rogelio had lost his mother and was supporting his brothers and sisters. But the woman was clever, and Althea suspected she was not the only one who had been sent out fishing.

'I'm getting . . . she says that there's a cloud in her stomach. I'm thinking it might be cancer.'

'You are sure it is her?' Rogelio said. 'My mother did not speak English.'

Althea hid a smile behind her hand.

'We all speak the same language when we've passed over, my darling,' Mrs del Ray said with a tinge of irritation. 'I'm sensing it was a long illness.'

'Yes.'

'My darling, I know how hard it must have been for you. Know this, your mother wants you to know that she's right here with you, right now, and will always be with you. Know this, your mother forgives you and understands the life decisions you have made.'

Rogelio covered his face with his hands. '*Inay*. Mama.'

He sat down and Jimmy and Annabeth fawned over him.

Now would be a good time to go. She must check on the boy. See if he was waiting for her in her cabin. He'd curled up with her again last night like a cat. It had been comforting. But perhaps first she should go and see Maria. Just because Mrs del Ray had recruited her, Althea had no intention of abandoning her post all together. That would be short-sighted. When help did arrive, when the storm on shore was over, she would be among the few who had done their jobs. She had even delivered fresh bags and water this morning, leaving them outside the staterooms, although she'd allowed herself to ignore the waste bags dumped in the corridor. She would find time to do her station properly later. Except for the Linemans. They were on their own. Whatever she did for them they would be ungrateful. They could rot.

Another twinge in her stomach. She hadn't felt sick, but now she was certain she was pregnant. She could feel it. Sense it. But they couldn't fire her if she had been diligent, could they? If she was one of the few who had stayed strong. And if they did, she had a back-up plan. She had also proven herself to Mrs del Ray. Perhaps she would agree to take her on as her assistant. Althea hadn't seen Maddie anywhere in the theatre, so perhaps she'd quit or been fired. That would be a good job to have; it might even lead to her getting a green card, getting out of Joshua's clutches once and for all. She didn't trust the old woman, but Mrs del Ray was just taking advantage of the situation for her own reasons.

She crept through the side door that opened out into the wings, and padded past the black curtains. The backstage technician – Althea didn't know his name – was snoozing, his head resting on a hand. Mrs del Ray's muffled voice drifted through the fabric.

Althea hurried to the I-95 and along to Maria's office. She knocked on the door. No answer. She tried the handle. It was unlocked, and with a quick look around to make sure no one was watching her, she slipped inside. Althea had never been in here unsupervised before. She crept over to the desk and tried the drawers, but they were locked. The rest of the crew decks were below the waterline, but this office was light and airy. She peered through the window and out over the water. They were still drifting, the ship dragging the oil slick of filthy red plastic bags in its wake, like a bride with a bloody wedding dress. Like her. Her wedding had been a grand affair. Her mother had borrowed money for it. Stupid. A waste.

She jumped as the door opened and Maria walked in, dressed in tracksuit bottoms and a stretched T-shirt.

'What are you doing here, Althea?'

'I was looking for you.'

The woman swayed and seemed to have trouble focusing. Drunk. Another sign of weakness. Maria weaved over to the desk, flopped into the visitor's chair and dug a crumpled packet of cigarettes out of her tracksuit pocket. Smoking was banned on the ships. Perhaps she would get fired. Maria lit it and blew the smoke out of the corner of her mouth. Althea tried not to breathe in. Joshua smoked; she hoped one day that it would kill him.

'I have done my station, Maria.'

'Good for you.' Maria coughed. Still no eyebrows and her hair was striped with grease. 'That what you wanted to tell me? That you are a good little worker?'

'I have not abandoned my station.'

'Then you are stupider than you look.'

Althea was hit with the tingling sensation she always got in her chest just before she and Joshua had a fight. 'I am doing my job.'

'There is no job anymore, Althea.'

'You are firing me?'

Maria laughed through the smoke. 'No. That isn't what I meant. I meant that there is no point you doing your job.'

'Why?'

'Why do you think? You are not stupid, Althea.' She waved her cigarette in the air. 'The ship. It's fucked.'

'Is there any news?'

'News about what?'

'The ship. The storm on shore. Rescue. The radio.'

'No.' She was lying. Althea could see she was lying.

Althea smiled sweetly. 'Can't you ask your boyfriend? Is he not one of the officers?' Those officers worked their way through the women. Only the ones dumb enough to think it would benefit them bothered sleeping with them.

A flash of anger – a spark of the old Maria – then: 'There is no outside communication. No ships. No planes in the sky.' Maria dragged in another cloud and coughed. 'Something has happened to the world.'

Althea had heard this theory as well. Like what? The world could not fall apart in four days. Perhaps she should bring Maria to Mrs del Ray. But no. She wasn't sure she could be bothered and she wanted to find the boy. 'I must go and check on my station.' She moved out from behind the desk, making for the door.

'Althea . . . wait.'

'Yes?'

'Be ready.'

'Ready for what?'

'Just be ready.'

Althea nodded. She was always ready.

She left the office and headed down to the entrance to the crew deck. Trining was leaning against the wall outside her cabin. *Shitballs.* She was not in the mood for more conversation.

'You are feeling better, Trining?'

'I am still sick. Althea, I heard you talking to yourself last night.'

'So?'

Trining coughed. It sounded fake to Althea. 'That woman is the devil. I've heard what she can do.'

'What woman?'

'The woman in the theatre, Angelo says that—'

'He knows nothing.' *Fuck-darned Angelo.* 'It's better there than down here. No one is sick.'

'Be careful, Althea.' Trining turned away from her.

Althea shrugged. Perhaps Trining was right. Perhaps Celine was the devil. It was one explanation. She didn't care. Althea left her and went to see if the boy was waiting for her in her cabin.

The Suicide Sisters

Helen couldn't see the woman's face, she was on her hands and knees on the other bed, her hair hanging in her eyes, her fingers gripping the pillow. But Jaco was looking straight at her. Thrusting and smiling. Thrusting and smiling. She turned her head away.

She heard him laugh.

Elise was burning up, she could feel the heat radiating through her nightdress. Helen prayed she was sleeping and wouldn't wake up while this sickening display was going on.

Jaco was now making grunting sounds and the girl was screeching along in time.

She could do it now, jump off the bed and bash him over the head with her laptop. Thwack. Slam it into the bastard's jaw with a satisfying crack. She'd thought about it many times. But they were stronger than she was, they would overpower her in no time. And she'd been agonising for hours about whether or not to leave the suite to go for help. She didn't dare leave Elise alone with them. They might barricade themselves in, and what if she couldn't find anyone to help? The situation outside had to be getting more desperate.

Trapped in her own cabin. A prison.

But what else could she do? Elise wasn't strong enough to be moved. Last night, Helen had tried to help her to the bathroom, but Elise had barely made it off the bed before her legs collapsed under her. Jaco and Lulia had reluctantly helped Helen heft her upright, but they'd been rough and she didn't want to risk that happening again.

She hated them. She loathed them with an intensity she didn't know she had in her.

They'd been smart. Fooled her. She'd been grateful to them at first. Yes! Grateful. Jaco had gone down to the crew mess to bring her a sandwich and extra bottles of water, saving her from having to leave Elise alone and queue at the Lido buffet. Lulia had cleaned the shower and bathroom and although Helen had quickly tired of her blow-by-blow run-down of every show she'd ever been in, she'd appreciated the help. It had been hard looking after Elise alone; exhausting. And it had been cathartic discussing the possible reasons why help had not arrived yet. Jaco was adamant that there was a storm raging at port and the coastguard was unable to send out rescue tugs; Lulia had heard that the ship had drifted out of commercial waters and it would only be a matter of time before they were picked up by another vessel's radar. Lulia had even promised to watch over Elise while Helen slept. Reluctant at first, Helen had given in. She'd slept for hours, a deep dreamless sleep. It was after she'd woken that things had started to turn sour. While she was sleeping, Jaco and Lulia had helped themselves to the two bottles of champagne Elise and Helen had brought on board. The champagne they'd meant to drink just before they threw themselves over the ship's stern.

Helen had said something along the line of: 'at least you could have asked', and in a flat venomous voice, Jaco responded: 'I could kick you out right now, you old bitch.' It had been as shocking and sudden as a slap in the face.

Helen had told him to leave.

He'd told her to 'make him leave'.

Helen had turned to Lulia for support, but she'd laughed.

She'd given up trying to plead with them. She was eloquent, she could talk her way out of anything, but it was obvious they weren't going to budge, and they were drunk. She'd moved onto Elise's bed to be closer to her, deciding that if they attempted to throw her friend out of the room she would fight them to the death. And she reckoned they'd seen that resolve on her face. She'd prayed that Althea or Maddie or the doctor would show up. All morning she'd been on tenterhooks in case there was a knock at the door. Jaco had put the 'don't disturb' sign on the door, so that might explain it, but she was still furious at them too for allowing this to happen. Why had no one come to check on them? Her friend was dying. She knew that. Elise was dying and she deserved to die in peace and with dignity, not stuck in a room with two thugs. She'd thought about telling them that there was little they could do to her that would make any difference. She'd been the lowest you could get. She'd faced death full on and won, but that was a lie. She'd never actually taken the tablets, or climbed over the railings on the Tranquillity deck. She'd read somewhere that the few people who'd jumped off the Golden Gate Bridge and survived, regretted their decision to jump mid-fall.

'Urguuuuuuuuurgh.' Jaco finished. 'Hey, Helen. Enjoy the show?'

Lulia laughed.

'Hey, Helen. I'm talking to you.'

Despite herself, she turned to look at him. He was wiping himself on the sheet, preening and smirking at her. He didn't have a good body in her opinion. Graham was the only man she'd ever slept with, but they'd once been to a nudist beach, where all kinds of comparisons were on show. Jaco's stomach was too round, his legs too thin. He stomped off to the bathroom, and she tried to block out the trickling sound of him relieving himself.

You've got squatters, girl, she heard Graham say, clear as day.

It was so unexpected, it made her laugh.

'What is funny?' Lulia snapped. 'Are you laughing at me?'

'No.'

'I think now you must leave here. The old lady, she will die anyway, yes?'

'Lulia, you know Elise can't be moved.'

'I do not want her to be pissing and shitting in here again.'

'That won't happen.'

'If it does, then I will—' Lulia clamped her mouth shut. Her eyes widened and she let out a little yipping noise, not dissimilar to the sounds she was making just minutes ago. Helen followed her gaze. A man, a tall man, was standing in the corner of the room, next to the television, his face in shadow, wringing his hands. Helen couldn't tell if he was doing this in consternation or in a threatening manner. She found that she didn't care.

And she found that she wasn't afraid.

'Jaco!' Lulia screeched, the raw terror in her voice filling Helen with glee. Good, she thought. Good.

Jaco bolted out of the bathroom, his penis flapping ridiculously. 'What?'

'Look!' She pointed at the dark figure.

Jaco jumped. 'Yah!' It was almost comical. 'How the fuck did he get in here?'

The man stepped forward.

'Helen,' Elise whispered, and Helen's heart leapt – she was speaking. Thank God. 'Humming. You hear it?'

'No.' But then she could. It was the same tune they'd heard before. The tune they'd heard in Celine's bathroom when they sat with her on the night the ship stopped moving.

The closet creaked open. A throaty giggle.

'Did you let him in?' Jaco was saying to Lulia. 'Well, did you?'

'No.'

The man with no face shuffled forward another step.

'I am not staying in here!' Lulia shrieked. 'Jaco—'

Something the size of a large dog scrabbled over the carpet towards Lulia.

'Helen,' Elise whispered. 'Helen.'

Helen turned away from what was happening in the room, hugged Elise to her and buried her face in her hair. She really was burning up; a spicy sweat blasted off her skin.

Lulia was sobbing now, and she was muttering something in her own language.

Someone screamed – Helen hoped it was Jaco, and then he said: 'We're going! We're going, okay?'

Thump, thump.

The door slammed.

The humming stopped, and only then did Helen look up.

The room was empty.

The Angel of Mercy

He'd thrown in the towel after the passenger tried to smack him across the face.

The morning had been a non-stop conveyor belt of scared passengers shouting at him to fix their girlfriends/husbands/wives. All had stories of the injustices they'd experienced; all were going to sue. Among other things, he'd dealt with a broken hand that would probably need surgery in the future; a food allergy (thank you, EpiPen); a woman with stomach pains who thought she might be having a miscarriage (all she was incubating was the beginnings of the noro); a thirtyish man with chest pains, convinced he was going to die (a severe panic attack). All of them were terrified, all of them were angry. All of them seemed to hold Jesse personally responsible for the ship's predicament. Damien's latest message was a version of the 'storm on land' bullshit that the captain had spouted. This didn't reassure the passengers he'd encountered. If anything, it made it worse.

'Are we lost?' *I don't know.*

'Have we drifted off course?' *I don't know.*

'What if the storm heads this way? Is there going to be a hurricane?' *I don't know.*

'Isn't there a transponder on board? Why can't they track us with that?' *I don't know.*

'Can you die from the norovirus?' *No.*

In the end, he'd sent Bin to request a security presence, but none had been forthcoming. All security personnel were needed up on the main deck, where he'd heard fights were breaking out continually. And he had to cope with the repercussions. Several blood-soaked faces and two possible concussions.

It couldn't go on.

When the clinic visitors had finally dried up – Martha and Bin had their hands full with the crew complaints – Jesse moved on to check on the passengers consigned to their cabins. The infected passengers who'd been forced to abandon their staterooms on the lower levels had quarantined themselves in the Dreamscapes Dining Room, sections of which resembled a painting from the Crimean War. He'd supervised the cleaning of the bathrooms there, both of which looked like the site of an alien birth. Jesse thought he'd become inured to the squalor: the soiled red bags left willy-nilly – sometimes dumped on the floor right next to a hazardous-waste bin – the plastic bottles and tissues and condoms and God knows what else, but that had shocked even him. The staff were thin on the ground; most appeared to have deserted their posts. He'd been snappish with one of the crew – an assistant waiter who was clearly going above and beyond his job description by venturing into the dining room – and Jesse hated himself for that.

It had been past noon when he'd made it up to the VIP suites. And that was when it had happened. The woman had cornered him as he was about to knock on Elise Mayberry's door. His heart sank. He recognised her as the wife of the man who'd abused him yesterday. She insisted that her husband be airlifted off the ship immediately. He patiently explained why that wasn't possible. She accused him of lying. He said that her husband only had a virus and it would pass. She insisted on seeing the captain. And then she'd gone to hit him. She apologised immediately and then became hysterical. She'd snapped: she'd been pushed to the limit. He knew how she felt. He also wanted to break down and cry. He hurried back to the medical bay for some Xanax – she wouldn't last the day without a helping hand – and that's when he'd done it. It had been so easy.

The ampoules were waiting for him in their little soldier rows. *Howzit, Jesse. Knew you'd pitch eventually. Come on in and join the party.*

Tap, tap, find the vein, *it's just a little prick, it'll be over in a*

second, trust me, I'm a doctor. A faint feeling of nausea and then . . .
It had rolled in on him, a gentle surge of warmth and calmness
and utter, absolute peace. All of it had faded: the worry about the
virus, about their situation, the gut-twisting regret about Farouka.
The pethidine oozed through his veins and soothed and caressed
and worked its magic. He should have given into it ages ago.

It even numbed the guilt.

After that first hit, he'd returned to his cabin – grateful, at least,
that he was housed on the passenger decks, and not one of the
lower ones – and for the first time since it had all kicked off, he
slept, waking at around four p.m. feeling refreshed and almost . . .
almost happy. He rubbed toothpaste over his teeth – noting that
his gums were numb, a side effect that he remembered from the
old days – swilled his mouth out with bottled water, and decided,
fuck it, he wasn't going to bother shaving.

Damien's voice crackled over the intercom. 'G'day, ladies and
gentlemen. We appreciate how patient you're being.' Jesse laughed.
Damien sounded almost bored. As if he didn't give a shit. As if
he'd given up. As if he'd finally found some self-awareness and
become tired of the platitudes and bullshit and the sound of his
own voice. '. . . and just to let you know, we've decided, for your
convenience, to open the bars and we will be serving complimentary drinks from now onwards.'

An open bar! Brilliant idea. Add alcohol to an explosive situation – that will help.

Jesse made for the door. He'd need some caffeine to counter-
act some of the wooliness. Or, he could just stay in his cabin until
help finally arrived (*it wasn't coming, nobody was coming for them
– they'd be here by now if they were*), and drift. But that would
mean leaving Martha and Bin to deal with the evening's horrors,
and he might be a *doos*, but he wasn't that much of an arsehole.
He wafted his way down to the officers' mess. Two white-trou-
sered men were having a harsh whispered conversation with
another officer – one of the assistant pursers, he thought. They
barely glanced at him. The bread was stale, and he helped himself
to a few slices of tomato, a handful of olives and a warm can of

Coke. He could afford the calories now he was back on the old pethidine diet. The crew member serving the food looked like she'd been crying. Jesse was attempting to formulate something comforting to say to her (*like what, dude? If in doubt, take drugs?*), when the floor dipped and he staggered. The ship's movement, which he'd become accustomed to, was more pronounced. It wasn't bad, but he was definitely aware of it. Rough weather. Could a storm be brewing? Perhaps the captain's 'bad weather on shore' spiel wasn't bullshit after all. Perhaps it had made its way across the ocean to their position.

But he could handle it. He could handle anything now. People talked all the time about how drugs were bad for you and fucked up your life, but no one ever really said that in some cases drugs could actually make you a better person. Martha was a case in point. She was a high-functioning alcoholic. It put her on an even keel.

Jesse cracked the can of Coke, and headed towards the medical bay, hesitating when he came to the entrance to the corridor that led to the laundry room. He wasn't sure he really wanted to know if the *malletje* fuckers had been back, but he had his pethidine shield to protect him, so he decided to make a quick detour to the morgue. There was no sign that anyone had tried to break into the storeroom. It looked like the circus had moved on.

But that wasn't true. It may be quiet here, but Celine del Ray was no doubt still putting on her show, wasn't she?

Nope. He wasn't going to go there.

He opened the storeroom door to double-check that all was kosher. The morgue door was firmly closed, and the storeroom's dark depths looked oddly inviting. He could hide in here. Zonk himself out and sleep forever. No one would look for him here.

No. Bin and Martha needed him. He shut the door with a slam and got moving.

Baci was waiting for him outside the medical bay. Jesse cursed under his breath. He'd meant to tell him about seeing Alfonso in the Dare to Dream Theatre, but that business about the morgue had wiped it out of his mind. Baci's pristine male-model exterior was becoming tarnished. Yellowish sweat moons stained his shirt; two-day-old stubble shadowed his cheeks. 'I have been looking for you, doctor.'

'How can I help?'

'Alfonso is back at his station.'

'Oh. Well that's good, isn't it? He fixed the ship yet?' *How droll.*

'No. He is only sitting there at his station, doctor.'

'Is he speaking?'

'No.'

'Nothing about the dark man?'

'No.'

'I am worried about him. I do not know what to do.' *Well, you could take some lovely lekker pethidine and you won't actually give a shit.* Not true. Jesse did give a shit about Bin and Martha. 'You will come and see him, doctor?'

'Now?'

'*Sì.*'

Jesse thought about it. It would be a way of killing two birds with one stone. Alfonso's burn pad needed to be changed. He had to do it sometime. The engine room wasn't the perfect place to do it, but where was? The whole ship was a festering pile of faecal matter.

'Let me get my bag. Wait here.'

'Thank you.'

Jesse hurried to the pharmacy cabinet. A fresh burn pad, forceps and what else? Stupid question. He slipped another three ampoules and another injector pen into his pocket just in case. And maybe just a soupçon of morphine too. Why the fuck not? They were supposed to sign for it, be accountable for every cc that was used, but hey, he was accountable. *It's going straight into my fucking bloodstream.*

'Jesse.'

He jumped guiltily at the sound of Martha's voice. How long had she been there? He hadn't heard her entering the room. Had he seen him helping himself?

'Bin's sick, Jesse.'

Fuck. 'Where is he?'

'In his cabin. I took him some . . . some rehydrate.'

Her words were stilted and her eyes were bloodshot. She was drunk. But who was he to judge? In some ways he was relieved. She was sharp, intuitive, if she wasn't impaired she'd probably pick up on the fact that he was spacing out big time. Or maybe not; it had taken the other doctors at his old surgery six months to figure it out. 'I'll go see him when I'm done.'

Her eyes were half-lidded and puffy. She really was off her tits, as she would say. 'Jesse. There's something going down. I've been hearing things.'

He didn't need to know about another round of superstitious crap right now – the staff burning an effigy in the casino or whatever. '*Ja?* Hold that thought. I'll be back now-now. Alfonso is back at his post.'

'He is?'

'*Ja.* But it sounds like he's still out of it. I'm going down there to change his dressing.'

Before she could stop him he joined Baci in the corridor, and accompanied him to the entrance to the lower levels. They headed down past the garbage-sorting room, and through the areas of the ship Martha dubbed the sweatshops. The metal ceilings seemed to press down on him, and the smell down here was deeper, thicker, like breathing in shit soup and diesel. The floor dropped again. Whoopsie. His stomach tried to push itself into his throat.

Down another level, around a corner, past a deserted workshop, and then on into the engine control room. It looked exactly as he expected it to. A wide desk strewn with buttons and knobs, screens on the walls, clocks, dials, charts, a plan of the ship's underbelly. Who knew what it all meant? Not him.

Alfonso was sitting on a chair behind the desk, staring straight ahead, his mouth half-open, crusty flakes at the corner of his lips. Jesse hoped he wasn't dehydrated.

'You see, doctor?' Baci said. 'He has not moved from there.'

'And he hasn't spoken?'

'No.'

'Remember me, Alfonso?' Jesse moved behind the desk to join him. A Ferrari badge was stuck on the display directly in front of him.

No response. Jesse took out his penlight and shone it into Alfonso's eyes, although he'd checked there was no sign of any abnormal dilation when he'd first been brought to the medical centre. Whatever it was that was causing the catatonia, Jesse was certain it wasn't a head injury. The ship fell again. *Christ.*

'Careful, doctor,' Baci said. He rode out the movement with ease, transferring his weight from foot to foot like a dancer. 'Rough weather. Not good for us with no stabilisers.'

'We're in danger?'

'If there is a rogue wave, *si*, of course.'

Thanks for that. Jesse concentrated his attention on Alfonso. 'I'm going to change your dressing now, Alfonso, okay?'

Alfonso didn't flinch as Jesse carefully removed the burn pad, examined the wound without touching it – it was progressing well, and the weeping had stopped – and after riding out another of the ship's dips, pressed a new one in place.

'What else can we do for him, doctor?' Baci asked.

'That's it.'

The ship rolled again, seemed to hang, then dropped. Jesse held onto the desk. He prayed that the pethidine would help prevent him from getting seasick, but if he stayed down here for much longer, not even a lorry-load of Dramamine would be enough. 'Alfonso? I am leaving now.'

'I am waiting,' Alfonso said in a loud, clear voice.

'Waiting for what?'

With a dying hiss, the fluorescent lights blinked out.

The Keeper of Secrets

It was spreading. The panic was spreading.

The staff had abandoned the bar next to the pool, and a cluster of passengers, male and female, were clambering over the counter, lashing out at each other, the ship's increasingly violent rolling motion doing little to slow them down. A deckhand wheeling a trolley laden with fresh red bags clocked the chaos, shoved his trolley away from him, and ran for the nearest service entrance. A couple of passengers tried to follow, but he made it through in time and had the sense to secure the door behind him. Down on the Promenade Dreamz deck, the shops were being looted, and a guest was using the statue of a cherub to smash through the Sandman Disco's glass doors. A small group (one of the men looked familiar) was attempting to prise open the service hatch behind the Guest Services desk. The only oasis of peace was the Dare to Dream Theatre. The doors were shut, with several darkened figures parked outside them.

Devi clicked back to the screens showing the main deck. A woman with wet hair plastered across her cheeks was waving frantically at the camera, lurching as the ship yawed to the side. There was no doubt the wind was increasing. Sudden squalls were common in the Gulf, and the rough weather had come upon them with no warning. Devi knew enough to know that without power to manoeuvre the vessel, a rogue wave could flip the boat as if it were made of matchsticks. If it got much worse, he had little doubt that the captain would order an evacuation.

If he wanted to find his prey, he didn't have long.

He tried radioing for assistance once more. 'Come in, control. Come in. Pran? Madan? Ram? Come in, please.' It was an impotent gesture. He hadn't seen his superior since their altercation last night, Madan was drinking himself to death, Ashgar was still sick, and Ram had instructed Pran to join him on the bridge. Pran said that Ram had caught a group of passengers roaming the crew area behind the stage, and the captain had ordered that the service doors be secured at all times.

He couldn't go up to the main deck alone. He would be able to subdue four men at the most. The only choice would be to deploy the MRAD, but it was probable that he would need back-up to keep the passengers at bay while he reached the box in which it was housed.

It would be suicide.

And Devi had to prioritise. Gary Johansson had to be on the ship somewhere. He'd eluded him on the main deck yesterday, after Pran had pointed him out, but Devi was almost positive that Kelly's assailant and the violent passenger who'd escaped the medical bay were one and the same man. He'd scoured each cabin on the lower decks last night after Pran had alerted him to the open doors, but he'd seen nothing untoward. No hands covering camera lenses, no Ladies in White. And no rapists and murderers. He'd swept the common areas twice, including the bathrooms and alcoves, and had scoped out the passengers holed up in the Dare to Dream Theatre early this morning. The set-up in there had impressed him. The area was tranquil, clean, the fug of bad air kept at a minimum thanks to frequent cleaning.

He clicked through to the lower decks again. Could Johansson have thrown himself overboard? He sat back and rubbed at his temples. It wouldn't be long before the generators ran out of stored power. The emergency lights would be extinguished, and so would the screens.

He couldn't stop the yawn – he'd been awake now for forty-eight hours.

Breath on his cheek. He flinched, craned his neck, saw Rogelio standing behind him. He didn't feel any trepidation that they might be caught together – all he cared about was that he had been stupid enough to doze off; he'd lost time that he could have used to track down the monster. 'What time is it?'

'Devi, I have something to say to you.'

'Wait.' He scanned the screens again. The passengers had moved on from the bar and were now gathered in clumps next to the entrance to the indoor buffet seating area, clutching at each other as the ship rocked. The pitch was getting worse. Devi swallowed. He could not allow himself to get sick now.

Rogelio gripped the back of the chair. 'Devi, I can help you.'

'Help me do what?'

'Find the man. The man you are looking for. The one who killed Kelly.'

A surge of hope. 'You've seen him? You know where he is?'

'No. But Devi, please. You must come with me to the theatre. She knows things, Devi. She can help you. I've spoken to her. She wants to see you. She says she knows what you want and she will give it to you.'

'Who are you talking about, Rogelio?'

A flash of movement on the screen capturing the I-95 caught his eye. Three crew members were running along it, using the wall to steady themselves. They were wearing life jackets – had an evacuation already been ordered? No. He would have heard the alert. Perhaps they were just being cautious, pre-empting the captain's decision.

'She can help you, Devi. You want to find the man who killed Kelly, don't you? She can help you.'

'Rogelio, go to your muster station.'

'The captain has not ordered—'

'Just do it.'

'I am not leaving you, Devi.'

'Go!'

Rogelio winced.

Devi softened his voice. 'I will join you soon. There is something I need to do first.'

'Devi, we'll be safe in the theatre. You have to trust me on this. And Celine can help you.'

Devi scanned the screens again. Out on the exercise deck, people were fighting to get down the stairs, presumably to get inside. Aft of the ship, water splashed up in an arc.

'Rogelio. I will come and find you.'

'You promise?'

'I promise.'

Devi tried the radio again. Nothing. Then he scanned through the lower decks once more. He was zooming in on Kelly Lewis's cabin door when the screen blipped and died. A second later the lights faded, leaving him in darkness. He removed his flashlight from his belt. The ship was really lurching now.

He stood up, intending to head to the bridge, when he saw twin lights bouncing towards him. He focused the beam of his own flashlight in their direction. Pran and Madan approached, flinching and blinking as his light caught their eyes.

'Devi, what are you doing here?' Pran asked. He sounded anxious, on the verge of panic.

'Did you not hear me radioing for you?'

'Devi . . . You have to get out of here. The crew is evacuating the ship.'

'I didn't hear the alert.'

A pause. 'It . . . there was no signal. Perhaps it is broken.'

'Have the passengers been alerted?'

'We have to do something first,' Madan said.

'What?'

Madan gave him a savage grin, walked over to the back-up hard drive and fired the twin pins of his taser into it. A sputter of sparks erupted out of it as it popped and hissed.

Devi lunged for Madan. 'What – why?'

Madan slapped his hand away. 'We're getting off the ship, Devi. I was ordered to do it.' Madan did not sound inebriated. He sounded completely lucid.

'Who ordered it?'

'Ram, of course.'

The rage came. 'You cannot destroy the equipment, Madan – it is a criminal offence! And there is proof on there that a crime has been committed.'

'The crew are leaving the vessel, Devi. I told you I had to get off the ship. I thought you understood. Without power it won't survive this storm. It could go down at any moment.'

And then he understood. 'You are not planning on evacuating the passengers. You're planning on just leaving.' And if the ship survived the storm and was eventually recovered, they didn't want proof of what they had done lying around.

'You have seen the passengers. You have seen how they are behaving. We could not possibly organise them in time—'

'You can't do this, Madan. You can't leave these people.' He looked to Pran, but the boy had turned his head away.

'The passengers can leave if they want to. They know where the lifeboats are.'

'But they don't know how to operate them!'

'There is nothing we can do. Come with us, Devi.'

'You cannot leave these people on the ship!'

'The people are shit, Devi. They treat us like rubbish, what do you care?'

'I will not let you go.' Devi placed a hand on the stun gun at his side. 'You cannot do this.'

'Devi. Don't do this, man.'

Now Devi couldn't see Pran anywhere. The boy must have fled.

'I am sorry, Devi,' a voice said from behind him. Ram's voice. With no warning, Devi's muscles seized, agony sizzling and fizzing through his nerve-endings. Unable to control his body, he dropped, hitting his head on the hard floor, panic shooting sparks through his skull. And then, he knew. He knew what had happened: Ram had tasered him. His flashlight rolled away across the floor as the ship tilted.

'I am sorry, Devi,' someone said – he could no longer tell if it was Ram or Madan.

Devi tried to move; desperately, he fought to speak. *Don't do this, I have something I need to do.* And then—

The Wildcard Blog

Fearlessly fighting the fraudulent so that you don't have to

Jan 03

Predator's group is growing. So far only met 2 or 3 people who have been to one of her shows and haven't been taken in by her bullshit. Even Emma and Donna from the singles group are convinced their dead friend Kelly spoke to them 'through Celine'. They said the usual, that Celine knew stuff she couldn't have known. Got them to break it down fact by fact, none of which were that specific, or anything Celine couldn't have picked up from ship gossip.

People are flocking to the theatre because it's clean and they're being fed and no one is freaking the fuck out. Pure cultish behaviour: make new arrivals feel special.

Unsure how Celine is influencing the rest of the ship. Auto suggestion? Must be. It's that or a hysterical reaction to a stressful situation, hallucinations caused by electrical impulses, low frequency sound or suggestibility. Even Maddie, who knows for a fact that Celine is a fake, has been seeing things. (NOTE TO SELF: If we ever get out of here, must check up on Celine's magical negro spirit guide. Figures she'd have one. Forgot his name – Papa Norris??) Maddie says she heard a humming sound before she hallucinated. Manifestation of The Hum on the ship?

4 p.m. People are really freaking out now. Quality of food dropping fast. Nothing at the Lido but bananas and tomatoes in hotdog rolls. Just heard the bars will be opened. BAD IDEA.

Captain has really fucked us. Reckon he went way off course. Most popular theory is that there's major bad weather on land preventing anyone from coming for us. Only other explanation is that something cataclysmic has happened. Like 9/11 or Black Thursday. Or worse. Nuclear War. The Rise of the Machines, an alien attack. Zombies. Ha fucking ha.

5 pm. Feeling a bit gross as the ocean is getting choppier. Maybe the ship will go down, put us all out of our misery.

Need to lie down. Will finish this later.

The Witch's Assistant

The lights had died ten minutes ago, and Maddie was still hoping that they'd miraculously come on again. Beneath her, the ship writhed and creaked. Even with the balcony door shut, the shouts from the deck above her filtered down.

Xavier groaned, and then she heard the liquid cough of him throwing up again. She'd given him some of her Dramamine, but it hadn't helped. And it seemed that *The Beautiful Dreamer* had cured her of her squeamishness. Now, in the dark, where anything could be lurking (*like Lizzie Bean, perhaps?*) she had other things to fear than someone getting ill.

The ship dropped, leaving a hollow feeling in her gut. Air, fresh air, that would help. She crab-walked over to the window and stepped out onto the balcony, lunging for the railing to steady herself. Rain swirled in her face; the ocean heaved below her. And something else – lights. There were lights in the water. She squinted, wiping moisture out of her eyes. Boats, there were boats out there.

She lunged for the door. 'Xavier! There are ships in the water. They're here!'

'Huh?'

'There are boats in the water! Someone's coming to rescue us.'

She heard him groan and stagger over to the window. Gingerly, he dragged himself out to join her. The ocean surged, and now she could make out a triangular-shaped silhouette – some kind of inflatable boat? – before it became subsumed in the swell.

Xavier grabbed her shoulder. 'Maddie. Those aren't rescue boats. They're lifeboats.'

A cold wash of panic. 'But . . . but I didn't hear the signal for an evacuation!'

He grasped her wrist. 'Come on.'

Together they reeled to the door, crossed the suite and stumbled out into the corridor. The only light came from the emergency strips on the floor and ceiling. She clung to the wall as the ship dropped again. Shapes loomed towards them from the far end of the corridor. The brother-and-sister couple lumped past them, clutching at each other. 'You got to get outta here,' the woman shrieked at them. 'Oh sweet Jesus. Abandon ship!'

Maddie hammered on Helen and Elise's door. 'Helen! Helen!' No answer.

'Come on,' Xavier yelled.

She turned to him. 'Where's your muster station?'

'Fuck that. We're going to the main deck where the fucking lifeboats are.'

Using the wall for support, they staggered past the elevator bay and across to the atrium. The door to the main deck didn't want to open at first, the wind was pushing against it, but then the pressure eased and she fell through it, almost going down as her feet slipped on the deck.

Chaos. Pure chaos greeted her. Mattresses had slid into the pool, the water around them sloshing violently. A sun-lounger was wrapped in a strange embrace with the railings, and the deck glittered with broken glass. To her left, passengers were rooting through the life-jacket boxes, pushing and shoving at each other. She spotted the brother-and-sister couple over by the bar. He appeared to have slipped and fallen, and his wife crouched over him, cradling his head to her chest. Should she help them? Shit – she didn't know what the fuck to do. She looked around for Xavier, but she couldn't see him anywhere. Water stung her eyes.

A piercing whistle sounded, and then the sky exploded with red light (*flares, they must have set off flares*) and for several seconds the deck was lit up clear as day. People were fighting to get up to the side decks, where the lifeboats were housed, their faces distorted masks of panic and pain. The ship rolled again, and several lost their grip, falling back into each other.

Someone thumped into her, and she turned to see Ray, holding the hand of a petite woman. 'Maddie! Come on! Gotta get . . . lifeboats.'

A security guard slammed past them, yelling: 'Wait! You cannot operate the davits from—', his voice was snatched away by the wind.

Again she searched for Xavier. The knot of panicked passengers clogging the area around the life-jacket boxes cleared, and she spotted him. He was on his knees, scrambling to keep his grip on a couple of life vests.

'Maddie!' Ray roared again.

'Does Celine know?' she shouted back.

'Maddie. You gotta . . . crew . . . the ship.'

'What about Celine?'

'Fuck her, Maddie.'

'But what about the Friends?' Jacob and Eleanor and Leila and Jimmy and Annabeth and . . .

The girl with him was tugging at his hand. 'Come with us,' she shouted at Maddie.

But she couldn't. She couldn't just leave the Friends. Maddie just couldn't do it. At the very least she needed to make sure they knew to head for the lifeboats. She turned and slid back to the glass doors, fighting against the tide of people trying to get out of the ship.

She'd reached the main staircase when the ship dipped into another steep pitch, so severe that her feet felt like they wanted to push up into her knees. A whooshing in her ears. A grinding, and then a metallic scream. Using the handrail for support, she half ran, half tumbled down the stairs to the Promenade Dreamz deck, grateful for the green glow of the emergency exit signs. The doors to the theatre were slamming open and closed, open and closed, but the stairs in front of it were deserted. She dragged her way up to the entrance, kicked the door open and crawled inside. There was a lull in the roaring in her ears and she heard Celine shouting: 'If you leave, you will die. It's your choice!'

'There is no death,' Maddie thought – or maybe she said it aloud, she wasn't certain, because then the floor disappeared beneath her.

The Condemned Man

He liked his hiding place. Snug as a bug in a rug. A boat within a boat! And he liked the movement of the ship, he always liked it when he could feel the sway of the sea. The wind was picking up, which he also liked, and it was raining. The tap-tap-tap on the tarpaulin roof was soothing. It swallowed the sound of the shouting.

He was safe in here. They'd never find him. Those security men would never find him. It was inspired. He was aware that he still wasn't quite himself. Everything was still a little bit out of focus, distanced really. He liked that, too. The bench he was lying on wasn't comfortable, but that was a small price to pay, wasn't it?

The old cautious Gary – the one who didn't have friends to help him – would have been paranoid about being caught in here. He knew that the lifeboats were all monitored to stop passengers fooling around in them, but this didn't deter him now. He trusted his friend. He'd tried to talk to him about the girl, but he'd come and gone, and sometimes Gary found he was talking to himself. The big man was mostly silent, but Gary didn't think he was judging him. Gary had explained that he wasn't sick. He wasn't really hurting anybody. It was just something he did. They didn't remember anything, and everyone knew that secretly, they wanted it. It was a biological imperative. People were hard-wired like that. Men were the hunters and women were the hunted. It was pointless trying to dress it up in any other way.

He didn't hate women. He didn't have 'unresolved anger issues'. He did it because it was in his nature.

And no. He didn't want to think about the other things. The dark things, although his mind did try and root around in his memory like a tongue straying to a tooth cavity. He was getting good at blocking it. It was a skill. You could build a wall and slot things behind it. It was something he'd done for years without thinking about it.

She's got a message for you . . .

Nuh-uh. Not listening.

She says she's going to make you suffer. She says she's going to make you suffer over and over and over and over again and it will never end.

She didn't say that. There was no message.

Shhhhhhh.

The boat rocked violently; a thump. The tarpaulin around him rippled, hands and arms stretched towards him, and he heard himself scream. People – there were people climbing into his hiding place. They were scrambling over each other and he felt himself being squashed against the side – he couldn't breathe.

He had to get out. Get away. He pushed against them, shut his eyes and fought. Someone pulled his hair, his cheekbone exploded, but he kept going, ignoring their yells of protest. Something slammed into the side of his head, and he saw stars, burped out bile, and then, like a cork fired from a bottle, he landed on his hands and knees on the deck, wind and rain lashing at his face. Someone stood on his hand, and he curled himself into a ball and rolled until he reached the railings on the other side.

He looked up, thought he could see Marilyn in the crowd, but then she was gone. Using the railing for support, he pulled himself to his feet and looked down at the pool deck below. A man had fallen into the pool. He flailed his arms, then disappeared under one of the mattresses in the water. Then, whoosh, the sky exploded with red light and he saw him. His friend. Waiting for him next to the glass doors that led into the ship. The floor rocked and bucked under his feet, but Gary kept his eyes glued to his friend as he shrugged past the people pouring up the stairs.

Someone smashed into him as he reached the main deck and screamed in his ear, but Gary brushed him off and kept going to the door. He shoved through it, pushing a woman who was attempting to exit out of his way. He couldn't lose sight of his friend. But it was dark inside the ship, and he was struggling to see. Then, a hand slipped into his left palm, and a smaller one slid into his right. He felt a moment of pure, primeval revulsion – *this was familiar he remembered this was familiar* – and then the hands tugged him forward.

The Devil's Handmaiden

Mrs del Ray had stopped calling out to people. Now she just sat there on the stage, lurking in her wheelchair. It would tip over soon. Althea had no doubt of that. Althea couldn't see her face. It was too dark to make it out, but she had the feeling the woman was watching her.

The only light came from the few people who still had battery life on their phones and the weak sickly glow of the exit signs. She had been helping Pepe hand out the water when she'd heard a man thumping down the aisle shouting that the crew were abandoning the ship and everyone 'must please go calmly to their muster stations'. She'd caught sight of him as he ran past her. One of the security guards – not the inscrutable one she'd encountered in the dead girl's cabin, but a young one with a weedy moustache. The panic hadn't lasted long. Those who were going to leave had already left. Those who remained were sitting quietly, huddled in groups. Most were getting sick.

The ship rolled beneath her, and she clutched at the back of a seat until it passed. She shouldn't be here, but she had no one but herself to blame. Maria had warned her yesterday that something like this was on the horizon. She should have figured out what she meant: that the crew was planning to evacuate the ship.

She would find the boy, and then she would leave. She made her way up to the stage, almost falling as she climbed up the side stairs. Avoiding looking at the woman in the wheelchair, she pushed through the curtain. She navigated by memory, gingerly picking her way around the obstacles at the back of the stage until she found the door that led out into the passageway. The boy had been with her a few hours ago in her cabin when she'd slipped away for a nap. Being with him was . . . it gave her energy. She was sick of everyone wanting something from her. Joshua wanted to suck the marrow from her bones and steal her money; the housekeeping managers and that *puta* Maria wanted her to be grateful for her job and put up with the poor working conditions and pay; Mirasol wanted her to tell her what to do; Mrs del Ray wanted her to bring others to the theatre. Her guests wanted her to smile and make them fuck-darned towel animals and not make them feel guilty about their shit-stained toilets and bad tips. The boy didn't want anything from her except just to be in her presence.

Keeping her eyes glued to the emergency strips on the floor – in places they were scuffed away – and using a hand on the wall to steady herself, slowly, carefully, and without allowing herself to panic, Althea made it to the I-95.

The beam of a flashlight came wobbling towards her. She squinted, then made out Rogelio, bulked out in a life jacket, face made ugly with terror. 'Have you seen Devi?'

'Who?'

'Devi. He's one of the security men.'

She clung to him for a second while the ship pitched. 'No.'

He shoved her away and moved on. A spectacular heave pushed her over to the other side of the corridor, but she found her balance and carried on. She wouldn't get sick. She couldn't afford to get sick. Now using both hands to steady herself, she inched down the stairwell to her crew deck. There were no strips down here. Nothing to guide her way. She was disorientated, and it took all of her self-control not to panic. This time, she navigated by feel, and when she turned the corner, she saw a faint light radiating out of one of the cabins.

A dark shape threw itself into her arms knocking her off balance. A surge of hope that it was the boy, but then she heard Trining sobbing: 'Althea! What's happening, Althea?'

'Everyone is evacuating the ship.'

'There was no signal. Why haven't they come to get me?'

Because they do not care. No one cares anymore.

'Please give me your flashlight.'

'No! Why? Don't leave me, Althea.'

'Give me your flashlight and then I will take you to your muster station. I have to get something from my cabin.'

Trining handed it over, and Althea raced into her cabin and shone it over the bunks, underneath them and into the tiny bathroom. Nothing. He wasn't here. Could he be on Five where she'd first seen him?

'Althea!'

'Go, Trining. Go to the muster stations.'

'You are not coming with me? Please, Althea. I still feel weak. And I'm scared.'

Fuck-darned Trining. 'Come on.'

She took Trining's hand and pulled her along the staff corridor, using her for balance now that she could no longer use the wall. The ship yawed, and she slammed into Trining's shoulder.

'It is going to sink!' Trining screamed.

'It is not going to sink.'

They made it past the bar and out onto the muster deck, where a cluster of crew members were waiting to climb into the chute that fed into the inflatable lifeboats. Althea had only ever seen this done in calm weather; she didn't dare look down over the railing. Someone shoved a life jacket over her head, the wind blew salty spray into her face. The ship groaned and the ocean raged and roared.

A hand pushed her forward.

'Althea!' A waving hand. Maria. Maria was near the front of the group, helping people clamber into the chute's mouth.

'I have to get the boy,' she said to Trining.

'What? I cannot hear you.'

The boy isn't real.

He was real.

'Don't be afraid!' Maria was shouting. 'Althea, come! It's your only choice.'

The Suicide Sisters

Screaming. She could hear screaming.

The ship's movement was far more pronounced – up, down, side to side – rolling and pitching, rolling and pitching.

Helen had closed the curtains and locked the balcony doors after their uninvited visitors had left. Once or twice she thought she'd heard sounds from the corridor outside. The sleeping pills had held her under. She'd only taken two (*for now*), but they'd done their job and blocked almost everything out. She sat up, unable to bear looking over at Elise in case she'd slipped away to join Peter. *For God's sake! Died. Not 'slipped away'. Died.* The room was dark, but she didn't remember turning off the lights.

Steeling herself for the yaw of the ship, she moved carefully over to the window, and with a flourish like a magician whipping a tablecloth away, she ripped open the curtains. She jumped – there were shapes, dark shapes, crawling just metres away from her.

They're back.

But no. They were just people, people crawling over the lifeboat in front of her balcony. A bloom of red light exploded above her, turning the foam flecks that tipped the ocean's meaty rolls into rubies, and for several seconds the scene unfolding in front of the balcony was clearly visible. A man and a woman, their clothes clinging to them, were frantically pumping the winch that worked the lifeboat's davits. A large figure (no, it wasn't him, her saviour), was balancing on top of the boat, attempting to unclip a rope. The ship tipped, he lost his balance, slipped and disappeared.

She stepped back and shut the curtains.

'Helen?'

The relief at hearing Elise's voice nearly floored her. 'They're leaving the ship. People are getting off the ship.'

'Oh.'

Oh indeed.

Helen crept over to what she hoped was Elise's bed. After the bright red light (flares, they had to be flares) – she was having trouble adjusting her eyes to the darkness.

'There a storm?' In between words Elise huffed like a bagpipe with a hole in it.

'The sea's getting rough.' It was worse than rough.

Helen resisted turning on the light (and who knew if it even worked anymore?); she didn't want to see her friend's pallor. She didn't want to see how close she was to the end.

'Thank you . . .' huff, puff, gasp . . . 'for taking care of me, Helen.'

'You would have done the same for me.'

'Is the . . . is the ship in trouble?'

'What, more so than before?'

Elise tried to laugh, but this set off a wheezy coughing fit. Water on the lungs, Helen thought, although she had absolutely no idea what that actually meant. 'You go. Leave me. Get to safety.'

There is no safety. The boat dropped again, and she felt like she was on a funfair ride, her stomach doing a loop-de-loop. It was exhilarating. 'I'm not going to leave you.' She lay back and fumbled for her friend's hand. 'You think it will be like a scene from *Titanic*?'

Another wheezy sound. 'I'm dying, Helen. I can feel it.'

'You're not dying.'

'I'm not scared. Thought . . . thought I'd be scared, but I'm not.'

Another roll, or pitch or yaw, or whatever the hell it was called. She heard something crash in the bathroom, and the sound of what had to be her laptop – the laptop with her final message on it – tumbling from its perch next to the television and thwocking onto the carpet.

The Angel of Mercy

The door of the storeroom opened, letting in a faint sliver of greenish light from the exit sign in the corridor outside.

Uh-oh, Jesse thought. *The aliens are here.*

The silhouette of a man stood in the doorway. Jesse watched as he shuffled in and looked around. There was something familiar about him – Jesse couldn't be certain, but judging by his body shape, he looked very like the missing patient. The one who'd gone AWOL. The one Devi thought might be responsible for the girl's death.

Jesse didn't speak, and the man didn't seem to sense he was in here. It was laughable really that someone would show up and invade his hiding place. The whole point of coming here in the first place was to regroup and have some alone time after the lights died. And by regroup he meant spike his veins full of Demerol, ha de fucking ha – and let's not forget the morphine chaser. Jesse had made himself a little nest next to a pile of empty cardboard boxes that had once held tinned tomatoes. He'd been planning on staying in here until the storm blew over or the ship sank. And lucky for him, the pethidine did seem to be keeping the seasickness at bay after all.

The man said something to someone and grasped hold of the morgue's hatch.

'It's full,' Jesse opened his mouth to say. 'Already occupied.' Flippant, trying to be funny, but really, what else was there to say? The guy appeared to know what he was doing. And Jesse hadn't forgotten how he'd acted after attacking the steward. Crazy. *Befok.* Best let him alone. Jesse was in no state to defend himself if the man went for him.

The patient carried on with his imaginary conversation, yanked the morgue's hatch open – Jesse winced at the whiff of putrefaction that wafted out of it – and then, without even a moment's hesitation, crawled inside, right on top of the deceased passenger. He leaned out, scrambling to shut the door, but he couldn't reach it.

The ship pitched steeply, seemed to hang, then rose up again, leaving Jesse's guts somewhere on the storeroom's ceiling, the movement dislodging the door's safety catch and slamming it shut.

Jesse blinked. Fuck. Now what? It was the passenger's choice to crawl inside there. Best place for him. He was dangerous, nobody wanted someone like that running loose through the ship causing havoc. They were in enough shit as it was.

He fumbled for another ampoule, but he was out of stock. Had he dropped the others as he'd stumbled through the dark heart of the ship? He must have. If he'd taken them all he'd be dead by now.

The ship rose again, then appeared to change its mind and tip sideways.

Time to return to the clinic. He'd rather go out whacked off his face than drown in a morgue storeroom next to a crazy man. He dug in his pockets for his penlight, and shuffled on his knees to the door. It took him several tries to open it. The second he lurched onto his feet, the ship threw him across to the wall, but that was fine, he couldn't feel a fucking thing. Using the penlight to guide his way – the light was ridiculous, but it was all he had – he edged up the stairs to the I-95.

Shuffle, shuffle, you can do it. And then, instantly (he must have spaced out), he was at the clinic door. Through you go, shuffle shuffle, easy does it, and on to the pharmacy cabinet. Light in his eyes. He blinked. A flashlight. He wasn't alone.

A hand grabbed his arm. 'Oh thank you, Jaysus. Jesse, Jesse, we've got to go.'

Martha. And she was wearing a life jacket. He shone his penlight into her face. She was crying, bright spots of colour on her cheeks. 'What have you been doing to yourself?'

'I killed a girl, Martha.' Where did that come from? It had just popped out by itself.

'Jesse, we have to leave now. I've been waiting for you, but they won't hold it for much longer.'

'Where we going?' He fell against her as the ship dipped again.

'Off the ship.' She almost dropped the torch and swore under her breath. 'I can't hold you up, Jesse.'

'What about Bin?'

'Bin's sick, Jesse.'

'We can't leave Bin.'

'We don't have a choice.' She was dragging him now. 'You think I want to? They won't let him on if he's sick.'

'I'm sick too.'

'You're pissed.' She was sobbing now. 'Please, Jesse. Come on.'

'I'll go get Bin. I'll catch up with you.'

He was glad he couldn't see her face. 'No, Jesse.'

'Really . . . I'll go get him. Make them take him.'

'Are you sure?'

'I'm sure.'

She released his arm, the light danced over to the door, paused and then it was gone.

Now. To business. He made for the pharmacy cabinet, another roll taking him off guard. Time slowed, his legs slid up from under him and he landed on his tailbone. A numb shock, no pain.

Jesse could hear glass breaking and something sliding across the floor. The door slammed. He fumbled for the penlight. Someone was standing right in front of the cabinet. He trailed the light upwards. The man put his fingers to his lips.

Jesse realised he knew who he was.

The dark man. Alfonso's dark man had come for a little visit.

And Jesse began to laugh.

The Keeper of Secrets

Devi spat out a mouthful of blood and bile, and rolled onto his back, the movement causing a white-hot flare of agony at the back of his skull. Slowly, carefully, he took stock. Every muscle was burning. His hands and feet felt like they'd been dipped in ice. His ears were filled with a roaring sound – he was unsure if it was coming from inside his head or not. And then a creaking and an ear-splitting screech, as if nails were being scraped along the ship's sides.

Ram. Ram had done this to him.

Something soft tickled his forehead. Light spiked his eyes. A voice: 'Devi. You are awake.'

'Where am I?'

'In the control room. I couldn't leave you. I came to find you. I couldn't leave you, Devi.'

Devi tried to sit up, but his muscles didn't want to obey him.

'Did they leave the ship?' Speaking made his jaw feel like it was going to splinter. 'Did it get evacuated?'

Rogelio didn't answer him. 'Many of the passengers have gone, I think.'

With a monumental effort, Devi made his arm move and touched his face. It was wet. Sticky. 'Help me up.'

'No. You mustn't move.'

But he had to. He could still be on the ship. The murderer. The man who had killed Kelly Lewis. The hard drive had been destroyed on Ram's – or the captain's – orders and the proof of what he'd done was gone.

But he still couldn't make his body do what it was supposed

to do. Sparks danced in front of his eyes when he lifted his head.

The ship seemed to throw itself upwards. Then it fell.

Whichever way he looked at it, he'd failed.

The Wildcard Blog
Fearlessly fighting the fraudulent so that you don't have to

Shitfuk a storm crazy bad.

this is my last will & testememtn. So so sickI leave evefything to the james randi foundati Christ I can't write anymore and I oep that someone reads this

The Witch's Assistant

The ship was listing badly to the left once more, but the violent motion had stopped. Maddie didn't recall this happening gradually; it had felt like it had ceased within minutes. Her ears ached, but the creaks and howls and what sounded like the rending of metal had also faded away. Not once, not even when the ship's movement had been at its most extreme, had she heard anyone in the theatre scream. No screaming, no begging for mercy, no prayers. They'd got sick. Of course they had. The smell of vomit was thick in the room, but Maddie fought to ignore it. She was hit with a sudden flood of euphoria. She was still screwed, of course she was. She was still on a ship drifting to nowhere, but she was alive, and that was something. She'd made the choice not to leave – *if you leave, you will die* – and she would now find out if she'd made the right one.

'Is anyone hurt?' A tremulous voice. It sounded like it belonged to Eleanor.

A groan from her left.

She dragged herself to her feet – she'd ridden out the storm on the floor beneath a row of seats – and focused on the stage. It was dark, but there was a darker shadow in its centre. She should help the Friends, but first, she had to see. Maddie crept towards the stairs that led up to it, picking her way through the detritus on the floor – bags, a scatter of water bottles and bizarrely, a whole salami – wincing as her foot slipped in something wet.

A woman was moaning from somewhere, but Maddie ignored her and continued onto the stage. Celine was still in her wheelchair (how had that not tipped over during the storm?), and her head was hanging forward, mirroring her pose on the night the ship had stopped.

'Celine.'

No answer.

'Celine.'

And then, like a doll coming to life, her head jerked up. 'Madeleine. Did you think you were going to die?'

'Yes.'

'Scary, wasn't it?' Her voice was cold.

'Celine. Just what the fuck is going on? Who . . . are you?'

'I'm Celine del Ray, medium to the stars.'

'The Celine I knew would have told everyone to sod off a long time ago. She wouldn't have bothered to gather all these people together. No way. The Celine I knew would have been the first person off the bloody ship.'

'You've got me. You can call me what you like. Jessie, or Stacy, or Tommy. Or Nonanthla, or Hiroko, or Jeremiah. Whatever you prefer. Your soul, my soul, all just old souls together. What's the matter with your matter?'

'Oh Jesus.'

'Him, too. Brain damage. It can change the personality. Isn't that what you think?'

'Celine . . . I saw . . . I saw . . .' *I saw Lizzie Bean, sitting in your bathtub.*

'Ghosts? Spirits? Ghouls?' She laughed. 'That was fun. I enjoyed that part. Although I'm not sure I got Papa Noakes quite right. Celine didn't give me much to work with.' Celine patted her hair, tapping a few stray strands back into place. 'What is it you want out of life, Maddie? I've been thinking about you, trying to figure you out.'

'I want to get off this ship for a start.'

'You'll get that wish soon.'

'How?'

Surprising her, Celine yawned. A huge jaw-cracking yawn. 'Run along now, Maddie. It's time to get moving. You haven't seen anything yet. This was just the appetiser. The main course will blow your fucking mind.'

The Condemned Man

The darkness was so pure that he couldn't tell if his eyes were open or shut. He breathed in. Sniffed. There had been a bad smell when his friend had brought him here at first, but he had got used to that quickly. He'd felt sick for a little while, but that had passed, too.

He wriggled his toes, hearing the crackle of the lumpy mattress beneath him. Sometimes it squished. Soft and hard in places. He had to contort his body to make himself comfortable.

A churning, grumbling sound. He reached out a hand; the snug sleeve walls of his hiding place were vibrating. Was this what had woken him? He couldn't feel his left arm – he was lying on it, and it had gone dead. He flexed his fingers, feeling the tingle of blood circulating again.

He said a silent prayer of thanks to his friend for bringing him here. A large storage locker. Yes, that was what it was. That's all it was.

His fingers found the wall again. A low throb, as if he was connected to a heartbeat. Gently at first, he pushed against the hatch. Just checking. Just checking it opened. He was safe in here and didn't want to leave, but he just wanted to make sure it did open in case he had to run again.

It didn't move. But that was okay, he wasn't pushing very hard. He shifted his position to get more leverage, the mattress crackling beneath him.

Not a mattress.

Shhhhhh.

That's not a mattress, Gary. You know where you are.

Shhhhhh!

He pushed against it with his shoulder this time. Nothing. His foot. Yes, he could kick at it.

Getoutgetoutgetoutgetout.

He scrunched his body around, but there wasn't space. He lashed out with his left leg, making a hollow bonging sound, but still it didn't move.

Getoutgetoutgetoutgetoutgetoutgetoutgetoutget

He just had to—

The mattress rippled beneath him.

The Devil's Handmaiden

She'd waited it out in her cabin. And still the boy hadn't come.

Trining had handed Althea her flashlight just before she'd been funnelled down into the life raft, and Althea was grateful for it now. Who would have thought that she, Althea, would ever be grateful to Trining of all people? Her wrists were bruised where Maria had tried to drag her into the escape chute, but she hadn't been sick. Queasy, yes, but that was all.

The crew corridors were deserted, all she could hear was the sound of her feet sloshing through the water that had pooled on the metal floors. Her shoes were soaked, her toes numb. She stepped over a discarded life jacket, a sodden suitcase and the tangled insides of a smashed radio.

Mrs del Ray would know where he'd gone. If she hadn't decided to abandon the ship too. Perhaps Althea was the only one left on *The Beautiful Dreamer*. Sailing alone forever until she starved.

The ship was listing badly now, slumping like a drunk. She trekked past the entertainment staff's cabins, and through the door into the back of the stage. Voices. She pushed through the curtains, saw flashlights dancing over the darkened seats and aisles of the theatre. Broken lights, the crumped body of a rolled-up backdrop that had fallen.

And there was Mrs del Ray. Sitting in her wheelchair in the centre of the stage, as if nothing had happened. Down below, people were helping others to stand. She could smell the sickness; the storm had been bad, of course people would have been sick. Althea hurried up to her and dropped to her knees.

'I can't find him. The boy. I can't find him.'

'Shhh. Listen.' Mrs del Ray cocked her head to one side. A low groan, as if the ship was sighing in despair, the lights flickered, died, then flickered back to life. Althea detected a slight vibration under her feet. It stopped, then started again. Mrs del Ray gave her a wide, hungry grin. 'Here we go.'

The Suicide Sisters

The storm had blown itself out. The ship was no longer being thrown around like a toddler's toy.

Helen was glad of the darkness. She didn't want to see. She didn't want to know. Elise hadn't made a sound since the ship's movement had ceased. Deliberately avoiding looking too closely at her, she sat up and slid off the bed, moving carefully across to the TV cabinet. A shard of glass stabbed into her foot. Her legs protested as she got down onto her hands and knees, scrabbling on the sloping floor for Elise's handbag. Her fingers found it, and she dug through it until she found what she was looking for.

Keeping her eyes averted from Elise's direction, she pocketed the Zopiclone, carried the last bottle of water over to her bed, and lay back.

The ship shuddered beneath her, and then the lights flicked on.

She didn't care. It was too late.

Better together.

The Angel of Mercy

'Wake up. Wake up, doc.'

Jesse covered his face with his arm as light pierced his eyes. 'Go away.'

'Jesse.'

He was lying on his back, something digging into his spine. A silhouetted shape was standing over him. The floor rippled under him. Gah. He swallowed. His mouth tasted of bile. 'Who's that?'

The dark man.

'It is me. Bin.'

A low hum, and then the lights came on, sputtered out, then shone at full wattage. A growling sound came from somewhere. The floor was vibrating.

'Are you hurt, doc? I thought that you had left with the others.'

Jesse's gorge rose as he raised his head, but there was nothing in his stomach to throw up. 'Martha?'

'I don't know, doc.'

'There's power?'

Bin nodded and grimaced.

'We're moving again?'

'No. But soon.'

'How do you know?'

Bin pulled a face again. 'There are crew down there. I saw them when I came here. Not everyone left the ship.'

'They can make it work? Drive it?' Did you drive a cruise ship? He didn't know the word. Christ, his head . . .

Bin helped him to his feet. The place was a tip. Files and vials everywhere. A tangled mess of drip stands. A flood of panic as he glanced at the pharmacy door. It looked intact. Thank fuck for that.

'People are hurt, doc.'

'Where?'

'The atrium, the main deck. They're being take to the Dare to Dream Theatre.'

'Anything serious?'

'Nothing that is life threatening. Maybe some fractures. I have done what I can. One I think has a concussion.'

Bin grimaced again, held up a hand, then stepped away neatly to be sick in a kidney bowl. Jesse noted that the nurse seemed to do even this with grace and precision. He handed Bin a cloth. 'Bin. You go on up. You're in no state to be helping anyone. I'll bring whatever I think we might need.'

'You are sure?'

'Yes.'

Jesse held his breath while Bin left the room. Fingers trembling, he hurried over to the cabinet.

Then it hit him. He'd just survived a major storm at sea relatively unscathed. Did he really want to continue along this path?

Fuck it.

He shoved the remaining ampoules in his pockets, and pulled the plastic wrapping off a syringe with his teeth. Within minutes, he'd have his armour back.

They were gathered in the foyer of the theatre, lying on the stairs and the carpet in front of the door. The interior of the ship hadn't fared too badly: he'd crunched over broken glass, and water had pooled in places, mostly in the crew decks, but it was nowhere near as bad as he'd imagined it would be. If anything, the storm had freshened the ship; it now smelled salty and damp, instead of like the inside of a sewage farm. And the wind would have swept away the blight of red bags that had followed in its wake.

Crew members were handing out water – reverting to old habits – and those who could walk were helping others out of the theatre. Safely swaddled in his pethidine embrace, he scanned the passengers, looking for who might be in the most need of his services. Bin was right. There didn't appear to be anything too serious. Several people looked green – but whether this was from

seasickness or the ongoing effects of the noro he couldn't say –
and there were a few minor contusions. A large woman who was
sitting next to a guy with a bandaged arm gave him a tentative
smile of recognition. He smiled back automatically, trying to recall
where he'd seen her. Then he got it – the hysterical passenger from
the VIP deck. She'd tried to hit him, and he'd meant to bring her
some Xanax. If she hadn't have lashed out at him, would he have
been tempted to fall into his old habits? But he knew the answer.
Ja, he would. He would have found an excuse sooner or later.

The rumbling of the engines stopped, there was a moment of
silence as everyone appeared to hold their breath, then they started
up again. Those who could gave a watery cheer.

Jesse supposed he should do something other than hang around
like a spare part. He was heading for the VIP passenger, when
someone shouted: 'Doctor!' A pretty Filipino guy standing at the
top of the stairs was waving at him. Jesse made his way through
the casualties and over to one of the pillars, against which a guy in
a blood-soaked white shirt was leaning. Christ. Jesse realised it
was Devi, the security guard who'd helped him sort out that *kak*
at the morgue. The left side of his jaw was swollen, and the cut
behind his ear would need stitches. He barely flinched as Jesse
examined the wound behind his ear; his eyes darted around, graz-
ing and assessing everyone around them.

'Looking for someone?'

'That man. Gary Johansson.'

The man who'd invaded his hiding place last night. Jesse hadn't
given him a thought until now. He'd had more important things to
worry about. 'Now *that* I can help you with.'

The Keeper of Secrets

Devi gripped the railing, which was slippery with moisture, clunked down the steps and staggered out onto the corridor that housed the laundry room and the morgue. Every muscle throbbed, every time he moved his elbow a spike of pain jolted to his fingers, and his head was a dark blur of ache. He touched his lip with his tongue – it felt like it was the size of a cricket ball.

The vessel trembled around them. Rogelio had been to the bridge and said that Baci, one of the few officers who had not abandoned the ship, was scrambling to assess which port they should make for. The storm could have pushed the ship far from the last known navigational point.

Rogelio held onto the back of his shirt as he shuffled along, and Devi was grateful for his support. Rogelio had stood by him every step of the way. When this was over, Devi promised himself he'd make it up to him.

Finally, they reached their destination.

Devi opened the storeroom door, stepped inside, and tapped on the morgue hatch with a finger.

An anguished howl came from within. 'Letmeoutletmeoutletmeout.' Then, sobbing.

Rogelio joined Devi in the storeroom. If he was frightened or horrified by what he had heard, it didn't show on his face. 'You are sure it is him, Devi?'

'Yes.'

'Will he die if we don't let him out?'

'I don't know.' *But he will suffer.*

'Can you live with yourself if you do this, Devi? Will it be over?'

Devi didn't need to think about the answer. 'Yes.'

The Wildcard Blog

Fearlessly fighting the fraudulent so that you don't have to

So I'm alive. Made it. Thought I was going to die for sure, but I didn't go down with the ship after all. I'm back in The Predator's cabin with Maddie. Caught up with her when she came back to the suite an hour ago. She found me lying on the carpet. Still don't know how I made it here. Feeling a bit better now, but that's a recent development.

Maddie isn't looking so good. Not sick exactly, but spooked. She didn't even look that surprised to see me.

Here's how it went down:

Wanted to die after a major bout of seasickness which was almost as bad as having the noro. Wrote a will if you can believe that, but I've deleted it.
Maddie saw lights out in the water, and assumed that rescue boats were on their way, but I could see straight away that they were inflatable lifeboats and we needed to get the fuck out of the cabin. We ran out onto the main deck, and I tried to grab a couple of life jackets (and got punched on the ear by some bastard in the process) and Maddie and I got separated.
One of the security guards was trying to get everyone organised. Some of them listened, most of them didn't. The lifeboats are up on the main deck, and that's a long drop, they have to be winched down. Not easy if you don't know what you're doing.
The adrenalin stopped the pukiness, but I didn't have any sense of balance, and I was slipping and sliding everywhere.
Saw some bad stuff.
A lifeboat falling, people clinging to the top of it and hanging off its sides.
Some fucker lit a flare inside one of the boats that was being

lowered into the water. It hissed and sputtered and burned like a firework. Could hear the screams of the people trapped inside it even above the wind.

I'd almost made it up to the lifeboat deck, when someone bashed into me, and I skidded, slipped into the pool and inhaled a ton of water. Got out, slipped into the pool again, this time almost got eaten by one of the mattresses that had been swept in there.

By that time, all of the lifeboats on my side were gone. Tried to make it across to the other side, but the panic was full on: Pushing and shoving and people were just throwing themselves into the remaining boats. Missed the last one by seconds, although the woman next to me went for it and leapt on it as it was dropping. Unbelievable.

I don't know what happened to her.

By now, the sea was beyond rough.

Heard someone shout: 'Come to me!' Looked over and saw the security guy waving his arms over his head just below me. People were trying to make it over to him, stragglers like me. Don't know how I got down the stairs to him without breaking my neck. Shouting at the top of his lungs, the security guard made it known that there were inflatable rafts on the crew muster station. Told us to follow him back into the ship.

I don't know for sure how I lost him. It was dark in there, and the movement was so bad by then I literally couldn't walk. I crawled. And I mean crawled to what I hoped was at least a railing or something I could hold onto. Managed to wrap myself around one of those angel pillars. The ship was groaning and screaming and it sounded like it wanted to rip itself apart.

How long did it last?

I don't fucking know. How long is forever? Fucking glad I'm not on one of those boats though. We must have got caught in a hurricane or something, because it

holy fucking jesus the engines I can hear the engines how the fuck did that happen?

DAY 8

The Witch's Assistant

Maddie and Xavier sat side by side on Celine's balcony, their legs propped up on the railings. The ship had started moving an hour ago. She looked out into the darkness, listened to the swoosh-slap of the water against the ship's side, the low thrum of the engine. A breeze tussled her hair. It was almost pleasant.

Xavier opened his mouth to speak.

'Don't,' she said. 'Just don't.'

She took his hand and intertwined her fingers through his.

Together, they waited in silence.

IT'S BACK!
Missing cruise liner found near key west

Breaking news: Yacht Captain spots *The Beautiful Dreamer*
At 4.30 a.m. EST, Jose Ferrigno, the captain of the yacht *Instant Fame*, reported seeing a ship floundering five miles east of Key West. Ferrigno informed the Port Authority that the vessel was listing dangerously to port side. It has now been confirmed that the stricken vessel is the cruise ship *The Beautiful Dreamer*, which has been missing for five days. Despite extensive searches of the Gulf of Mexico and surrounding waters, no trace of the vessel or its passengers has been found until now, and the ship's disappearance has baffled industry experts. With estimated casualties topping even those of 2012's Black Thursday air disasters, the disappearance of *The Beautiful Dreamer* was already being dubbed the biggest maritime disaster since the *Titanic*.

Follow our up-to-the minute report and live blog:
Our reporter Jonathan Franco is at the scene.

@jonf667
Ship listing badly. Looks like lifeboats are all gone.
Some damage evident to hull.
@jonf667
Rescue vessel & helicopters on scene. Still no word on survivors
@jonf667
Rumours spreading that Jose Ferrigno saw survivors on board.
@jonf667
JF's recorded message to the CG: '[There is] a light
on the port side. I think there are people on board.'
@jonf667
Jose Ferrigno allegedly has a history of substance abuse.

@jonf667

No sign of survivors being airlifted out but reports coming in that there may be bodies on board.

Update:

10:32 a.m.

An NTSB spokesperson has now confirmed that no survivors have yet been found. *The Beautiful Dreamer*'s parent company, Foveros Cruise Lines, has disclosed that there were 2019 passengers on board, of which 716 were British, two German, and the remainder US citizens. Most of the maritime officers and engineers were Italian, whilst most of the service crew were from developing nations. All 2964 passengers and crew are still listed as missing.

Update:

10:57 a.m.

A spokesperson for Foveros Cruise Lines says he is reluctant to speculate at this point in time, but went on to say, 'Structural damage and the deployment of all lifeboats suggests that the ship must have encountered severe weather and ocean conditions, precipitating an evacuation order. This is standard maritime protocol for such an eventuality. The fact that the vessel is damaged and all the lifeboats appear to have been lost at sea, suggests an Act of God is the most likely cause of this terrible tragedy.'

Meteorologists confirm that there was a mild to strong tropical storm brewing a few miles west of the Bahamas three days ago. Official reports on weather conditions in the estimated vicinity of the vessel have not yet been released by the authorities.

Bodies Found on Nightmare Cruise Ship

The Dade County Coroner's Office has confirmed that the bodies of two women have been found on board *The Beautiful Dreamer*. One of the deceased has been identified as Kelly Louise Lewis (32) a hair salon receptionist from Essex, UK. The second, that of an elderly female, has not yet been identified.

Melanie Zindell, a close friend of the Lewis family asks that the press respect the privacy of the bereaved family. She did, however, say that Ms Lewis's parents send their condolences to the families of the other missing passengers and crew.

A spokesperson from Foveros Cruise Lines, the cruise company that runs the line of 'Beautiful Class' ships, including the *Dreamer* and the *Wonder*, which was stranded for two days last year in Cozumel after its propulsion system broke down, said the company extends its sympathies to Ms Lewis's family and friends and will do all it can to cooperate with the NTSB in their investigations.

Voices from the Deep?

Long Island, NY.

Hundreds of mourners flocked to the streets of East Meadows, Long Island last night to pay tribute to controversial psychic medium, Celine del Ray, who is believed to be one of the victims of *The Beautiful Dreamer* maritime disaster.

Del Ray hit the headlines in 2014, when she publicly stated that 'she had proof from her spirit guides' that Lori and Bobby Small, two victims of one of the four Black Thursday plane crashes that occurred on January 12, 2012, were alive and suffering from amnesia. Lori Small's mother, Lillian Small, reportedly exhausted her life savings hiring detectives to search for her relatives, despite DNA evidence confirming that her daughter and grandson had died in the crash. Last year, Lillian Small gave notice of her intention to sue del Ray for emotional distress.

Among the mourners was Elisha Cobalt (47), a 'psychic healer' from Brooklyn, New York, who said she has been receiving daily 'updates' from Archie, one of Celine del Ray's spirit guides. 'Archie says that he and Celine are together now, and Celine wants everyone to know that she'll be sending through information about the missing passengers soon.'

Cobalt has offered her services to the families and friends of those who are believed to have drowned when the cruise ship hit troubled waters in the Gulf of Mexico.

The Beautiful Dreamer:
A Modern Day Marie Celeste?

It's been a month since *The Beautiful Dreamer* suddenly reappeared, after five days of mysteriously being lost at sea. And it seems the NTSB still has no idea what has become of the 2962 people on board.

Could the crew and passengers of *The Beautiful Dreamer* have suffered the same fate as those of the *Mary Celeste* and other ghost ships throughout history?

After all, in this day and age, how does a ship that could comfortably house three thousand people simply disappear? There were extensive searches for the ship during the five days following its mysterious disappearance, yet no traces of its whereabouts were found. Conspiracy theorists are already polishing their foil hats, and there are predictably many whispers online and in the media about *The Beautiful Dreamer* falling victim to the notorious Bermuda Triangle, despite this myth being debunked on numerous occasions.

According to a statement from Foveros Cruise Lines, the Captain's log, CCTV footage and GPS black box seem to have been compromised and 'have nothing conclusive to add'. And the only thing experts seem to agree on is that the captain must have ordered an evacuation, as all lifeboats were missing. However, no one can explain why an unmanned ship in the middle of the Gulf Stream wasn't sucked out into the vast Atlantic Ocean.

There are also signs that a norovirus raged throughout the ship. A salvage expert, who has asked not be named, said, 'The place was a mess. There was no food, there was broken furniture everywhere and the place stank like a mix between a sewage plant and a binge drinker's bathroom.'

The official line is that the ship must have drifted off course, a fire briefly disabled the propulsion system, and mindful of the bad press and drop in profits Foveros Cruise Lines has been suffering recently, and fearing a reprisal from Foveros Cruise Lines' executives, the captain held off on sending a distress signal. The ship was caught in a storm, and an evacuation was then ordered.

And what of Jose Ferrigno, the man who discovered the ship and alleges he saw survivors on board? Ferrigno is far from a reliable witness given his history of drug smuggling, substance abuse and depression, but he has adamantly stood by his claims. Is he simply giving the world false hope?

One thing is certain, *The Beautiful Dreamer* (or should we say, Nightmare) is far from the first ship to confound the world.

- In 2003 a mysterious tanker with no name or registration was found 35 miles from the coast of Australia. It was believed to have harboured refugees but no one was found on board, and the only sign of habitation was a child's soft toy animal.

- In 1872, *Mary Celeste*, perhaps the most famous 'ghost ship', was discovered floating entirely unmanned, but with all her cargo and supplies intact.

- The *Jenny* was found 17 years after it went missing in the Antarctic in 1823. The captain's last message read: 'May 4, 1823. No food for 71 days. I am the only one left alive.'

Sailor Who Discovered Mystery Cruise Ship Found Dead

The man who discovered *The Beautiful Dreamer* has died of a suspected drug overdose. Jose Ferrigno (49), who also had a history of depression and substance abuse, was found dead at his home yesterday evening at approximately 7 p.m. Initial reports suggest that he took his own life.

Ferrigno, who achieved notoriety after discovering the missing cruise liner three months ago, was adamant that he had seen survivors on board. This was continually denied by those who arrived first on the scene, the US Coastguard and the NTSB.

Conspiracy theorists, who have backed up Ferrigno's assertions, believe there is a global cover-up and say that this is further proof that authorities are hiding something.

A spokesperson from the Dade County Coroner's Office declined to make a statement about these allegations.

Ferrigno lived alone. His body was discovered by a neighbour.

NSA Denies Survivors' Existence. Describes Leaked Documents as 'A Clever Hoax'

The National Security Agency has once again come under scrutiny after several documents, which purport to be fragments of interviews with several passengers and crew who were listed aboard *The Beautiful Dreamer*, went viral yesterday.

Leaked by @anonymous998, the source of the documents is unknown.

The documents have surfaced amidst widespread speculation about the fate and whereabouts of the 2962 passengers and crew who were on board the vessel when it left Miami on December 28, 2016.

According to the National Transportation Safety Board findings of the 'most likely' sequence of events, the ship ran into difficulties after losing power due to a fire in the engine room. Fearing that it would capsize in high seas, the crew ordered an evacuation. It is believed that a tropical storm may have sunk the lifeboats and claimed the lives of any survivors.

Critics from a wide spectrum argue that the theory lacks coherency and is not corroborated by the known facts. Some critics have accused the Coastguard and the NTSB of being complicit in a cover-up of critical facts and of the survival of at least some of those aboard the ill-fated ship.

The National Security Advisor took to Twitter this morning to refute the claims: 'We categorically deny that these documents are anything other than fake.'

'They are a clever hoax designed to undermine our security efforts.' And: 'There were categorically no survivors found on board *The Beautiful Dreamer*.'

TOP SECRET

DO NOT COPY DO NOT EMAIL

Herein please find the abridged transcripts of the interviews conducted with the five subjects discovered on board *The Beautiful Dreamer* on January 05, 2017.

The transcripts are in English. There are two additional transcripts that were issued as reports; they are summaries of the first three transcripts and omit the non-substantive and repetitive statements. Some of the information has been deleted from the enclosures because it was found to be currently and properly classified in accordance with Executive Order 12988, as amended. This information meets the criteria for classification as set forth in subparagraphs (c) and (g) of Section 1.4 and remains classified TOP SECRET and SECRET as provided in Section 1.2 of the Executive Order. The information is classified because its disclosure could reasonably be expected to cause exceptionally grave damage to the national security.

The accounts have been listed chronologically for purposes of cross-referencing. A summary of the findings will be forthcoming.

The interviews were supervised by ███████████ ████████████ ███████████████ ████████████ and ████████████████ all of whom are trained in ███████████████ approved interrogation techniques. Parapsychologists ████████████ and ████████████ ████ were also present. The interviewers were instructed to extrapolate information in as non-confrontational and physically non-intrusive manner wherever possible. The primary intent was to ascertain the whereabouts and fate of the other 2957 passengers and crew who were on board *The Beautiful Dreamer* when it left the Port of Miami on December 28, 2016.

Day Four

The subjects were kept separately at ████████████ facility, which has a ████████████ security rating. Their only interaction was with staff, which was monitored at all times.

We have taken into account the possible correlation with the recent Costa Rica Incident where a fishing trawler allegedly carrying fifty-five illegal immigrants disappeared off the coast of Spain, and the events known to the media as 'Black Thursday'. [See addendum 17a of Section 18c]

Please review the material and provide your recommendations as to how to proceed, no later than 31/3/17.

DO NOT COPY DO NOT EMAIL
>>Smith, Xavier L/ Interview #1/ Page 1

SUBJECT NAME: Xavier Llewellyn Smith
DOB: 17/11/88
ADDRESS: 47 A Street, South Beach, Miami
OCCUPATION: Freelance writer. Writes a daily blog entitled 'The Wild Card Blog', the purpose of which is to debunk psychics and faith healers. Purports to be a member of the American Society of Skeptics. See addendum 34a for copies of blog entries extrapolated from Smith's laptop computer. Smith is financially supported by a trust set up in his name by his deceased maternal grandfather. Smith is estranged from his biological parents.
NOTES: Smith was initially hostile. Psychiatric evaluation shows no sign of delusional activity or personality disorder. No history of mental health issues. Tests reveal him to be occasional user of alcohol and marijuana.

Mr Smith, please start by stating your name and date of birth for the record.

XS: I told you people, I'm not saying anything else until I'm lawyered up. Seriously, what are you, NSA? Homeland Security? What?

Mr Smith, we would appreciate your cooperation.

XS: Go fuck yourself. I'm not some illegal immigrant. I'm an American citizen. You can't do this to people like me.

[Interview suspended due to subject's agitation]

[Interview recommences]

Mr Smith, previously you have said that the vessel was drifting for five days with all communication and the majority of operational systems out of action. During this time, where was the ship located?

XS: How in the hell would I know? I'm not a navigator. Ship got lost. Drifted into the Gulf Stream, maybe. Got lost in the Bermuda Triangle. I don't fucking know.

And you were on board the vessel in order to confront Celine del Ray about the Lillian Small case, is this correct?

XS: Yeah.

What is your interest in Celine del Ray, Mr Smith?

XS: I don't like what she does. Conning people.

You have no personal history with her?

XS: No.

What was it that sparked your interest in Ms del Ray's activities?

XS: I heard her on that radio show. Kavanaugh's show. She was saying how she knew that Bobby Small and his mother were alive. That pissed me off.

And your intention was to confront her on the cruise ship?

[Subject pauses for several seconds]

XS: Yeah. Only that backfired on me, didn't it?

In what way, Mr Smith?

XS: Jesus. I've told you this. Because of what she did. Putting us under group hypnosis or whatever. I told you people that when I was first brought here.

Please calm down, Mr Smith. We are only trying to help you.

X S: Yeah, sure you are. Don't think I don't know that I've bought myself a one-way ticket to Gitmo. No one knows we're here, right? The least you can do is answer that.

Mr Smith, I can assure you, as soon as we have debriefed you, you will be free to continue your life as usual.

X S: [Laughs] Yeah right.

To recap: You believe that everything you experienced since day four of the cruise is the result of being under a delusion?

X S: You tell me. It's possible. What I saw wasn't possible.

We would appreciate hearing what it is you saw, Mr Smith.

X S: I bet you would.

Where are the missing passengers and crew?

X S: You really want to know?

[Subject leans forward]

We poisoned their Mai Tais with cheap vodka. Added extra refined sugar to the chocolate fountain. One by one they succumbed, so we had no choice but to throw them over the side.

Mr Smith, we are simply trying to understand this situation.

X S: You and me both. I don't know where they are.

[Subject raises his voice and thumps his fist on the table]

I don't know where they fucking are. Celine del Ray was heading up some sort of suicide cult. After the captain and crew abandoned ship during the storm, maybe she got them all to jump over the fucking side. I don't know. Why are we here? What are you not telling us?

[Interview suspended]

>>Gardner, Madeleine/ Interview #1/ Page 2

but yes. I knew Celine was a fake when I took the job. If you want me to say it, I'll spell it out. So what? But that didn't explain Lizzie Bean or Archie or what some of the other people said they saw on board that bloody ship.

You believe these were actual physical beings, Ms Gardner?

M G : You think I don't know how this sounds? Listen, you asked me to tell you what I saw in my own words. That's what I saw. I saw Lizzie Bean. Is it crazy? Then I'm crazy. Xavier has his own theories about that – group hypnosis or whatever. But you know when something feels real. Lizzie Bean shouldn't have existed, but she did. The others shouldn't have existed, but people saw them.

Did you ask Celine del Ray about them?

M G : No. But I have my own theory about why they were there.

And what is that?

M G : She used them to manipulate us. Scare us. It amused her. There's nothing more potent than fear if you want to control someone. Xavier says I saw what I wanted to see. That I bought into Celine's bullshit. But . . . all the stuff that happened later . . . there's no way that was all in my head.

You've said before that 'Celine wasn't Celine'.

M G : All her actions after the ship stopped – after she had her episode or whatever the hell it was, were out of character. She wasn't Celine. The old Celine, I mean. She spoke like Celine, had her memories, but . . . you could see in her eyes. No. It wasn't Celine.

Are you saying you believe she was possessed?

M G : Christ. No. Maybe. I . . . look, I'm still trying to work through all this, wrap my head around it.

Is this going to take much longer? When can I go?

You are not under arrest, Ms Gardner.

MG: But I can't just get up and leave, can I?

As we told you when you were first brought here, this is merely a debriefing. A necessary formality. The people who were on the vessel with you are still unaccounted for.

MG: You hear stories, that's all. About what you people do. [Laughs] Shady agencies, people disappearing, that kind of thing.

We understand your concerns. To return to Ms del Ray. You have stated that she was possessed.

MG: I didn't say that exactly.

If she was possessed could you speculate by whom? Or what?

MG: I'm not ready to answer that yet. I'm not sure I even know the answer.

Let's go back. What happened after *The Beautiful Dreamer* became operational again?

MG: Oh God. When the ship got moving again, Xavier and I stayed in Celine's suite for a while. I guess we felt we'd be safe in there, and . . . I suppose I wasn't ready to see where we were or what we might be facing. I don't know about Xavier, but by then I was convinced something awful must have happened on land that prevented rescuers getting to us. Or that we'd drifted into unchartered waters somehow, only nothing's unchartered these days, is it? So yeah . . . That fear, it froze me at first.

I don't know who made the decision to get out of there in the end. Don't think we even discussed it, we just stood up and left. I knocked on Helen's door again to double-check she wasn't in there. I'd tried many times, so at that stage I didn't know if she'd left on the lifeboats or not. I couldn't see how, with Elise so sick. So yeah. We left the cabin and went outside to the pool deck. It was still dark – around four a.m. or so.

Who was there?

MG: Almost everyone who was left on board. Most of Celine's contingent. Two hundred people maybe. And a couple who'd been on Celine's deck. The Linemans or Linekers their name was – something like that. I remember seeing them when Xavier and I ran for the lifeboats. No one was speaking. Eerie is probably the best word to use. By then I should have been used to things freaking me out, but it still made me shiver. There was no sign of Celine. Then a man's voice, Italian, came over the intercom, and said we were approaching Miami. He sounded nervous, his voice wobbling. Later I learned that was Baci. He'd stayed behind when the other officers abandoned the ship. I don't know why he didn't leave. He was never part of Celine's group. I don't think he'd even met her until the engines came to life.

Why Miami? Why not another port?

MG: I don't know. Maybe that was the closest port to us. Xavier said the crew were able to track where the ship drifted using manual navigation, so it's possible. Maybe Baci just wanted to get home. Maybe it was Celine's idea.

Did you talk to anyone while you were on deck?

MG: No. Everyone was shell-shocked, still recovering from the storm. I saw Jacob, one of Celine's original followers, if you can call them that, and he acknowledged me, but that was all the interaction Xavier and I had with anyone at that point. We'd all been through so much at that stage. Oh wait . . . I tell a lie. Xavier went up to a girl he knew. Lisa, he said her name was. She looked out of it, barely seemed to see him.

We stood in silence and waited. Five, ten minutes went by, and Xavier said that the officer must have made a mistake about our location.

Why?

MG: Because if we were approaching Miami, we should have seen lights. But there were no lights. The coastline was completely dark.

I'm tired. Can I have a break now?

[Interview suspended]

Day Four

the cruise line for five years.

And were you happy in your position, Ms Trazona?

AT: It was a good job.

Did you have any dealings with Celine del Ray while you were on board?

AT: Yes.

Could you tell us what those were?

AT: No. I will not say anything more unless you guarantee me a green card. You cannot make me speak.

[Subject refused to speak at this time despite several attempts to encourage her to do so]
[Interview suspended]

DO NOT COPY DO NOT EMAIL
>>Zimri, Jesse C/ Interview #1/ Page 1

SUBJECT NAME: Jesse Clarence Zimri
DOB: 17/11/84
ADDRESS: 7 Acacia Road, Sun Valley, Cape Town
OCCUPATION: General Practice Medical Practitioner. Dr Zimri voluntarily left his former practice in Tokai, Cape Town after misdiagnosing a sixteen-year-old girl, Sasha Lee Abrams. Ms Abrams was complaining of stomach pains, which Dr Zimri diagnosed as colitis. Abrams subsequently died from complications from an ectopic pregnancy. Subject was addicted to pethidine but did not enter a rehab facility at that time.
Subject is married to but separated from Farouka Majiet.
NOTES: First interview with Dr Zimri was aborted. Subject was delirious, vomiting, and suffering from pethidine withdrawal.

307

>>Fall, Helen/ Interview #1/ Page 2

the British Embassy? This isn't an interview. This is an interrogation. Does anyone even know we're here?

Ms Fall, you are in a unique situation.

HF: Where are we? I assume we're still somewhere in Florida. How did you manage it?

Manage what, Ms Fall?

HF: Spiriting us away like this. I'm assuming no one knows we're here. It's all very Tom Clancy, and I'm very impressed. Now. Let me make something clear to you. I will not talk to you whatever you do to me.

Ms Fall. You have our guarantee that as soon as we have finished debriefing you to our satisfaction, you will be released from the facility.

HF: And what exactly does 'to your satisfaction' mean?

We need answers, Ms Fall. We need to know the fate of the passengers and crew who were absent from the vessel when it was discovered.

HF: How are you going to do it?

Do what, Ms Fall?

HF: Dispose of us after we've answered your questions, of course. Do you have a system like the mafia where you feed us to the pigs? Make us disappear in some porcine bowel track? There are worse ways to go I suppose.

Ms Fall. We have your computer. We have reason to believe that your intention and reason for being on the cruise ship was to take your own life.

[Subject shows symptoms of distress]

HF: That is private. You have no right to access my personal belongings.

We understand that you find this upsetting, Ms Fall. There are many families out there who need answers.

HF: They won't get them from me. Where are the others? Where's Maddie? Althea?

They are being extremely helpful and cooperative, Ms Fall.

HF: Then you don't need me.

[Subject refuses to respond to further questioning at this time] [Interview suspended]

>>Gardner, Madeleine/ Interview #2/ Page 2

and then when the sun came up . . . well . . . We saw it for the first time.

Saw what, Ms Gardner?

MG: Look, I'm going to tell you what I experienced, but I want it on record again that I know it's unbelievable. It's nuts. Beyond nuts, really, but you asked me to be honest about what I saw, so I'm going to do that. If you want to lock me up in the funny farm afterwards, then so be it.

Duly noted. Please continue. What was it that you saw – or believed you saw?

The ship moved closer to the coastline, heading for the channel that leads to the harbour, and the closer it got, the more we could see. God. I suppose the first thing that hit me was that I couldn't see anything move. No one on the beach, no boats in the water. Nothing.

Then Eleanor, one of Celine's core group of Friends, had the idea to look through the view-finders on the exercise deck. But I didn't need to look through them. As we got closer still, we saw blocks of holiday flats stained with smoke. There were vehicles – big army trucks – and huge white tents all along the beach.

God. I think it was then that the smell hit us. Just the thought of it now makes me feel sick. The slightest breeze blew it towards us. Have you ever smelled a dead body? I hadn't. Not until then. Imagine the stench ten thousand bodies make when they've been rotting in the sun. It was making people sick all over. I retched several times, but I had nothing to bring up.

Baci came over the intercom again and said that he couldn't get any closer without a harbour pilot guiding the ship in. The engines were still running, but the ship slowed right down to a stop.

I know you don't believe me, but the others will back me up. I mean, why would I concoct a story as crazy as this one?

And the others on board? How did they react?

M G : I suppose at first we couldn't believe what we were seeing. People started crying, a few started saying that it must be terrorists. You know what I mean, 'Fucking ragheads got us in the end,' that kind of bullshit. We all knew that something had to have happened while we were stranded. It's what we all expected, I guess. Seeing it like that though . . . your worst fears realised. God. It was . . . Can I have some water, please?

[Interview suspended for seven minutes]

Where was Celine del Ray at this point?

M G : She was now on the main deck, parked in front of the Lido bar. I don't know how long she'd been there. I didn't see her arriving. Jacob wheeled her over to the railings and everyone turned to look at her. And then she said . . . she said something like: 'What a mess. We really made a mess with this one.' I can't be precise. I was pretty shaken up at that point.

What did she mean by that?

M G : I don't know. She didn't seem to be too surprised at what she was seeing.

Xavier was next to me, and he squeezed my hand so tight I could feel the bones crack. That's the kind of detail that makes it real. He was saying, 'I knew it, I knew it, I knew it,' over and over again. 'I knew something had happened.'

Someone said, and I don't know who it was – Eleanor again, maybe – said, 'Should we go and see if there are any survivors?'

No one answered her for a minute or so. It was clear that Miami was fucked – sorry. We didn't know if we'd stumbled into the aftermath of a war, or a plague, or what. Then the dam burst and arguments broke out, some people saying we should head for land and check it out, others saying that that would be madness if a biological weapon had been let loose or whatever. Celine just let them rage on. I suppose she knew they had to get it out of their systems.

When there was a lull in the shouting, Celine said, 'Go and see if you like. I wouldn't bother though.'

We all turned to look at her. Then she said: 'Any volunteers?'

No one spoke up for what felt like ages, and then one of the security guys, Devi, stepped forward and said that he'd go. He looked terrible, like he'd been hit by a bus, his face all puffed up and bruised. Rogelio, one of the assistant cruise directors, begged him not to go.

I think it was then that it really started to hit people, and they started asking, 'What if it's not just Miami?' and talking about their friends and family. Celine spoke up again and said something like: 'It is not just Miami, my darlings.' And then she began . . . God, I suppose you'd call it preaching. She spoke for at least half an hour, promising people that they'd see their loved ones again 'in spirit' and reminding them that she'd kept them safe so far, and they must continue to trust her. The people there wanted to hear that. They wanted someone to tell them what to do. They were terrified, traumatised, broken. She was good at talking. That was her real gift. When she spoke, people listened. Not even Xavier interrupted her.

Devi was still insisting he wanted to leave the ship and see for himself what had happened. Then out of the blue, Xavier said, 'I'm going too.' I remembered that he lived in South Beach. I'd seen his address on his driver's licence. Celine gave him a huge smile and a wink. It was almost as if she wanted him to go. And then I found myself stepping forward. Christ knows what made me do it.

I still don't know.

Jacob was demanding to know how we'd reach the shore, and one of the deckhands said there was one tender boat left that had jammed when the davits had been incorrectly released or something like that. He said it hung off the ship at a crazy angle, but he should be able to free it. Devi suggested we take the ship's doctor with us and sent me and Xavier off to find him. No one had seen him for hours.

We found him sleeping on one of the hospital beds. He looked like he'd been drinking, and barely reacted when he saw the coastline for the first time. He'd been pretty crap when he'd dealt with Celine, so I couldn't really see the point of bringing him along with us, but Devi insisted. A nurse, Bin, who was as sick as a dog, also said he wanted to come along. And then other people started volunteering. Devi put paid to that. He said that whoever was going had to wear protective gear and breathing apparatus in case of infection. He'd collected the ship's fire-fighting suits, which included helmets and oxygen tanks – God, they were so heavy – and there were only five suits. We would only have an hour of oxygen, so whatever happened it was going to be a short trip.

While the tender boat was being freed, Xavier and I hung out on the main deck. He was withdrawn and didn't want to talk. He kept glancing at the coastline. Celine was busy organising everyone, getting them to right the chairs that had been thrown everywhere during the storm, sending Althea and other people to get bottles of water and whatever they could find. She was telling people not to worry, that they were the lucky ones. They were safe on the ship for now.

For now. That's what she said.

People worked together, having something to do helped them. One of the passengers – a woman I hadn't spoken to before – asked Celine if she could organise a prayer group and Celine told her to go ahead.

Paulo, one of the stewards, was going to be driving the boat, and Devi said we'd have to climb on board it via one of the loading bays, which sounds easier than it was. Paulo didn't have one of those awful heavy suits and he was terrified, really shitting himself. I tried to reassure him, but what could I say? 'Don't worry, it's not the end of the world'?

Xavier was still spaced out, and the doctor and Bin were taking it in turns to throw up over the side. I felt . . . God, I suppose vulnerable would be the right word as we pulled away from *The Beautiful Dreamer* and she loomed over us, casting her shadow around us.

Can I get a coffee or something?

[Interview suspended]

>>Trazona, Althea/ Interview #2/ Page 2

AT: Do you have my green card?

We are working on that Ms Trazona. These things take time. It would help if you would show that you are willing to cooperate.

AT: I am not stupid. I know how this works. You help me, I'll help you. I have seen too many people deported to trust you.

We assure you that isn't going to happen Ms Trazona. If you cooperate, we will guarantee that you and your child are safe and secure.

AT: The boy? You have found the boy?

What boy, Ms Trazona?

[Subject refuses to answer]

Ms Trazona, our medical tests show that you are eight weeks pregnant. Again, you have our assurance that—

AT: If I help you, you will guarantee me citizenship?

Yes.

AT: I want that in writing.

[Interview suspended for several hours]

[Interview recommences]

AT:What do you want to know? I will only answer what I want to answer.

That is understood. Ms Trazona, could you please tell us about your relationship with Celine del Ray?

AT:What about it?

Did you like Celine del Ray, Ms Trazona?

AT: Like her? No. I did not like her.

Could you explain why?

AT: I could see what she was. She was not to be trusted. I knew that from the beginning. And I was right. She tricked me. Used me. Just like everyone else.

Earlier you mentioned something about a boy you spoke to on the ship.

AT:There was no boy.

When you were first brought here to this facility you told our medical representative that the rescuers must return to the ship and find the boy.

AT:There is no boy.

[Subject refuses to speak again at this time]

[Interview suspended]

>>Smith, Xavier L/ Interview #2/ Page 3

XS: Maddie's delusional. I could see that straight away when we met back in the suite after the storm. Celine had said something to her. Infected her with her bullshit.

Mr Smith, earlier you say that 'what you saw wasn't possible'. Could you clarify?

XS: I didn't see anything. Let me break it down for you again. The ship got stranded. There was a big fuck-off storm. The captain and crew abandoned us, people panicked, and escaped in the lifeboats. Everyone who was left behind became the victim of a mass delusion where they believed they'd returned to an alternate Miami. One that was fucked up. Then . . . shit, I dunno. Celine convinced everyone to jump overboard, whatever.

Why would she do that, Mr Smith?

XS: People like her want to be talked about. Maybe she wanted to go down in history or something.

Mr Smith. You say that the ship was drifting for five days before the engines started up again. Where was the ship in the two days following that?

XS: Going round and round the Gulf Stream. How would I know?

You categorically deny that you at any time left the ship?

XS: Jesus H. Christ. How many more times?

[Subject becomes agitated. Interview suspended]

>>Fall, Helen/ Interview #2/ Page 5

I felt the ship stop. I didn't move for a while. I didn't want to leave her.

You are speaking of Elise Mayberry?

HF: Yes.

So you were not on deck when the ship reached its first destination.

HF: No.

You saw nothing? You weren't curious?

HF: I was in mourning. And I'd seen enough. I'd seen the lowest people could go.

We are sorry for your loss, and appreciate you talking to us.

HF: I'm not doing this for you, or for the families of those who have lost people. All I ask is simple, that after you've done whatever tests or whatever it is you have to do, that Elise's ashes are scattered next to her husband's.

And where is that?

HF: I don't know. You can find these things out, can't you? What have you done with Elise's body?

I can assure you Ms Mayberry's remains are being—

HF: I should have gone with her. I should have gone with her when I had the chance. Only . . . only . . .

[Subject becomes visibly distressed]

[Interview suspended]

>>Zimri, Jesse C/ Interview #2/ Page 2

JZ: I'm not well. I'm in no state to answer your questions. I got to . . . I think I've got the noro. About fucking time.

Dr Zimri, according to Madeleine Gardner, you were among the party who left the ship. Can you confirm this?

[Subject continues to protest that he be allowed back to his room]

[Interview recommences after medical intervention]

JZ: Jesus. What did you give me? Diazepam?

Day Four

You are feeling stronger, Dr Zimri?

JZ: *Ja*. Much. Achy, but okay.

Dr Zimri, according to Madeleine Gardner, you were among the party who left the ship. Can you confirm this?

JZ: *Ja*.

Can you confirm who was with you?

JZ: Bin – Jesus, Bin . . . Fuck. That security guy, Devi, though he was still in a bad way. Maddie, the woman who worked for Celine del Ray. And some guy I hadn't met before.

Paulo, my old cabin steward, if you can believe that, was driving the boat. I didn't know he had it in him. I didn't get much of a chance to speak to him, because although we didn't have to go far, less than a kay, probably, I got sick almost the second I climbed on board. So did Bin. The closer we got to shore, the realer the whole thing became. I was zonked when I saw the coastline for the first time on the cruise ship. Thought I was imagining it. Now we were coming face to face with buildings with smashed windows, no cars, no noise except the burr of the engine and this low buzz which I later learned was from the flies on the beach.

The channel was blocked by another cruise ship. It looked untouched but it was jammed right in there – it was bloody huge and I could read its name: *The Beautiful Wonder*. Paulo manoeuvred the boat towards the end of the jetty wall and tied us off. He still looked terrified. Devi instructed us to put on our gear. I started sweating the second I pulled on the suit, which was like being wrapped in asbestos. He said he was going to head out and see if he could locate a police station or find any military personnel – oh *ja*, that's the other thing, there were a couple of army trucks on the pedestrian boardwalk. Empty, but you could see that at some stage there was a military presence.

Maddie's friend – intense guy, bad Celtic tattoos, I can't remember his name – said he was going to go and check out his apartment, which was around the corner from the harbour. He hadn't said a word the whole time we were on the boat. Maddie said she'd go with him.

Devi asked Bin and me to head along the beach and investigate what the fuck those giant tents staked out along it were all about. I was seriously worried about Bin and told him to stay with Paulo. He refused. I should have tried harder.

[Subject requests a five-minute break]

[Interview commences]

Did you go along the beach, Dr Zimri?

JZ: *Ja.*

Please continue, Dr Zimri.

JZ: Are you guys really buying all this stuff I'm saying?

Please continue, Dr Zimri.

Christ. Well. It was a nightmare right from the first second. For a start, I almost fell out of the boat when I climbed out of it. The tanks and helmet . . . Jesus, you'd have to be super-fit to carry all that weight even in perfect conditions, and we had to climb over a fence and scramble over the rocks to get to the bloody beach. It was unbearably hot walking along that beach, in that suit. I don't know if the smell could cut through the breathing apparatus, or if I was just imagining it. Jissus, it was like . . . And Bin, I really felt for him. He'd doped himself up with Solu-Medrol and Imodium, but they wouldn't stop the noro.

After a minute or so, I didn't think about what I was doing. I just walked.

Then we reached the first tent. There were about six of them, I think. Placed all along the beach. I knew what they were straight away. I knew it was where they must have taken the bodies to store them from the flies. Why there I have no idea. Maybe everywhere else was full. It was clearly a mass operation of some kind. Maybe they were planning on chucking them into the sea. There was a huge pile of body bags just thrown on top of each other around the entrance. Someone had covered them in lime powder, and sand and other crap had blown in on top of them. Didn't stop the flies though. They were so thick in places, you couldn't see a hand in front of your face.

I knew I had to open one up, see what we were dealing with.

And did you?

JZ: *Ja.*

Could you please describe the condition of the body?

JZ: *Ja.* It was fucked. That's a medical term, by the way.

In your opinion, what was the cause of death?

JZ: I'm not a pathologist.

We would appreciate hearing your opinion.

JZ: Christ. I don't know. I didn't want to touch it. What we were doing, getting so close, it was already dangerous. The suits wouldn't protect against an airborne pathogen.

[Subject sighs]

Look, from what I could see, it looked like it might have been some kind of super-flu or Ebola-type infection. It was hard to even tell the gender of the body it was so bloated. There did appear to be some lesions and swelling of the glands, but that could have just been putrefaction at work.

In your opinion, how long had the bodies been dead?

[Subject remains silent]

Please answer the question, Dr Zimri.

JZ: I asked Bin his opinion, but he just shook his head. Without another word, he walked off down the beach and I shouted at him to stop. He didn't hear me, or didn't want to hear me. We only had forty-five minutes of oxygen left or so. Like I say, the whole thing was incredibly short-sighted.

And then Bin started yelling and pointing at something. I ran up to him, which almost killed me. The helmet's visor was steaming up, and the oxygen I was breathing tasted like diesel. And then I saw it too. A flash of red in the sand about five hundred metres away.

Bin said he thought it might be a lifeboat, but it was difficult to be sure with the flies and the spray and the fucking helmet. He set off, and I ran after him. We jogged past another of those tents, this one had earthmoving equipment around it and an overturned army jeep.

It was a lifeboat. One of the triangular inflatable ones. It had collapsed, which isn't supposed to happen, so fuck knows what it had been through, and the sea was trying to tug it back in. Bin was there first. There was something tangled in the ropes attached to it.

A body.

Did you recognise the body?

JZ: *Ja.* It was Damien. The cruise director.

[Interview suspended]

>>**Gardner, Madeleine/ Interview #3/ Page 2**

all he would say, over and over again. 'This is impossible. This is impossible.'

Why impossible?

MG: The ship had lost communication for . . . God, what was it? Five days by then. You could see that what had happened must have taken longer than that. And a cataclysm hasn't hit Miami in actuality, has it? I'm here . . . sitting here. Talking to you. We're in Miami, right? Or close to it.

Please continue, Ms Gardner.

MG: We headed away from the beach and towards the highway. The apartment blocks to our right were barricaded with rolls of razor wire. I couldn't tell if that was to stop people getting out, or getting in. We passed the gate to the harbour. There were still boats there, yachts, but I saw something lying behind that gate . . . sprawled out, covered in flies. None of it felt real. None of it. Xavier led us to the end of the walkway, around a corner and towards a wide boulevard. Behind us, a few hundred metres away, where the main road met the highway, it looked like the army had set up some kind of barrier there. More wire, huge army trucks, I think there was even a tank. I don't know. Sweat was running in my eyes, it was becoming difficult to see, and my shoulders were aching and shaking under the weight of the suit and the oxygen tanks. I did try to peer past it, hoping that maybe I could see towards the airport. Stupid, really, as I knew it was miles away.

We passed by a large strip mall. God, that freaked me out. A huge pet store, all kinds of graffiti smeared across the windows. A CVS pharmacy that looked like it had been turned into some kind of church. And the billboards . . . instead of adverts for McDonalds or whatever, they . . . um . . . One said nothing but 'repent' in huge red letters that looked like blood. Another showed a series of photographs of teenagers, the word 'sinner' slashed across each of their faces.

How were you feeling at this point?

M G : Numb, I suppose. Light-headed. Part of this was the equipment. My entire body was wet with sweat. I was running out of energy and I asked Xavier how much further it was. He told me it was just three more blocks. He kept moving, and I kept following. Part of the main road was flooded where a water pipe had burst and we had to detour around it. Um . . . God. There was so much to take in. And flies. Flies everywhere. I had to keep brushing them away from my visor. Whatever had killed the people, it hadn't killed the flies.

Finally he turned down a residential street that looked reassuringly normal. Only . . . several of the houses' windows were boarded up and notices were stuck onto every door or garage door that we passed. Most were ripped or weathered, but I found one sealed in plastic. Have you seen it?

[Subject is referring to the following document scanned in here for convenience:

What to do if you suspect your family is infected with the Ishi Virus.
Do NOT approach the authorities or attempt to leave the vicinity.
Call the 0700 hotline.
WE WILL COME TO YOU.
Quarantine the infected in a room and seal and secure the entrance and exit. All items that the infected has touched must be incinerated.
Those attempting to flee the quarantine line will be prosecuted.
May Jesus and Lord our God have mercy on all our souls.

NOTE: There is no known strain of disease classified 'the Ishi Virus'. 'Ishi' was the codename for Unit 787, the covert biological and chemical research undertaken by the Japanese in World War II]

Xavier eventually stopped outside a house three blocks down the street, a park of some kind behind it. Semi-detached. Not high-end or anything, but nice enough, apart from the fact that the windows were covered with newspaper. The door was locked, but he flipped up a pot outside the door and retrieved a key.

Then we went inside.

In your opinion, what was Mr Smith's state of mind at this point?

MG: You mean Xavier?

Yes.

MG: It was difficult to see his face clearly through the visor, but I could tell he was trying to hide his emotions. But when I asked him if he'd put the newspaper over the windows, he snapped at me, said something like, 'Don't be so fucking stupid.' The place was cramped and dark. We tried the light switch, but the electricity was out – no surprise there after everything we'd seen. The kitchen and lounge were on the ground floor, and it looked like the bailiffs had just been. The floor was covered in dust and filth, there was sod-all furniture, nothing but a desk and an empty bookshelf, and someone had spray-painted a peace sign on the fridge door. Xavier had told me he was a trust-fund kid. I wouldn't have expected him to live in such a squalid place.

Did Mr Smith comment on the condition of the residence?

MG: He said something like: 'This can't be,' then he ran up the stairs. I don't how he moved so fast in that suit.

Did you follow him?

MG: Not right then. I snooped around for a few minutes, looked in the kitchen cupboards – they were all empty – and checked the desk drawers. That's where I found the e-reader. I'm not sure why I pocketed it. Maybe because it seemed to be the only thing of value in the place and I thought Xavier might want it. Time was really running out by then and to be honest I was getting spooked. As if I was in a haunted house or something. I called out that we'd have to hurry as we'd need enough air to get us back to the tender boat, but he didn't answer. I shouted again, and he still didn't respond. I had no choice but to go after him.

And where was he?

MG: He was standing in the doorway of what had to be the bedroom, staring down at something. I touched his shoulder and he screamed. I told him once again that we had to get the hell out of there, and this time he listened to me and headed for the stairs.

What was it that he was looking at?

MG: The room was empty but for a mattress with a lumpy duvet piled on top of it. Look, I can't be sure or anything, but it was possible that there was something . . . God, someone – okay? – under there. All I know is that the window frame was black with dead flies.

Did you investigate further?

MG: No way. Do I look insane? No. I got the hell out of there. Can I get some water, please? My throat is aching.

[Interview suspended]

>>Fall, Helen/ Interview #3/ Page 2

It was Althea who came to find me. She was kind, I'll give her that. The whole time we were on that ship, she was kind to me and Elise. She said Celine wanted to see me. She said Celine was waiting for me in the spa.

Did you go and meet Ms del Ray, Ms Fall?

HF:Yes. I was reluctant to leave Elise. Probably you're thinking I'm some dotty old woman, but even though I knew she was gone, that there was nothing else I could do for her, I didn't want to leave her. But I did.

I was curious. I suppose I wanted to hear what Celine wanted to say to me.

I wasn't shocked at the damage inside the ship. I'd been expecting it. And as for the spa, do you know, Elise and I hadn't even been in there the whole time we were on the ship. It was relatively untouched. Smashed bottles, which made the whole place stink like a prostitute's boudoir, and it had clearly been looted, but it was quiet.

She was waiting for me in the hair salon. Sitting in her wheelchair, flicking through a magazine – yes, really! – as if she was a client waiting for her stylist.

She greeted me like an old friend. It was . . . it was . . . and I don't like to use this word . . . but there is no other. Surreal. Two old women at the beauty salon or the hairdresser's, swapping small talk.

Please continue.

HF: She thanked me for coming. I asked her why she wanted to see me. She said she'd taken a shine to me. That I had proven myself to her. She said . . . I do have an excellent memory, but . . . hold on. Yes. She said, 'It gets dull after a while. Going round and round and round again. Far better to be a puppet master than a puppet. Tearing down worlds then building them up again. Setting wheels in motion to see where and how they'd roll.'

She went on like this, talking clichéd nonsense, for quite a while. It was all rather annoying, if you want the truth.

Do you know what she meant by that?

HF: I assumed she was talking about her parlour tricks.

>>Smith, Xavier L/ Interview #3/ Page 2

and then there are those medical tests you did. Have you tested us for drugs? Hallucinogenics?

Mr Smith, to confirm, you state that you never returned to your house?

XS: I never went back to my house! Ask my fucking neighbours.

I was never off the fucking ship.

The captain and crew ditched us, people panicked and fled, only to lose their lives in the storm. And the rest of us . . . Celine convinced us that we were experiencing something we could never have experienced.

[Subject is shown the e-reader that Madeleine Gardner states she collected from his residence]

Can you please explain what this is, Mr Smith?

XS: It's a Kobo. You can read books on it. It's like a Kindle, only more ethical.

Mr Smith, would you mind reading the content list from it? Just the first page.

XS: Yes, I would mind.

[Subject is shown the list of books stored on the device purportedly taken from his apartment: *From Crash to Conspiracy* by Elspeth Martins, *Beyond Black Thursday* by Carter Edwards, *The Truth About Black Thursday* by Ace Kelso, and *Dangerous Belief* by Michael Shermer.

NOTE: It has been ascertained without a doubt that the authors of the books named have not written or published this material]

XS: I've never seen those before.

[Subject refuses to comment further]

[Interview suspended]

>>Gardner, Madeleine/ Interview #4/ Page 7

drag him back to the boat. By now I was absolutely exhausted. Xavier kept saying 'it isn't happening, it isn't happening'. I didn't bother to argue with him. My back was sore, I was dying of thirst. *The Beautiful Dreamer* had drifted further out, and I remember this weird panic that we wouldn't be able to get back on it. After what we'd been through on it! . . . God . . .

Devi was the next one to arrive. He'd been at the cordon, the place that I said looked like some kind of military blockade. He said he'd tried the radio and they had satellite phones and all sorts of equipment, but there was nothing. No signal.

None of us said the obvious. That this damage couldn't have taken place over five days. The damage we'd seen would have taken months.

The doctor came back alone.

[Subject requests a ten-minute recess]

[Interview suspended]

>>Trazona, Althea/ Interview #4/ Page 2

she told the old woman that she could have her husband back. That there were ways. That she could have everything she wanted. That someone like Helen could learn to do what Mrs del Ray did. We all could. It was hard to make sense of what she was saying. For example, I heard her say that we could all learn to come back again and again in a vessel of our own choosing. It sounded like religious nonsense to me.

How did Ms Fall respond?

AT: She was staring at Mrs del Ray as if she was mad. Perhaps she was. Or is. I liked Helen and Elise. Very good guests. Clean. Quiet. I was sorry that Elise died. Then Mrs del Ray said I could leave them alone. So I did.

Where did you go?

AT: I went out onto the main deck. People were clearing up the area. Most of them were helping with the work, but Mr and Mrs Lineman, who were guests on my station, were sitting by themselves at a table next to the Lido bar. Mrs Lineman called my name and asked me to go to their cabin and collect Mr Lineman's medication.

How did you respond?

AT: I was tempted to tell them to go and fuck themselves, but they looked so lost that I agreed. They had been punished enough. Mr Lineman had broken his arm, and she was very pale and tears were running down her face. On my way to their cabin, I met Rogelio, one of my paisanos. He was very worried about a friend of his, the security guard who had gone with the others to the mainland. I could see he wanted to talk. I let him.

He knew I'd found the body of the dead girl.

Kelly Lewis?

AT: Yes. Rogelio told me that the man who had murdered her was locked in the morgue. He said that Devi, the security guard, wanted him to stay in there as punishment for what he'd done.

How did you feel about this?

AT: I didn't know the man. Rogelio said he was worried about Devi and how he would feel if the man died in there. He said Devi was sensitive and might blame himself and regret it, even though the man was a rapist.

I suggested that we should go and see if the man was still alive.

We went down to the morgue, and Rogelio banged on the door to see if there was an answer.

And was there?

AT: Yes. A soft tap. Weak. I didn't hear the man cry out or anything like that, but it sounded like he was still alive.

Then what did you do?

AT: I told Rogelio to wait for me there and then went to ask Mrs del Ray what we should do with him. If we should leave him in there, or let him out.

What did she say?

AT: She said it was Rogelio's choice if we wanted someone like that to join them.

Did you question what she meant by that?

AT: No.

Rogelio and I had a long discussion about what to do. Devi had given Rogelio his taser gun, and he held it in front of him while I opened the hatch. The smell! I thought I was going to vomit. The man had messed himself and he was moaning and sweating and talking all sorts of nonsense. He tried to climb out, and then Rogelio shot him.

The man jerked like a puppet, and then he seemed to pass out.

Moving him out of there was hard. We had to drag him part of the way. He was heavy. But when we reached the I-95, we were able to use a gurney from the medical bay.

Where were you planning on taking him?

AT: I knew the crew members had opened one of the loading bays.

It was simple. Rogelio took his legs, and I took his arms and we carried him to the edge. He moaned, and Rogelio thought that he would have to use the taser again, but then he was quiet. We rolled him into the water.

I would like to make it clear that we weren't planning to kill the man. He was not dead when we put him into the water. He deserved a chance to live. Everyone does. He could have woken up and swum. But I will admit we didn't check if he did. Perhaps we didn't want to know. We weren't far from shore. And at least that way, Rogelio said, Devi would not be haunted by the man's ghost and his conscience. He said that Devi would assume he had escaped and had thrown himself overboard. That way he would not blame himself.

What did you do next?

AT: I had something I had to do. I had someone I had to find.

Who?

AT: Trining. One of the other stewards. I thought she might still be on the ship.

Did you find her?

AT: No. But I promised myself I would keep looking. Mrs del Ray said that he – she – was no longer on the ship, but I didn't always trust what she said. I needed to make sure.

>>Gardner, Madeleine/ Interview #5/ Page 3

Why did you not leave Miami and go overland to attempt to see if there was life elsewhere?

MG: Because we were running out of air. And anyway it was obvious that there was *no* life elsewhere. That level of destruction didn't just happen in isolation. The extent of it was . . . I've told you how bad it was.

How did the other passengers react when you told them what you had discovered?

M G : Not well. And it was up to me and Devi to do the honours. The second we got back to the ship, Xavier disappeared and locked himself in Celine's cabin. He couldn't cope with what he'd seen. Jesse also left us. He was gutted that he'd let the nurse go off by himself and he hadn't tried to stop him. Yeah, so Devi and I did our best, but they didn't want to hear it. They hadn't seen what we'd seen, so they kept insisting that we were mistaken, that it'd happened recently, while we were at sea, and that was why no one had come to rescue us. A few of them – Jacob especially – got quite angry with us. Celine just listened, an infuriating smile on her face.

What is your explanation for what you saw in Miami, Ms Gardner?

M G : There's only one, and it's batshit insane. That somehow we'd arrived in . . . I don't know. Another version of reality. One where the world had been hit by a cataclysm. One with a history that had never happened. Celine – or the ship – had taken us somewhere else.

Yeah. Trust me, I know how that sounds.

What happened next?

M G : Celine spoke up and gave another one of her speeches. She said that we must move somewhere where we could live until the dead bodies had had time to putrefy and wouldn't be a health hazard. And, surprise, surprise, she knew exactly where we should go.

She had it all planned to a tee.

And where was that?

M G : Foveros's private island. Dream Cay. We'd stopped there on the second day of the cruise. Celine – the old Celine – had got drunk at the beach bar there.

Why there?

MG: According to Celine, very few people lived there, so body disposal wouldn't be too arduous. It was large enough for all of us and there were plenty of food sources. There were horses and chickens everywhere. A bar styled to look like a pirate ship on the beach. Fishing. And let's not forget the enormous Duty Free shop. If you were going to spend eternity somewhere, that would be the place. All set up for you.

>>Zimri, Jesse C/ Interview #4/ Page 2

JZ: I felt *kak*. Worse. I couldn't believe I'd let Bin go. I mean, the man shouldn't have even come with us. But he kept talking about getting back to his family, although how the fuck he thought he'd manage that, I have no clue. Perhaps he just couldn't face getting back on the ship. The whole 'girl coming alive in the morgue' thing had spooked him badly, and the passengers had treated us like shit while it was all going on. But I should have stopped him.

When we got back . . . fuck it. When we got back I went back to the medical bay to see what I could take to zonk myself out. And it wasn't just Bin. I didn't understand how any of this could be happening. The bodies, the devastation. It was all . . . Christ. I don't know.

Baci caught up with me before I had a chance to dig into the Demerol. He was in a bad way. He'd stayed behind with Alfonso when the rest of the crew had abandoned ship, and he was asking if I'd seen any sign of the lifeboats. I lied to him and said I hadn't. I told him he'd made the right decision staying on the ship. I lied about that too. He said Alfonso was much better mentally, and said 'the dark man' – the ghost or devil or whatever it was he kept hallucinating – had gone.

One of the engineering guys came and found Baci and said that Celine wanted to talk to him. It sounded like they were planning on moving to another port, I heard them discussing fuel ratios and power and blah-de-blah before they left. I didn't care where we were going. I had other plans.

And what were they?

JZ: [Laughs] To block everything out with the help of medical science. And I succeeded with that, alright. Next thing I knew I was being carried into a helicopter by a couple of giant marines.

That's it. That's all I've got to say.

And you stand by your version of events, Dr Zimri?

JZ: I'm telling you what I experienced. Nothing more, nothing less. Whether you want to take the word of a drug addict is up to you.

[Interview suspended]

>>Fall, Helen/ Interview #4/ Page 2

to the suite. I prepared Elise's body. Washed it down. In some ways this helped.

How long did you remain in the suite, Ms Fall?

HF: I remained there until my door flew open and I found men in black SWAT uniforms milling around out there. I was taken to a helicopter, inside which I saw Althea and Maddie. I felt so sorry for Althea. She was hysterical, and one of your medical thugs gave her some sort of tranquilliser. Maddie didn't speak, but she was smiling. It wasn't a relieved smile that we were being rescued. I . . . can't really describe it. She said she'd knocked on my door earlier, and assumed Elise and I had left the ship. And she was half right. One of us had left the ship. In spirit, anyway.

And that is all I can tell you. And no, I won't speculate any further on Celine del Ray. Not that whatever I say about her will matter now.

Could you clarify what you mean, Ms Fall?

HF: You know what I mean. You're going to bury us. You're not going to let us go. You're smarter than that. We're not terrorists. We're not a threat. But there's a reason why you will never let us go.

And that reason is?

HF: It doesn't matter.

What does not matter?

HF: Any of this. This charade. Maybe you believe in heaven or hell, maybe you believe in Nirvana or Narnia, or that when you die, that's it. That's what concerns you. That's why we're here, isn't it? Maybe if the story got out, our story got out, people wouldn't believe it. But what if they did? How do you think people will react if that's taken away from them? If they have proof?

Proof of what, Ms Fall?

HF: That it's out of our control. Life. Death. That we're being manipulated, played. I am a rational person, but I saw things on that ship that could not – and should not – exist.

And . . . I keep thinking . . . What if she's right? What if it never ends? What if there is no death? If I don't believe what I saw, why am I now so afraid to die?

[Interview suspended]

>>Gardner, Madeleine/ Interview #6/ Page 3

How long did it take us to get there? Not long. Along the way we saw other signs of devastation. Half-submerged oil tankers, a couple of other cruise ships in the distance, both of which looked like they were on the verge of giving up the ghost. Baci and the crew sailing the ship couldn't bring it right up to the island, and Celine said we would have to use the tender boat to ferry people to the shore. She told everyone to collect anything they thought they might need, and to hurry down to the loading deck.

I tried to get Xavier to come out of his room, but he told me to 'fuck off, this couldn't be happening'. I had no idea Helen was still on board. I feel bad about that.

The Friends got everyone organised in no time. And they all helped each other. Several passengers had been injured in the storm – that couple who were on Celine's deck, for example – and Eleanor made sure they got down there first so that they could be comfortable. There were still some inflatable crew lifeboats aboard, so some of the crew dropped those into the water and were using them to travel onto the island.

I felt a bit isolated. Almost everyone was giving me a wide berth because of what Devi and I had told them when we returned from Miami. Devi was one of the first to go to the island. He didn't look reluctant about it. He looked . . . I never got to know him, but he seemed to be happy. He knew the truth, that the world we were in wasn't our own, but even if he'd been offered the choice Celine gave me, I got the feeling he would have stayed.

Celine asked Jimmy and Annabeth to carry her wheelchair. Then she asked me to help walk her down the stairs.

And did you?

M G : Yes. I think she wanted to be alone with me – talk to me in relative privacy. And she said that I didn't have to come with her to the island. She said that I could choose to stay on the ship and take my chances.

Then she said, if I wanted to, I could 'go back'.

What did she mean by that?

M G : She wouldn't say what she meant. But it was fairly obvious. She either meant back to the Miami that was destroyed, or back home. Here.

I said yes. That I would take my chances. I didn't even hesitate.

The other choice – to spend an eternity with the Friends, sweet as they are, in a giant Duty Free shop – wasn't an option.

How did she react?

M G : She was pleased. I don't know if she knew for sure who else was on board or not. I was shocked when I saw Althea and Helen in the rescue helicopter. I knew Xavier was in Celine's suite, but I thought everyone else had left the ship.

How was your return to be achieved?

M G : She said she would instruct Alfonso and Baci to turn the ship around. She said the rest would be up to me.

When the last of the Friends had left, Baci got the ship started. I thought he might stay on it, but he didn't. The tender boat chugged alongside it, and although I didn't see him do it, he and the other crew who were needed to keep it going must have jumped onto it from the loading deck.

You were on a ship with no one controlling its direction or speed?

M G : Yeah. I know. It sounds like suicide.

Did Celine say anything to you before she left for the island?

M G : No. Not even goodbye.

Why did she send you back?

M G : I don't know. Maybe she wanted us to tell you what we saw.

Did Celine tell you why *The Beautiful Dreamer* was chosen for this 'venture'?

M G : Yes. I asked her when she made her offer to send me back. She said it could have been anyone. A boat full of Cuban refugees. A ship of Somalian pirates. A 767 packed with commuters. But this, she said, seemed like it would be more fun. 'This way, the vacation never ends.'

In your opinion, who or what took over Celine?

M G : She told me what she was. Just after the storm.

She said that she was like us once. You don't die, she said. You just move on. There was no death. She said the only difference between her and everyone else was that she could decide how and when she came back. She said she was us. All of us. She said they'd done this before. Countless times.

She said they would do it again.

They?

Yes. They.

[Interview suspended]

>>Smith, Xavier L/ Interview #5/ Page 1

We understand that you believe you were under the influence of a shared delusion, Mr Smith. We would appreciate it if you could share your opinion on what this delusion was.

XS: Jesus. Okay. The delusion was that Celine had somehow taken the ship into another reality. A reality that was fucked.

Hypothetically, how would she achieve this?

XS: How the hell would I know? Even hypothetically, I don't think she moved it with the power of her mind. Maybe the nuts are right, maybe we did just drift into the Bermuda Triangle or whatever you want to call it.

Hypothetically, what was her intention?

XS: Isn't it obvious? The world she brought us to was dead. And *The Beautiful Dreamer* was her Noah's Ark.

[Subject laughs]

[Interview suspended]

>>**Trazona, Althea/ Interview #6/ Page 3**

They came and found me in my cabin. The men. The soldiers. That's when I found out that Mrs del Ray had left. She told me I would get what I wanted, but she lied. She used me.

In your opinion, who or what is Celine del Ray?

AT: I don't know. How would I know? She was just an old woman who used people. Trining said she was the devil.

Do you believe that?

AT: No. She was too cruel for the devil.

[Subject remains silent for several seconds]

AT: If she is anything then she would be God.

The Prisoner

It's too late. She's left it too late. If only she'd made the decision yesterday, she might have had a chance to get out of here. She's been telling herself to 'give it just one more day' since she arrived ten days ago. It's not the hours, or the city, or the work, or the loneliness. It's the kid. The bloody, buggering kid. She bites into the ragged flesh around her thumb until she draws blood, a habit she thought she'd quit years ago, and whips through the sites again.

The Reddit and Zoop forums are going crazy, and she's been hopping from one link to the next, hoping against hope that they'll discover that the plane has simply run into difficulties; landed on some obscure airstrip perhaps. Or even that it's crashed. That would be better than this. But still there are no reports of any wreckage. It happened in an instant. One minute it was on the radar; the next, gone. Blip. The second one in a month, only this one isn't a China Airlines internal flight, it's an Airbus ferrying passengers – mostly American and British – from Heathrow to JFK.

She skims through the headlines, occasionally sliding to audio. It's impossible to keep up with all the theories: terrorism, the Bermuda Triangle effect, the beginnings of the Rapture, environmentalists blasting the planes from the sky. Everyone and her dog has a theory, just like when all those people went missing from that cruise ship four years ago – and the nuts still haven't let up about that. She had a boyfriend for a while who totally bought into that bullshit story about the survivors.

Again, she searches for flights to London. Then Europe. Nothing. According to CNN, air traffic is being suspended 'for the foreseeable future'. Could she get home via ship? She imagines herself hitching a ride on a trawler – a cabin girl. She googles cruises leaving from New York to Europe, but even the cheapest is way out of her price range, and there are no berths for the next month. She doesn't have the money to find a hotel or an apartment – she's emailed her parents, but they can only spare a few hundred quid, nowhere near what she'll need to pay the rent or put down a deposit until she can find another job.

For now, she's trapped.

She stands up, stretches. Rubs her socked feet over the polished wood floors. There's a single photo of Joshua as a baby on the mantelpiece – the same one they sent to her when she applied for the job. He looks cute, wrapped in a baby-blue blanket, his eyes peeking through the swaddling. There are no pictures of him past the age of two. She doesn't know where they got him from, if they adopted him from an agency or used a surrogate. They haven't said, and she can hardly ask. Desiree and Marcus. Figjams, her mum would call them: *Fuck I'm Great, Just Admire Me.* Marcus, a biochemist; Desiree, a psychiatrist. They're exactly what she expected from watching movies about New York: a brownstone apartment in Brooklyn Heights, both fit and shiny-haired and fast-talking and hardly ever here. And she isn't the first au pair. She'd overheard them talking about it one night. The one before her – Clara, from South Africa – had lasted all of three days.

Her alarm beeps. Almost time for his piano lesson. She breathes in, then pads up the stairs. Desiree and Marcus have made sure his days are filled with activities: Young Einstein classes, swimming lessons, French. Desiree let slip that a woman used to come in once a week to teach him Tagalog, 'so that he wouldn't lose touch with his culture'; she didn't say why the lessons had stopped. The piano teacher, a brittle Eastern European woman, who Tracey finds almost as intimidating as Joshua, is the only person she's met so far who isn't affected by the boy's weirdness.

'Hi, Joshua! Almost time for your piano lesson.' She hates the overly bright voice she uses when she speaks to him. 'You ready to get going?'

He gives her one of his, *what are you, stupid?* looks. He's already dressed, sitting on the bed, waiting for her. She's tried to articulate what it is about him she finds so repellent. It's not just that he never smiles; there's a weight to him, as if he's always silently judging her. The neighbourhood kids are also wary around him. She's tried to connect with the other au pairs and nannies, the little club that gathers every day around the benches in the park, but they won't let her in. She knows she shouldn't take it personally. It's not her, it's the fear of their charges being sucked into a playdate with Joshua. Whenever they go to the park, he always ends up playing by himself. Although he never really plays – just watches, with that slightly sardonic twist of his mouth.

On her third day here, it had all got too much and Marcus caught her crying in the kitchen. He confided that up until he was three, Joshua had screamed almost continually. It had stopped overnight; as if a switch had been thrown inside him. Marcus laughed humourlessly, and said he didn't know what was worse, the non-stop crying or how he was now. Tracey gets the impression that he's been avoiding her since then.

She ushers Joshua out of the front door, and it begins to drizzle the second they step onto the top step. 'What a nasty day!' she chirrups. He stands absolutely still while she puts on his gloves. 'You warm enough, Joshua?'

'Yes.'

'Shall we get going then?'

'Yes.'

'Good.'

It starts spitting with more force as they reach the pavement. Autumn in New York. The sky heavy and low. She hasn't even been across the bridge to Manhattan; the skyline taunts her. The boy's hand is a small, repellent lump of wood in her hand. Back when she'd mistaken his reticence for shyness, she'd chattered away to him every time they left the house: 'Look! A dog,' or, 'One day we must go to the museum,' but now she doesn't bother. They walk the five blocks to Fulton in silence, the leaves slick and slimy under her cheap boots.

At the crossing, they wait for the 'walk' signal to flash and then hurry across with the rest of the people eager to get out of the rain.

They pass a boutique, the clothes costing more than a month's salary, and a deli stocked with cheese wheels.

'Nearly there!' she sing-songs, wishing she could just fire up her music and forget about him. Tracey usually waits in the Starbucks on the main drag while he has his lesson, which is pretty much turning into the highlight of her week. They turn the corner. A woman in high black boots and an oversized knitted cap placed artfully over bobbed hair, weaves around them, giving Joshua an 'aw, aren't you cute' look. And he does look cute in his Baby Gap boots and Paddington Bear overcoat. The woman moves to cross the road, raising a lofty hand to forestall the truck moving towards her. Tracey feels a twinge of envy, wishing she had the kind of confidence it takes to hold up traffic. The truck slams on its brakes to let the woman cross, but she hasn't counted on the motorbike behind it. An engine revs as it speeds up to zip around the truck. It happens, like these things always do, in slow motion. The motor-bike brakes sharply, attempts to swerve around the woman, wobbles, then tips and slides, knocking the woman's feet from under her. For a split second the woman's eyes lock with Tracey's – *this can't be happening* – and then: *fwump*.

Tracey grips Joshua's hand and drags him back. 'Don't look,' she screams. 'Don't look.'

She tries not to, but she can't help fixating on the mess where the woman's head should be, and . . . and . . . there's something spattered on the pavement. She hustles Joshua over to the Starbucks and drops to her knees in front of him, the damp pavement soaking through the knees of her jeans. The coffee-shop window is filling up with rubberneckers; several are pushing their way through the door, looking through their gel-phones' screens, filming the carnage.

She brushes rain from the front of Joshua's parka. The kid's face remains slack. 'Joshua. Are you okay?'

He nods. She takes his gloved hands in hers, scrambles for something to say, ends up burbling: 'The lady who fell is just sleeping. The ambulance will come in a minute and she's going to be fine, you'll see.'

He gives her a look of such contempt, she drops his hands and finds herself wiping hers on her jeans. *Just a kid, he's just a kid.* 'She's not sleeping,' he says. 'She's dead.'

'We don't know that for sure, Joshua.'

'Yes we do. But don't worry,' he says, with a lazy grin. 'Know this. There *is* no death.' And then he laughs.

Acknowledgements

Many thanks go to my fabulous editor Anne Perry and agent extraordinaire Oli Munson for their endless patience and support: you both rock. Lauren Beukes, Kate Sinclair, Alan Kelly, Paige Nick, Helen Moffett and Alan and Carol Walters kindly read the novel in its fledgling stage and offered fantastic comments, advice and arse-kicking when it was most needed. Thank you all.

I'm also in debt to Ben Summers, Becky Brown, Vickie Dillon, Hélène Ferey, Jennifer Custer, Veronique Norton, Jason Bartholomew, Conrad Williams, Oliver Johnson, Reagan Arthur and the hard-working publicity and production teams at Hodder & Stoughton and Little, Brown.

The majority of people who generously gave me insider info about the cruise industry and/or information about all matters maritime requested not to be named here for various reasons (primarily because they work for the cruise industry). You know who you are and I'm extremely grateful for your time and kindness. All mistakes are mine.

Charlie Martins and Savannah Lotz patiently bore the brunt of reading endless drafts and endured being kept awake by the grind of the coffee machine at 3 a.m. As always: thank you for having my back.

About the Author

Sarah Lotz is a novelist and screenwriter with a fondness for the macabre. She is the author of *The Three* and lives in Cape Town, South Africa, with her family and other animals.